Flight from Berlin

FLIGHT FROM BERLIN

A Novel

DAVID JOHN

BOURBON
STREET
BOOKS

An Imprint of HarperCollinsPublishers
www.harpercollins.com

FIRST BOURBON STREET BOOKS EDITION PUBLISHED 2013.

Designed by Fritz Metsch

The Library of Congress has catalogued the hardcover edition as follows:

John, David.
   Flight from Berlin / David John.—1st ed.
     p. cm.
   ISBN 978-0-06-209156-7 (hardcover)
   I. Title.
PR6110.O33F55 2012
823'.92—dc23   2011032501

ISBN 978-0-06-209159-8 (pbk.)

13 14 15 16 17   OV/RRD   10 9 8 7 6 5 4 3 2 1

For Claudia

He, the blind one, always had a map before him in spirit, and created or destroyed kingdoms by a single word.

—ERNST WEISS, *The Eyewitness*

A number of historical figures appear as characters in this story. Some background information on them is provided in the Notes on the Characters section on page 367.

This book is a work of fiction. References to real people, events, establishments, organizations, or locales are intended only to provide a sense of authenticity, and are used fictitiously. All other characters, and all incidents and dialogue, are drawn from the author's imagination and are not to be construed as real.

Flight from Berlin

He landed hands first on the wet, sandy soil and rolled over on his side. Wind roared inwards towards the blaze, sucking the air from his mouth. His skin was paper; his hair tinder.

Run, for God's sake.

Richard Denham moved to get up, but the next blast flattened him, sending a huge jet of flame over his head.

He crawled forwards through showers of brilliant white stars. Some fifty feet away a man in a sailor's cap was beckoning, shouting through the rippling glow.

'Over here, buddy, *come on.*'

I'm coming, friend, he thought, seeing in his mind that first day on the Somme twenty years ago. *Which way are the Jerry lines, pal?*

He staggered up and began to run, but a roll of burning diesel smoke engulfed him. Stumbling, he hit his head against something metal.

The next thing he knew he was being carried away at a run, jiggled over the sailor's shoulder like a sack of oats, the man's lungs heaving under the load.

The sailor swore as he lowered Denham to the ground.

A light drizzle was falling. He touched the swelling lump where he'd hit his head.

People were moving, dark figures silhouetted against the glare of the fire. He caught the obscene reek of roasted flesh.

Suddenly he thought, *Where is it?*

'Can't hear what you're saying, buddy. We're giving you mor-phine, you understand? You're burned.'

Bundles of paper, he knew, had a knack of surviving blazes. He remembered that from crime reporting. Eleanor would have made it safe.

A needle pricked his arm. He felt the cool flow of the injection.

Where was Eleanor?

How strange, how small the things that change history, turn it from its darkened course, send it eddying off down new, sunlit streams.

He lay back on the wet grass, feeling the ropes that tied him to consciousness begin to loosen. In the blackness above, embers traced the air like fireflies.

How strange.

Part I

Chapter One

Eleanor Emerson arched her body through the air and broke the surface with barely a splash. In the world below she glided through the veils of sunlight, the bubbles of her breath rumbling past her ears. She surfaced, and air, sound, and light burst over her again. Her muscles were taut, ready for speed.

Weekday afternoons were quiet at Randall's Island, the periods when only the dedicated furrowed the lanes, marking lengths as mechanically as electric looms. But today the pool seemed far from the world. She was the only swimmer in the water.

At each fifty-yard length she tumble-turned back into her wake, cleaving the water, faster, beginning to warm up. After all the training was she close to her peak? Lungs filled; legs thrust. Steadily she was rising through her gears, reaching for *full steam*, when something tapped the top of her bathing cap, causing her to stall and choke.

For a second she hoped it was Herb, coming to surprise her, but a lady with a rolled parasol stood at the pool's edge, the sun behind her, so that all Eleanor could see was the light shining through a floral-print dress and a pair of Ferragamo shoes.

'Jesus, Mother. What are you doing here?'

'It came, sweetheart,' the woman said.

Eleanor stood, dripping, shielding her eyes, and saw that her mother was holding out a Western Union envelope. Only now did her heart start to race.

'Oh no, Mother dear. Read it to me.'

Mrs Taylor began an exploration through her handbag for a pair of reading glasses, ignoring the mounting agitation in the pool. Finally: 'On behalf of AOC am pleased to confirm your selection for US team congratulations Brundage . . .'

Eleanor had started screaming before her mother had finished, her wet hands fanning her face as if there weren't air enough.

'Really, sweetheart . . .'

She screamed again as she did riding the chute at Luna Park, breaking into a high, girlish laugh and smacking the water with both hands, splashing and kicking with her feet, so that her mother opened the parasol.

'You're soaking me.'

'Mom, I *made it*!'

'Well, did you think you wouldn't? You'd better break the news to your father. I'm certainly not going to.'

JOE TAYLOR HANDED the telegram back to her and looked out of the open window. It had turned sultry. The breeze moving the flag next to his desk carried the smell of traffic fumes, coffee, and a promise of rain. Below, a fire engine wailed up Madison Avenue.

'I see,' he said eventually. He stood still, his shoulders rising in a sigh. His back towards her, he said, 'Do you intend going?'

The question filled the room.

'I'm going,' Eleanor said.

'Well, my girl, I won't pretend I'm not disappointed.'

'Dad, please—'

'It's all right.'

He looked tired. With a pang of sadness she noticed that his hair had completed its change to white, making him seem much older. And there was a lack of vitality about him, an incipient infirmity. He turned to face her and smiled in the worried way he had with her, hands in his waistcoat pockets with his thumbs sticking out, a posture she knew usually signalled a speech. If only he'd lose his temper, shake his fist, and rave like a Baptist. Then at least she could shout back. This was the worst thing about the whole business. His tolerance. His disappointment.

'I know I should congratulate you. Any father would be proud of a daughter who's made the Olympic team, and of course you must follow your own star . . .'

Here we go.

'Your mother and I have given our blessing to whatever choices you've made. We welcomed Herb into the family . . . We supported your *singing* career. But Germany?' He shook his head vaguely. 'We send our athletes there and we will be *condoning*, lending *respectability* to the most iniquitous . . .'

'Dad.'

' . . . the most *unconscionable* regime ever to—'

'*Dad.*'

Exasperation flared in her eyes. 'Quit the speech. It's about competing. That's all.'

They held each other's gaze.

He said, 'I fought hard to stop Brundage winning that vote. I lost. And now I'm entrusting you to his care?'

'I can handle him.'

'Can you?' He sat slowly down at his desk, his shoulders slumped. 'Everything's a game, isn't it? A high school dare, a challenge. Rules are to be broken; advice to be ignored.' Thunder rolled and a splash of rain hit the windowsill with a thump. 'One day, my dear, you'll see the world for what it is. And that'll be the day you quit being a Park Avenue playgirl and grow up—'

His desk intercom buzzed.

'Yes?'

'Senator Taylor, sir, I have the *New York Times* on the line.'

'Well, well,' he said, looking up at her. 'News travels fast in this town.'

*   *   *

HER CAB MADE a right at West Twentieth Street, and Eleanor braced herself for the barrage of flashbulbs. One enterprising reporter waiting on the corner had already spotted her and was running alongside her window, trying to jump onto the running board.

'Eleanor, how's it feel to be going to Berlin? How's it—'

She put her sunglasses on and ignored him.

'Hey, lady, don't be a snob.'

It was just after rush hour on a humid July morning. The ship wasn't sailing until eleven, but the boardwalk was already filling up with hundreds of well-wishers and passengers preparing to embark. Her cab inched past a sidewalk crowded with athletic teams in club sweatshirts, some laughing, some chanting a college yell, all heading towards the pier, holding Olympic flags and banners with goodluck messages. Hot dog vendors had set up stalls.

Directly ahead, the bow of the SS *Manhattan* towered above the crowd like a sheer rock promontory, shimmering in the haze of heat. Cranes lifted cargo to the top deck, where the United States Lines had painted the liner's two funnels red, white, and blue, and festooned the rails with bunting in honour of the team.

The cab pulled up as close to the boardwalk as it could get and was mobbed.

'Will you break the world record for backstroke again, Eleanor?'

'I'm going to Berlin with no other aim,' she said, stepping into the fray, long legs first, and posing briefly in the bias-cut skirt and tilted cream hat she'd chosen with this moment in mind. Flashbulbs popped.

'Is Senator Taylor mad at you for going?'

'My father wishes me well in whatever I do.'

'Will your husband be joining you?'

'No, my husband will be on tour with his orchestra.' She pointed in the direction she wished to go, and the reporters moved aside. 'Take it easy, boys.'

'Say, if you meet Hitler what're you going to say to him?'

'Change your barber.'

The reporters laughed, and scribbled.

She pushed her way into the crowd, swatting aside an autograph book. *Will your husband be joining you?* They sure knew how to ask a sore question. She was still raw from her fight with Herb last night. Since she'd qualified for the team he'd acted like he'd lost his top dog status in life, one minute spilling her the sob stuff, the next, a real asshole. Same story every time she achieved something. Then this morning he'd claimed some phoney engagement as an excuse not to wave her off. Hadn't her dad been enough to handle? What was it with men?

Nearer the barrier to the pier a group of her teammates were sitting on steamer trunks and talking in high, excited voices. Some had never been out of their home state, let alone on board an ocean liner. A few veterans, like Eleanor, had competed at Los Angeles in '32, but most were doe-eyed college kids, plucked from the boondocks. All wore their USA team straw boaters, white trousers or skirts, and navy blazers embroidered with the Olympic shield.

'Hey, you guys,' she said. 'Who's up for a little first-night party on board later?'

Just then, the sound of screams was carried on a wave of applause from near the entry to the pier, where another cab was inching its way into the dense mass of people. Jesse Owens's coach jumped out, followed by the man himself in a pinstriped navy suit, and the press jostled to get a word from America's star athlete. Photographers shouted his name.

'Make way for the golden boy,' she said. Her teammates stood on their steamer trunks to wave and whistle.

Eleanor and Owens were the same age, twenty-three, and both were world-record holders. She'd never figured him out. The less winning seemed to concern him, the more effortlessly he won. The more courtesy he showed, the farther he left his rivals behind. For her, winning required a dedicated mean streak—and a desire above all else that the others should lose. She watched him ponder each reporter's question, brow furrowed, and answer as though to his father-in-law, nodding and grinning modestly.

The heat on the pier was rising, and the noise and the wafts of diesel oil and dead fish were making her feel nauseated. She decided to board and made her way up the gangway. *So long, New York*, she thought. *When I set foot here again it'll be with shame or glory.*

At the entry to the deck stood a stout, middle-aged matron wearing the team uniform and hat. She was holding a clipboard.

'Welcome aboard, Mrs Emerson,' the woman said with a faint, whiskery smile. 'You're on D deck, sharing with Marjorie Gestring and Olive McNamee. Your trunk's in your cabin.'

'Thank you, Mrs Hacker. D deck sounds delightful.'

'If it's luxury and glamour you were after, you should have booked your own first-class fare.'

'You think I didn't try?'

The woman ticked her list. 'Count yourself lucky, my girl. The Negroes are sleeping below the waterline. You'll wear your uniform at dinner, please. Bed is at ten o'clock.'

Eleanor walked on before her irritation showed. She'd had enough evenings ruined by chaperones.

'Old drizzle puss,' she muttered.

'I heard that, young lady.'

SHE FOUND HER two cabinmates unpacking to shrieks of laughter and felt herself tensing slightly. At school she'd stood out from the other girls in so many ways that she'd learned to endure their frequent unkindnesses. Swimming had often been her way of escaping them.

'Hi there,' said the nearer, a broad-shouldered blonde chewing gum. 'I'm Marjorie, and this is Olive.' The second girl, who wore oyster-thick eyeglasses, grinned at her. 'It's a privilege to dorm with you.'

'Likewise.' Eleanor smiled, embracing them both in turn, and suddenly realised that she recognised them from the trials. 'Jesus, you can rely on old Hacker to put swimming rivals in the same cabin.'

'I'm a diver,' Marjorie said, a little crestfallen. She looked about fourteen.

Eleanor didn't want to be a bad sport. She'd been green, too, before her Olympic debut at age nineteen. Her gold medal at Los Angeles had made her the belle of the press corps, celebrated on the covers of magazines as an all-American beauty. 'Your body's a head turner,' Sam Goldwyn had told her, 'and you've got a lot of class.'

She wanted to say something friendly, but Olive spoke first.

'I heard your husband's band at the Harlem Opera House.'

'You're from New York?'

'Queens,' said Olive.

'Los Angeles,' said Marjorie, chewing.

'Town girls, thank God,' Eleanor said, sitting on the bed and testing the springs. 'I was worried I'd be with some of our sisters from Ass-End, Nowhere.'

Olive's laugh sounded like an old windscreen wiper. 'So what's it like singing?' the girl asked. 'With a dance orchestra, I mean.'

'As a career I wouldn't recommend it,' Eleanor said, taking a Chesterfield from a tortoiseshell case and lighting it. 'Late nights, loose ladies giving your husband the eye, and the perpetual disappointment of your father . . . But I guess it's taught me to hold my liquor.'

Marjorie tittered behind her hand.

'Your father opened my school,' said Olive. 'He doesn't like the band?'

'Senators tend not to get along with bandleaders. Especially when a daughter marries one and gets talked into playing nightclubs wearing a one-piece bathing suit and a pair of high heels.' She exhaled a long plume of smoke, remembering the dismay on her dad's face when she'd sung him her version of 'Whoopee Ti-Yi-Yo.'

Whatever the excesses of her second career, she'd never let it interfere with her training. She recalled a night at the Century

Club in Chicago, the place smoke filled and reeking of scotch. A hoodlum crowd if ever she'd seen one. After the show she'd stood drinks for the boys, but Herb went to bed, licked. And at two in the morning she was at the Lakeshore Pool, lap swimming, ploughing up the lanes as a mist billowed over the water. Her nose and throat were raw from the cold air, her every muscle honed to its purpose—not just to win, but to win spectacularly, with all the speed in her power.

A knock at the door, and a uniformed cabin boy entered with a bouquet almost as large as he was.

'One o' you ladies Eleanor Emerson?'

Eleanor took the flowers and opened the card. *Good luck, Kid. No hard feelings? Herb.*

A scent of lilies settled heavily in the confined space. But before she had time to dwell on Herb's gesture, Olive was holding up a small sheet of paper.

'Hey, who put this here? It was underneath my pillow.'

Eleanor and Marjorie lifted their pillows and found the same anonymous printed message. Eleanor read it out loud, her voice hardening as she realised what it was.

MEN AND WOMEN OF THE USA TEAM! GERMANY WILL SHOW YOU A SMILING FACE THAT HIDES ITS EVIL HEART. EVERY DAY CITIZENS WHO DO NOT THINK LIKE THE NAZIS ARE TORTURED AND MURDERED. PROTEST AGAINST THIS CRIMINAL REGIME BY REMAINING ON YOUR STARTING BLOCKS AT EACH RACE! DO NOT ALLOW YOURSELVES TO BECOME PAWNS OF NAZI PROPAGANDA!

'Gee, those boycotters don't let up,' said Marjorie, who had picked up a copy of *Vogue* and began flicking through it. She held up a page with an airbrushed portrait of Hannah Liebermann posing with her foil. 'Doesn't she look like Myrna Loy?'

'My mom got a letter from her union telling me I shouldn't be going,' said Olive. 'That the Nazis have banned the trade unions . . .

or something like that. Didn't sound like such a bad idea to her. If the AOC says it's okay for us to go, that was fine by her.'

Eleanor crumpled up her copy of the note and tossed it straight through the open porthole. A thought crossed her mind—that her father had arranged for these notes to be placed here, that he was aiming one final guilt-tipped arrow at her before she sailed. But equally, she supposed, they might have been left there by any hot-head from the boycott movement. There were enough of them.

'What I cannot understand,' she said, opening a compact mirror and inspecting her lipstick, 'is what the hell's it to do with Olympic sport?' She snapped the mirror shut. 'Why would *anyone* think there's something wrong with wanting to win gold medals for the USA?'

Two trombone blasts from the ship's funnels reverberated through the floor, and they heard feet running along the corridor outside. 'Come on,' she said to the girls, 'I think it's time for bon voyage.'

THE AMERICAN OLYMPIC team members, all 384 of them, were pressed against the rails, waving to the thousands come to see them off, along with the ship's other passengers—the reporters, diplomats, and socialites—on their way to the Games as supporters and spectators. Eleanor spotted Mary Astor and Helen Hayes standing on the first-class promenade.

On the pier, a high school athletic team unfurled a banner reading GIVE 'EM HELL, GLENN. Tugs, yachts, and liners tied up at the neighbouring piers began sounding their horns in a raucous medley, with each blast echoed by vessels farther up the Hudson. Overhead, a biplane circled. It seemed as though the whole of New York City was there to wish them luck. Every window in the towers of Midtown was filled with faces.

On the ship's top deck five girls from the women's high jump team hoisted a vast white flag emblazoned with the Olympic rings. The crowd roared and stamped their feet, breaking into a chant.

'U-S-A! U-S-A! A-M-E-R-I-C-A!'

Eleanor basked in the happiness and goodwill of the thousands of faces, and felt their energy. Not a single protester as far as she could see. Not one angry face.

The funnels sounded their bass notes again, the companionways were cast off, and three tugboats pulled the *Manhattan* out into the harbour. The athletes waved and whistled in a frenzy. Some held paper streamers linked to the hands of parents and sweethearts on the pier, wept when the streamers broke, and hugged each other. Gradually the pier slipped away in a tumult of spray, foam, and engine noise. The band struck up 'America the Beautiful' and tears welled in Eleanor's eyes. *Who needs a damned husband anyway*, she thought.

Chapter Two

*A*chtung . . .'
    The ferry's loudspeaker announced each stop along the shore as a U-boat might alert its torpedo room to targets.

'Unsere nächste Halt ist Friedrichshafen! Friedrichshafen!'

Richard Denham was the only passenger to disembark onto the narrow quay. As the weather was mild and his luggage light he decided to walk the half mile up the high street towards the hotel. He carried a flaking leather case that contained his portable Underwood and a change of clothes. In his breast pocket was the letter of invitation, in case he should be obliged to produce it at the reception desk. He could imagine doubts about his liquidity at the region's smartest spa resort when they saw his unshaven face and the slept-in flannel suit he'd worn on the long train journey from Berlin.

A breeze swept across the lake from the Alps, rimpling the glassy surface and dispelling the oppressive heat of high summer. Clouds and sky reflected.

The high street of Friedrichshafen, narrow in places, was a pretty, cobblestone affair, with baker, coffee shop, and butcher, all with window boxes in bloom and high-gabled roofs of red tiles. This could be any small town in southern Germany on a peaceful Saturday in summer. Even the sound of approaching drums, from some distance away, was depressingly normal.

The day after he'd received a call from his press agent in London, demanding more 'human interest' stories and less politics, Denham had cabled an old colleague of his father's. To his surprise he received a response by return:

> *My dear Richard,*
> *I am indeed very happy and pleased to receive a message from you. With the greatest pleasure I remember the visits of your father to us here in Friedrichshafen, and we Germans live in remembrances. It would be my pleasure to welcome you Saturday. I insist please that you stay at the Hotel Kurgarten as the guest of the Luftschiffbau Zeppelin. You shall of course have whatever access you require to our work and I promise to do my utmost to answer your questions.*
>
> > *I remain sincerely yours,*
> > *Hugo Eckener*

The dismal boom of the drums was getting nearer, so Denham slipped into a shop out of sight. This was the second time in as many weeks that he'd taken refuge somewhere to avoid saluting some passing banner. He'd seen them beat up people who didn't salute. As his eyes adjusted after the glare of the street, he saw that he'd entered a post office and remembered the stamps his son, Tom, had asked him to find.

The walls of the narrow street amplified the advancing sound, the drumbeat now underscored by the crunch of marching feet.

He watched from the post office window as the brigade leader passed, holding high a banner with the words DEUTSCHLAND ERWACHE—'Germany, awake.' Shoppers along the pavement raised their right arms, holding groceries in the other. Row after row of Brownshirts followed the banner, caps strapped under their chins, boots smacking the cobblestones. Each man carried a tall swastika flag of scarlet, white, and black and sang what sounded like a hymn, except that it was about sharpening daggers on kerbstones.

Denham folded his arms and swore under his breath. Warm weather in Germany brought out a tide of shit these days.

Just out of sight, a car horn blared once, and then persistently, causing the marchers to break step. Something must have blocked their way, because as the rows in front came to a sudden halt the ones following collided into their backs, throwing the parade into disarray. Caps were knocked off, flagstaffs whacked into faces, and fronts shoved against rears. The men swore and yelped, shouting, '*Halt!*' to those in the rear.

'*Haaaalt!*'

Denham snorted with laughter. What was going on? He pulled his Leica out of the case and tried to get a couple of shots of the farce unfolding.

'*Mister Denham.*'

He usually got a better fee for an article with photos.

'*Mis-ter Den-ham.*'

Denham froze.

A man's voice was yelling his name over the commotion outside. It was coming from the direction of the car horn, which sounded again.

'*Mis-ter Rich-ard Den-ham?*'

The voice was addressing him in English. So, chances were it didn't belong to a Brownshirt. In fact, it sounded familiar. He stepped outside into the crowd of uniforms and saw, about twenty yards down the street, a black, open-topped Maybach parked half up on the pavement. The old street was so narrow, however, that it left barely six feet for the marchers to pass. Standing in the car was the tall, plumpish figure of Hugo Eckener, waving with his hand high in the air.

'My dear Richard,' he yelled, 'I saw you go in. Have you just arrived?'

'Dr Eckener,' Denham said, unsure how to return such bonhomie with a brigade of aggrieved Brownshirts looking on. He sensed trouble.

'Come on, get in. I'm giving you a ride to the hangar. You can check into the hotel later.'

Reluctantly the marchers began manoeuvring around the vehicle, casting malign looks at Eckener and Denham.

Self-conscious, he walked to the car, put his case on the backseat, and was about to hop in when an iron hand gripped his shoulder and yanked him around. A thickset, sunburned man glowered into his face. He wore the cap and insignia of a Scharführer. The brown collar strained around a neck that was like a rump of cured ham.

'You took photographs of this?' he said.

Denham felt the Leica become hot in his hand.

'You thought it was amusing?' The man's breath came in short snorts. Violence hung in the air like static.

'Comrade,' Denham said, attempting a smile. 'Hasn't this week before the Games been decreed a Week of Jollity and Cheerfulness?' He heard the Anglican vowels in his German as if his voice were a recording on a gramophone.

A brown bank of uniforms was moving in around him, penning him with no gap for escape.

'Your name, sir.'

'My name's Denham. I'm a British reporter resident in Berl—'

'British?' the man said, parodying Denham's voice. 'And what is your business here?'

His mouth began to dry. 'Your esteemed Dr Eckener has asked me here. I'm writing a piece on the new Zeppelin.'

The Scharführer looked over the heads of the men and stared at the doctor.

'Our esteemed Dr Eckener closes his heart to our national awakening, yet feels free to do whatever he pleases.' For some reason the men chuckled, as if this were some local running joke. He turned back to Denham. 'But you, sir, are coming to the barracks.'

Denham opened his mouth to protest, but it was Eckener's voice that sounded, filling the length of the street on the warm air.

'This man is here at my invitation.'

Standing in the open-topped car he towered over the Brownshirts, the chin beneath his goatee wobbling with rage. Elijah addressing the followers of Baal.

'You're harassing a foreign guest of the Reich's, and believe me, that will not go well for you in the week before the Olympic Games.'

The Scharführer seemed to waver. The men glanced at each other.

Denham saw his moment, shoved his way through the uniforms, and jumped into the passenger seat. The Maybach's engine roared. He took a ten-reichsmark note from his wallet and held it towards the Scharführer.

'Here. No harm done,' he shouted. 'Buy your men some beers.'

The man snatched the note just as the car jerked forwards and accelerated up the street, forcing the men bunched at the back of the brigade to step quickly out of the way.

'Do you often ruin their parades?' Denham said over the noise of the engine.

'Criminals and gangsters,' Eckener shouted. He was furious.

Denham leaned back in his seat and laughed, pulling the brim of his hat over his eyes. 'Always keep your head down and stay out of fights. I should have learned that lesson from the war.'

He had to admire the old man's effrontery, but then Hugo Eckener enjoyed an immunity afforded to few other opponents of the regime. In 1929 he'd become the most famous German in the world when he circumnavigated the globe as commander of the *Graf Zeppelin*—the first voyage of its kind in an aircraft. Immense crowds turned out to greet the silver machine when it landed in Tokyo, San Francisco, and New York, fulfilling his dream that the Zeppelin should forge links of friendship among nations. He was an ebullient, courageous, driven man, an enormous personality who counted kings and presidents among his acquaintances. So high was his standing at home and abroad that the Nazis dared not touch him, and he knew it.

'It's wonderful to see you again,' Eckener yelled. 'How long has it been?'

Denham saw familiar houses, gables, and barns speeding by. 'I haven't been here in six years. Not since we flew with you on the *Graf* to Brazil.'

'Ha! Yes. Your dear father saved our skins on that one . . .'

But Eckener's mind, Denham sensed, was still seething with Brownshirts.

'You told those devils that you're living in Berlin. Is that true?'

'It's true.'

The old man shook his head. '*Unglaublich.*' Incredible. 'You mean you *choose* to live in this lunatic asylum? What about your family?'

Denham shrugged. 'My wife said I was more intimate with the typewriter than with her, and left me. Besides, Berlin is where the news is. I sell a lot of stories from there.'

'You have a son, though, yes?'

'That's right. Tom. He's eight years old.'

'Surely you miss him?'

'Of course. But . . .'

'The British,' Eckener said with admiration, 'are intrepid.'

Denham's other reason for living in Germany was harder to explain, but he knew it had something to do with the hysteria gripping the country. The shrieking, stamping monstrousness of it had the odd effect of making him feel sane and normal. There'd been times in the quiet civility of Hampstead, in the difficult years after he'd returned from war, when he'd felt he was losing his mind.

They motored out of the town and along lanes where the air was sweet with mown hay. In the far distance across the lake he saw Säntis, the nearest of the Swiss Alps, still blue with snow, its peak hidden in a thundercloud.

'*Hindenburg* is a good name for the airship,' Denham said.

'It was a compromise. The first name they gave me was *Adolf Hitler.*'

THE MAIDEN FLIGHT of the D-LZ129 *Hindenburg* to New York in May had made headline news. Denham had followed the story of its construction, sending cuttings for Tom's scrapbook. At 804 feet in length—one-sixth of a mile long—it was only a few feet shorter than the *Titanic*. At its middle, widest point, it was the height of a fourteen-storey building, and had a gas volume of more than seven million cubic feet.

Possessed even with these statistics, he gasped at his first sight of it, moored to its mast under an azure sky. The ship was a giant, the largest flying object ever made. Streamlined perfectly from nose to fins, it lay facing into the breeze, sheathed in a silver fabric that reflected the early-evening sun. The shadow of a summer cloud passed slowly over its hull, giving Denham the impression of watching a vast fish basking in the shallows of a warm sea.

For several minutes he stood next to Eckener in silence. The ship's side was adorned with the Olympic rings in honour of the Games. Two of the four propeller-engine cars were visible, sticking out of the lower body like flippers. A row of promenade windows ran along part of the midship, where the luxury passenger accommodation—the lounges, bar, cabins, and dining room—were recessed entirely into the body. The control car was the only part of the structure that hung below the hull, like a single eye, resting on its landing wheel.

'Beautiful, isn't she?' Eckener said. 'Even with those filthy black spiders they made us put on her.' He gestured to the enormous swastikas emblazoned on the upper and lower tail fins.

'Sublime,' Denham mumbled. It was the most marvellous thing he'd ever seen.

'I wish your father could see her.'

'How fast is she?'

'Top speed is a hundred and thirty-five kilometres per hour,' said Eckener. 'Faster with a tailwind. She's the quickest vessel over the Atlantic. Frankfurt to Rio de Janeiro in one hundred hours and forty minutes; to New York in fifty-nine hours. Not as quick as I'd have liked, but we can't take a direct route. The French don't want us over their rooftops . . .'

They walked towards the *Hindenburg*. To the left of the field, the doorway of the nearest hangar was open, revealing the vast nose of the *Graf Zeppelin*. The tiny figures of some mechanics were making checks on a propeller-engine car, but otherwise the field and two hangars were deserted, giving a deep stillness to the place.

As they reached the ship the contours of the immense hull spread out above them like the surface of another planet. Eckener led Denham to a small ladder hanging down from the control car, and up they climbed into the nerve centre of the Zeppelin.

Inside, the fittings were of gleaming aluminium, like those of a rocket ship in *Flash Gordon*. An array of instruments controlled the ship's course, speed, and buoyancy. Eckener pointed out each in turn. At the front of the bridge was the rudder wheel that steered with the aid of illuminated gyrocompasses; on the left was the elevator wheel, which maintained altitude and trim. Above these were the ballast control levers, and a gas-cell pressure gauge with warning lights that flashed—the very latest in long-distance airship-flight technology. A telegraph, like those on ocean liners, sent messages to the propeller-engine cars. But most dramatic of all, high, slanted windows surrounded the bridge, giving a superlative view onto the world: left and right, below, and far into the horizon, so that any approaching lightning storms could be circumnavigated. Everything smelled metallic and new.

Denham felt as if he were in a dream. In another life he'd have been a Zeppelin commander, he realised. The age of fast, luxury Zeppelin travel had begun. He imagined fleets of these giant ships linking the distant continents of the earth. Their time was at hand. They were the future.

'How about a spin over the lake,' he joked, knowing the ship couldn't go anywhere without some three hundred ground crew present.

'How would you like to fly next Saturday?' Eckener said, slapping his shoulder. 'The *Hindenburg* will make a pleasure trip over the opening ceremony of the Olympiad in Berlin. And in the meantime, enjoy a few days here on the lake, as my guest of course.'

'I would like that very much,' Denham said.

'Excellent. There will be a movie crew on board, too.'

This man is the other Germany, Denham thought. The Germany of decent, kind people who stand like rocks against the flow of the times.

In the navigation room next to the bridge, Eckener motioned for him to sit at the chart table. A golden light burnished the dials and switches of the radio instruments. The old man's face seemed rejuvenated in the sunset. At sixty-eight he had the appearance of a man years younger, though his hair and goatee beard were white. His face was large, jowly, and intelligent, with flinty blue eyes, one of which, disconcertingly, was higher than the other.

'Let's have a schnapps,' he said, unlocking a drawer and taking out a bottle and two glasses. 'I sometimes permitted the night watch a nip on board the *Graf* at the end of the shift. It gets very cold over the Atlantic in spring.' They toasted each other in silence, and knocked it back. 'And now, my dear Richard, I have something for you.' He opened a cupboard beneath the table to reveal a small safe. 'I keep a precious relic in this chest, but by rights it belongs to you.' He turned the dial slowly. 'The combination is five-ten-nineteen-thirty.'

Denham was puzzling over why the doctor should give away the numbers to his private safe, when it struck him. They made the date of his father's death. Eckener removed a small felt bag and handed it over with what seemed to Denham a look of earnest pity. He opened it and a pocket watch fell into his hand.

'I've been waiting for a chance to give it to you in person,' Eckener said.

For a fleeting moment he had a sense that his father was present in the room, as though he'd slipped in through some fissure in time. The watch lay cool in his palm. He turned it over and saw in tiny engraved italics the words:

For Arthur Denham—On his retirement—Royal Airship Works— Cardington

An overpowering sense of love and loss welled inside him. His eyes filled, and hot tears rolled freely down his cheeks. Eckener put his arm around Denham's shoulders.

'You were young to lose your father.'

'Not that young. I am forty next year.'

Denham fell silent for a while, staring at the watch as he turned it over in his hand.

'I thought there was nothing . . .'

'It was found near the site,' Eckener said. 'Somehow it must have been thrown clear.'

Later, as they walked back across the Zeppelin field in the gloaming, Denham turned to look again at the *Hindenburg*. Dully it reflected the purple light.

Chapter Three

Eleanor, paddling her legs as hard as she could, strained against the rope that attached her waist to the side of the tiny swimming pool on deck. But it was no use. As the ship pitched and rolled, she found herself flailing in two feet of water at one end of the pool, with six feet at the other end, before it all slopped back the other way. She stood up and undid the rope.

'Another twenty minutes, please.' The women's swimming coach was pacing the edge of the pool.

'I can't train like this.'

'It's the only pool we've got for the next few days.'

'Yeah, with water straight from the goddamned icebergs.'

'Where do you think you're going?'

'For a shower,' Eleanor said, plucking up a towel. 'And a cigarette.'

She headed along the deck, leaving a trail of wet footprints. A fresh wind had been blowing all afternoon, whipping spray from the crests of the waves high into the air. Patchworks of cloud skittered overhead, breaking now and then to admit flashes of hot sunshine that coloured the ocean a deep verdant green. The ship was making slow progress as it seesawed through the weight of wind and water.

As she turned the corner towards the stairs that led back to D deck—*smack*—her shoulder collided with a strapping blond running laps.

'Hey, mister,' she said, clutching her shoulder. 'Oh. Sorry, Helen.'

'No problem, sis,' the woman growled and continued her lolloping stride.

Her guess was that poor Helen Stephens, the hundred-metre champion from Missouri, was forever being mistaken for a guy, but she didn't seem to care. All the same, her flat-chested manliness was sure to raise eyebrows when they got to Berlin. Helen had even more brawn than her archrival, Stella 'the Fella' Walsh.

Eleanor washed her hair as best she could under the thin trickle, then slipped into her bathrobe and lit a Chesterfield. The cabin vibrated from the hum of the engines below. One by one, she pulled out the gowns hanging in the tiny closet, cocking her head as she appraised each in turn, before settling for a shining pearl grey chiffon number to wear with her white-sable stole. She laid it on her bed and was choosing some jewellery when Marjorie and Olive returned.

'So, guys,' she said, 'how was your turn in the Olympic paddling pool?'

Marjorie stared at Eleanor, wide-eyed. 'Is that what you're wearing to dinner?'

'Sure. Why, what are you wearing?'

'Our team uniforms.'

Eleanor wouldn't even be joining them for dinner if Mrs Hacker hadn't ordered her to be present for Brundage's speech. But she had no intention of sticking around afterwards for whatever entertainment the team had organised. The playwright Charlie MacArthur, whom she'd run into on deck earlier, had invited her to join him and his wife, Helen Hayes, for a little drink with the press corps up in first class. Now that sounded like a party worth going to.

There was a knock on the door, and the cabin boy entered, smirking, with Eleanor's curling tongs.

'Got them heated on the chef's grill, ma'am.'

'Thanks, kid,' Eleanor said, handing him a second pair. 'Girls, whatever you want, just ask Hal.'

'That's right. Coffee . . . tea . . . *me*,' the boy said as he left.

She took out her small beauty mirror, balanced it against her trunk, and blew smoke thoughtfully into her reflection.

'Eleanor,' said Olive in a schoolma'am voice. 'You're smoking *again*.'

'Haven't you heard?' Eleanor said as she set about waving her hair. 'I train on cigarettes and champagne.'

SHE FOUND MOST of her teammates already assembled in the noisy C deck dining room. They were so many that they ate in two sittings, but all had gathered to hear Avery Brundage's speech, with dozens standing around the edges of the room. Jesse Owens entered, looking a little delicate, she thought. She'd heard he'd spent the day in his cabin, seasick.

Eleanor found herself sitting at a table with the decathlete Glenn Morris, the five-thousand-metre runner Lou Zamperini, and two relay runners, Sam Stoller and Marty Glickman. Morris had matinee-idol looks: six foot two, with brooding, Cherokee eyes and a chin like a DC Comics superhero.

The noise subsided as Avery Brundage strode in, followed by two AOC officials and Mrs Hacker, the team chaperone, self-important with her clipboard. She'd applied some lipstick, Eleanor noticed.

Brundage, the president of the American Olympic Committee, had on his buttoned-up double-breasted suit and rimless eyeglasses, which, together with his bolt-upright posture, gave him a trim, conceited appearance. He was a tall ex-pentathlete, broad shouldered, and at forty-nine wore his age well. Not handsome exactly—his chin and forehead were large and plain—but he had the charisma of conviction. Eleanor knew from the public beefs he'd had with her dad that Brundage took himself seriously in the extreme. Both were men of strong principles, but where her father's were inclusive and egalitarian, she suspected Brundage's were quite the opposite. He stood still, waiting until the dining room had fallen silent.

'Fellow Olympians,' he began, 'we are finally on our way.' Cheers and whistles from the audience. 'You, America's finest, are

participating in an event that enshrines the world's noblest sporting
ideal: the Olympic Games. It is an ideal that exemplifies all that is
good in man's nature, an ideal that transcends the quotidian strug-
gles of everyday life . . .'

'The *what*?' mumbled Lou Zamperini.

'Hold the spirit of this ideal in your hearts and remember that
you represent the grandest country in the world. You are going to
Germany to win for the honour of your country and for the glory
of sport.'

The athletes applauded with wild enthusiasm, but now Brundage
wagged a finger in the air.

'It has not been an easy road. Only a few months ago, it was still
uncertain whether we would be competing in this Olympiad. Those
in the so-called boycott movement—the Communists and the cos-
mopolitans who understand little of sport—sought to make the
American athlete a martyr for a cause not his own . . .'

'He means Communists and Jews are not real Americans,' Eleanor said in a low voice.

' . . . but common sense has prevailed. The Olympic ideal rises
above all those issues of politics and skin colour, and let no one tell
you otherwise.' Again, the athletes applauded and whistled. 'Whatever misconceptions people may have about Germany, whatever
distortions are perpetuated in the press, let one thing be understood.' Pointing into the audience, he paused, looking at everyone
in the room. 'Germany appreciates the Olympic ideal better than
any other country I know. It has made athletic excellence the highest priority in its national life—a policy our own government would
do well to emulate. For I believe that in striving for this ideal we
may one day witness the development of a new race. A race forged
through sportsmanship, a race physically strong, mentally alert, and
morally sound . . .'

'Jesus,' said Eleanor.

Brundage stopped for a moment and seemed to be looking in her
direction, his eyeglasses flashing in the light.

'A race that scorns injustice and will fight for fair play and what it believes is right.'

The applause this time was less certain, as the arcane articles of Brundage's faith passed over the heads of most in his audience.

'Sounds like fascism to me,' said Marty Glickman.

Eleanor looked at him, this almond-eyed relay runner from the Bronx, still in his teens, and wondered if he and Stoller were the only Jews on the team.

'Finally,' Brundage said gravely, 'I must give you a word of warning about your conduct over the next few days at sea. You will be tempted by an unlimited variety of rich food. If you are undisciplined in controlling your appetites, your medals will be lost at the dining table . . .'

Even as he spoke, waiters were preparing the tables for the first course, placing baskets of bread rolls on each.

'Will you look at that?' said Lou Zamperini in hushed amazement. '*Six types* of bread roll.'

' . . . Second, I would remind you all of the AOC handbook rules, which demand that you refrain from smoking, the drinking of intoxicating liquors, gambling, and other forms of dissipation.' He looked slowly around the room to make sure everyone was hearing. 'Anyone who violates these rules will be dealt with severely. Thank you.'

'I'll take that as a challenge,' Eleanor said, to laughter from those around her. She'd heard enough of Brundage's views to know that if Communists and Jews didn't fit into his Olympian ideal—whatever bunk he spoke about sport transcending all—then, frankly, neither did she. Athletes, in his world, were supposed to be poor and pure, but she had made money of her own and had tasted plenty of what life had to offer. But she was a sure bet to win a gold—and Brundage knew it.

'What's on the menu tonight?' Lou asked a waiter.

'Pumpkin soup, roast chicken with gravy and mashed potatoes, roast beef with French fries, tomato salad, baked apple, cranberry Jell-O, and ice cream.'

'Oh my Lord . . .' Lou's eyes filled with wonder.

'Careful, Lou,' Eleanor said. 'Fatty Arbuckle never won the five thousand metres.'

After coffee, she slipped on her white sable stole. 'Well, see you boys around,' she said. 'This joint's a little clean for me.'

'Have fun,' said Lou, into his second ice cream.

The rolling seas had calmed, and Eleanor stepped out onto the deck to a beautiful night. She leaned back against the rail and watched the Olympic flag on the top deck flutter gently against a sky already filling with stars. Water lapped away from the ship, which hummed gently. The lights of a distant vessel twinkled and bobbed, and she felt a sudden yearning in her heart, a void that longed to be filled, but with what, she wasn't sure. Didn't she already have love? Phrases of music from the upper decks carried down on the breeze. She turned and climbed the stairs up to first class, trying to push Herb from her thoughts.

Some of the ship's grander passengers were walking off their dinner with a promenade on A deck. Eleanor caught the sparkle of diamonds around the women's necks and the scent of expensive perfume. Inside, a piano was playing a familiar song, 'The Glory of Love.'

She followed the music down a wide corridor to a small lounge decorated in the modern style. The lighting was soft and low.

At a bar made entirely of polished chrome, Charlie MacArthur and his wife, Helen Hayes, were standing drinks for a number of men Eleanor guessed were the reporters. Helen, fair haired and delicate in a white gown and corsage of apple blossom, looked lovelier in the flesh than she did on the silver screen, and, unlike Eleanor, had received the benefit of the A deck hairdresser.

Charlie spotted her in the doorway and clicked his fingers several times to get the attention of the pianist, who obliged him by playing the signature tune Eleanor sang in her shows with the band.

'Charlie,' she said, arching an eyebrow. 'I'm on board as an athlete.'

'Eleanor, my rose, you know Helen of course? Come and meet our friends.' The men stood up. He introduced her to Allan Gould of the United Press, and two journalists, John Walsh of the *Chicago Tribune* and Paul Gallico, the chief sportswriter of the *New York Daily News*.

'The pleasure's ours, ma'am,' said Gallico. 'We're fans of yours.'

He had a fresh, square-chinned face, glasses, a college tie, and an Ivy League manner of the shy sort. She liked him immediately.

A groomed young man with an Errol Flynn moustache stepped forwards, holding a half-pint glass brimming with champagne. He was the only one wearing white tie. 'William,' he said, handing her the glass. And she realised he must be William as in Randolph Hearst Jr. 'You've got some catching up to do, my dear. We're all getting pleasantly soused here.'

'You can't shake your shimmy on tea,' Eleanor said, raising the glass and downing it in one.

'Now, where did you learn to do that?' said Hearst, slipping his arm around her waist.

'An Illinois roadhouse called the Sudsbucket,' said Eleanor, gently removing his hand.

Another gentleman, introduced as George Kennan, an American diplomat returning to Moscow, joined them. 'Seems you've got the run of the decks here,' he said to Eleanor, a pipe clenched in his teeth. 'I've been dodging gum-chewing Tarzans all afternoon.'

'Mr Kennan, some of those Tarzans were Janes,' she said.

Helpless laughter.

'So I guess you finally told those boycotters where to get off,' said the diplomat.

'Oh please, George, this is a party,' said Helen, clutching his elbow. 'Did Charlie tell you I've returned to Broadway? California was simply ruining my skin . . .'

Eleanor considered for a moment, reminded of something that had irked her in Brundage's speech. She'd heard every boycott argument over this last year and shrugged them off. Politics, as far as she was concerned, was supremely irrelevant to the Games. Not once had her conscience been troubled by the thought that she shouldn't go to Berlin; not a wink of sleep had she lost. But tonight? She found herself very reluctant to side with Brundage, whose pro-German argument had struck her as highly unsavoury, with its mysticism and horseshit about forging a new race. The text of that anonymous note from under her pillow flickered across her mind like a title card in a silent movie—*every day citizens who do not think like the Nazis are tortured and murdered*—and now she caught herself wondering how much truth was in it. And yet . . . her mind reached for an argument that trumped them all: Jesse Owens. Wasn't he the key?

'The fastest man on earth is on board this ship,' she said, interrupting Helen, 'and he's a Negro. He's going to win gold in Berlin in front of the whole world. Don't you think that'll be one in the eye for stupid, hokey race theories? I think it's damned right that we're going to these Games.'

Mumbles of 'Here, here.'

But for the first time along the contours of her brash and uncomplicated worldview, there were buds of doubt.

They were joined by a dozen more friends and acquaintances of Charlie's and Helen's, who arrived to squeals and cheers—'My dear, what a surprise seeing your name on the passenger list'—and the party progressed noisily through its indistinct stages: sociable, elated, raucous.

Eleanor was enjoying herself. Enjoying herself more and more as the champagne went down. Two hours later, after repeated requests from Paul Gallico, and now more than a little refreshed, Eleanor was persuaded to sing.

'Name your song,' she said.

'"Let's Misbehave,"' someone shouted to howls of laughter and encouragement. She stepped unsteadily up to the piano, which played her in, and began, in her low voice:

'We're all alone,
No chaperone
Can get our num-ber,
The world's in slum-ber
Let's misbe—'

She stopped midnote. Her face froze, and the piano fell silent one bar later. The revellers turned, following the line of her gaze towards the doorway of the lounge, where a stout woman in the Olympic team uniform was standing with her arms folded. Mrs Hacker stared straight at her ward with a slow nod of her head.

'Eleanor Emerson,' she said. 'Go to bed. Now. Or shall I fetch Mr Brundage?'

Someone snickered as everyone in the room looked back at her. But Eleanor wasn't going to feel embarrassed.

'Friends . . . ,' she began, with a straight face. 'Do we need to go to Germany to see a notorious dictator with a moustache? We have our very own right here. Folks, meet our team chaperone, Mrs Eunice Hacker,' she yelled, throwing her arms out as if introducing a star act. The party cheered and raised their glasses.

A flash of alarm in the chaperone's eyes, but then her face hardened, and so did Eleanor's resolve not to have her evening spoilt.

'What're you gonna sing, Hacker? *Hey*, this is first class. You can't wear that movie-usher's uniform up here.' Mrs Hacker turned and waddled away, to more applause from the revellers.

'Oh boy,' said Eleanor, collapsing in a fit of laughter. 'That's done it.'

Chapter Four

Denham smoked an HB between courses, staring out over the great expanse of the lake at dusk. The place had drawn him into its mood—placid, untroubled, deep—and he remembered why people took holidays. He stubbed out the cigarette just as two white-gloved waiters arrived to serve him the duckling with champagne cabbage; a third showed him a Moselle from the Kurgarten's cellar and uncorked it for him to taste.

For something to read he'd brought the *Berliner Illustrirte Zeitung*, the publication with the most pictures and the fewest lies. It was full of features on the Olympic athletes and the hopes for Aryan victories. One story, titled 'Seven Beautiful Girls from the USA,' caught his eye. The magazine saw movie-star qualities in the American team and had given one girl a full-page photo. Wearing a white, one-piece bathing suit and a white cap strapped beneath her chin, her long legs crouched at the edge of a pool as though she were about to dive, the girl faced the camera, wide mouth smiling provocatively, her nose puckered. She had a long neck and a beauty spot to the right of her nose, one of those little imperfections that only seem to magnify loveliness. ELEANOR EMERSON FROM NEW YORK, the caption read, WAS THE 1932 GOLD MEDALLIST IN THE BACKSTROKE. SHE IS ALSO A SINGER AND THE WIFE OF A POPULAR BANDLEADER.

The hotel's restaurant was filling up. He heard the rough sounds of Swiss German from one table—bankers and their wives on an evening out from across the lake; at another, two English ladies keeping diaries seemed to know all the waiters by name; at a table near the door, a solitary woman in expensive Italian clothes kept giving him the eye.

The maître d' was showing another couple to a table.

Oh, *shit*.

It was Willi Greiser, the Nazi press chief, dressed in Teutonic weekend wear: a green Bavarian jacket trimmed with braid. The blonde with him must be his wife. *What the hell is he doing here? Let's hope he's not staying the week*, Denham thought. Fortunately, Greiser didn't seem to have spotted him.

He finished eating, refilled his glass, and walked out onto the terrace. Lights twinkled around the shore, and the air was heady with the scent of honeysuckle. In the distance, the Alps gave off a pale glow in the crystalline air. He leaned on the stone balustrade and listened to the laughter and fragments of conversation from couples walking the promenade below.

'Good evening, Denham.' A man's voice.

Denham screwed his eyes shut. So he'd been spotted after all.

'This *is* a pleasant coincidence,' the voice continued. 'I thought I saw your name on the hotel register. What brings you to Friedrichshafen?'

'The scenery, Greiser,' Denham said, turning round. 'How about you? Aren't the local papers printing all the good news from Berlin?'

A match flared behind Greiser's cupped hands, illuminating the low-lidded eyes, the heavy hair that fell in blond slices over his forehead, and the ridiculous college duelling scar down one cheek, the badge of a phoney pedigree. His lapel held an edelweiss.

'Just a few days' relaxation before the Olympiad,' he said. 'It's going to be a busy time for me. Half a million foreign visitors expected in Berlin.'

'That's a lot of people to fool.'

Greiser grinned with genial menace. 'There's only one thing that would bring you here, Denham, and I don't recall receiving your request to visit the *Hindenburg*, much less endorsing it.'

'I'm here to see Hugo Eckener, who is an old friend of my fa-ther's.'

Denham touched the engraved watch in his pocket, fearful now of the raw emotion it had released in him.

'Really? A social visit?' Greiser chuckled, breathing out a mix of sarcasm and smoke. 'You're here to write a feature, and this time you'll clear it with my office—before that fucking agent of yours sells it all over the world. The chief read your piece on National So-cialism in football and was highly annoyed by it.'

'Goebbels read that?' Denham punched the air.

'In German. It was syndicated in one of the Austrian dailies. I had to calm him down, tell him you're not a bad sort. But this is a warning to you, Denham. I'm serious. Any more damage like that and your press accreditation will be revoked. You'll be expelled . . . or worse.'

'Greiser, what could be worse than that?'

He fixed Denham with a hard stare. 'Watch your step,' he whis-pered and turned back through the terrace doors into the restau-rant.

Denham jabbed two fingers up and down at Greiser's departing head, then turned and slumped onto a stone bench. Somewhere off to the left, in the hotel ballroom, a string orchestra was playing the waltz from *The Merry Widow*.

He'd clashed before with Greiser over pieces he'd written and had got away with it. But this time it sounded like the Bank of Cheek and Luck was calling in the loan. He cupped his face in his hands and rubbed his eyes. Meeting the combined demands of Greiser and his agent was like finding his way through a fantasy castle riddled with mirrors, mines, and trapdoors.

Someone had left a wineglass on the stone paving of the terrace. On a sudden impulse Denham jumped up and kicked it, sending it high into the air in a great arc that ended in the lake.

He'd known Greiser for years. They were the same age, both re-porters, but the similarities ended there. Greiser was an opportunist

with a diabolical talent for manipulating the foreign press. His cos-
mopolitan background was unusual in the Nazi hierarchy—he'd
spent a year at Cornell, spoke fluent English, and had something
of the college jock about him, which made him popular with the
United Press boys. Yet he was the worst type of careerist fostered
by the regime. Even the fanatics had the integrity of their faith,
however loathsome, but Greiser believed in nothing. He'd begun
his career reporting the truth and had switched to suppressing it,
as though it were a natural evolution. He was wholly without conscience. Whatever grim fate he was threatening at the end of that
exchange, Denham had no doubt that he meant it.

Feeling a sudden urge to speak to someone human he returned to
his room and placed a telephone call. The operator called him back
after a few minutes with his connection to London.

Tom answered. Their conversation was stilted at first, talking
about school and cricket, but that changed when Denham mentioned he'd been inside the *Hindenburg*. His son had question after
question, some of them highly original, in the way that only children can be.

'You didn't smoke a cigarette on board, did you?'

'No, I didn't. But there is a special fireproof smoking room.'

'But how do they light the cigarettes?'

'I don't know.'

'Did you get me those stamps?'

'Of course,' Denham lied, hitting his forehead. 'I've put them in
the post.'

He remembered that none of Tom's school friends had got their
hands on a recent Zeppelin issue. By such small tokens are status
and respect conferred among eight-year-olds.

Denham said, 'How's Mummy? Is she there?'

'She's gone for a walk with Uncle Walter.'

Who's Uncle Walter? 'Ah, I see.'

'When are you coming home?'

'Soon.'

Their chat concluded after Tom gave him a trumpet recital he'd been practising for school. It was an uncertain performance, full of breathy squeaks and duff notes, but Denham could picture the concentration on his small face.

When he replaced the receiver, a valve in his heart opened and flooded him with sadness. He imagined for the thousandth time how it might have been if he'd made a success of things with Anna. He knew how hard it must have been for her to cope with him: his sudden departures on trips lasting weeks, his silences and secrets. His craving for solitude. He didn't blame her for leaving him. But he missed Tom. Could they ever have been a happy, carefree family? The three of them living in that house in Hampstead, pottering in the garden on summer days like today or roaming on the heath . . .

Or had there, in truth, been no real choice for him?

He took out a small framed photograph he kept in his travelling case: of Tom holding up a slow-worm he'd found in a flowerbed, a squeal of horror and delight on his face, and Anna sitting on a deck chair behind him looking cross—a disjunction that never failed to make him smile. He placed it on the bedside table, lay his head on the pillow, and angled the frame so that his face was reflected in the glass. Then he imagined that he, too, was in the picture with them.

But he was slipping into that slough of loneliness.

He looked at his watch. It was still early.

With an effort he got up and wandered downstairs to find the bar, thinking how much he was in the mood to hear a slow trumpet melody, pulled along by the lazy rhythm of a double bass. The orchestra, however, had moved on to a medley from *Der Rosenkavalier.* It seemed to be working its way through all the Führer's favourites. Nothing with any Negroid syncopation, which pretty much ruled out anything that might set your feet tapping. Perhaps they saved the Wagner for cocktail hour.

As he passed the reception desk Denham saw that he'd caught the eye of a young man sitting with a group of four others in the corner of the lobby, and was immediately on his guard. He walked into the deserted bar, sat at a tall stool in front of the barman, and glanced in the mirror behind the crystal and bottles. Sure enough, the man followed him in, accompanied by the others, and they all sat at a table nearby.

Were they watching him?

He ordered a large whisky. The young man glanced again at Denham, but the others, deep in some boisterous discussion, didn't seem to be looking. Nothing unusual if the local police were keeping a tab on him, he supposed. Especially after he'd come so spectacularly to the attention of the area Brownshirt division on his arrival. He lit an HB and watched the reflected smoke coil into the air. Couldn't a man have a quiet drink without being spied on?

Before he could even sip his whisky, the young man was standing next to him at the bar, waiting to order. He turned to Denham with a broad smile.

'You're American?'

First Greiser, now this. Why hadn't he stayed in his room?

'English, actually.'

'Wonderful. I love your Cary Grant.'

The remark was more unexpected for being spoken in English.

'So what do you like about Friedrichshafen?' the man said, still smiling. 'The friendly locals?' This he said with a slight tip of his head towards the barman, who was polishing a glass and eyeing them both with suspicion.

It was hearing the actor's name pronounced with a German accent that made Denham smile, despite himself. 'I'm here as a guest of the Zeppelin Company.'

The man's eyes widened. 'That's why we're here,' he said, 'for the *Hindenburg*, I mean. We're the movie crew filming the opening ceremony of the Olympiad on Saturday. We were just arguing about how to set up the shot as we fly over.'

Denham turned to look properly at him. He was quite young, perhaps about twenty-seven, slender, good-looking, and dark for a

German, with glossy black hair sleeked stiffly back. His features
were delicate, Italian almost, with a straight nose and long eye-
lashes. He had on a white sports sweater over an open-necked shirt,
like a tennis player.

'Friedrich Christian,' he said, extending his hand. 'But everyone
calls me Friedl.'

Denham introduced himself. 'You're a cameraman?'

'I'm training to be one. I used to be an actor,' he said with a shrug,
'but there are not so many roles for dark-haired boys these days . . .
I write poetry, too. And you? You must be a reporter. You don't look
like a tourist.'

'Is it that obvious?' Denham said with a wink and straightaway
wished he hadn't. The young man gave him an odd, private smile.

Denham shifted on the bar stool and mentioned that he'd be on
Saturday's flight, too.

'Excellent—then together we'll descend through the clouds to
Olympus, like gods.'

'Where did you learn such good English?'

'In Berlin. I lived with a poet from Corpus Christi College, Cam-
bridge. He taught me. But so did Agatha Christie and John Buchan
. . . and Jean Harlow, Bessie Smith, and Cab Calloway.'

Denham felt sorry for him. He would have to hide his nature a
bit better if he was to avoid a visit from the Gestapo's queer squad.
All the same, there was something not wholly trustworthy about
him—in the hustlerlike way he grinned and stood a fraction too
close for comfort.

'Who's starring in the film?'

'It's a documentary, called *Olympia*. The athletes are the stars I
suppose . . . although in a way I don't think the film is about sport
at all. May I?' he said, pointing at Denham's matches on the bar
and producing a very fine cigarette case. It was a beautiful object,
Denham noticed, fashioned of engraved silver and inscribed with
the initials *KR*.

'Let me guess,' Denham said as Friedl lit up. 'The film is really about showcasing the might of the new Germany to the world? No one knows that better than the reporters. Everything serves politics now, including the *Hindenburg.*'

Friedl pondered this as he inhaled. 'No, not that even,' he said. 'It's about perfection, physical perfection. The whole film is about the power and beauty of the body . . .'

That's probably the biggest Nazi obsession of all, Denham thought.

Later, on the way back to his room, he wondered about the Nazis' attitude towards homosexuals. A boy caught with a boy faced conviction under Paragraph 175 and a long stretch in a camp, where the '175ers' got a worse time than the Jews. Yet no other regime in history had done more to throw boys together with boys, not to mention kitting them out in a fetish of straps, belts, and boots.

Other things about that lad rang warning bells, too, all of them faint except for one: the initials on that silver cigarette case meant that either his name wasn't Friedl Christian, or it wasn't his. And if it wasn't his, he'd probably stolen it.

The Alpine air had made Denham drowsy. He lay down on his side in the same spot as before and was gazing again at the photograph next to his bed when he realised that his reflection was no longer in its frame.

He sat up, all his suspicions coming alive.

Had it been moved?

Warily he looked around the room, at his case, his typewriter.

Maybe he was being paranoid.

Chapter Five

The summons was swift in coming. At ten-thirty Eleanor was still slumbering when Olive shook her. 'Hey,' she squeaked, sounding for all the world like Betty Boop. 'Mr Brundage wants to see you in the C deck coffee room.'

She sat up slowly and felt her temples with her fingers. 'Jesus.' Her eyes felt too small for their sockets, and there was a bilious, grapey concentration coating her tongue.

Show them what you're made of, sister, she told herself. 'Kid, pass me those Alka-Seltzers next to the washbasin, would you?'

Half an hour later she entered the coffee room, fresh, made up, and wearing her team uniform for the first time. Avery Brundage was sitting behind a table with three other committee members she didn't recognise. But at least Hacker wasn't there to gloat.

The door opened again, and Mrs Hacker plodded in and took a seat.

'Good morning,' Eleanor said with a bright smile. 'What's this about?'

'I think you know what this is about, Mrs Emerson,' Brundage said, tapping his thumb with a pencil. They each had a copy of the AOC handbook in front of them. 'Mrs Hacker discovered you drunk and abusive at two o'clock this morning.'

'That's hardly true,' said Eleanor. 'It was one-thirty for a start.' She noticed one of the committee members suppressing a smile, but Brundage was not amused.

'Don't screw with us, young lady. I made the rules perfectly clear. If you set yourself above everyone else you will disrupt the team's morale and discipline, and I will not *stand* for that.' His voice rose to a shout. It was a shock, like a clap of thunder on a fine day. 'I spent two years fighting old man Taylor. Tell me, am I fighting you, too? Because you *will not win*.' His eyes were blazing. For several seconds he glared at her. Then, in a calmer voice, he said, 'I should tell you that I am minded to drop you from the team. However . . . my colleagues, in their wisdom, think it fair to give you one more chance.'

Eleanor glanced at the other men, grateful to know she had allies who had restrained him.

'You will not be seen on the first-class deck again. Do you understand me?' He slammed his fist on the table. 'One last chance. Now get out and train.'

She was close to tears. As she rose to leave, she saw victory playing around the edges of Hacker's whiskery lips. Well, the old buzzard got her revenge all right.

Eleanor strode out of the room, onto the deck, and around the corner to look for the quietest spot she could find, which was in between two lifeboats. She leaned against the rail, hidden from view. Most of the team were training on the sunny side of the ship.

She wanted to scream. Her father, with his righteous speeches and—once she felt guilty enough—his damned forgiving smile. Now Brundage. She felt whacked between these men like a hockey puck.

All she wanted to do was dive into that pool and win.

TWO DAYS LATER the *Manhattan* docked for a few hours at Cobh in southern Ireland. Team members of Irish descent crowded the ship's rails to see the colourful terraced streets along the waterfront and the towering cathedral, their young eyes rheumy with nostalgia for a country they'd never set foot in. That evening the ship sailed into the English Channel to dock for the night at Cherbourg.

'Nothing again today, ma'am.' The radio telegraph operator

checked through the telegrams in his in-tray. 'Sorry. Does your husband have the correct ship's name and code?'

Eleanor had called by the small telegraph office on each day of the voyage. She had received messages from well-wishers in New York and one from her parents, expressing a hope that she was behaving, but not a word from Herb, despite her cabling several notes she thought were lighthearted and conciliatory enough not to make him feel upstaged. What a stubborn child he could be.

Last night and again this evening Mrs Hacker was standing near her at dinner, like a prison warden, the dull gravity of her presence sucking all the fun out of the atmosphere. She wore a black pleated dress with cavalier cuffs and collar. Her hair was scraped back into a knot. Where the hell did they get her? She could be Bela Lugosi's mother.

At first Eleanor thought the old crow was simply keeping an eye on her, but tonight the chaperone's malevolent glances in her direction convinced her she was being goaded. Go ahead, try your luck, my dear, the whiskery smile seemed to be saying. You'll be expelled from the enchanted kingdom and sent home in a pumpkin.

A round of applause. Some of her teammates had decided to put on a show, and Eleanor looked over to see Olive taking the stage dressed as Shirley Temple, with a large bow in her hair. She did a childish curtsey and began singing in her squeaky voice 'Animal Crackers in My Soup.'

Eleanor closed her eyes. That *does it*, she thought and threw down her napkin. She got up, walked between the tables to the door, out of the dining room, and onto the deck. It was an overcast night threatening rain. The harbour lights of Cherbourg threw unnatural colours onto the oily seawater, and the port looked grim and unenticing. She wandered along the deck, with snatches of Olive's whiny song following her on the damp breeze.

One last time, she thought, and stopped by the door of the telegraph office. What will it be tonight? A telegram from President Roosevelt, but nothing from Herb?

'Oh, Mrs Emerson.' The radio operator seemed to avoid her eye. He wasn't supposed to peruse the content of passengers' telegrams, but he took the messages down. He retrieved an envelope from his tray and handed it to her. She opened it in front of him and knew she had trouble when she saw the sender's name, Louella Parsons, LA queen of the gossip columnists. The message read:

ACTRESS VELMA DELMONT PHOTOGRAPHED LEAVING YOUR
HUSBANDS HOTEL ROOM SANTA MONICA THIS MORNING STOP
PLEASE CABLE REACTION STOP

The operator had found a hole-puncher to empty.

'Well,' she said tartly, reading the words a second time, 'I guess that explains his cable-shyness.' She crumpled up the piece of paper and tossed it into his waste-paper basket. 'Good night.'

She strode into the hallway where the main stairs led down to D deck, a fury rising inside her. The lousy, childish, jealous, cheating *shuckster*. The dirty, worthless, two-faced—

'Eleanor, bed in half an hour, please. It's nine-thirty.'

She looked round to see a bald-headed AOC official with a bow tie who had been present during her coffee room encounter with Brundage.

'Oh, take a jump overboard,' she shouted without stopping.

She had never heard of Velma Delmont, but the fact that Louella Parsons had seen the need to put 'actress' in front of the name meant she was either a showbiz nobody or a streetwalker.

'Herb, my man, I hope you got everything you deserve. Velma Delmont has VD written all over her.'

In her darkened cabin Eleanor shut the door and slumped against the wall, seeing the faint disc of light from the porthole begin to blur. For a long while she stood there reddening, her teeth bared, her face streaking with tears.

'Damn it,' she whispered, the breath juddering in her chest.

In a corner of her heart perhaps she'd known he was no good.

Perhaps she'd even known that he didn't love her. She'd been a fool. His music had captivated her. And that night at Radio City when they'd first met, his pomaded hair a touch too long, his patterned tie with a diamond pin, she'd seen his potential for shocking her parents. She was young and rich, and he'd married her. Why wouldn't he? It wasn't as if she hadn't tried to make it work. But the more she'd done to win his affections the worse his behaviour seemed to get. And for the first time in her life she'd been vulnerable.

Where does it go from here? she thought.

She wiped her eyes with the palms of her hands and told herself that she refused to cry. She absolutely refused.

At the end of her corridor she put her head round the steward's door and found the cabin boy, Hal, dozing with his feet on a stool, a Lone Ranger comic book across his lap. She shook him gently.

'So,' he said, opening his eyes, 'we're alone at last.'

'Kid, do me a favour. Go find out if there's a return party for Mr and Mrs Charles MacArthur on A deck?' His eyes bulged when she showed him a silver dollar.

'Yes, ma'am.'

Minutes later she was half changed into a gown when Hal knocked on the door and handed her a note.

My dear, what's keeping you? Humdinger of a party up here!! Put your dancing shoes on. Charlie

Much later, when she tried piecing together the fragmentary memories of the evening, she wasn't sure if it was Herb's betrayal or the certain knowledge of consequences from Brundage that made her drink even more than usual. Either way, the champagne flowed and she had raised her glass with no thought for tomorrow. When the band had played 'Let's Face the Music and Dance,' she'd heard an omen and a direct appeal.

She remembered Paul Gallico stepping through the throng to greet her.

'Darling, do you have a match?' she asked him.

'Have you been crying?'

She mingled with Charlie, Helen, and John Walsh before dancing with Hearst Jr to 'Let Yourself Go.' Throughout the evening Charlie brought over people eager to meet her. It seemed she'd become something of a celebrity for defying Brundage—who, she learned, was unloved among the great and the good—and her exchange with Hacker at the MacArthurs' party had become the best piece of gossip on A deck. This is probably what had emboldened her to further indiscretion.

In the final throes of the party, with the few loyal revellers-in-arms still standing, she had a memory of inventing an uproarious new dance called 'the Avery,' which involved making jerky, chicken-enlike steps, arms flapping and rear ends stuck out, in a burlesque parody of the Charleston.

Sometime in the early hours, Paul Gallico had carried her down to D deck and had found Mrs Hacker blocking the corridor to Eleanor's cabin. The chaperone, in her bathrobe and hairnet, cocked her head as she saw them approach, relishing the moment of Eleanor's vanquishing.

'The cabins on this corridor are for females only,' she said.

'You can carry her yourself if you like,' Gallico said. At this, Eleanor tried standing but listed towards the corridor wall.

'Are you slithering around after me again?' she slurred to Hacker, with a dangerous look in her eye.

'I knew you would disobey Mr Brundage's orders to—'

'Why are you still up? Let me ask you that, why are you still up . . . you sneaking, snitching old witch?' Eleanor staggered backwards, and Gallico caught her.

'Well, I've never in my life been spoken to like—'

'You creeping, crawling old spider!' Eleanor shouted. Doors along the corridor opened, and a number of girls popped their heads out to listen.

'You dried-up fossil cat's turd . . .'

'I'm going to fetch Mr Brundage this instant,' the chaperone shrieked, but she seemed rooted to the spot, shrinking before the onslaught of Eleanor's rage.

'You do that, old girl, you do that,' Eleanor said, pointing an unsteady finger.

Then she stumbled into her cabin and passed out on her bed.

Sometime before breakfast, she heard afterwards, the ship's medic was called and failed to revive her. He thereupon diagnosed, no doubt at the prompting of Brundage, a condition of 'acute alcoholism.' Later that morning she found herself once more summoned to appear in the coffee room before the committee. As she was climbing the stairs to C deck, Gallico stopped her.

'Eleanor, John Walsh and the press boys want a quick word before you see Brundage.'

TEN MINUTES LATER she walked into the coffee room. Brundage was tight-lipped, eyeing her as though she were some repellent specimen pickled in alcohol. The bald-headed committee member with the bow tie who'd told her to go to bed last night was the nominated spokesman, but she already knew what he was going to say. She had no time for bow ties, which she associated vaguely with frivolity and penile inadequacy. Brundage nodded to him.

'Mr Penworth, if you please.'

The man cleared his throat and began reading from a statement.

'After due deliberation with my colleagues concerning your violation of the AOC training rules in the early hours of this morning and Tuesday last, and after consideration of the various complaints from the team chaperone thereunto pertaining, and of the medical diagnosis of your condition, we regret to inform you that your entry into the Olympic Games is cancelled.'

He looked up, a sheepish blink behind his eyeglasses.

'Look, gentlemen,' Eleanor said in a bleary voice, 'please don't do this. I know I had a few glasses of champagne, and I'm very sorry about the whole thing, it was wrong of me to—'

'We gave you every chance, Mrs Emerson,' said Brundage, 'but you forced our hand. You have not demonstrated the Olympic spirit, nor indeed any team spirit.' Eleanor had expected him to be angry, but he seemed relaxed, as though vindicated and relieved to be rid of her.

'Please,' she said, the composure starting to drain from her voice. 'I've spent four years training for these Games. You know I can win the gold. I want to apologise for my—'

'I'm afraid the committee's mind is definitely made up.' Brundage snapped his rulebook shut and got up to leave. 'You will disembark at Hamburg later today and return immediately to New York on board the *Bremen*. Mr Penworth here will make the arrangements. Goodbye, Mrs Emerson.'

As the other committee members began to rise, Eleanor felt her face flushing and adrenaline pumping—the instinct that kicked in when she was in danger of being beaten in the pool.

'Now just hold on one minute,' she said, leaping towards the entrance and barring the men's way. She was damned if she was going to let them close the door in her face. Avery Brundage, accustomed to having the last word, looked surprised. The committee members stood still.

'Sir, last night my friends in the press corps realised, probably before I did, what my fate would be this morning.' She stared Brundage full in the face. 'So they offered me a job.'

'A job?'

'Yes, a job. As a reporter, at the Games. They're not hiring me for my writing—they'll do that for me—but for my name. It seems, thanks to you, that I've already acquired a certain infamy in the dailies back home.'

Brundage removed his spectacles, his eyes narrowing with irritation.

'Didn't I make myself clear? I said you will disembark at Hamburg and return immediately—'

'I heard what you said. If you've fired me from the team, that's my hard luck, but you have no further rights over me.' Her eyes glistened, but her voice held. 'I'm from a free country, and if I want to be in Berlin to support my friends, there's not a damned thing you can do to stop me—unless you want to make an ass of yourself in the thirty daily newspapers of William Randolph Hearst.'

Brundage opened his mouth to speak and closed it again. For a moment he seemed ready to yell something that far exceeded the strict parameters of his own code of conduct.

Eleanor walked to the door with her back straight and her head held as high as it would go, keeping her hands in her jacket pockets so they would not see her shaking.

'See you at the opening ceremony,' she said.

Chapter Six

Zeppelins had been a part of Denham's life for as long as he could remember. The serene giants first floated into his imagination in pictures on cigarette cards. Every day after school he'd walk home to Pound Lane, a quiet row of terraced houses along the river in Canterbury, daydreaming of airships—imagining fleets of them in the sky over the cathedral, humming like giant bumblebees. He'd draw them and make models from household litter. He wanted to know everything about them. Luckily his father, Arthur, a mechanical engineer, had caught the Zeppelin bug, too.

Even in those pioneer days there was no doubt in Arthur Denham's mind that lighter-than-air ships were the future of long-distance travel. Aeroplanes, he said, were flying hedge-cutters. They'd never be good for anything but deafening, hair-raising hops. 'Not for sailing through the clouds,' he'd say with a twinkle in his eye, 'across continents and oceans.'

The Great War was into its second year when Denham finally saw a Zeppelin. He was eighteen. He and his younger brother, Sidney, were on a day trip to London with their mother's sister Joan, a nervous, childless woman who doted on them. Her surprise treat for them at the end of the day was a musical revue at the Strand Theatre.

Over the years the events of that night would assume a luminous clarity in Denham's memory. It was a chill evening in October and an air raid blackout was in force. Only the yellow lights of trams and taxis lit the faces of the crowds along the pavements—the theatregoers, the office workers heading home, the soldiers on leave from the Front. Hollow-eyed lads lost in a gloomy limbo. Above the grand buildings of the Aldwych the constellations stood out as keen as diamonds.

The show was *Sunshine Girl*, and the audience was encouraged to join in the songs.

When the final curtain call ended, the audience rose and began making their way along the rows towards the exit. They hadn't quite reached the auditorium doors when the floor shook and an ominous rumble sounded from outside.

'And here's us come without a brolly,' Aunt Joan said.

The next rumble silenced the crowd and stopped them cold. Fragments of plaster dropped from the ceiling, and the stage curtains swayed. Sidney looked up at him wide-eyed, wanting reassurance.

When it came, the explosion was almost a direct hit.

A blast ripped through the foyer, sending rolls of plaster dust into the auditorium. The crowd fell to the floor, clutching their hats to their heads. In the commotion outside a man yelled, 'It's a Zepp! It's a bloody Zepp!' A woman screamed, and unrestrained panic broke out as the crowd surged towards the exits. Sid began bawling and hid in the folds of his brother's overcoat.

'Ladies and gentlemen. Ladies—and—gentlemen—*please*,' a voice boomed from the stage. Mr George Grossmith, the show's star, was addressing them. 'Remain inside until the danger has passed over, I beg of you.' His peremptory tone seemed to take control of the crowd, making the panic subside somewhat. People hesitated, and one by one, they began to sit. 'Now, all of you, sing along with me to calm yourselves down.'

The orchestra played 'Pack Up Your Troubles in Your Old Kit Bag,' and slowly people joined in the singing. Aunt Joan's voice came in short, rattled breaths, but she persevered, as if fearful of bringing on her asthma if she succumbed to hysteria.

As the explosions and rumbles outside grew fainter, voices that had sung out of terror sang out of defiance, and by the time the orchestra played 'Keep the Home Fires Burning' the audience was a chorus of patriotic fervour. Soon, a Boy Scout appeared in the emergency exit to call the all-clear, and they ended with 'God Save the King.'

When Denham, Sidney, and Aunt Joan followed the crowd in single file through the wreckage of the foyer someone was again screaming. Outside, they stared in disbelief. People bloodied by flying glass were being tended on the steps until ambulances arrived. The grand crescent of the Aldwych, lit by the blazing roof of a building, was strewn with masonry and cobblestones. An acrid stench of cordite hung in the air. In his shock Denham was not certain what he was seeing among the flames and shadows. An omnibus overturned, its axle shattered. A dying horse's snorting and whinnying. A number of clothed forms, limbs at unfamiliar angles, sprawled over a mosaic of smashed glass.

'Oh, gosh, *look*,' said Sidney.

In the distance to the east were the cigar shapes of four Zeppelins, golden in the lights of the fires, the drone of their propeller engines clear on the night air. Arc lights swept the sky, holding one gleaming ship, then another, in the fingers of their beams. Artillery fire boomed, making chrysanthemum blooms of flame in the sky beneath them, but nothing touched them.

'It's a battlefield,' said Aunt Joan, holding a handkerchief to her mouth. 'London's a battlefield.'

Denham continued to stare, after his aunt and Sidney had turned to leave. He could not take his eyes off the four magnificent messengers of death.

HE AWOKE CLAMMY with sweat. Sheets writhed around his body, leaving striations and gullies across his neck and chest, like an artist's impression of the canals on Mars. His dream of the Zeppelins had merged—as his dreams often did—into one of the trenches. After a few weeks' training in the London Rifle Brigade he'd been shipped to France. Only a few days after that he'd seen his first man killed. And then more men killed than he could ever count.

A breeze from the lake moved the curtains, and light bouncing off water played on the ceiling of the elegant room.

He looked at his watch, and leapt out of bed.

'Damn.'

He had a Zeppelin to catch.

AT ELEVEN O'CLOCK Denham found the hangar in a frenzy. Beneath the vast tethered bulk of the *Hindenburg*, hundreds of ground crew were moving through the shadows, preparing the ship for the voyage to Berlin. Surfaces buzzed with the roar of the propeller engine cars, which were running a thunderous preflight test. The ship almost filled the hangar's cathedral space. From the rows of tall windows along the right-hand wall, shafts of light were given mass and texture by the dust in the air. Where the ceiling could be glimpsed above the leviathan, a galaxy of electric lights twinkled.

Dr Eckener was directing proceedings from the top of a truck loaded with hydrogen canisters, booming through a megaphone his demands for pressure readings, weather reports, and general haste. How soon all this purposeful mayhem would become chaos, Denham thought, without the concentrating effect of the old man's magnetism—the force that kept the whole enterprise going.

Behind him a whistle sounded, and with an echoing clang the building's great doors began to roll apart. Denham saw rays of sunshine blaze across the ship's nose and along the streamlined ridges of its hull, and felt his suitcase become light in his hands.

Eckener spotted him, and climbed down from his perch.

'Good morning, good morning,' he bellowed, without the megaphone. He was wearing his commander's cap, an old leather flying jacket over his tweed suit, and a waistcoat smudged with cigar ash.

'My dear Richard,' he said, shaking Denham's hand warmly. 'I hope everything on board will be to your comfort and satisfaction.'

'I don't doubt it. How are the skies looking?'

'A low drizzle over the Reich capital this morning. Also a stiff northeasterly. So we'd better depart before the weather plays any dirty tricks—and hope the clouds clear for our moviemakers. They're on board, together with a pair of our local Party big shots, along for the champagne and the free ride.'

Eckener held up his pocket watch for all to see and shouted, 'Ten minutes.'

'I don't know how to thank you,' Denham said.

'Richard, my boy, just come back and see your old friend soon. I hope you get the story you want. You're in Captain Lehmann's hands now.'

'You're not commanding the ship?'

'Unfortunately, no . . .' The old man hesitated. 'It seems I'm being moved aside for incurring the wrath of the Propaganda Ministry once too often.' Eckener chuckled, but there was worry in his eyes. 'I have apparently "alienated myself from the Reich," and you reporters are no longer to mention me in the newspapers.'

Before Denham could respond, a young steward was beside them, pointing at the leather case hanging from his neck.

'No personal cameras permitted on board.'

'Oh for goodness' sake, man,' Eckener barked. 'He has *my* authorisation to take his camera on board.' The young man stepped back, smarting, and Denham noticed the small Party pin in his lapel. 'Make yourself useful by offering Herr Denham whatever information he requires to write his article.'

'Yes, sir.'

Eckener smiled at Denham apologetically. 'You will have to hand him your matches, however. Not even you are exempt from that rule.'

The noise of the engine test stopped, filling the hangar with an iron silence. Eckener leaned towards Denham's ear.

'I'm sure I don't need to advise caution to you of all people. The Party has members among the crew. They'll be watching you . . .'

Denham winked. 'Don't you worry. I won't tell them your joke about a little girl going up to Hitler and—'

'Till we meet again,' Eckener said in a loud voice, cocking his head towards the offended steward, and then giving a wheezy laugh despite himself. 'That was a good one. If you hear any more, remember them for me . . . now hurry.'

Denham turned and climbed the narrow aluminium stairway, thinking of the joke Eckener had told him. A little girl approaches Hitler and his entourage with a bouquet of flowers but stumbles. Hitler catches her, cups her face in his hands, and kneels down to say a few quiet words. Afterwards people crowd around her. 'What did the Führer say to you?' they ask. The little girl is puzzled. 'He said, "Quick, Hoffmann, a photo!"'

He was concerned about Eckener. Why did he have to go on making a stand like that, jeopardising his life's work? It would not make one iota of difference.

Denham continued up into the belly of the ship. It was like boarding a flying ocean liner. He nodded to a bust of old Hindenburg on the landing, then turned the corner into a lounge furnished with modern, comfortable armchairs. On the wall a large mural map of the world traced the routes of the great expeditions, from the voyages of Magellan to the globe-trotting flight of the *Graf Zeppelin*.

The lounge was separated by a low rail from a long promenade, where wide windows slanting outwards offered panoramic views. Most improbable of all in a craft where everything was designed to save weight, a baby grand piano built of aluminium stood at the far side of the lounge. Above it hung the obligatory portrait of the dictator, whose hyperthyroid glare followed Denham across the room. The soft red carpet deadened his footsteps. The area was deserted.

The *Hindenburg* was truly an airborne hotel, and a luxurious hotel at that. It was the mother lode of his fantasies, and even greater than he'd imagined—more beautiful, more spacious. He touched the Plexiglas window, almost expecting it to dissolve as he woke from a dream.

'*Zeppelin marsch!*'

Outside, Eckener shouted the order to move, and the hundreds of ground crew picked up the ropes and pulled, walking the giant craft out through the hangar doors like Lilliputians heaving Gulliver into the sun.

In the open, as the men waited for the signal from the control car, Denham caught himself wondering whether a thing so large was really going to fly.

'*Schiff hoch!*'

The mooring ropes were thrown off, and together the men gave a mighty upward shove, pushing the ship into the air. He heard laughter and a smatter of applause from a crowd of bystanders as water ballast was released from the prow, dousing some of the men.

Within seconds the ground was receding at an alarming speed. At about three hundred feet the ship slowly stopped rising and drifted in silence for a few moments, over the Zeppelin field and towards Lake Constance. Sunlight danced among the sailboats, and rippled like satin over the distant foothills of the Alps. Among the gabled roofs of Friedrichshafen, cars seemed like toys moving among matchbox houses.

Suddenly the four diesel engines sputtered into action; the propellers churned the air and pushed the great ship forwards.

Denham swept his hat off and laughed, holding his arms wide. He was charged with an electrifying freedom, as though he were slipping the world's chains, floating free of all its fear. How sublime, he thought, how miraculous, how—

'Hello, Richard,' said a voice in English.

He turned, embarrassed, as if he'd been caught pulling faces in the shaving mirror.

'Ah. Hello there.'

The young man he'd met at the bar, Friedl something, stood at the entrance to the lounge in knickerbockers and a sleeveless cricket sweater over a white shirt. His mop of black hair was swept under a Basque cap, as though he were a weekend guest of the Great Gatsby.

'We've almost got the ship to ourselves,' he said with that hustler grin. 'Just a few guests, my colleagues in the movie crew—and you.'

'Yes, it's rather a privilege.'

'Tell me something . . . do you listen to swing?'

Surprised, Denham said, 'I do.'

'Good. I want to know what grooves these days'—he raised a hand to the side of his mouth in a mock whisper—'and about all the other things that are banned here . . .'

Again, he was struck by the man's candid nature. It seemed hard to believe that it hadn't got him into trouble. And he listened to swing. If there were two things utterly anathema to National Socialism, they were Jews and hot jazz.

'We'll do an exchange,' Denham said. 'I'll tell you what's hot and you can tell me any gossip you've heard about the Games—and I mean real news, not official stuff.'

On the port side of the airship a long dining room filled the length of the space, separated by a low railing from another promenade, also with panoramic views.

Tables were laid with white linen, fresh-cut flowers, and silver cutlery; the china plates bore a Zeppelin motif. White-jacketed stewards were arranging ice buckets and dishes of cured ham and roast venison for a buffet lunch. Halfway along the promenade Friedl's crew was adjusting a rig holding a telephoto-lens movie camera pointed through an open promenade window. Denham recognised the men from the bar at the Kurgarten. The two Party big shots Eckener had mentioned—for whose enjoyment the sumptuous lunch was provided—were admiring the view with their wives and two young children, a boy and a girl. Both were colourless men in their late thirties, complacent in their light brown tunics, gold-trimmed swastika armbands, and booted legs, set wide apart. In any normal society they'd be town clerks or farm inspectors, Denham supposed, but in Germany the Party could elevate the most humdrum official into a Caesar, free to build an empire from which to draw homage and fealty.

'A pair of golden pheasants,' Friedl said.

They walked to the windows at the opposite end of the promenade from the Party men and watched the Rhine wind its way into
the horizon through steep, wooded valleys. The castle tower of
Meersburg passed below. As it gained height, the ship tilted gently,
and a broad patchwork of cabbage fields and hamlets filled the view
for as far as the eye could see. Horses pulling a hay cart reared their
heads at the sight of the giant ship looming above; a farm dog chased
its shadow across a field, barking.

Corks popped and champagne was poured, and shortly after,
lunch was announced. Denham joined Friedl at a table for two.

'That's our director of photography, Jaworsky,' Friedl said, pointing at an older man talking to the captain. 'The best cameramen
in Germany today—made his name shooting Alpine movies, our
equivalent of the western, you could say. And over there is Gerhard,
our gaffer.' He nodded with a flash of shyness towards a tanned lad
in shirtsleeves who was lifting reels. The lad smiled back at them.

'He's your boyfriend?' Denham asked, before he could stop himself.

A change of pitch in the propeller engines and the ship picked up
speed.

Friedl stared at his plate, reddening, as though he'd been slapped
across the face. When he looked up, his fine features hardened.

'No, he is not.' After another pause, he said, 'As you yourself
might have said, is it that obvious?'

Denham wanted to kick himself.

'Please forgive me. It's a reporter's bad habit. I spend too much
time with hard-nosed hacks. I hope you'll excuse it.'

Friedl was about to speak when his eyes froze on something over
Denham's shoulder. He turned to see a dull-eyed, freckled boy of
about ten, the son of one of the Party men, standing near their table, watching them. The type of boy who'd stone birds for fun. He
wore the Jungvolk uniform. The belt around his shorts had a dagger
hanging from it.

'It's rude to stare,' Denham said in German.

'Why are you speaking English?'

'We're American gangsters planning a bank robbery in Berlin.'

The boy looked from him to Friedl. 'He doesn't look like a gangster,' he said, then ran off to report this observation to his father.

'You wait,' Denham said. 'He'll be telling them he's discovered a spy ring on board.'

Friedl didn't seem to be listening. For a few moments his eyes were naked, and Denham saw the truth of his existence: a secret life, of courage poisoned by fear. Fear of whisperers and informers. Of midnight knocks on the door.

'You must miss the old republic,' Denham said, still trying to atone for his gaffe. 'I mean, no one in Berlin cared who was a warm boy then, did they? What happened to the old El Dorado on Motzstrasse?'

'Closed down,' Friedl said, his face sullen. After a long silence, he spoke in a distracted voice, as though his mind was riffling through banks of old memories. 'Berlin was the centre of the world, you know. Jazz to rival Harlem's, great movies, new things happening in art every week. Nightlife, atmosphere, freedom. I had work at the UFA studios; friends I'd meet in the cafés on the Ku'damm. It was a great life. Look at the city now . . . The only atmosphere left is fear. Everyone's afraid. Even those golden pheasants over there will worry over what their children say about them on Jungvolk evenings . . . There is a shadow over everything.'

He looked at Denham, his face suddenly animated. Speaking in German, he said, 'Didn't we meet at a poetry reading in Mainz last year?'

Denham waited for him to elaborate, but he said nothing more. 'I don't think so,' he said, pulling a dubious face. 'Not sure I've ever been to Mainz.' He knocked back his champagne.

Friedl continued to watch him for a moment, but a light seemed to go out in his face, and his eyes drifted to the windows.

They waited until the Party men and their families had heaped their plates; then he and Denham helped themselves to smoked ham, black bread, pâté, and pickles, and Friedl asked him what was new in Harlem and who was recording on which label, revealing an obsessive's knowledge of jazz that petered out after about 1934. He listened keenly as Denham told him of Count Basie's new tenor sax, and Benny Goodman's move to Chicago.

'Believe it or not,' Friedl said, 'something like the old life may return to Berlin for the duration of the Games. All part of this relaxed image they want to present while the city is full of foreigners. The police will tolerate jazz, and the Jews will get a break.'

A waiter refilled their glasses. They toasted each other, and Denham regarded his new friend with a mixture of respect and concern.

Friedl explained that nothing was being left to chance with the movie, *Olympia*, and with a blank-cheque budget from the Propaganda Ministry, they had more than forty cameras ready for every contingency. Any shots that could be filmed beforehand had been. 'I've been on set at the stadium for a month,' he said. 'She films *everything*.'

'She . . . ?' Denham wasn't sure why he felt surprised. 'You work for Leni Riefenstahl?'

'Yes.' Friedl gave him a quizzical look, as if unaware of the opprobrium and awe that attached to the woman's name in equal measure. Denham had seen *Triumph of the Will* and remembered being dazed with disgust and admiration. It was an astonishing work, casting Hitler as a nation's Messiah, glowing with a monochrome aura. The bastard had literally given her a cast of thousands.

'Well then,' Denham said, buttering a slice of bread, 'what stories going round would you care to share with a discreet reporter?'

Friedl munched slowly on an apple. 'None that wouldn't get me into trouble . . .'

'So you do have a story.'

'I didn't say that.'

'Come on. If it's the one about the German lady high jumper who might be a man, I've heard it.'

'No . . .' Friedl shifted in his seat. 'It's about the Jewish athletes, the ones who trained for the German team . . .' He turned again, to make sure they weren't being overheard. The Party men and their wives were taking second helpings, but the boy was nowhere to be seen. 'Sorry, but if I tell you, they'll trace it back to me . . .'

This was a familiar situation for Denham, and he seldom felt proud of himself when he had to use the old hacks' tricks.

'Look, if it's a story that damages the Nazis, the world needs to hear it. Don't you agree?'

'Yes, but—'

'These people aren't your friends, Friedl. If you keep quiet you're sort of helping them . . . aren't you?'

Friedl fell silent. Denham waited.

'Do I have your word you'll protect my name?'

'Naturally,' Denham said.

'The Jewish athletes in the Olympic Games . . . ,' he began, and started again. 'The Reich Sports Office had to allow some Jews to try for the German team; otherwise the IOC would have removed the Games from Germany . . . or countries would have boycotted.'

Denham searched his memory. There had been an outcry about this in the international press last year, before the Winter Olympics in Bavaria. The Americans sent a delegation to make sure the German-Jewish athletes were being given a fair chance.

Friedl leaned in closer. 'It was a deception. The Nazis set up some fake training session for the benefit of the IOC, the press, and the Americans, with Jewish athletes present. But in fact the Jews got no facilities—nothing. They had to train in farmers' fields. After all, they're banned from every sports club in Germany . . .'

A buzzing noise, and an old Fokker biplane appeared alongside the airship's promenade. The pilot, in cap and goggles, waved, and most of the diners interrupted their eating to watch at the windows. The boy was still not there.

'It gets worse,' Friedl said. 'Last week, when all the countries' teams were safely on board ships heading for Germany, the Reich Sports Leader simply told the Jews that they hadn't been selected for the German team after all. I guess he calculated that it was too late for anyone to complain or take official action.'

'"Germans Drop Jews from Team"?' Denham said. 'Nothing new there.'

It was a depressing and familiar story, although this deception sounded more brazen than most.

'They had to make a single exception, however. Hannah Liebermann. You've heard of her?'

'The fencer? Are you joking?' Denham reflected for a moment. It hadn't occurred to him before that she was Jewish. 'She's one of the most famous athletes in the world.'

'Exactly. She's so famous they couldn't *not* include her. But how is this for irony?' His voice dropped to a whisper. 'She *refused*. The one Jew they gave the honour of competing for the Reich told them where to put their invitation . . .'

'Good for her. So she's not on the team either.'

For a minute Denham had thought this was leading up to a scoop. He called the waiter over and asked for a whisky.

'She is on the team,' Friedl said, his expression dark. 'They're forcing her.'

'What?'

'They're forcing her to compete on the German team by threatening her family if she doesn't.'

'Christ.' Denham put his glass down. 'Wasn't she living abroad?'

Friedl was distracted again. The cameraman, Jaworsky, was calling him from the far end of the promenade.

'She's been in California since '33. When she refused their invitation the Gestapo started arresting her family. She boarded the next ship back to Germany.'

'How do you know all this?'

Friedl shrugged. 'Call it pillow talk between me and someone who knows.'

'I've got to interview her,' Denham said.

'Excuse me.' Friedl got up. 'I have to work.'

Denham had a story. A vital, personal story of courage and deception, a *political* story that even his agent, Harry, would like. It moved him. It went straight to the heart of all that was wrong with these Games. An innocent woman made to act in the charades of a boundlessly criminal regime in its bid to appear decent before a watching world. They were holding her up as proof of their fairness when they had nothing but hatred for her. To cap it all, she was a sporting superstar—with cover-girl looks.

He drained his glass and got up, noticing as he did so the white cloth on a nearby table twitch, and the scabbard of a Jungvolk dagger poking from underneath. Glancing over his shoulder to make sure no one was watching, he delivered a brisk kick to the bulge where the boy's backside was. He was out of the dining room before anyone could locate the source of the howling.

As usual when he was preoccupied Denham wanted to pace. He returned to the deserted lounge on the starboard side and ambled along the promenade window, drumming his fingers on the sill. Beneath him beech forests and fields heavy with crops rolled by, but in his mind's eye he saw Hannah Liebermann, lithe and silken-haired, pointing her foil, arm straight. She was one of the greatest athletes Germany had ever produced, whose fighting style had an extraordinary grace.

He'd have to reach her in private somehow. An approach through the official channels would almost certainly be refused. In fact, Willi Greiser would surely expel him for this one. No doubt about that . . . Was it worth it?

He was sitting at the baby grand piano, looking up at the portrait of the tramp turned dictator, trying to remember the notes for that Bessie Smith number 'Nobody Knows You When You're

Down and Out,' when he saw the red jug ears and ginger hair of that steward approaching from the far end of the lounge. The one who'd asked for his camera earlier. The Party pin in his lapel glinted like an evil eye.

'Herr Denham? I'm at your disposal.' He spoke with a marked Swabian accent. 'Captain Lehmann suggested you may like a tour of the ship.'

'You read my mind,' Denham said. 'Could we start with the smoking room?' He was dying for a cigarette.

They descended to B deck. The steward, who introduced himself as Jörg, led him to a small bar, which connected via an airlock to an intimate smoking room, pressurised, he explained, so that no hydrogen could seep in. It had small café tables and a comfortable leather bench running around its walls.

He lit Denham's HB. On the far side of the room was a wide window set into the floor. Wisps of white cloud passed beneath the glass, filling the room with a pale light reflected from forests and valleys below. *Surely this must be the acme of all smoking experiences*, he thought.

'Do you have mail to post?' the steward asked.

'Mail?'

'We drop a postbag when we reach Berlin. Letters are franked in the mailing room.'

'With *Hindenburg* stamps?'

'Of course.'

'You may just have saved a father's reputation with an eight-year-old.'

Jörg grinned and fetched a blank postcard from behind the bar. Denham scribbled:

Dearest Tom
Here are the stamps I promised. Your old dad's writing this from the smoking room of the 'Hindenburg.' To answer your question,

my cigarette was lit with a car lighter attached to the wall. How
about that? Be nice to Mummy.

Love, Dad

He handed the postcard to the steward, stubbed out his HB, and
the tour continued. The young man gave him a pair of canvas shoe
coverings in case his heel should make a spark on the metal grill
floor, and they entered the keel corridor—no more than a narrow
catwalk—which led deep into the stern of the ship. Denham took
notes in shorthand of the statistics Jörg gave him as they passed
storerooms with space for two and a quarter tonnes of fresh meat,
poultry, and fish and 250 vintage wines; and the freight room, which
was large enough to hold an aeroplane and the huge duralumin
tanks filled with diesel fuel.

As they neared the end of the corridor the steward did an extraordinary thing. Beneath them stretched the silver fabric of the
airship's outer cover. To demonstrate its strength he leapt twelve
feet off the catwalk and bounced up and down like a boy on a tram-
poline. For an instant Denham glimpsed the unremarkable lad beneath the Nazi persona he'd acquired like a greasy sheen on his skin.

Onwards they went until they reached a vertical shaft, which they
climbed for what seemed like half a mile until it joined the main
axial corridor, the bone that ran through the centre of the vast ship
from fins to nose.

'Amazing,' Denham said, laughing.

It was like a film stage built from an Erector set. A gargantuan
spider's web of bracing wires and girders radiated out from the central axis, and looking along the corridor's length was like seeing infinity reflected between two mirrors. The air was much colder.

Together they walked along the corridor between towering gas
cells, which hummed quietly with the vibration of the engines.

'There are sixteen of them,' Jörg explained, 'maintained around
the clock by duty riggers.'

Denham touched one of them with the palm of his hand. That such a delicate membrane separated safety from catastrophe was unimaginable. What risks man takes in order to fly.

Soon the corridor intersected with another airshaft.

'Wait here,' said Jörg. 'I must pass an instruction to the duty rigger.' With that he disappeared down the shaft.

Seems a good moment to give him the slip, Denham thought. He continued alone along the axial corridor, eventually reaching a bay in the very tip of the ship's nose, where huge coils of mooring rope were stacked on the floor.

Outside the bay window, fields of cumulus billowed, brilliant and numinous in the afternoon sun. The ship had gained considerable height while he was inside its hull and was now beginning its descent through the clouds. A minute later his vision filled with grey, and the rain of a summer squall flicked at the window, fanning across the glass in the headwind.

Suddenly, there was Berlin, vast and sullen.

The metropolis spread out in every direction. He hadn't even realised they were near. The sun broke through for an instant, casting a shaft of gold over the eastern outskirts. He saw the River Spree snaking around the landmarks, opalescent in the metallic light. He saw coal barges, trams, and traffic moving.

The *Hindenburg* maintained its downward tilt and was soon gliding over the rain-washed streets and rooftops, casting its shadow. As it slowed, the propeller engines changed gear into a deep, pulsing drone.

He could see the entire Olympic route: all the way from the Brandenburg Gate, through the Tiergarten, where the road was hedged with flag-waving crowds, along the Kaiserdamm and the Heerstrasse between double rows of sycamores, until in the distance to the west he saw it: the granite colonnade with banners flying, the thousand-year stadium of the new order.

Within minutes he could make out the brazier on the Marathon

Gate and the top-hatted heads of officials. The athletes, in their blazers and white shoes, stood in long rows, preparing to parade onto the track behind their flags.

Now the airship was passing slowly over the stadium's stone rim, and Denham's line of vision dropped into a vast crater seething with life, deeper than the surrounding ground. Half the bowl was plunged into shadow by the ship, and a hundred thousand people raised their heads towards him.

'My God,' he whispered.

The ship hovered for a moment, the engines humming so that the propellers seemed to caress the air.

A fanfare sounded faintly, distorted through loudspeakers, and then the movement of a wind over a field of barley passed through the hundred thousand, which rose as one, right arms raised, and he realised that the man himself was making his entrance, the tiny, striding figure in brown.

High in his vantage point, Denham heard the crowd's roars, like waves crashing on a shingle shore.

Chapter Seven

The roar of propeller engines set Eleanor's teeth on edge.

'Ain't that something?' shouted Paul Gallico, his mouth full of bratwurst. The crowd applauded in a frenzy. He was sitting next to her in the Associated Press box, rather too close for comfort. They were really crammed in on these benches.

She didn't even look up as the Zeppelin droned overhead. She felt slightly sick to her stomach, imagining she still sensed the tilt and sway of the *Manhattan* beneath her. Of more interest to her was a shouting match going on nearby between some guards and a tough-looking young woman in flared slacks who seemed to be in charge of a camera crew positioned near the rostrum. According to the AP reporters in front of her, the guards had been ordered by Dr Goebbels to remove the cameras. The woman insisted she had permission to film.

'See, these guys put on a great show of order,' Gallico said, 'but their whole setup is chaotic. The country is a jungle of personal empires.'

Eleanor said nothing.

'Aw, cheer up, sweetheart. It's not like you've never won an Olympic gold before.'

'Buddy, I'm okay,' she said, sharper than she'd meant. She squeezed his hand. 'You boys have been swell.'

He offered her the bratwurst, and she took a bite.

'Hey . . . ,' she said, chewing. 'I always knew I'd go from bad to wurst.'

That gave Gallico helpless giggles at the moment of Hitler's entrance.

They'd guessed the great man was near. Loudspeakers around the stadium had kept up a hyperactive commentary on the progress of his motorcade across the city, and the crowd simmered with excitement. Contingents from five continents were singing football-terrace songs and a dozen national anthems that boomed around the bowl in a cacophony of competitive cheer. Soldiers in uniform; members of hundreds of sporting and youth organisations in their white shirts; diplomats, the press, socialites, and families of Berliners with children waited in high spirits, enjoying the Olympic truce that lay over the city.

Eleanor was a stone in a field of waving grass, consigned here to the bleachers to look down on all she had lost. To hell with her newspaper column. She considered slipping away while she had the chance, and before her ex-teammates marched in.

Too late.

An earth tremor of applause. The loudspeakers rose to a shriek, and the crowd stood to greet the distant figure entering between the towers of the Marathon Gate. At the same moment sunshine dazzled on the wet granite, as if the elements were in abeyance to some diabolical luck that accompanied him. A fanfare sounded, drowned out by yells of *Heil!*—the first few shouted with hysteria before finding their measure in a deep chant.

The American reporters remained in their seats, which shook beneath them with the noise. To the right, beyond the glass partition of the box, a group of Italian air force cadets were whooping and whistling.

Hitler descended the monumental steps to the track, followed by an entourage of Olympic officials, military brass, and Party satraps. His left hand grasped the belt buckle of his uniform; the right acknowledged the rolling roar with a type of benediction—a limp, upturned palm, held at shoulder height.

Around her Eleanor saw faces twisted in the type of ecstasy she'd once seen among the Holy Rollers in Tennessee. Only the Italian cadets next to the box were laughing, not taking the moment seriously.

On the track, the dictator stooped to greet a small girl, who curtsied and held a bouquet towards him. Finally, he climbed the steps to his box and saluted with an outstretched arm. The crowds stamped their feet and began singing the Party anthem. Eleanor lit a cigarette.

'Jesus H Christ,' Gallico said. 'Where's the spirit of international harmony? Is there any song less appropriate?'

'"Ma Rainey's Black Bottom,"' said Eleanor.

The singing petered out as a great bell tolled, and sailors standing around the rim of the stadium synchronised the raising of each nation's flag. It was the moment Eleanor had dreaded.

The French, in blue berets, were the first large team to emerge, marching from a tunnel beneath the Marathon Gate. As they passed Hitler's box the tricolour was dipped and they gave the fascist salute, which he returned, to the crowd's intense delight. The British were next, but gave him nothing but a brisk eyes-right.

'Which hotel are you at?' Gallico said.

'Every hotel's full. William Dodd and his wife are putting me up.'

The Italian team entered, shambolic, like the chorus of a comic opera, but the air force cadets next to the box swept off their caps and yelled, proclaiming them heroes of the *patria*.

'William Dodd . . . our ambassador?' Gallico was impressed.

'He's a college buddy of Dad's.'

The Indian team passed by in their turbans. A single Costa Rican, carrying his flag, was given a tremendous cheer. The Australians, in cricket caps, waved at the crowd and ignored the Führer. A large Bulgarian team marched in with a high kick, to much mirth in the stadium.

Soon, the crowd was reserving its biggest applause for those teams that saluted. Eleanor watched Gallico scribble: '. . . *like Romans in the Colosseum of yore, condemning or reprieving chariot teams before their emperor . . .*'

At last, the Americans. Seeing their sheer numbers, the largest team, beaming and relaxed, felt like a stab in the heart. She stood and waved, struggling to keep the quiver from her lip, but soon her shoulders sagged.

Eleanor, you damned fool.

As they passed Hitler they took off their straw boaters and held them to their hearts, and the crowd seemed to warm to their easy manner.

'I guess we're not too hot at marching,' Gallico said, watching the athletes' loose-gaited walk. 'Apart from Brundage, that is.' Even from this distance they could see the determination on the man's face as his arms swung stiffly behind the Stars and Stripes. 'Is that a goose step?'

Eleanor spoke through a loud sob. 'His big head's so far up his ass I think that puffed-up chest is his forehead.'

'Hey, hey.' Gallico put his arms around her. She leaned her head on his shoulder, smelling cigarettes, Brylcreem, and bubble gum, and hugged him, starting to feel foolish.

'I'm such a chump.' Thick tears rolled down her cheeks, which he dried with his handkerchief.

'You're one of the nicest people I know,' he said.

She linked her arm in his and tried to compose herself.

'Listen,' he said. 'Me and the boys, we're going to talk to Brundage. See if we can't change his mind . . . He may not want to cross a unanimous US press corps.'

Eleanor's breath quaked in her chest. 'Paul, honey . . . I don't deserve you.'

The team was still passing by on the track below. She spotted Glenn Morris and Lou Zamperini and waved at them with Gallico's handkerchief. Towards the back she saw Olive and Marjorie, their faces flushed with pride. She called their names, and to her great surprise they spotted her and waved back.

Finally, a tumultuous roar greeted the home team. The Germans, dressed in white, marched in immaculate drill and executed a flaw-less salute.

All the teams now stood in formations behind their national flags, and a hush fell as an elderly Olympic official stepped up to the rostrum to begin a long speech. The crowd began to fidget, and Eleanor sat back, drained by tears.

Her eyes came to rest, vacantly, on the straw boater of one of the American reporters, and her mind drifted. She was remembering the long, hot family summers on Long Beach. Her father had worn a straw boater to work each day in the sweltering city. How had she forgotten that? In the afternoons her mother would drive her and her younger brother, George, to swimming lessons to keep them out of mischief—playing alone in the dunes or along the trolley tracks. When she was eleven George died of polio, but she carried on swimming, almost as an act in his memory. He was eight years old, and a really sweet boy.

She came out of her reverie to a heavy silence. All eyes were upon a tall blond runner, carrying the Olympic torch, who stood in the gap at the stadium's western side. Gracefully he ran down to the track and cantered around the rows of athletes before sprinting up the steps of the Marathon Gate on the opposite side. The crowd held its breath. The runner paused, holding the torch high, then plunged it into the bronze brazier. Flames leapt into the air, and another huge roar shook the stadium.

Eleanor felt the noise cast her adrift, decoupling her from the existence she had known, and she was struck by a conviction that a chapter in her life had closed for good.

Chapter Eight

The warm weather made the whiff from the Schultheiss Brewery more than usually rank. Denham told the driver to stop on the corner of Kopischstrasse, and saw the man's nose wrinkle in the mirror. A second smell, of paraffin, followed a dog that tore past with a burning rag tied to its tail. Some children on the corner were laughing.

'You live round here?' the man said, pocketing the tip. 'It stinks.'

Denham got out and slammed the door.

Welcome to Berlin!

After a day riding the world's finest passenger aircraft he couldn't face the crowds on the Ringbahn and had treated himself to a cab home from the airfield. The drizzle of the afternoon had eased off, leaving the air heavy and the streets smelling malodorously sweet.

Kopischstrasse, in the Kreuzberg district of the city, was a row of Wilhelmine buildings standing in the shadow of a Gothic brick water tower. The solemn balcony facades with wrought iron work were relics of grander times, but now each monumental house was carved into small, run-down apartments.

In the sepulchral hallway of number five, radio music was coming from the ground-floor apartment of Frau Stumpf, his landlady. He put his head round her door, but saw she had company. At her kitchen table, back towards him, was the balding fat head of his downstairs neighbour, Reinacher. The man was a tireless bore. If he wasn't collecting for one of the Party's endless relief drives, he was knocking on doors, enlisting the tenants into some sort of activism. The red collection tin sat on the table. Frau Stumpf, hunched in her shawls, shot Denham a look that said, 'I have to listen to this *Quatsch*,' so he placed the bottle of schnapps he'd brought for her next to the door and closed it without Reinacher hearing.

He was fond of Frau Stumpf, a delicate, absent-minded woman who treated the tenants with an old-fashioned courtesy. She'd lost her only son at the third battle of Ypres and had led a kind of half life since. He'd sometimes keep her company and eat her terrible stollen cakes.

The two-room apartment he rented on the third floor smelled scorched and musty after his week away, and a jade plant had withered in its pot beside the tile stove. He opened a window onto the courtyard, with its lines of greying laundry, threw his hat onto the corner of the door, and noticed the thin layer of soot covering everything. A sour smell of hops wafted in.

He wound the handle of the Victrola and placed the needle on the record left there a week ago, the Hot Five playing 'Alligator Crawl.' Humming the riff and lilt of Armstrong's trumpet, he lit an HB and sat for a few minutes, watching the smoke unfurl in the dusty light.

Hannah Liebermann.

He'd give Rex a call. The old hack usually had good sources and might even have a lead on how to contact her. There even was a chance he was still in the office.

He answered after one ring.

'Rex, beer at the Adlon?'

'Be there in half an hour, old boy.'

Denham put his hat back on, but before leaving the building climbed to the fifth floor and knocked gently on the door of the attic apartment.

'Everything all right, Frau Weiss?'

After a while a chain rattled and the bolt turned. The door opened ajar and an old lady's face peeped out like a bird's. Her eyes moved fearfully in their sockets, but she smiled like a little girl when she saw him, then unhooked the chain and took his forearm in her avian claw.

'Could be better; could be worse,' she said with a shrug. 'It's these children. They don't behave the way they used to. Would you get me some coffee and sugar this week?' She fumbled for a note in her apron pocket, but he waved it away.

Frau Weiss, the building's only Jewish tenant, had not left her apartment in two years. Not since her husband had gone out to buy a newspaper and never returned. A week after his disappearance his bloated remains were dredged from the Landwehr Canal showing fatal wounds to the head, but the police had declined to investigate.

BY THE TIME Denham arrived at the Hotel Adlon it was a fine summer's evening. Unter den Linden was closed to traffic for the opening of the Games, and crowds of strolling Berliners and tourists were out enjoying the heat. Loudspeakers along the avenue played Strauss waltzes in between official announcements, as though the city were one great carnival. He was ready for a cold beer.

Rex Palmer-Ward, chief correspondent for the *Times*, was waiting for him at their usual corner table in the upstairs bar, puffing on his calabash pipe, the long strands of his salt-and-pepper hair tumbled down over his forehead. He'd been a friend of Denham's for years in ways for which Denham would always be grateful. God-father to Tom and, during the hollow days of Denham's divorce, comforter and fellow sorrow-drowner.

The place was packed with press, shouting and chatting in a dozen languages. Rex rose to greet him, extending a stick-thin arm. Denham had rarely seen him eat. He seemed to subsist on nicotine, alcohol, and salted nuts.

'Hello, old boy. Did you catch the opening of the Games?'

'I made a flying visit,' Denham said and ordered a beer for himself and another for Rex. 'Are your chaps over from London?'

'Yes, the *Times* and *Daily Mail* boys were mightily impressed, of course.' He began stoking his pipe with a cocktail stick. 'Took them to the press briefing at the zoo ballroom this morning. The little Doctor was as quick as a whip as usual . . . made a ringing speech about how the Games had nothing to do with propaganda— Germany merely wanting to show its best side—this from the world's master propagandist . . .'

Their beers arrived.

'Look at this,' Rex said, lifting the *Berliner Morgenpost* from his side pocket. 'I had to read the Nazi press to find out the King is holi- daying on a yacht in the Med with this American woman, Wallis. Our boys are pretending he's at Balmoral.'

'That's game of them.' They both laughed.

Denham said, 'You wouldn't happen to know of a Jewish sports organisation I could contact? Got a story about an athlete I'm fol- lowing up.'

Rex frowned. 'Not likely. Independent sports bodies are banned as far as I know. Can't you simply doorstep this person?'

'Maybe. If I can get close. But I suspect this one's protected in case people like me come along asking questions. The athlete is Hannah Liebermann. She's competing under duress.'

'Good God.' Rex looked up from his pipe. 'Be careful. They're twitchy. If they think you're snooping behind their Olympic stage scenery they'll throw you out. And then who will I drink with? So, where on earth did you hear that?'

'A source I had to charm and coax,' Denham said, seeing in his mind's eye the intensity of Friedl's face on the airship, the light of ploughed fields and sky reflected in it. That bizarre question. *'Did we meet at a poetry reading in Mainz last year?'*

Rex was watching him, curious.

'You know, you've got one of those faces, old chap. People confide in you . . . They trust you. It's why you get the good stories.' He tapped out the carbonised debris and cleaned the bowl of the pipe with his finger.

They were silent for a moment; then Rex changed the subject.

'Been invited to any of the parties?'

'Not one.'

'Here.' He pulled an envelope from his jacket and slid it across the table. 'Can't make this one—if you want to go you'll have to pretend you're me.'

Denham removed the thick card invitation with embossed italic lettering. 'Ah, the language of diplomacy.' The inscription, in French, began:

On behalf of the Reich Government
Reichsminister for Public Enlightenment and Propaganda
DR JOSEPH GOEBBELS
requests the honour of your company for dinner
at an 'Italian evening'

The party was to be held on the Pfaueninsel, a nature reserve island in the Wannsee, where many of Berlin's rich and powerful had their homes.

'I'll dust off my dinner jacket,' Denham said.

'Won't do. It's white tie and tails.'

Over the noise of the bar a pianist began playing 'Frauen Sind So Schön Wenn Sie Lieben,' a tango Denham had been hearing a lot on the wireless. *Women are so beautiful if they're in love.*

Rex said, 'Phipps will be at that reception. Introduce yourself to him.'

'Sir Eric Phipps? Are you serious . . . ?'

Rex nodded. 'He may look like a squirrel with stage fright, but our ambassador's no fool—and he doesn't have the time of day for the appeasers. Phipps is one of us. Tell him you drink with me.'

'You've pulled him up a peg in my estimation,' Denham said. 'I didn't know you knew him.'

Rex leaned towards Denham, his face grave and confiding. 'By the way, old chap . . . with that trustworthy face of yours . . . if anyone were to pass you some intelligence—significant intelligence—I know you'd act in the nation's best interests. Keep yourself above reproach and all that. Am I right?'

Denham put his beer down. 'If it's important I'd put King and country first, if that's what you mean.'

His old friend's expression was hard to read.

'Rex, this is cryptic even for you. Was there some intelligence in particular?'

But Pat Murphy from the *Daily Express* had appeared at the table, rubbing his hands. 'Evening, gents. There's a rumour going around that one of the German lady high jumpers is, in fact, a man.'

'Only one?' Rex said, his face amused again.

Two Americans from the Reuters Bureau also pulled up chairs, and soon the table was in a haze of smoke from Rex's reignited, smouldering pipe. Denham decided it was time to eat.

He was leaving the grand lobby when he found himself sharing the revolving front door with two women who were entering. One was short and chattering, the other a tall blonde with a stylish pillbox hat tilted low to one eye. She had a long neck, a wide, full mouth, and a beauty spot just to the right of her nose. No makeup. For a long moment they exchanged glances through the glass.

HIS FAVOURITE BISTRO on the Bergmannstrasse usually put him in a good mood. On quiet evenings, and if there were no uniforms in the place, the *patron* tuned the wireless to a Parisian jazz station that played live sessions of Django Reinhardt and Stéphane Grappelli. But tonight the place was crowded and noisy, along with every other restaurant on the street. He tried jotting some shorthand for his *Hindenburg* piece, but the evening's conversation with Rex had riled him.

It seemed to confirm something he'd long suspected about his old friend: he had links to the British Secret Intelligence Service, the SIS. Not so surprising, perhaps. Spies and journalists alike were in the information game, courting contacts, mining for secrets. In times like these the jobs were almost identical. And as the chief *Times* correspondent Rex had sources all over Germany.

Phipps is one of us. Tell him you drink with me.

First an entrée to the ambassador at a high-level reception—what had prompted that?—then a heavy hint that any intelligence passing Denham's way should be handed in to the British authorities. In other words, his longest-standing journalist friend was asking him not to be a journalist. He chewed his bread slowly as he considered this.

By the time he asked for the bill he'd decided that intelligence work, divining meaning from the tea leaves of figures, rumours, and whispers, or whatever it involved, was a game he'd leave to Rex.

THE STREETLAMPS WERE lit when he returned to Kopischstrasse, whistling 'Frauen Sind So Schön Wenn Sie Lieben,' which echoed around the gloomy hall. Why was it only the annoying tunes stick in your head? All was dark behind the frosted glass of Frau Stumpf's door.

At the top of the stairs he switched on the landing light, only half registering the smell of an unfamiliar cigarette. He was putting his key in the lock when his door swung open from within. An enormous man in a hat and raincoat lunged from the darkness inside, shoved his fist into Denham's chest, and sent him crashing against the landing wall. He had barely slid to the floor when a hard blow struck the right side of his head, knocking him flat. A mewling pain cried from his jaw and ear, and blood filled his mouth where he'd chomped down on his tongue.

Chapter Nine

Since the final month of the Great War, Denham and violence had shunned each other like repelling magnetic forces. Lately something had switched, and he seemed to be attracting it. He'd been attacked. And a week ago in Friedrichshafen, in the brush with those Brownshirts, he'd sensed how near violence was. As near as rain after catching its scent on the breeze. One ill-judged word, one ambiguous glance, would have released it.

From somewhere in the dark along the landing came the scratching of a mouse. Easing himself up, he leaned against the wall, closed his eyes, and concentrated on breathing.

The blood in his mouth tasted sour and ferrous. It was both unexpected and familiar, like the taste of strong liquor after years of temperance. The taste of violence.

He'd had a sense of two, maybe three men rushing past him down the stairs. In the dim light of the landing he'd seen only the departing back of the shot-putter in the raincoat. The front door of the building had slammed with a ghostly echo.

He nudged his door open with the tip of his foot. A soft light from the courtyard reflected on the ceiling of his sitting room, enough for him to see the devastation. His books were strewn across the rug, and opened, as if each had been individually searched; there was almost nothing left on the shelf. The armchair had been turned over and the threadbare cushions pulled from their covers.

He stood up and heard the blood singing in his ear, but the pain in his back where he'd hit the wall was abating. He picked up his hat and entered the apartment, noticing his hands shaking. His few pictures—of Tom's junior cricket team, and a sepia photograph of his parents on their wedding day—had been pulled from the walls and the backs torn off the frames. In his bedroom the mattress was turned over and all the drawers pulled out, emptied, and searched. Again he noticed the rich, hempy smell of that cigarette.

When he saw his father's gold cufflinks untouched in the saucer on the chest of drawers, he knew for certain his visitors were not burglars.

Who were they?

He lit an HB and watched the glowing tip.

If they were police of some sort then he had plenty to choose from. Apart from the regular police—the Orpo, who patrolled the streets, and the Kripo, who caught felons—there were also the Gestapo, the secret police, sadists who sifted through denunciations, and the SD, the Sicherheitsdienst, who controlled state security and intelligence. This last one was the Gestapo's shadowy twin, and he had little idea of what it did, apart from sending shudders up everyone's spine. But the more he thought about it, the less he believed that any of them would do such a crude job and allow themselves to be surprised in the act. If Gestapo professionals were investigating him he would never know they'd been in his apartment.

His head began to ache. Under the bed he found a quarter-full bottle of Johnnie Walker, uncorked it with his teeth, and took a generous swig. A rough anaesthetic, but it did the trick. Lying back on the bare mattress he focused on Tom, and on Anna, and on beautiful girls, and on the soaring sensation he'd experienced that afternoon from the prow of the airship, the sunlit white clouds like a child's picture of heaven.

He opened his eyes.

'Seven Beautiful Girls from the USA' . . . the feature article with photos in the *Berliner Illustrirte Zeitung*. He'd read it over dinner at the Kurgarten. That's where he'd seen that girl before. The lovely tall girl who'd walked into the Adlon as he was leaving.

Chapter Ten

Martha Dodd, the daughter of the ambassador, linked her arm in Eleanor's and led her towards the reporters seated around an open-air table at the Tiergarten Café. Gallico walked behind them. 'Don't be shy,' Martha whispered. 'Thomas Wolfe's a sweetheart.' The low cloud of the day before had returned, but Eleanor wore her sunglasses nonetheless. Somewhere in the trees a loudspeaker was blaring out the *Radetzky March*.

The four men stood as Eleanor's party approached. *What an odd pair we must look*, she thought. Martha was so short her head barely reached Eleanor's shoulder.

'Lord, don't say you've eaten breakfast already,' Martha said in the high, silvery voice she reserved for male company. 'We're starving. Hello, Walter. Hello, Tom. Hello, Bill. May I introduce Eleanor Emerson, who is staying as our guest for the duration of the Games?' Pat Murphy introduced himself.

'Mrs Emerson,' said Thomas Wolfe. 'Your fame precedes you.' He was a hulking great man; her hand seemed lost in his.

Eleanor groaned. 'You're too kind, but please don't offer me champagne. I don't want to get thrown out of Berlin tomorrow.'

The men laughed politely.

Wolfe said, 'You know, news of your being, uh, released from the US team has been all over the dailies back home, and not just the sports pages.'

'Well, it's not exactly what I wanted to be famous for.'

Coffee, eggs, and strudels were ordered; then to Eleanor's

embarrassment Martha began recounting for the men's amusement the incidents of the voyage, with her run-ins with Brundage and the moments of her shame and disgrace told in an uproarious parody, so that by the end of the story she'd been made to sound like some tipsy Mae West in a game of truth or dare with Ming the Merciless. The reporters barked with laughter, drawing the attention of people at the other tables. This set off an intense round of gossip and rumour swapping as the men dished up what they'd heard about the regime's stage management of the Olympics. Eleanor glanced at Gallico for support, and met a look of ferocious sympathy. *What a dear man you are*, she thought, *and thank God I didn't tell Martha about Herb. I'll never see the funny side of* that *story*.

Martha Dodd was twenty-eight years old, and petite, with a girlish round face and widely set eyes of a startling blue. She hosted literary parties, adored intrigue, and relished arguments—most unlike her father, the solemn Ambassador William E Dodd. Unfortunately for Eleanor, the girl's sharp repartee could often sound like bitchiness; she seemed to think Eleanor's 'news column' at the same time important and comical, which probably meant that she saw her guest as a bit of a joke. *And why wouldn't she*, Eleanor thought. *I was good at one thing and one thing only, and I blew it*.

'Now, boys, we need to find some scoops for Eleanor to file— some proper news, mind you. Bill? What about the links between German athletic training and rearmament?'

Eleanor rolled her eyes at Gallico, the one person she didn't mind knowing how much this was getting on her nerves.

'It's okay, Martha,' she said. 'There's an important story for me right here.' Eleanor turned to the *Daily Express* reporter. 'Mr Murphy, tell me more about this kraut lady high jumper who might, in fact, be a man.'

BY MORNING DENHAM had a high ringing in his ear from the punch to his head, and a purple contusion across his cheek.

He ignored the mess in the apartment, simply returning the table and chair to their place so he could type up the *Hindenburg* piece from his notes while his courtyard neighbour, a locksmith, changed the lock on the apartment door.

Denham worked through the day, tapping away at the Underwood in a sleeveless undershirt, an HB hanging from the corner of his mouth. A warm, gritty breeze brought the sounds of the city through the window.

By late afternoon he was satisfied. He gathered the typewritten sheets, put them in an envelope addressed to Greiser's press office, and set off by tram to the Friedrichstrasse to deliver it. If he was going to find Hannah Liebermann and tell her story to the world, he'd be wise to play things safe with Greiser in the meantime. Do nothing to upset the bastard.

Berlin's transformation was complete—as though a long siege had been lifted. The streets were colourful and welcoming, with garlands hanging from every lamppost and shopfront along the Leipzigerstrasse. The Olympic rings billowed from the flagpoles of the Wertheim department store, and the JEWS NOT WANTED signs had disappeared from shops, cafés, and parks.

With the state's sadism hidden from view, the Reich Labour Front had ordered a week of 'jollity and cheerfulness' prior to the Games, fearing that foreign visitors might be disheartened by the *Berliner Schnauze*—the surly local manner. *Only in a tyranny*, Denham thought, *are citizens ordered to be happy.*

He delivered his article at the reception to Greiser's office and emerged through the glass doors back onto the Friedrichstrasse, thinking he'd walk home. As he made his way along the shopfronts, tilting his hat against the sun, feeling for his matches in his jacket pocket, it was a few moments before he noticed the dark vehicle in the reflection of the windows. A forest green Humber Pullman with fat whitewall tyres was keeping pace alongside him in the street. A British car? He turned to look at it. A blind in the rear side window was pulled down, concealing its passenger. The car pulled over next to him; the back door opened, and a man in a bowler hat got out. He spoke in English.

'Gentleman in the car would like a word, sir.'

Denham hesitated.

His expression blank, the man stood to the side of the door and gestured for him to step in.

With as much curiosity as suspicion he climbed the running board and into the back. There was enough headroom to wear top hats, and such a wide seat that he might have mistaken the tall, bony man sitting to one side for a discarded coat and hat. Another seat faced the rear, like a London cab's.

'Mr Denham? Get in,' the tall man said, smiling. 'Can we give you a lift somewhere?' A light South Wales accent.

'I was on my way home.'

Bowler Hat Man got into the backseat facing Denham, and the car purred into the southbound traffic before he'd given his address.

'Sorry to ambush you like that,' the tall man said, 'but no one's going to overhear us if we have a little chat in the car, you see. My name's Evans. I'm attached to the embassy here.' He offered Denham his hand across the seat, releasing a faint smell of mints. His long face was framed by white sideburns, and there was something lugubrious about his black homburg and wing collar. He paused, his eyes falling on the darkening wound on Denham's cheek.

'A chat about what?' Denham said.

'Yes, of course. You may like to know that your printed articles have been read with satisfaction in our embassy here, and in certain offices of Whitehall.'

This was news to Denham. 'But . . . most of my pieces are published in American weekend newspapers and magazines.' He glanced at Bowler Hat Man, who observed him without expression.

'Quite so, quite so,' said Evans, 'which is why Sir Eric Phipps takes an interest in them. It is vital that the wider American public is not kept in the dark about the way things are heading in Europe. Things you capture very well in your features.'

'I see.'

Evans looked out of the window as the car sped past buildings decked with long white pennants displaying the Olympic rings. 'With so many of the American press here for the Games, one might hope their eyes would open, although you'll have noticed that the scale of the cover-up is impressive . . .'

'Yes . . . I've noticed.'

Still looking out of the window, Evans said, 'Which leads me to the purpose of our little chat.'

Denham felt himself squirming. 'May I smoke?'

Evans looked at him and nodded.

'Mr Denham, we know you're a discreet sort . . . and one whose sympathies may coincide with the work of certain like-minded people here who render the occasional service in the national interest—'

Denham cut him off. 'I'm flattered, Mr Evans, but if you're talking about passing secrets and so on, that type of work's not for me.'

'Of course, we may never call, but—'

'I'm happiest when I stay out of trouble.'

Denham caught himself touching the wound on his cheek.

'That's quite all right. I understand,' Evans said primly. 'Not everyone wants that sort of responsibility, or the risk, indeed.'

The car glided across the Landwehr Canal at Hallesches Tor. His home was only a few minutes' walk from here, and he thought of asking the driver to stop.

Evans was eyeing him carefully now.

He said, 'We would, however, ask for your help with one particular matter . . .' Leaning forwards he closed the sliding glass partition that separated the back of the car from the driver. 'We've received intelligence that a certain German dossier . . . which we believed had been lost or destroyed . . . has resurfaced.'

Despite Denham's mentally dismissing Evans, the man had a foot
in the door. Denham's gaze returned to him. 'And you think someone may try to pass it to a British journalist?'

'To a British journalist with a reputation for writing the truth,
yes.'

'What's significant about this dossier?'

'If you're given it, you will know. All we ask is that you bring it
to us. We'll see that you're compensated for your trouble.' He took
a card from his wallet and passed it to Denham. It read DAVID WYN
EVANS—PASSPORT OFFICER. Underneath were two telephone numbers, one for the Mitte District of Berlin; the other a Whitehall
number.

'Diplomacy's not going to work, Mr Denham. If there's any hope
for Europe it lies in intelligence . . .'

They regarded each other in silence for a moment until Evans's
nose caught the waft from the Schultheiss Brewery. He began to
wind down the window.

'It's worse if you let the air in,' Denham said.

Bowler Hat Man let him out without a word, and the Humber
rolled away. Denham watched it go, staring down the street long
after it had disappeared.

When he turned the corner into Kopischstrasse a small crowd
had gathered outside his building. He recognised some of the locals
from Chamissoplatz; they were watching a stretcher being carried
out by two Orpo men. Strands of fine white hair trailed from beneath a blanket as it passed. Frau Stumpf was holding the front door
open.

'What happened?' he asked her.

'Herr Denham. Oh dear me. Frau Weiss fell.' The landlady had a
tremor in her voice. 'She's dead.'

The men loaded the stretcher roughly into the back of an Orpo
wagon. He stood watching, dumb, suppressing in his head the horrible possibilities that were presenting themselves. Frau Weiss had
lived in the building all her married life.

'How did she fall?' he asked.

Frau Stumpf looked at him with fear in her eyes, shook her head and said nothing.

'On the stairs?'

The woman seemed to shrink into the door.

'Tell me,' he said. Faces in the crowd turned to look at him.

'From her window,' she said breathlessly.

Someone sniggered.

Two Jungvolk boys and a girl were watching the scene with interest. One of the boys had a look Denham had never before seen on a child. He was laughing with his tongue out, his eyes narrowed to sharp slits.

Chapter Eleven

A pontoon bridge lit with Roman candles connected the shore with the Pfaueninsel—the Peacock Island—in the broad lake of the Wannsee. After days of intermittent rain, the skies had cleared and a warm evening light gilded the tall trees of beech and elm.

Ambassador Dodd gave Eleanor his hand as she alighted from the embassy car, followed by Martha and her mother.

Martha had not stopped talking since they'd left the ambassador's residence on Tiergartenstrasse. She'd been studying a thick booklet that showed them all where to sit.

'If you ask me, Mother, you're on the most prestigious table.' She held the seating plan to Mrs Dodd's face. 'Sir Robert Vansittart, Dr Goebbels, Mrs William Dodd, Lady Aberdare, Count Baillet-Latour, Countess Szembek, Ambassador François-Poncet, the Prinz von Liechtenstein, and General Ernst Udet. Do we know him?'

'A flying ace, dear,' said Mrs Dodd. 'Just your type.'

'Daddy, I declare you've been snubbed. I should mention it to the State Department. You're the second-ranking diplomat here—'

'Please, Martha,' the ambassador said drily. 'I shall greatly dislike shaking our host's hand. If I am not required to sit at his table, I count myself fortunate indeed.'

'Try to smile at him this time, dear,' said Mrs Dodd.

'You know what they say, Daddy,' Martha said. 'If you're not at the table, you're on the menu.'

Ambassador Dodd's friendship with Eleanor's father made him

a dear, if somewhat forbidding, figure to her. The two men were colleagues years ago at the University of Chicago, where Dodd had been a professor of history. He was given the ambassadorship, Martha told her, for being a Jeffersonian Democrat and a liberal—qualities the president said would be powerful charms against Nazi sorcery.

'Now, where is Eleanor seated? I can't see her table,' continued Martha, turning the pages. 'Oh, ha-ha, here it is. They've seated you with the athletes. Lord, what a gaffe.'

'That suits me just dandy, thank you, Martha,' said Eleanor. She was ready to staple that booklet to Martha's head.

Again her stomach knotted at the thought of what she had to do. If there was any hope of being reinstated she would have to face Brundage this evening and say something. Show her repentance. Anything. She wasn't sure how. She doubted her pride would allow her to plead.

A steward in a powdered wig and knee breeches escorted them over the bridge, past an honour guard of naval cadets who snapped to attention and presented their oars.

The ambassador, hunched in his tailcoat, walked in front, mustering all his forbearance for the handshake ahead, while Eleanor, Martha, and her mother glided behind him in a whishing of taffeta and silk.

Eleanor felt the eyes of the cadets passing over her figure and decided she'd chosen well this evening: a midnight blue cocktail gown of light silk with transparent sleeves and a narrowed waist. It was set off with a corsage of white orchids and the pearl necklace she'd been given for her twenty-first. In heels she towered over the two other women. Martha teetered along just in front of her, her tight satin dress riding up her hips. *Satin's such an unforgiving fabric*, Eleanor thought.

They entered a grove of trees glowing with coloured lanterns in the shapes of butterflies. Page girls in plaits and dirndl skirts lined the way, beckoning them along a bend in the path as though into an enchanted wood. A sound of violins mingled with the breeze in the trees.

At the top of a small rise, the wooded path gave onto a broad lawn where the Reichsminister's guests were mingling in front of a Gothic folly—a fantastical medieval keep, all white turrets and machicolations.

Barring their way, however, was the welcoming party.

While the ambassador presented his wife and daughter, Eleanor gaped at their host with wonder. He was a diminutive, club-footed man with a large head, rodent ears, and eyes she thought far from benign. In white tie and tails he looked bang out of place. It was like seeing Al Capone in a mortarboard and college gown.

Beside him stood his wife, Magda, a handsome, fearless-looking blonde, who, Mrs Dodd whispered, was effectively Germany's First Lady, as Hitler was unmarried.

Ambassador Dodd introduced Eleanor last, and Dr Goebbels bowed to kiss her hand. He said a few words of welcome in German, and the depth of his voice surprised her. As he looked up, his dark eyes flared and the tip of a red tongue flicked across his lower lip.

'Jesus,' said Eleanor, when they'd moved onto the lawn. 'His wife saw that.'

About two dozen groups of people were talking in the rich evening light, with more guests arriving. A fine roasting smell was coming from a kitchen marquee on the far right of the lawn, mingling oddly with the colognes concocted by the barbershops of the Savoy and the Hôtel Ritz.

Eleanor was offered champagne by a footman. Then, with irritating whispers and tugs on her elbow, Martha directed her eyes towards dozens of people she had never heard of: Himmler, the chief of police, waddling among groups like a country curate out of his depth; Lída Baarová, a stunning Czech movie siren and the current object of their host's affections; a conceited knucklehead called von Ribbentrop, whom Hitler had just appointed ambassador to Britain;

and the Mitford sisters Diana and Unity. 'They're a pair of English roses who've caught the Nazi bug real bad.'

'Like blackfly,' suggested Eleanor.

Eventually dinner was announced by a bugle. Eleanor excused herself and went in search of her table, which she found beneath an oak tree hung with lanterns. It was seated with young women athletes, all in team uniforms of different nations, and she realised then that only the females had been invited, which, given her brief experience of their host, kind of figured. The girls eyed her gown, perhaps thinking she had the wrong table.

'Eleanor, over here,' came a husky voice she knew, and the gentle, giant figure of Helen Stephens unfolded to its full height, beckoning her over. 'Sit with me.' They hugged, and for a precarious moment Eleanor felt all the raw hurt that had made her weep in the stadium.

'You won't believe my day,' Helen said, banging the table so that the cutlery bounced. A childhood operation on her throat had left her sounding like a longshoreman with a hundred-a-day cigarette habit. 'I won. I won the hundred metre. I beat that damned Polack, Stella Walsh . . .'

'Sis, that's wonderful. You were the only woman man enough to beat Stella the Fella.'

Waiters placed a selection of wines in the centre of the table and served panini and small Italian delicacies as a tenor serenaded the tables with a tub-thumping aria. None of the girls touched the wines, and for once Eleanor decided she'd enjoy herself sober.

The surface of the Wannsee reflected a crimson sky. Soon, candles were placed on the table and tiny electric lights turned the trees into sparkling candelabra.

Later as the plates were cleared away couples got up to dance on the terrace in front of the Gothic folly. The string orchestra had withdrawn and was replaced with a large, black-tie dance band that immediately swung into a foxtrot.

'Oh, ha-ha, *there* you are.'

Martha was gliding towards her through the crowd, her eyes

lit with champagne. Once again, Eleanor got the faint impression
that she'd been made the butt of some joke and noticed, not without
some satisfaction, that the shorter woman had lipstick on her teeth,
giving a carnivorous leer to her smile.

'Lord, what a head we'll have tomorrow,' Martha trilled, taking
Eleanor's arm. 'Over here, there's a *fascinating* man I know you'll be
dying to meet.'

'Okay, but I'm married, remember?' Eleanor muttered.

She was led between clusters of people until they reached a group
of men with their backs towards them. With an instant dread she
recognised the broad shoulders and bolt-upright posture of the man
addressing the group. He was winding up some story with booming
emphases and hand gestures.

'Some joke, Martha.'

'You said you had to talk to him.'

Martha tapped his elbow. He swung around, and Eleanor was
faced with Avery Brundage.

The man's nostrils flared.

'Mr Brundage,' Martha cooed, sliding a glance at Eleanor. 'Look
who I've found.'

'Hello, sir,' Eleanor said, trying her best smile.

For two seconds his indignation visibly battled self-control.

'Good evening, Mrs Emerson,' he managed. There was perspiration on his brow.

'There, ha-ha, you've made up. A diplomatic coup on my part, I
think. Mr Brundage, Eleanor is our guest during the Games.'

'Sir,' Eleanor continued, 'would you be kind enough to spare me
a minute of your—'

But before she could finish, a British voice was saying, 'My word,
who have we here?'

Brundage stepped aside to allow the women into the circle. A
short, dapper gentleman with a monocle and a pencil moustache
was observing Eleanor with a poker face. His chest was heavy with
medals and decorations.

Martha said, 'Eleanor, dear, this is Sir Eric Phipps, the British ambassador.'

'Delighted,' he said, his face giving nothing away, but she noticed his monocle casting a miniature spotlight up and down her body.

He, too, kissed her hand, and something about his courtly manner charmed her.

'Eleanor won the hundred-metre backstroke at the last Olympics, Sir Eric,' Martha said.

'The backstroke? How very interesting.'

'And you, sir,' Martha continued, turning to the third man, 'I don't think we've met.'

'Richard Denham, madam. I'm a journalist.'

'At last, a colleague,' Eleanor said.

He offered his hand, and their eyes met.

She'd held the gaze of umpteen people this evening, so why this one was different she wasn't sure, but she felt an instant quickening of her heart, a tightening in her chest. Her hand lingered in his before he released it. He had cool, greenish eyes that seemed a little sad. His tailcoat was an obsolete cut, but it revealed a pleasing figure, even if he was a tad shorter than she was. He was in his late thirties, she guessed. He wore no ring.

'Mr Denham here has been very sporting in not jotting down my indiscretions,' said the ambassador, 'and Mr Brundage has been delighting us with a thoroughly comprehensive account of the American Olympic training regimen.'

Denham caught Eleanor's eye, and she turned to hide a smile.

Brundage seemed to bristle at the women's intrusion. He gave a curt nod to each of them. 'Ladies. Your Excellency. Sir.' And stomped away.

'You're a Brit?' Eleanor said to Denham.

'I am, but I live in Berlin.'

'Been in the wars, huh?' she said, looking at the bruise on his cheek. 'Say, didn't I see you leaving the Adlon yesterday?'

There was a reticence about this man. She wondered what his

story was. Martha was already making eyes at him and had begun to pout her lips out in a way she seemed to think attractive.

Sir Eric was smiling at them and was about to speak, when a young woman appeared at his side and slipped her arm in his.

'Dear, I think Sir Robert and Sarita need rescuing from the Ribbentrops.'

'Ah. Please do excuse me.' He bowed and left.

'So, Mr Denham,' Martha simpered as she accepted yet another glass from a passing tray, 'are you for the Games, or are you one of these Olympic spoilsports, too?'

'I'm afraid,' Denham said, looking at Eleanor, 'that I'm one of those spoilsports. Simply by coming here you're helping them.'

'Helping who?' said Eleanor, grinning, thinking there was a punchline coming.

'You're helping the Nazis muscle into the fold of decent nations. They're using you.'

Eleanor laughed with dismay. 'I am not—*we* are not—anyone's pawns.'

Martha had already drained most of her glass and seemed to have lost the thread of the conversation. 'Exactly, everyone should just get along . . .'

Eleanor held his gaze. The last thing she wanted was an argument at a party. All the same, she couldn't let this pass.

'Can't some things in life be above sordid politics?' she said, conscious that she was sounding just like Brundage. 'I think the Olympic ideal is one of the few things that is.'

Denham's brow furrowed with understanding. It was the same mannerism her father had when arguing with her, and it drove her nuts.

'The Olympic ideal is being twisted by some very unscrupulous people. The racial discrimination on the German team, for instance—'

'Race?' said Eleanor with a little shake of her head. 'We've got the fastest man on the planet competing in these Games, and he's a Negro. Doesn't that give the lie to race theories? Who cares about race?'

He chose not to take the baton and seemed to wait for her to cool down. Martha had given up on the lip pouting and was trying to lock eyes with him.

In a conciliatory tone he said, 'Look, for the Germans these Games have little to do with sport. This fortnight is a huge show of power, a propaganda display. The whole country is in training, but not for sport . . .'

Eleanor had had enough.

'I don't know what you're talking about,' she said coolly, 'but it sounds like total garbage.'

'Madam, I am sorry, but you are naive.'

'You want to know something?' she said, pointing her finger at him. 'You're one of the most annoying people I've met.' And with that she turned on her heels.

As she walked away she heard Martha slurring, 'Say, now she's gone how about a dance?'

Eleanor slipped among clusters of people, trying to find a way out of the crowd. Voices were talking freely now, lubricated by champagne.

She made it to the edge of the lawn without anyone buttonholing her and went in search of a place where she could be alone. A garden path circled the lawn and led back towards the grove they'd entered earlier. The chattering groups of guests petered out; just a few couples were strolling. She followed the path along a garden wall.

Damn that guy, she thought, wishing she was home in New York.

Turning a corner she suddenly spotted Brundage striding away down the path some distance ahead of her. *Last chance*, she thought. Feeling that she had nothing to lose, she was hurrying to catch up with him when he turned sharply right and entered a low pergola set into a dense beech hedge. Where on earth was he going? She followed him into a darkened tunnel of vines that emerged into a circular arbour. Roses burgeoned over trellises, and small, intimate benches were set into secluded nooks.

She'd lost him. His black tailcoat had vanished in the shadows beneath the trellises. Treading with caution she moved along the arbour path. Crickets chirped, and a keening cry from one of the island's peacocks made her jump. A scent of roses was heavy in the air; the noise of the party a background murmur.

Then she heard men's voices only a few feet away, and quickly stepped into a nook where she couldn't be seen.

' . . . I'm grateful for an opportunity to speak with you,' came a voice with a mild German accent. 'May I call you Avery? Please, let's sit. There's no one here.'

The men sat in a recessed bench about twenty feet away, separated from her only by vines and rosebushes. The voice continued in impeccable English.

'Your friendly attitude towards German sport has been noted in the highest circles here. As such I am emboldened to broach with you a matter of some considerable delicacy . . .'

'I'm listening.'

Chapter Twelve

There was a pause as the speaker seemed to gather his thoughts. In the stillness beneath the trellis, Eleanor could hear her heart beating.

'The United States is a new power in the world, Avery,' the voice began, 'a power that, happily, does not feel threatened by enemies. Perhaps because it feels so assured, so safe, it has not seen the need to strengthen its national fibre through policy . . .'

'I'm not sure that I follow.'

'You are a loose body of amateur sports organisations, are you not? What you need is training through a national organisation on the German model . . .'

'I wholeheartedly agree, sir. That is exactly what I've been advocating—'

' . . . and that means a more scientific approach to athletics, and to the—how shall I put it?—the *biology* of your athletes.'

Brundage fell silent. She heard a match being struck and the German inhale.

'Success in the Olympic Games reflects the moral and racial quality of the competing nations, Avery—nations whose help Germany may one day need in fighting the threat of Judeo-Bolshevism. Communism.'

Eleanor leaned her head farther into the roses.

Brundage seemed to hesitate. 'It's true that I believe the United States must take steps to stamp out communism, but—'

'I knew we would see, how do you say, "eye to eye."' The voice sounded pleased. 'So perhaps as a small token of your solidarity with me on this matter . . . you might reconsider the selection of certain athletes—on your relay team, for example.'

The man's voice had dropped so low that Eleanor strained to hear.

There was a baffled silence from Brundage before he spoke. 'On our relay team?'

'Yes. Let's say it may not be helpful to our cause if your two Jewish athletes should win.'

Brundage was silent, at an apparent loss. 'Marty Glickman and Sam Stoller?'

'We Germans have had to allow one Jew on the German team, of course, to show the world we're being fair, but with the pressure she's under I doubt she'll win. Your two Jews on the relay team, however, seem certain to win. We've been watching them train at the Olympic village.'

Eleanor winced. *Was he being serious?*

'Mr von Halt—Karl—I don't understand. We have Negroes running on our team. Why object to the Jewish athletes?'

'Oh-ho, the niggers, yes. I watched your Jesse Owens win today. Quite a spectacle, and he had the crowd with him. But there you are cheating.'

'Cheating?'

'Of course! The blacks have an enlarged heel bone, like jungle animals. They have an unfair advantage. You may as well enter race-horses.'

'Sir—'

'But the Führer does not care about the blacks, Avery.' Again the voice lowered to a hush, like a supplicant in a confessional box. 'It is the Jews that concern him.'

Eleanor felt the nape of her neck crawl. Another long pause, and she pictured this man, this von Halt, looking straight into Brundage's eyes.

'To him the threat of the Jews to our lifeblood, to all that is vital in our folk community, has a . . . spiritual significance. You understand that the prospect of Jews winning races, breaking records, receiving medals on the podium in front of the German people, has a most unfortunate symbolism . . .'

'Karl, I want to help but I don't see how I can simply—'

'He has spoken lately of his vision for the Olympiad. We will send our athletes in Zeppelins to Tokyo for the 1940 Games, but thereafter it is his desire that the Games should take place in Germany for all time to come. Germany is the only nation willing to give the resources the Games are due . . . the only nation with the strength to lead the world's struggle against Judeo-Bolshevism. It is a vision of the future, Avery. Think about it. The British Empire grows old and weakens. It is America's help that Germany will need to stop the Jews from Bolshevising the earth, and the fight starts here'—there was a smack as a fist hit a palm—'with the selection and training of our finest men and women. In this fight I foresee that you, my friend, will have an important role to play . . . To begin with, I can tell you in confidence that you are our preferred candidate for the presidency of the IOC.'

About a minute seemed to pass without either man speaking. *Jesus Christ, Avery Brundage, don't do it*, Eleanor thought.

'The two Jews,' Brundage said at length. She heard him inhale as he made his decision.

'Thank you, Avery. I assure you that I will mention this gesture of friendship to the Führer in person. Now let's drink to it. This is a party after all . . .'

Eleanor caught a glimpse of the man slapping Brundage on the shoulder as they departed across the arbour.

She lifted her heels onto the nook's stone bench, drew her knees up to her chin, and began to rock backwards and forwards. She did not look up from her knees because of a sickening feeling that the arbour had begun to spin.

She did not snap out of it even when the first explosion split the sky. A bloom of fuchsia-red light lit the arbour like a ship's flare, casting fast-moving shadows through the trees. Rockets whistled upwards, with one burst overlapping the next into bouquets of coloured sparks. The crowd on the lawn applauded as the display became louder and more lavish. She felt each detonation reverberate like a mortar in the hollow of her chest.

THE CARRIAGE JUDDERED over the points, shaking Denham's bones on the wooden seat. His head lolled against the window. He'd undone his tie and taken off the rented woollen tailcoat, which in the warmth seemed to give off the accrued odour of a thousand dinner-dances. An elderly couple watched him with sour faces, sniffing the alcohol on him. Berliners were not afraid to stare. He put a foot up on the seat opposite. The couple exchanged glances. An infraction of the S-Bahn rules. He put the other foot up and tapped his shoes together.

He'd had to wait a long time for a chance to meet Sir Eric. The ambassador was beset with introductions, talking to guest after guest in French, German, or Italian, nodding away, poker-faced. A monocled curiosity from the days of the Great Game. Now and then he'd laugh judiciously, allowing some Nazi boor to feel he possessed the wit of Voltaire. In the end, Denham caught him as he towelled his hands in the gents' washroom. His face registered no surprise, as if he'd been expecting this approach at precisely this moment.

'"The Rhineland—Backyard Belligerence,"' Sir Eric said, taking time to adjust his sash and buttonhole rose in the mirror. 'I've sent transcripts of that piece you wrote to every appeaser in the cabinet. Surprised you got away with that one.'

'My luck may have run out.'

They walked back to the party, the ambassador a foot shorter than Denham. His shoulder was hunched on one side, like an aged cat's.

'We're running a team of fielders at the moment, Denham. Play-ers who can only watch patiently in the hope of catching our op-ponents out and limiting their innings. Regrettably, we're not

Chapter Thirteen

Denham rose early and headed for the Café Kranzler on Friedrichstrasse. A full breakfast, he decided, was the best cure for his hangover.

He bought a paper at the station kiosk and climbed the steps from the U-Bahn. The air was cool and fresh, the sky marbled with cirrus clouds. It was going to be a fine day. Traffic was still sparse; a yellow tram clangoured along the tracks on Unter den Linden, bell ringing.

He took a table in the sun, ordered coffee, eggs, smoked ham, and pastries, and began to scan the *Deutsche Allgemeine Zeitung*. The report of Jesse Owens's victory in the hundred-metre sprint yesterday was tucked away inside. This time there was no mention of Owens's colour, despite weeks of unembarrassed references to *der Neger*. On a separate page Denham spotted a curious notice, evidently lifted from a Chancellery press release. 'The Führer cannot be present at all the final competitions and is therefore unable to receive the winners of different nations. Receptions for the winners in the Führer's box will no longer take place.' All that to avoid shaking a black man's hand.

Coffee at the Kranzler was the best in Berlin. He'd just ordered another cup when he saw her. She was crossing the street towards the café, hatless, and wearing a white suit and round white-rimmed sunglasses, like an advertisement for Lux toilet soap. He raised the newspaper to hide himself and was waiting for her to walk past when a sugar cube flew over the top of the page and hit him on the chin.

'Too late, mister, I already saw you.'

supported much by our home crowd . . . Plenty of them, you know, are very "pro." Quite a few here this evening. Lord Londonderry, for instance, thinks he can placate a monster by cooing . . .'

Beneath the tact and avuncular manner Denham detected a steely directness.

'So, my question is,' Phipps said, patting Denham's shoulder, 'are *you* willing to field for us . . . ?'

'Well sir, I—'

'*Good* man.'

They could say no more. Someone was presenting the tombstone figure of Avery Brundage.

And then that girl, that beautiful American from the magazine.

If she had talked of anything else—whatever girls her age talk about—he would have stayed as quiet as a mouse in stockings. Instead she and her friend had blundered with panache into the most loaded of subjects. Why hadn't he just let her be?

But he'd had to put her right, enlighten her.

The train careened into a tunnel with a metal scream. A loud crack, and he saw that he'd rammed his heel into the wooden slat of the bench.

WHEN SHE ARRIVED home at the Dodds' house on Tiergarten-strasse Eleanor placed a telephone call to Gallico's hotel.

'Eleanor? Too late for a drink. I'm in my pyjamas.'

'Paul, honey, I know you and the boys are planning to petition the AOC about getting me back on the team . . .'

'Yeah, we've got a meet with Brundage tomorrow. I think there's a pretty fair chance that—'

'Well, look. Thanks for thinking of me, but I don't want you to do it.'

'Are you drunk?'

'Stone-cold sober. I've changed my mind. I'm through. I don't want to be on the goddamned team, or have anything to do with these Games.'

Denham lowered the paper and put his hand up to shield his eyes. She stood hand on her hip, with the sun behind her. Light blazed through her golden hair.

'Relax, I'm not going to bite your head off,' Eleanor said, removing her sunglasses.

'Won't you join me?'

'Thanks. By a strange coincidence I was thinking of you. It's Richard, right?'

'Sorry that I upset you last night.'

She took a Chesterfield from a tortoiseshell case in her handbag. He lit it for her, and she inhaled.

'It's me who should apologise,' she said, the smoke coming out with the words. She waved at the waitress. 'Coffee, uh, *bitte*?

'Richard, I come from a long line of stubborn idiots, and my father is the most stubborn of them all. When he's convinced of the truth of something he runs with it like a dog with a bone, even if it's a lost cause . . .' She held her cigarette up at an angle, staring at nothing in particular.

'Surely lost causes are the ones worth fighting for,' Denham said.

She smiled. 'That's what Dad says. He tried talking me out of going to Germany, but being his stubborn idiot daughter, here I am. What I'm trying to say is . . . my old dad's cause may have been lost but that's not to say it wasn't right. We shouldn't have come here. None of us.'

Denham's breakfast arrived.

'Mind if I ask what made you change your mind?'

'Let's just say I got my rose-tinted glasses knocked off . . . of all places in a rose garden . . .' Her expression darkened, and she fell silent for a minute while he ate, before saying, 'Hey, what're you doing today?'

Denham took the Olympic programme from his jacket and showed her.

'There's a story I'm after about a German fencer. She's competing in the opening heats at the House of German Sport at ten o'clock.'

'Mind if I join you? As a fellow reporter I mean, not as a date or anything. I'm sorry, I don't even know if you're married. Not that that's relevant. Hey, why don't I shut up?'

Denham laughed into his napkin. 'As a fellow reporter I'd be delighted. And I promise you my former wife couldn't care less what I do.'

IN THE CUPOLA Hall of the House of German Sport every bench was packed. Smatterings of applause punctuated the female fencing elimination heats. Denham and his new associate sat at the end of a row, next to a rowdy party of Hungarian girls. A high amphitheatre surrounded a stage, behind which great frosted-glass windows admitted a soft light, almost silhouetting the contestants. The place smelled of fresh paint and floor polish.

'Who are we here to see?' said Eleanor once they were seated.

'Hannah Liebermann.'

'You're *kidding* me, right?'

'No, why?' Denham found the American habit of asking exclamatory questions tiresome.

'She and I have been in the same magazines plenty of times, but we've never met.'

They searched the faces of the competitors seated around the raised piste in the centre of the hall, but the famous Liebermann wasn't among them. Then the loudspeakers announced, *'Krisztina Nagy, Ungarn; Hannah Liebermann, Deutschland.'* The Hungarian girls screamed their applause, and the Germans in the hall turned their heads towards a slim woman of average height standing on the stairs to the side of the hall, away from the other competitors.

'That's her,' said Eleanor.

She had dark, plaited hair worn with a white band around her head. A small, straight nose gave her profile a certain nobility, Denham thought, something statuesque. She wore a tight-fitting white jerkin with an eagle and swastika emblazoned on her chest. Unlike the other contestants, who sat about with tense faces, awaiting their bouts like sprung traps, Liebermann was calm, and Denham imagined he saw melancholy in her—in the measured way she pulled on her gloves and slowly picked up her foil. Her coach was a short, full-bellied man with a small moustache and a few strands of hair ribbed gamely across the top of his pate. He was fussing about her, giving her some last-minute instruction involving a stabbing arm and finger action, to which she was paying not the slightest attention.

'I suppose your story has nothing to do with Liebermann having the type of beauty that launched a thousand ships?' Eleanor said.

He shook his head and kept his eyes on the fencer. 'I'll tell you what the story's about when you tell me what happened last night to make you think your dad was right about these Games.'

As Liebermann walked towards the piste in the centre of the hall her eyes seemed to be searching the crowd. Suddenly she found someone with whom she exchanged a charged look, a look that struck Denham as one of fierce love. He turned in the direction of her gaze and straightaway saw the dark young man in a brown gabardine coat. Although seated several rows back he was impossible to miss. His left eye was purple, puffed up, and surrounded with stitches, and his nose had been broken. Bandages covered one hand. The sight sent a cold shiver over Denham's back; it was as though the young man had crawled from a tunnel that led straight back to the trenches, twenty years ago.

'You're pale,' Eleanor said, when he turned back.

'Just a hangover.'

Liebermann stepped up to the piste, shook hands with her Hungarian opponent, and pulled on her mask. Both raised their foils to their faces in the swashbuckler salute, then poised with tips held at forty-five degrees. The umpire shouted, 'On guard!' and the bout began.

The two women inched towards each other like ghost crabs on a strand. Liebermann probed her opponent's defences with small strikes, testing her tactics. The Hungarian's reflexes were sharp,

and she had a long reach; she parried the strikes with confidence
and Liebermann lost the round, to a disappointed bray from the
crowd. The second bout began in a similar style with the Hungarian seeming to grow in confidence as she pursued her strategy with
wider, more dramatic strikes. Denham wondered if Liebermann's
misfortunes had knocked the fight out of her.

'Hannah,' Eleanor shouted, 'sock it to her.'

'This is not a heavyweight prizefight.'

It wasn't until the third minute of the second round that Liebermann suddenly changed tack, as though she'd just cracked her opponent's code, and lunged with surprising aggression. The crowd sat
up; the Hungarian lost her balance, and Liebermann pressed home
the attack with brilliant, precise movements. She won the bout.

The crowd shouted encouragement. If they knew Liebermann
was Jewish, they didn't seem to care.

In the final bout she smacked the Hungarian's foil aside and
lunged again and again with a shocking ferocity. Cowed, her opponent crumbled under the onslaught and stumbled back over the
warning line. Liebermann was through to the finals, and the hall
gave its noisy assent.

'Holy crap,' said Eleanor, clapping. 'Did you see that?'

They watched her shake her opponent's hand and take off her
mask and the band around her head, letting her dark plaits fall to
her shoulders. With only the briefest nod to the crowd she stood
down from the piste and left the hall through an exit in the base of
the amphitheatre.

'I'm going to speak to her,' said Denham.

'I'm coming with you.'

'You stay exactly where you are.'

He ran down the wooden steps and out through the exit Liebermann had taken. This led into a semicircular lobby, at the end of
which he saw her climbing a staircase and disappearing through a
door at the top. He dashed after her, taking the steps two at a time,
and entered a wooden corridor. At the far end, Liebermann stood

talking to the coach. She was holding open a door, as though she was about to disappear into a changing room.

'Fräulein Liebermann!' he called.

They turned to look at him.

'Congratulations,' Denham said in German.

She inclined her head without smiling, and he sensed that her trust wouldn't be easy to win. She really was quite beautiful.

The coach looked at him through narrowed eyes.

'My name's Denham. I'm an English news reporter and feature writer. Would you do me the honour of a brief interview?'

Her brown eyes seemed to widen at the mention of 'English.' She was about to speak when her coach cut in.

'Fräulein Liebermann is tired after her match. And any foreign press wanting an interview must apply for permission through the official channels.'

'Now is as good a time as any, Rudi,' she said. 'Which newspaper do you represent Herr . . . Denham?'

'I'm published in the London *Times*, the *Daily Express*, but mainly in weekend newspapers and magazines in the United States. Is there somewhere we can talk?' he asked, ignoring the coach.

'I said you need permission,' the coach persisted.

Liebermann opened the door of the room she'd been about to enter.

'We can talk in here. As you can see, I've been given a changing room all to myself. I'm either privileged or insulted. I really can't decide.'

'Not without permission.'

Denham put his foot in the door.

Liebermann said softly, 'I'm sure permission can be obtained straightaway from the Ministry official in the hall, Rudi. Why not go and ask him?' Her voice was cultured with a faint haughtiness.

From the hall the applause echoed like the roar of a phantom army.

The coach hesitated, then glowered at Denham. Turning to

Hannah he said, 'I will return directly. You will answer no questions until I'm present.'

He waddled off down the corridor, his rubber soles squeaking on the wooden floor. *A stroke of luck*, Denham thought. The man is an idiot.

The changing room smelled of sweat and sports unguents. Somewhere behind a tiled wall a shower dripped.

'We don't have long,' she said, sitting down and placing her foil into a long black case. 'And we can speak in English if you prefer.'

He'd thought hard about how he'd tackle the interview if he ever got it, but now he was lost for words. Whatever he'd intended to ask, he found himself saying in English, 'Who was that young man you greeted in the audience?'

She looked up, suspicious and fearful.

'I saw you make eye contact with him.'

There was a long pause before she said, 'My brother.'

'What happened to him?'

'It's a family matter,' she said in a small voice. 'Look, don't you want to ask me if I'm pleased to be back in Germany, or whatever you reporters normally ask?'

'I think I know how you feel about being back in Germany. I saw your brother's face, too.'

'I'm not sure what you're after, Mr Denham—'

'Was he roughed up by the Gestapo to make sure you do what they want? To make sure you compete?'

'For God's sake . . .' For an instant her face was livid with terror.

'Forgive me,' Denham said quietly. He knew he was going too far too quickly, but that coach would be back at any moment. 'Hannah—if I may—if there's something you want the world outside Germany to know, I can help you get it out there . . . the publicity may work to your advantage. It may stop them—'

'Stop them doing what?' Her voice was a baleful cry in the tiled room. 'Destroying my life and my family's? Do you know about that? Is that why you're here? Yes, it might,' she said with great bitterness, her voice trembling under the weight of tears, 'or they may decide to make us disappear altogether. After the Games.'

Sunlight from a narrow window near the ceiling dappled on the white-tiled floor and across her head, which bobbed as she cried, and he saw that her hair was not black, as he'd thought, but a dark chestnut, with strands of copper and gold.

After a few moments she composed herself, wiped her eyes, and looked up at him with a hint of the steel he'd seen earlier.

'What do you want from me?'

'I want to tell your story,' he said. 'The whole story.'

She looked into her lap, and her knee began to shake up and down.

Denham glanced towards the door. A sound of rubber soles came squeaking from the far end of the corridor outside.

'I don't know . . .' she said, her face contorted with strain. 'It might only make things worse . . .'

'They wouldn't dare harm your family if the spotlight of the world's press is on you.'

She rose and began pacing along the wooden bench, nervous, pulling at her fingers.

The footsteps were yards away.

Denham said quickly, 'The new laws have taken away any future for the Jews. You must know that. The pressure we bring could help get your family out . . .'

The door handle turned.

'How do I contact you?' she whispered.

The coach stepped in, gave them each a fishy look, and held the door open for another visitor, whose footsteps approached. Two seconds later Willi Greiser entered, accompanied by an SS man in black uniform.

The press chief's eyebrows shot up when he saw Denham but soon recovered an expression of urbane cynicism.

'Denham, I might have guessed it was you.'

'Hello, Greiser.'

The two men held each other's stare. A slice of dark blond hair had come unstuck and hung down over Greiser's left eye. He wore a pale linen suit and a tie patterned with the Olympic rings.

Greiser said, 'Fräulein Liebermann is here as a special guest of Germany's . . .'

'That's an odd thing to say about a German.'

' . . . under a unique arrangement that precludes her from giving any interviews to the press. Permission is refused.' He turned to Hannah and the coach. 'Would you excuse us while I have a word in private with Herr Denham?'

The SS man escorted them out to the squelch of the coach's rubber soles.

The door closed, and Greiser dropped any pretence of conviviality.

'If it weren't for the Olympic fortnight, Denham, I'd kick you out of Germany today.' He came closer, and Denham felt the warmth of his breath. 'Last week you were in Friedrichshafen snooping around the *Hindenburg*—I should have you charged with espionage—and today I find you attempting to speak to Hannah Liebermann. I warned you—'

'You warned me not to write any more damaging pieces, Greiser,' Denham said calmly, 'and I've taken your advice to heart. It's not in my interests to be expelled.'

Greiser paused. The duelling scar on his right cheek was flushed a pale purple. 'How much do you know about Liebermann?'

'I know she's the greatest woman fencer Germany's ever produced, and she's home after a long absence. That's a story in itself. It's the most natural thing in the world to want to interview her—'

Greiser exploded.

'Listen to me, you piece of shit.' He grabbed Denham's lapels and rammed him against the changing room wall, his head narrowly missing a hook. 'D'you think you can talk your way out of anything?' he roared. 'Stick your nose into this and you'll be too risky for us to expel! We'll make you vanish into night and fog. No one will ever hear of you again.' His nose was almost touching Denham, into whose eyes he peppered flecks of spittle. 'You—stay—away—from—Liebermann!'

Denham shoved him back, but Greiser made a grab for his neck. Denham tried to swing him into the wall, but Greiser's grip was strong. They lost their balance and together crashed onto the bench, then to the floor, both now with their hands around each other's throats.

'Hey, what the hell's going on in here?'

Eleanor was standing in the door. 'Richard?'

The two men released each other, and Greiser looked away.

'Who is this?' he said, getting to his feet. His head was all gold, puce, and pink.

Denham sat up onto the bench. 'Greiser, may I introduce Eleanor Emerson, a reporter with the Hearst Press; Eleanor, Willi Greiser is an old friend of mine. He's the press chief. We were just catching up.'

'You could have fooled me,' she said.

Greiser straightened his tie and his sleeves, replaced the errant strands of hair, and walked out of the room without another word.

'What happened? Why was that jerk mad at you?'

'I think he was scared,' said Denham.

'Of what?'

Denham rubbed his throat, grimacing. It was the only explanation for that extraordinary outburst. He'd never seen the man lose his temper before. Greiser was always the suave operator. His masters must be acutely sensitive about Liebermann, and Greiser was under pressure. Plus he'd patently screwed up—by leaving her in the custody of that idiot coach. Not surprising that he panicked, perhaps.

'Did you speak to her?'

'A few words.'

'Well?'

'She wants to talk.'

He leaned over and picked up a small black leather ID pass of some sort from the floor under the bench. Two silver runes flashed in the light. Inside were Greiser's mug shot and birth details, stamped with an eagle. It was a *Sippenbuch*, a racial record carried by all members of the SS. Greiser, it seemed, was an honorary SS-Standartenführer, the equivalent of a colonel.

'It must have come out of his side pocket,' Denham said.

He looked up and smiled at her. 'I'm glad you turned up, cavalry. Think I may have got my marching orders if you hadn't.'

'No problem. I was just worried when I saw her leave and there was no sign of you.'

'Hm. Well, anyway, thank you. I shouldn't have told him your name, though . . . I really shouldn't have done that.'

Chapter Fourteen

Denham bought lunch from a stall and they joined the groups of fencing fans on the lawn outside the House of German Sport, picnicking next to a flowerbed droning with bees.

'Your frankfurter looks nicer than my hamburger,' Eleanor said.

'Too bad.'

'I think I'll skip lunch.'

'All right,' Denham said. 'Have mine. I'll have your hamburger.'

The Reich Sports Field filled the horizon. Between rows of poplars, the new hockey and football fields were lurid with new grass. A quarter of a mile away the vast Olympic plaza led up to the stadium, which glared white in the sun. Every few minutes the breeze carried the roar of the crowd and the tinny strains of national anthems.

'Are you going to tell me what happened in there?' said Eleanor.

'It's tricky,' he said, picking at some sauerkraut with a wooden fork.

He watched her slip out of her shoes, hitch her skirt unselfconsciously, and sun her long legs on the grass.

'No rush,' she said, closing her eyes and facing the sun. 'You can tell me later . . .'

The plodding chords of 'The Star-Spangled Banner' reached them from the stadium. She nodded her head towards the sound. 'Mind if we go take a look?'

They walked across the playing fields towards the stadium. In the centre of the Olympic plaza were parked, bumper to bumper, a row of ten open-topped Mercedes-Benz touring cars, gleaming and

ticking in the sun like a demonic coal train. Each was guarded by SS
men in white gloves who stood about being photographed by tourists and answering questions from Jungvolk boys.

'Adolf's security,' Denham said.

They showed their press cards at the gates and passed into the
stadium's forecourt. With the flags of the competing nations flapping from its rim, it resembled some vast vessel in sail.

The stadium was full and murmuring. The long jump finals were
in progress as he and Eleanor squeezed along a row near the eastern gate. On the far side he spotted the gold flash of the pennant
that flew when Hitler was in attendance, but the man himself, surrounded by his entourage, was a brown dot in the distance.

Carl 'Luz' Long, the German long jump favourite, was on the
runway. The press had been idolising him for months, and it wasn't
hard to see why. Tall, graceful, and flaxen-haired, he was an Aryan
poster boy. But such was the curiosity about Owens since Monday, when the hundred-metre win had made a black man the most
famous figure in the Reich after Hitler, that the stadium's energy
seemed ambiguous to Denham. The members of the large American
contingent were easy to spot with their straw boaters and sunglasses.

Denham tapped the shoulder of a man sitting with his young son
in the row in front. 'What's happened?'

The boy answered. 'Luz Long jumped seven point seven three
metres, but Owens fouled again. This is the second jump out
of three. Maffei of Italy and, um, Tajima of Japan are still in, but
they're not jumping as far as Owens and Long.'

The stadium fell into an electrified silence as Long prepared. He
stood, frowning and rubbing his knees, his white shorts pulled up
high around his waist, then launched himself, blond hair waving,
with enormous strides. The leap was tremendous; his legs pedalled
thin air as if to force him farther forwards, and his landing was so
hard that it sent a shower of sand into the pit where a camera was
filming. The crowd applauded generously. There was a few seconds'
wait, and the speakers announced the result.

'*Seven point eight seven metres. New Olympic record.*'

The stadium rose to its feet and began chanting Long's name. Two German team members lifted him, beaming, up onto their shoulders and carried him around the pit. When they put him down, Owens walked over and shook his hand.

'What a sportsman,' said Eleanor.

Denham peered at the distant brown dot in the Führer box, picturing the man slapping his cotton gloves into his hand and muttering, 'Beat that, *Neger.*'

The stadium waited as Tajima and Maffei took their jumps, both far shorter than Long's. Finally a warm 'aah' surrounded Owens from all sides as he stepped onto the runway, his hands on his hips. He took a deep breath, tapped his heels on the ground and rocked his torso gently, as if moulding his muscles to the movement he had to make.

The Americans were on their feet.

'*Owens! Owens! Owens!*'

His body was supple, his limbs loose and lithe compared with the tension and power of Long's.

The stadium fell into a tense silence. Some American girls in the next row were wringing their programmes in agony. If Owens fouled again, the gold was Long's. Eleanor grabbed Denham's hand.

Owens broke into a sprint.

'Go on, Jesse, go on, go on, *go on!*' Eleanor said under her breath.

With his final stride the American catapulted into the air and, as he flew, bent his head forwards and brought his legs up straight, reaching for his toes. When he landed there was a look of mild surprise on his face as the applause broke around him. The measure was taken.

'*Seven point nine four metres. New Olympic record.*'

A tremendous 'ooh' from the crowd.

Owens dusted off the sand and gave his modest grin, waving at the crowd and trotting back to a towel he'd laid on the grass, as if he'd been for a dip.

The murmuring intensified as the minutes passed and Long finally returned to the runway for the third and final jump.

The crowd chanted his name, but his face looked far from encouraged. He was pale and kept screwing his fingers into his palms, as though he had dirt on his hands. Far away in the Führer box the entourage was on its feet and watching through binoculars.

Carl 'Luz' Long broke into the run of his life, and the crowd screamed their support. With the final two strides he leapt. But somehow, once airborne, he seemed to lose his balance, as if hands unseen were nudging him off course. He strained but couldn't recover as his body fell forwards and he landed badly on one foot.

The red flag went up, and the Führer's entourage sat down. The gold medal was Owens's, and he still had his third jump to make.

'He's won,' Denham said. 'He doesn't need to try again.'

Eleanor was watching Owens intently as he walked back to the runway. 'He's going to jump clear out of Berlin.'

Owens touched his nose and lips, crouched, and rubbed his hands over his buttocks and down his shanks.

Then he rocketed down the runway and shot into the air. For two seconds he flew, and landed with such force that he sprang upwards again, diving into the sand.

The tape measure was brought up, and when the announcement was made there was a half second's silence as the crowd took it in.

'*Eight point zero six metres. New Olympic record.*'

After the silence, the roar rolled across the stadium like an avalanche in the Tyrol, causing the seats to tremble and buzz. The crowd chanted, '*Yes-sy Oh-vens, Yes-sy Oh-vens.*' To Denham's surprise Eleanor threw her arms around him, laughing, so that he caught the white flower scent in her hair. When they parted, her face was close, her eyes on his. He felt her breath.

They turned back towards the field. Long, who'd won the silver, shook Owens's hand and embraced him; then, to everyone's delight, the pair set off arm in arm around the track, waving to the crowd, inspiring laughter, and even greater applause.

Denham looked up to the Führer box, but the man's seat was empty. He'd left.

He and Eleanor made their way to the end of the row. On the steps, she slipped her arm in his, as if it were the most natural thing in the world, and turned to look at Owens down on the track, so that Denham couldn't read her face.

Still staring down at the athlete, who was surrounded by reporters, she said, 'We still shouldn't be here. Not even Jesse. The whole setup stinks . . .'

Denham was stunned. What had happened to her last night? He decided not to press her, though. Not now. Instead he said, 'There's a friend of mine down there I want you to meet.'

He led Eleanor down the steps to the edge of the track, pushing past the departing crowds. The movie crew were still at work, lifting cameras out of pits in the ground where they'd filmed the action. He spotted Friedl wheeling a camera dolly. Denham called out, and the young man waved, then ambled over, flicking his sleek black hair out of his eyes. He had a white band around his arm with the word FILM. When Denham introduced Eleanor, Friedl's mouth gaped.

'"Seven Beautiful Girls from the USA,"' he said. 'You're the swimmer.' She rolled her eyes, but Denham saw from her tight smile that she was pleased.

'Think that long jump will make it into your movie?' she said.

'Of course . . . Unless someone says otherwise.' He put a surreptitious two fingers under his nose to make a toothbrush moustache. 'Tell me, Beautiful Girl from the USA, do you like hot music, too?' He put his arms around them in a confidential huddle. 'There's a dance tonight, and I would love you both to come.'

Eleanor looked at Denham.

'Be at the Nollendorfplatz Theatre by ten.' He dropped his voice. 'A band from Hamburg is playing some prohibited numbers in between the polkas and waltzes. *American swing.* If we're lucky the police will leave us alone because of the Olympiad. Every hepcat in Berlin will be there . . .'

As they joined the throng leaving the stadium through the eastern gate Eleanor said to Denham, 'What on God's green earth is a hepcat?'

'Shall I tell you over dinner?'

'Oh,' she said, smiling at the ground. 'All right. But tonight's my shout. You got my hamburger. My frankfurter.'

Outside in the forecourt, a large crowd, many of them young boys with autograph books, had gathered around the mobile radio car of the Deutscher Rundfunk, which was broadcasting live radio coverage of the Games.

'Jesse must be in there now,' said Eleanor. 'The press boys told me that all gold medallists are interviewed on live radio after their competition. Imagine that. A black man's voice is speaking to Germany right now. They wouldn't put him on the radio back home unless he was singing "Dixie."'

Chapter Fifteen

Eleanor was late meeting him at the restaurant, which was in a tree-lined street off Golzstrasse, not far from Nollendorf-platz. Denham was reading a newspaper at a corner table and rose, smiling, as she entered.

That shyness as he met her eye. 'No gown this evening?'

She was wearing a blue angora sweater, a red chequered skirt that came only to her knees, and short white socks.

'Ever seen a girl dance swing in a gown?' She pulled off her beret, so that her unwaved hair fell around her neck, and kissed him on the cheek. 'I hate those downtown swells who go slumming in Harlem dressed for the Ritz.' She sat down and looked around at the wood-panelled walls, the low lighting, and the couples murmuring over chilled bottles.

'A favourite place of yours?'

'Yes . . . it's hard to find, and the food's good. I hope you like French cuisine. To be honest I eat what the Germans eat only when I'm broke. I took the liberty of ordering this bottle.'

'And what gave you a taste for French cooking?' she said as he poured her a glass. He seemed younger in candlelight. The bruise on his cheek was healing darkly, giving an intensity to his face.

'The war,' he said.

For a moment the light focused in the stem of his glass reflected in his eyes.

'I ended the war as a first lieutenant. For a few weeks after the armistice we were quartered in a château in Picardy. The villagers were kind to us. They taught me a little about food and wine.'

'You had survived,' she said without thinking.

'After a fashion.'

Denham raised his glass in a silent toast, and she did the same, took a sip, and savoured the subtle vintage. 'A 1913 Petit Verdot,' he said. 'A relic from a less troubled world.'

'The year I was born.'

They were silent for a while, and then he said, carefully, 'Must have been hard for you, what happened at the end of the voyage over. Your friend Martha told me.'

'Sure, it hurt like hell. After four years of work it was a mighty blow to my pride. But it's really not the end of the world. I've won a gold medal before . . .' She smiled faintly and sighed. 'The truth is, my behaviour was pretty awful.'

'Sounds like you had quite a time on that ship. "Let's Misbehave" is my favourite Cole Porter.'

Eleanor put her glass down. 'Loyalty and discretion are the qualities I admire most in Martha.'

Denham's laugh dispelled any tension. 'So,' he said, breaking off some bread. 'I want to hear all about the Herb Emerson Orchestra.'

They drank more of the wine and ordered dinner: he a rainbow trout in a champagne sauce, she a simple ratatouille. For dessert they shared a tarte tatin with cream.

They continued talking long after the wine was finished and the waiter had brought them coffee and Armagnac. Eleanor relished the exquisite burn of the spirit on her tongue, took Denham's cigarette to light her own, and leaned back in her chair.

She said, 'Now, are you going to tell me what a hepcat is?'

'A kid who dances to swing,' said Denham. 'Usually a well-off kid who can afford the imported records and the English fashions. They've been a big worry to the authorities since jazz music, or rather the wilder "hot jazz," was banned from the radio last year. A stupid move if you ask me. Teenagers of every generation will rebel.'

'Ban jazz?' Eleanor's face slumped into her palms. She was feeling nicely inebriated. 'But why? That's as insane as banning booze. It just makes you want to drink. We should know. We had a failed thirteen-year experiment.'

'The Nazis are terrified of what wild jungle rhythms will provoke in the nation's youth . . .' He leaned towards her and lowered his voice. 'Which of course means only one thing . . .'

'And what is that?'

' . . . reckless, indiscriminate sex.'

The wine made Eleanor laugh freely, and she accidentally dropped her cigarette. He allowed her to light another one, for him this time.

They left the restaurant arm in arm into the humid night, and she remembered that she hadn't even mentioned the revelation in the rose garden, or asked him about Liebermann.

'Friedl's party is a few blocks away,' he said.

The sky was a deep cyan, flecked by the gold of the moths around the streetlamps. On the corner of the block a dozen or so people were gathered on the pavement, looking into the window of a café. Inside it was almost dark; there were no café tables but rows of seats packed with people watching a fuzzy square of light emitting from a large wooden box. Together they peered in at it. It wasn't cinema but a small, ghostly picture showing Carl 'Luz' Long running into his jump, followed by a cut to the Führer rocking back and forth in his seat and slapping his knee. Every few seconds a man in a white coat adjusted a dial to focus the picture. Eleanor was as mesmerised as everyone else. Neither she nor Denham had seen a television before.

They turned onto Motzstrasse, and Eleanor was about to mention the rose garden, when Denham pulled her roughly into a darkened garage entrance.

'Hey,' she said, more surprised than anything. 'There's a time and a place . . .'

'We're being followed.' He put his finger on her lips. 'Someone was waiting outside the restaurant as we left. He's been keeping pace behind us.'

Slowly, they craned their heads a fraction beyond the edge of the corner and saw, about twenty yards up the street, a man standing beneath a streetlamp, looking left and right. The moths cast tiny, fast-moving shadows across his dark coat and the trilby that obscured his face. Denham put his hands around Eleanor's shoulders and gently pulled her back.

He checked again and waited, holding her close, with her back towards him and his arm around her waist. She felt his heartbeat through his wrist. Suddenly they heard the man approaching, the beat of his footsteps loud and clear on the warm air.

'*Run*,' Denham said.

He caught her hand, and together they sprinted down the sidewalk.

The man shouted in German, and ran after them.

They rounded a corner onto a street of stores shuttered for the night and almost collided with a man walking a dog. Ahead, a yellow light spilt onto the pavement from an open doorway. They ran towards it. Smells of roast pork and cabbage came from inside, and the sound of accordion music and laughter.

Denham led her into the crowded *Kneipe*.

It was noisy and hot. They tried to walk at a normal pace, dodging an aproned waitress carrying a tray of foaming beers and another with platters of chops and mash. Eleanor looked over her shoulder, saw the dark trilby entering after them, and glimpsed the man's face. Her skin froze. Something *horrific* . . .

'Go,' she yelled at Denham.

They ran along a gangway between dining booths, weaving sharply around another waitress with a tray, which caused Eleanor to knock an ice bucket hard with her knee. Ice, wine, and glasses smashed across the floor.

A draught of cool air from ahead, and they saw, beyond the

accordion players and another dining area, an open exit. The *Kneipe* had entries on two streets.

In another moment they were on the sidewalk again. This second street, lit by bright streetlamps, was crowded with a departing theatre audience. She and Denham pushed into the throng.

Eleanor looked back. 'Have we lost him?' She'd barely broken a sweat, though Denham was breathing hard.

'Let's find that party,' he said, as if they'd simply taken a wrong turn.

She stopped and looked at him, incredulous, swinging him around by the elbow so that he faced her. The chattering theatre crowd flowed around them.

'Would you like to tell me what the hell's going on?'

'I don't know,' Denham said, shaking his head. 'Look, Greiser warned me this morning to stay away from Liebermann. But I have no idea if that is why we're being followed. I'll explain as we walk . . .'

He told her about the intruders he'd surprised as they ransacked his apartment.

'Who were they? Police?'

'I suspect not. The police would simply have arrested me, then searched.'

'Thieves then.'

'They didn't take anything. No, someone somewhere is under the misapprehension that I have something they want.'

'Well, what?'

Denham swept his hat off and put both hands in the air in exasperation. 'I have *no idea.*' It was the first time she'd seem him ruffled. Even in that locker room brawl he'd kept his nerve.

'So that guy following us . . . ?'

'Could have been one of Greiser's men keeping an eye on us; could have been one of my intruders; could have been anyone. Who knows?'

'His face . . . ,' she said with a shudder.

*   *   *

THE THEATRE ON Nollendorfplatz was an art nouveau palace
adorned with decorative turrets and frescoes of erotic figures. No
light came from inside, and heavy, dark curtains had been drawn
behind the door.

'We're in the right place,' Denham said, watching something
over her shoulder.

The first things she noticed were the boys' chequered jackets and
wing-collar shirts. These, together with fedoras and rolled umbrellas, which they swung as they walked, created an eccentrically sharp
look. The girls on their arms wore their hair waved, dyed, or curled;
there wasn't a Teutonic braid among them.

'What's with the umbrellas?' Eleanor said as the darkened curtain was pulled aside and a faint trumpet, whining high over a drum
rhythm, was heard from within.

'Is he with you?' said a voice in English. A young man in pin-
stripes and sporting a gorse bush of tangled hair nodded towards
Denham, and slipped an arm round her shoulder.

'Yes, he is,' Eleanor said brightly, flicking his hand off.

They entered a marble foyer, where a large notice on an easel
proclaimed in red letters:

SWING TANZEN VERBOTEN!
REICHSKULTURKAMMER

At the other end a second heavy curtain was pulled aside and
another door opened. It was a large venue, much too large for the
crowd of a hundred or so youths, not yet dancing but gathered in
front of the band on the stage where a vocalist was singing 'Min-
nie the Moocher.' He threw out the lines of the refrain, which the
audience repeated back in mangled English. The attraction seemed
to be the trumpeter, a chubby young man in a tuxedo who inflated
his cheeks like Louis Armstrong, producing Armstrong's coarse lilt.

A clarinet, two saxes, another trumpet, three trombones, a double bass, a piano, and a drummer completed the band. Not a violin in sight. *I'll be damned*, thought Eleanor. A serious swing band. Not large, but the acoustics filled out the sound nicely.

A glitter ball cast its revolving constellation through the veils of cigarette smoke. On the right-hand side a long bar stretched almost the entire length of the floor. The left was taken up by a seating area of café tables arranged among large potted ferns.

Eleanor thought that, seen together, moving in rhythm, soaking in the forbidden music, they were the most outlandish kids she'd ever set eyes on. They looked nothing like the English or Americans, more like some rebel faction whose appearance was exaggerated to look as unfascist as possible. Some of the boys had forelocks that extended into a bizarre whip down to their chins.

'Hey—'

Eleanor turned to see Friedl pushing his way towards them through the crowd. His black hair shone with brilliantine and a cigar stub was stuck soggily in the corner of his mouth. He stopped in front of her and Denham, exhaling a breath potent with rum. There was an edginess to him, and his eyes danced.

'What d'you think of the band?' he said, putting his arms around them. 'It's the "Flottbecker" from Hamburg. There are cats here from Leipzig, too, and Hanover. Here—' He began pulling the shoulders of the youths in front of him, turning them around. 'This is Ray, this one's King, here's Fats, Fiddlin' Jim, Old-Hot-Boy—he's from Hamburg, formed a huge club around *one* gramophone—and this is Eton-Charlie.' This last youth had excelled himself with a derby hat and a silver-topped cane. 'A *dead smart* look,' Friedl said to Denham, 'like your foreign minister, Anthony Eden, don't you agree?'

'Dead smart.' Eton-Charlie put his nose in the air making the others laugh. Two girls introduced as Blackie and Swing-Puppy smiled with cyclamen purple lips.

A waiter brought them drinks of iced Coca-Cola and rum.

Applause from near the stage, and the singer stood down. Then the drummer beat the first bars of 'Sing, Sing, Sing'—*Bam bam bam-bam barram bam-bam*—and the crowd went wild.

'Benny Goodman, King of Swing!' someone yelled.

The slim boy known as Fats grabbed Eleanor by the hand, and she allowed him to pull her onto the dance floor.

The crowd swung their arms high, kicked their legs out, and threw each other from the waist. Girls shimmied around the boys, hitched their short skirts up to reveal their panties; boys picked the girls up and banana-split their legs over their crotches. Many of the steps were crude, improvised by the youths themselves, or based on some variation of the old Lindy Hop. Eleanor found herself surprisingly moved by it all.

At the bar Denham stood with Friedl. The young man was pale and sinking his drinks at an alarming rate.

'Something wrong?' Denham said.

'Did you make contact with Liebermann?'

'Briefly, after her match this morning. But the press chief stopped the interview.'

Friedl's head slumped to his chest. When he looked up Denham saw anguish in his eyes. 'Go and find her. Interview her family, too. Publish the truth about these Games . . .' There was an off note to his voice, as if mania was only just being contained. 'I mean . . . it's a good story for you . . . isn't it?'

'What's happened?'

'I got a tip-off . . . a few hours ago. My name's on an arrest list. Probably tonight. Tomorrow at the latest.'

'Christ. I'm sorry.'

'I'm going away. Into hiding. I just came to see my friends. I shouldn't be here.'

'Are they coming for you because you told me about Liebermann?'

'No,' he said, managing a weak smile. 'Not because of that.'

'Where will you go?'

Friedl seemed to collect himself. 'It's safer if I don't tell you. I have friends. You shouldn't worry.'

The band was now playing a swing arrangement of 'Blue Skies,' and about half the youths were sitting at the tables to the left of the floor, chatting, sweating, drunk, and laughing. The rest were still hitting their stride in front of the stage.

The shrill note might have been the sax bringing in the next number until Denham realised, at the same moment as everyone else, that a whistle was being blown.

'Oh no,' said Friedl.

Some fifteen Hitler Youth were entering the hall from the back and spreading out along the walls to both sides. Short hair; clean, hard faces. Brown shorts with daggers hanging from their belts.

'Change the music,' the one in the lead yelled, waving at the stage. 'Hey you. Change the music.'

'I'll say goodbye,' Friedl said, his voice tight.

Denham embraced him. *Good luck.*

'Find Liebermann.'

He turned and pushed his way along the bar to the corner of the floor, slipped behind the stage curtain, and was gone.

The pianist struck up a halfhearted tango to whistles and jeers. 'Not kosher!' someone shouted.

Suddenly a lit cigarette was thrown at the Hitler Youth leader. He recoiled, his fingers frantically brushing the bright embers from his shirt; then he lunged in the direction it had come from, fist raised. The brawl began instantly.

Denham found Eleanor. 'Time to go,' he said, taking her hand and leading her towards the foyer.

Seconds later they were through to the street.

Behind them came shouting and the sound of a glass smashing.

Eleanor said, 'You don't think there'll be serious trouble, do you?'

'Probably not. One gang of kids fighting another. They'll all scramble before the Orpo get there. Those Hitler Youth were probably just looking for girls.'

He told her about Friedl's tip-off and his escape into hiding.

'Do you think he'll be okay?'

Denham said nothing.

A tram clattered over the carriageway. They meandered hand in hand down a deserted street. Denham had no particular destination in mind. The buildings were ornate, shuttered, and heavy, like old safe boxes. The air was still warm, carrying the sound of a far-off train whistle sighing into the night.

'I've had a great time,' Eleanor said.

Before them the cobblestones glinted like mackerel scales, and in one of the trees around the streetlamps a nightingale trilled, answered a moment later by another in a nearby street.

They turned and faced each other. Her eyes were swimming in the moonlight, her lips parted a little, her breath short.

They kissed slowly, her tongue hesitant, then insistent, his hands clasping her to him. It had been a long time since he'd held a woman who appealed to him for reasons beyond base need. For a few moments he was lost in her. But then an old demon breathed in his ear and he released her.

'What is it?' she whispered.

'You're a married woman,' he said, 'and I'm a lost cause.'

'Aren't lost causes the ones worth fighting for?' she said quietly.

They embraced again, her warm cheek resting on his neck, and stood still for a few moments, rocking very gently, when she gave a sharp cry and jumped away, sending Denham's heart into his mouth.

The shriek echoed off the dark buildings. Her eyes were locked on a point over his shoulder.

'What?'

'Goddamn it, he's there,' she said, pointing to the darkness beneath the trees.

Denham could see nothing.

Then from out of the shadows the figure in the black trilby came quickly towards them.

'Who are you?' Denham shouted in German.

'Please . . . ,' said a young man's voice. 'Don't run again.'

He stepped into the light of a streetlamp, took off his hat, and Denham recognised him. The mutilated eye and stitched-up cheek glistened.

'I want to talk to you . . .' The young man's voice was quick and rattled. 'My name is Roland Liebermann. I'm—'

'I know who you are,' said Denham. 'Relax, son, it's all right. You gave us a fright, that's all. How did you find us?'

'Hannah told me about you while you were in the changing room with that official,' he said in a hoarse voice. 'She asked me to follow you, but I couldn't risk approaching you in public . . . if they'd seen me talking to you, well . . .' He shrugged. 'I found you again as you left the stadium and, lucky for me, you took a taxi. I jumped in one and followed you home. Taxis are safe for me.'

'Walk with us awhile,' said Denham.

Roland Liebermann glanced down the still street. A light had come on in a nearby window, and now there was movement behind a curtain.

'There will be a *Portierfrau* with a telephone in every building along here,' he said. 'It's too dangerous. I must go. My sister said we could trust you, and, if I found you, to ask if you will come to us—tomorrow.'

'I'll come,' said Denham.

'We live at Winklerstrasse 80, in Grunewald. Will you remember that?'

'Winklerstrasse 80.'

'*Gnädiges Fräulein*,' Roland continued, turning to Eleanor but still speaking in German. 'I'm sorry I scared you. Tomorrow then,' he said to them both. 'But please, don't let anyone see you approach our house.'

Denham extended his hand to Roland. He hesitated, but then shook it firmly, before pulling the brim of his hat down and turning away. They watched him disappear up the street, darting through the shadows under the trees.

'I understood enough of that to know you're going to see Lieber-mann,' Eleanor said. 'And this time I'm coming with you. No arguments. What's the matter?'

Denham was looking down at the hand he'd just shaken with Roland Liebermann.

'He had no index or middle finger.'

THE HALLWAY IN Kopischstrasse was in darkness when Denham got home. Inside Frau Stumpf's apartment a clock chimed twice. Exhausted, he climbed the stairs, intending to fall straight into bed. He opened the door warily but found no sign of another forced entry. On the floor in front of him, though, was a telegram, which Frau Stumpf must have slipped under the door.

It was from Anna, asking him to call immediately.

A bud of anxiety popped into his stomach. He had a cordial friendship with his former wife, but they both knew that Tom was the only reason they kept in touch. Had something happened to him?

He picked up the telephone before his imagination ran riot, got through to the exchange at Charlottenburg, and placed an urgent long-distance call. Within seconds the operator called him back with the connection.

'Richard?' Her voice sounded strained. 'I've been trying to reach you since early this morning. There's been no answer . . .'

'What is it?'

'It's Tom . . .' Anna's voice wobbled. Behind the hiss and crackle on the line he heard her crying. 'He's disappeared.'

Chapter Sixteen

Denham pictured his former wife as he usually did: lying under a quilt, clutching the handset of the bedside telephone. She was prone to tension headaches and retreated to her bed when vexed, her face pallid beneath her dark hair. Denham waited for her to stop crying, and then asked her to explain.

'You see, on Monday evening I had some important news for Tom. Walter, the friend I'm sure I've told you about, has asked me to marry him—yes—and I thought Tom would be pleased. He's so good to him, Walter is, but anyway I'm afraid Tom took the news rather badly.'

'Oh.'

'I asked him to shake hands with Walter in the drawing room, but he was beastly about it, so I told him to apologise and he wouldn't, so I sent him straight to bed, and—' She broke off and began crying again. 'And now he's gone,' she wailed.

'Anna, try to keep calm. Any idea *where* he's gone?'

Denham was standing now, wishing he could pace, but the telephone cord wasn't long enough, so he had to settle for scratching his head.

But as she continued her account, he felt himself relax. The motive for Tom's little adventure seemed plain enough, and he'd almost certainly come home when his bread and corned beef ran out, his protest made and his tail between his legs. All the same, where could he be hiding this time?

'I'm sure it's nothing to worry about,' Denham said. 'Remember when he planned a long-haul expedition from the potting shed and you wondered where all the candles and Banbury cakes had gone? Or that time he spent the night in the Prendergast kid's garage with my army knapsack?'

Anna said nothing, which Denham knew better than to take as a sign of mollification. The line whistled and buzzed. 'I'll telephone again tomorrow,' he said, 'to see if there's any news.'

'You're not coming over?'

'Of course, but I'll be very surprised if the boy isn't back for breakfast. I'll call in the morning. There's a story here I'm investigating—'

'A story?' Her tone was sharp and accusing.

'It's a very big story, about a Jewish athlete who's—'

There was a rattle as she hung up.

Denham had blamed himself for the breakup of his marriage, although hearing Anna's reproachful tone made him doubt that things could have been different. He remembered her face when he told her he was leaving on a long trip to Brazil. Tom was only two, and she was right to be angry. But Germany was the last straw. He'd taken an assignment in Berlin—and when most foreigners began deserting it, had decided to stay. Anna had finally realised that he preferred to be alone and had cast him out. She couldn't understand him. But he had a sense that Tom did. Tom had a child's insight into his old man. He understood that his dad had to be by himself and that it wasn't anyone's fault.

IN THE MORNING he tried calling again but was told by the operator that he'd have to book his call for later. With so many foreigners in Berlin the lines were jammed. He didn't want to antagonise Anna by failing to make contact, so he popped into the post office on the Bergmannstrasse and sent a telegram asking her to cable him with any news.

At the kiosk outside the station he spotted a five-day-old copy of the *Daily Express*. He jumped onto the U-Bahn and read the paper's coverage of the Olympic opening ceremony. Gushing descriptions of Berlin *en fête* filled the columns, with no mention of the brutalities that had been swept out of sight. But it was the lead article that dismayed him the most. It was of the view that the British athletes had let the side down by not giving the Hitler salute. 'It would not have done the British any harm if they had made a gesture to the country housing the Games by following the unexpected example of the French . . .' He would have to tease Pat Murphy about that.

ELEANOR WAS WAITING for him as arranged: next to the flower stall of Berlin Zoo Station. He saw her first and smiled to himself. She wore a light raincoat and a black beret—an attempt, he supposed, at looking incognito—but coupled with her red lipstick, heels, and round sunglasses with white frames, the drab coat and hat only seemed to heighten her glamour.

'Sorry I'm late,' he said, and explained about Tom. Eleanor looked concerned.

'Aren't you worried?'

'I'll take the evening flight from Tempelhof if he doesn't show up today, but the odds are he's already come home for his toast and eggs, with dirt behind his ears.'

The morning sun streamed into the station, casting dusty shafts of light onto the tiled floor and long shadows among the scurrying rush-hour commuters. Denham led Eleanor up the steps to the platform. Trains disgorged passengers in a disorderly bustle; the station echoed with announcements. He and Eleanor were the only people embarking, and a minute later their deserted carriage was juddering out of the station and heading southwest to the suburbs.

'We're going to a smart address,' Denham said. 'Grunewald is the playground of Berlin's filthy rich.'

'Well, that figures. He's head of an international bank, apparently, but discreet, you know? Not like Rothschild with foundations and charities, splashing his money all over town . . .'

'Who is?' said Denham.

Eleanor took off her sunglasses and looked at him with exasperated amusement. 'Don't you research your victims, Mr Reporter? Jakob Liebermann is who. He's a multimillionaire, so no wonder he lives in a swell neighbourhood. Over breakfast I asked Ambassador Dodd all about it. Hannah's dad is some secretive art collector and head of this Jewish private bank with interests all over the place. The US would welcome him with open arms, but he's been denied an exit visa. Martha says that's because the Nazis want to strip his wealth from him before they let him out, and there's nothing the State Department or anyone else can do about it . . .'

The carriage door slid open and the beat of the rails came loudly in.

'*Ihre Fahrkarten bitte.*' They presented their tickets. '*Danke. Heil Hitler!*'

Eleanor inspected her lipstick in her compact mirror. 'Okay, now it's your turn. What exactly is the story here?'

'Hannah's family has been threatened. She's being forced to compete.' Denham turned to watch the city roll past the window. 'The trouble began when she told them no—to representing Germany in the Olympics, I mean. If it became public that she'd refused the invitation in protest over the Nazis' hate laws against the Jews, it could have finished these Games. Dozens of wavering nations might have pulled out, with a tremendous blow to German prestige. That could not be allowed to happen. So they had to act quickly, and resorted to the methods they know best.'

'Roland . . . ?'

Denham shrugged. 'My guess is that the Gestapo took her brother into "protective custody," worked him over, and kept some of his fingers as souvenirs. After that Hannah was on the next ship home to Germany.'

'And they made old Jakob's exit visa conditional on his daughter's good behaviour . . . ?'

'Most likely. And if they ever *do* let him out, like you say, they'll denude him first of every penny he's ever earned. Jews lucky enough to leave can take only a few marks in their pocket. It's the law.'

After a minute of silence Eleanor said, 'Jesus Christ.' She was staring at the trees and chimneys passing but didn't seem to be seeing anything. 'They torture people,' she mumbled. 'They rob them. . .' She looked at Richard. 'But it's too late to make any difference. The Games are taking place.'

'There's more than a week still to go. Plenty of time to get the story out there and ruin the show for them.'

'Isn't she taking a big risk seeing you?'

The train began to slow, emitting a great hiss of steam.

'We're all taking a big risk.'

WINKLERSTRASSE WAS IN the heart of what seemed like a social housing development for the overprivileged. Huge, polished cobblestones, mature horse chestnuts lining the avenues, and set back from the road, the great houses in their grounds, shuttered against the heat of the day and secluded by pines and magnolia in bloom. A green light filtered through the leaves. The place was in a deep hush, exuding an air of privacy and wealth; the only sounds were of birds calling among gardens.

As they walked Denham kept glancing back to see if they'd picked up a shadow. But he knew it was impossible to be sure. Heydrich, the head of the SD, the Nazi intelligence agency, had turned the whole country into an espionage state. Who was watching? Who was following? That gardener? The elderly couple walking a dog? The woman sitting in the parked car? Millions of willing informers.

They reached the high gates of number 80, fashioned in a design of wrought iron leaves, flowers, and ribbons. On either side two tall stone gateposts held iron carriage lamps in yellow glass.

'Think we should ring the bell?' Eleanor said.

Peering through the bars, they saw a gravel driveway that curved out of sight behind rhododendron bushes, over which a fairy-tale turret could be glimpsed.

'The gate's open,' said Denham. It yielded with a deep, ferrous groan, and they entered the grounds. Behind the foliage stood a tall house of glazed yellow bricks, with a pointed roof, arched Gothic windows, and two towers, one cylindrical, the other crenellated like a medieval keep. Beyond the building were mown lawns and a pier giving onto a boating lake.

Eleanor made a low whistle. 'A castle for a princess.'

On a curve in the driveway was parked a gleaming black Opel, its engine humming. The driver stood on the other side of it, smoking and watching them approach. It was several seconds before they noticed, through the glass of the car windows, the blood-red armband on his uniform.

'Now what?' Eleanor muttered as they crunched towards the porch. 'He's seen us. We can't just turn around.'

The front door of the house opened. Raised voices came from inside the hall, and two men emerged onto the steps, one of them saying, 'You'll hear from us,' to whoever was seeing them out.

The first man wore a fedora, a tailored suit, and cotton gloves. He had a white moustache twirled into pins, and a pince-nez, through which he cast them a curious look as he approached the car. Under his arm, Denham noticed, was a copy of *Die Kunst im Dritten Reich*, the Nazi art periodical. His companion, who'd made the abrupt farewell at the door, swaggered out in polished boots, a brown uniform with a gold-trimmed swastika armband and a collection of decorations glinting on his breast—a golden pheasant in full plumage. He was tall, with a florid face, fat lips, and a head of thick grey hair that clashed oddly with the brown garb.

Denham felt the pheasant's gaze fall upon him, before moving to Eleanor, whom he looked up and down. Eyes the colour of dishwater.

'You have business here?' he asked.

'We're calling from the Lutheran Church,' Denham said, in his best Berliner accent.

'Niemöller's lot?'

'Not us.'

The dishwater eyes sharpened for a moment, as if committing their faces to memory. 'You're wasting your time,' he said, getting into the car. 'They're Jews.'

'Ah. Thank you.'

The Opel's engine moved into gear, and the car sped off over the gravel and out of sight around the curve in the drive.

'We're not from the church,' Denham said to the maid standing by the open door at the top of the steps. 'We're friends of Roland and Hannah Liebermann's.'

'Who is it now, Lore?' came a deep voice from inside the hall. Denham gave the maid their names, and they were asked to wait. She returned a moment later and showed them into a large, brightly upholstered sitting room with a ceiling higher than a double-decker bus, where tasselled velvet curtains were half drawn against the bleaching power of sunlight. Denham could see why. Almost every inch of wall was hung with canvases—some small, others the size of billiard tables. Colourful, dynamic, modern works; some were even familiar to him, or rather the artist's style was familiar. His eyes were drawn to a large, dreamlike piece from the Blue Rider School, above the oversized stone fireplace.

'Beautiful . . . ,' Eleanor said.

Dozens of horses galloped towards the viewer, one over the other, moving in a great purple-blue wave.

'Franz Marc, the artist,' said a deep voice, 'was a friend of mine.'

They had not noticed the man standing at a walnut drinks cabinet next to the mantelpiece, pouring himself a glass of cognac, which he knocked back in one gulp. He was about sixty-five, bald, with a trimmed grey beard, a long nose, and pale, weary eyes. A port-wine mark covered part of his left cheek like a thumbprint. His dark suit and waistcoat cut a sombre presence amid such colour.

'My children told me to expect you,' he said in English, beckoning for them to sit. There was a strong Yiddish clip to his voice and he spoke ponderously, as though there was nothing left to hurry for.

'They said you are journalists taking a great risk to see Hannah, and for that you are welcome. In times like these courageous people are few. I am Jakob Liebermann.'

He wound a bell handle next to the fireplace, and they heard a distant chime. On the coffee table before them was a year-old copy of *Life* magazine, with Hannah on the cover, holding her foil. The photograph was a soft monochrome in which a makeup artist had given her the femme fatale treatment, with lips and hair dark and ravishing.

'Please understand I do not normally drink at this hour, but after the meeting that just took place here, I have given myself permission.'

'Unwelcome visitors?' Denham ventured.

'They had no appointment, and I was compelled to receive them, so, yes, you may say that.'

'Who were they?' asked Eleanor.

'Men from the Reich Chamber of the Visual Arts,' said Herr Liebermann, 'come to assess the value of my collection.' He gazed gloomily at a wall behind their heads.

Lore entered, pulling a trolley clinking with china cups and a teapot. 'Please see where Hannah and Roland are,' Herr Liebermann said to her, 'and ask Frau Liebermann to join us, if she's feeling well enough.'

'Those men want *your* art?' Denham said, surprised. The Nazis had strong views on 'degenerate art'—or rather, anything that challenged their parochial, reactionary tastes.

'Not for its own sake,' said the resonating, slow voice. Herr Liebermann rubbed the bridge of his nose and his eyes, exhausted from whatever exchange had taken place. 'Otto Dix, Paul Klee, Max Ernst . . .' He gestured vaguely to the walls. 'Their work is now *Verfallskunst*—the art of decay. Art to be *liquidated*.' He raised his eyebrows in an expression of beleaguered aloofness. 'That word—so much in vogue today. Those two men will sell this collection at auction in Lucerne and New York . . . to raise foreign currency for the Reich.'

Denham noticed an embossed business card on the coffee table for a GALLERIE HABERSTOCK, GERMAN DEALERSHIP. He'd seen that a lot recently—adding 'German' before 'lawyer' or 'doctor' to signify that the card bearer was of good Aryan coin.

'That man,' said Herr Liebermann, nodding to the card, 'specialises in these disposals. He's an art dealer, a businessman like me. Him I could talk to. But the oaf in the uniform told me my collection amounts to "Jewish artistic violence against the German spirit."' He sat down on a divan, shaking his head, seeming to shrink into the folds of his suit.

'You're giving them the collection in return for an exit visa?' Denham asked.

'Partly. They want a great deal more from me than the art.'

'But it's your collection,' Eleanor said suddenly. 'Why should . . .' Herr Liebermann silenced her with a raised hand and a melancholy smile.

'Please,' he said. 'Acceptance is the quicker route to wholeness, though I confess that today even I feel unequal to the complexities of our times.'

'If there's something we can do—' Denham said.

'Thank you, Herr Denham, but I take comfort from the fact that I am a difficult man to rob. By law my banking interests in Berlin will soon be Aryanised, but elsewhere—in Basel, in London, in Amsterdam—my wealth is held by trustees from whom deeds of transfer are required, and for those they need my cooperation. So we're talking about a deal . . .'

'And you think they'll keep their side of the bargain?' asked Eleanor.

'That,' said Herr Liebermann, 'is a question I cannot answer or know the answer to.'

Denham gazed at the walls again and his eyes fell upon one small picture that seemed not to fit at all. It had a grotesquely ornate, gilded frame and appeared to be a watercolour of some Baroque church.

'The painting you're looking at,' Herr Liebermann said, noticing Denham's interest, 'is my little joke. It is by our Chancellor Hitler.'

Denham looked at him in astonishment.

Hitler the failed artist, twice rejected by the Vienna Academy of Fine Arts. The entire Nazi movement was founded on disappointment. Goebbels the thwarted journalist. Heydrich the cashiered sailor. The salvation these misfits sought in racial revolution.

Footsteps echoed from the hall, the door opened, and Hannah entered, followed by Roland.

'Ah, here we are,' Herr Liebermann said.

Hannah greeted them dressed in knee breeches and a cotton jerkin, her hair tied up as if she'd come straight from training. Eleanor was introduced, and Denham thought he discerned a cool reserve as they shook hands, the two Olympians gauging each other, eyes locked. The fencer did not possess Eleanor's voluptuous beauty. She was trim, sharp, and pretty, but her real attraction lay in her formidable self-assurance and her poise—with a habit of turning her head so that it was in alignment with her shoulders, like an ancient Egyptian profile.

'I'm sorry you got into trouble on my account,' she began. 'That man Greiser warned me never to speak to you again, but I told him he's used all his arrows. Short of killing Roland, there really isn't anything else he can try. His quiver is empty.' Her voice was bright and crisp, as though she were addressing a town hall meeting.

Roland said nothing. He was in an open-necked shirt and a pair of Oxford bags—the relaxed garb of any upper-class young man at home, yet he was still the hunted creature they'd seen by lamplight. His leg slouched over the arm of a chair, and one arm lay around his sister's shoulders, his fingers stroking her hair. The mutilated right hand he had concealed in a kid leather glove, which rested on his knee. Something inside him had broken. Denham could see it in his eyes. Behind the fearful face was an intelligent boy, who, in any normal time and place, would be off travelling or thinking of a career.

When Denham was Roland's age his own hopes for the future had been smashed by events no less extreme.

No one spoke for a moment until Herr Liebermann said, 'Hannah, my love, what was it you were hoping Herr Denham and Fräulein Eleanor could do for us by coming here?'

'I was awake last night thinking about your offer, Mr Denham,' she said, her brown eyes wide and clear, 'and I would like to give you the interview you requested. Here. Today. Roland, too. For you to publish in England, the United States, and, really, wherever else you can.'

Denham hadn't expected such eagerness and wondered now about the wisdom of it. 'I'm not so sure . . . ,' he said.

'But we are sure. We signed away the art, but straightaway they wanted more. They won't let us go until they've taken the clothes off our backs, and even then . . .' She spread her arms in a gesture of despair.

'I'm sorry to say I think you're right about that,' Denham said.

'Then your article must say clearly what they did to Roland. Everything, now, while the Games are still on. The whole world must read about it. Then they wouldn't dare touch him again.'

Denham scratched his chin. 'It might not be expedient for them to arrest him again if they know the foreign press is watching, but don't think you can shame them or appeal to their nicer qualities.' And before he could stop himself he said, 'Shit doesn't have nicer qualities.' He put down his teacup and apologised. The faces before him were serious, but then a smile began to play beneath Herr Liebermann's beard, and the old man began to laugh.

'Shit doesn't have nicer qualities,' Herr Liebermann repeated, and with the release of one who'd been under months of unsmiling strain. Eleanor and Roland began laughing, too; only Hannah's face remained prim and slighted.

'Have I missed a good joke?' came a woman's voice from the doorway. They turned to see a heavy lady with unruly silver hair, a long pearl necklace, and an old-fashioned cameo brooch. Frau

Liebermann shook hands with them, offering the tips of her fingers, so that Denham half wondered whether she expected her rings to be kissed. She spoke in a singsong voice as though she were in a dream. He guessed she'd taken a sedative.

The whole family now sat looking at him and Eleanor, expectant, and not unhappy. Denham removed his notepad and Leica from his case.

'Where shall we start?'

Hannah's story was as grim as he'd expected. On the voyage from California she'd been kept under constant supervision, and her telegrams were censored. They'd forbidden her to win the fencing final, because a Jew could not be seen to take the gold, but she could win the silver. She was isolated from the rest of the team and given the world's worst coach. And on the podium, she was to give the Hitler salute, which they'd even made her practise in front of them.

Roland, as Denham had guessed, was the bait they'd used to bring her back. He'd been kept for four days in the Gestapo's basement cells. The young man's eyes told him everything, and Denham knew better than to ask.

When she had finished, Denham took several photographs of them together in the sitting room with the blue horses behind them, and many of Hannah by herself posing with her foil. Afterwards Frau Liebermann insisted that he and Eleanor stay for lunch around a table laid in the grounds at the back of the house. Small white yachts in sail circled on the lake, brilliant against the afternoon sun.

Roland stood to pour wine for them all. Thistledown floated through the warm air and some landed in his black hair. As he poured Eleanor's glass, his eyes met hers.

Ah well, Denham thought, and looked away. *He's much nearer her age than I am.*

Herr Liebermann said a brief prayer in Hebrew when the meal of baked carp and potatoes in cream was placed in front of them; then he raised his glass. 'To America,' he said, smiling at Eleanor.

'To America,' they all said, and clinked glasses.

*   *   *

THEY LEFT THE Liebermann house unseen by a disused door in the wall of the grounds and walked in silence for a while down the leafy avenue, which seemed even stiller in the heat of the late afternoon.

'It's happening, isn't it?' Eleanor said after a while, her head lowered.

'What is?' But Denham thought he knew what she meant.

'Everything.' She reached out and held his hand. 'Us. You and I. Our fight against these bastards.'

'Yes,' said Denham. 'It's happening.'

AT BERLIN ZOO station they made plans to meet that night.

'Look after these,' Denham said, handing her his shorthand notes and the Leica. 'They'll be safer at the ambassador's house.'

Back home, he put his head around Frau Stumpf's door. His landlady was sitting alone at her kitchen table in her long shawl, listening to radio music and staring at the wall, which was how he often found her. She seemed to jump when he entered, and then, unusual for her, avoided his eyes.

'Good afternoon, Herr Denham. Yes, you have another telegram.'

He tore it open, and felt the niggle of worry finally hatch and spread through his gut.

NO NEWS STOP POLICE TO ISSUE MISSING PERSONS NOTICE STOP
COME SOONEST STOP

Leaping up the stairs to his apartment, he tried to work out how fast he could get to London. First he would call Anna, then Tempelhof Airport in the hope that there was a seat on the evening flight.

From a crackling radio behind Reinacher's door the voice of Goebbels resounded in the stairwell. ' . . . *This day, I believe it is no exaggeration to say . . . that a hundred million people in Germany and*

beyond her frontiers . . . have been tuned to the broadcast of the eleventh
Olympiad from Berlin . . .'

He put his key in the door to his apartment and pushed, not even noticing that the new lock wasn't locked. His senses warned him but his brain was too slow on the uptake. He stepped into his sitting room and two men stood up.

'Richard Denham,' the nearer one said. He opened his jacket to reveal the warrant-disc hanging from an inside pocket. 'You're to come with us.'

Chapter Seventeen

Gestapo. Both men wore grey suits and black, snap-brimmed trilbies.

'May I make a telephone call?' Denham said. He felt a strange calm come over him, as if he'd expected them. Somehow, in his heart, he'd known it would come to this.

'You'll be back in the morning,' the man said, stubbing his cigarette out on the rug. 'You can telephone then.'

That, Denham knew, was a gross lie, but he wasn't going to argue.

They escorted him downstairs, one in front and one behind.

A storm of applause was breaking across the speech on Reinacher's radio as the speaker's voice moved into high gear. *'As for those seduced by the international Jewish press into doubting the Führer's desire for peace . . . I say this: . . . let them come to Berlin! . . . Let them come to Berlin! . . .'*

Frau Stumpf's door was shut.

Outside, a grey Horch waited. The back door was held open; Denham got in and sat next to one of the Gestapo men while the other drove. How brisk and businesslike they were. No handcuffs, none needed. Such fear did these men inspire that citizens meekly did as they were told.

The smell of the car's seat leather mingled with a faint odour of vomit.

'I thought you boys only came at night,' Denham said.

Neither answered.

The roads around Belle-Alliance-Platz were clogged with traffic

as the evening rush approached, and the Horch was caught in a
crawl behind a line of cars and yellow double-deckers. Neither Gestapo man seemed the least frustrated at their lack of progress. He
wondered how long they'd been in his apartment. Both wound down
their windows to smoke, but neither offered him a cigarette.

They turned onto the Prinz-Albrecht-Strasse, plunged in shadow
as the sun moved into the west. Göring's new Air Ministry passed
by on the right, wall after wall of granite, the city's latest pharaonic
monstrosity. The car slowed to a halt, and the gates of the darkened
Gestapo building swung inward without a sound.

THE MILD-SPOKEN GALLICO had to raise his voice to be heard
over the laughter, piano music, and clinking glasses in the Adlon's
upstairs bar. Reporters from every newspaper, radio station, and
wire service in the world seemed to be drinking there this afternoon. He hadn't touched his beer.

'Let me get this straight,' he said, leaning towards her. 'You go
hiding in a rosebush and overhear a private conversation between—'

'I wasn't hiding.' Eleanor was looking over the rail next to their
table. She could see right down into the lobby, where a couple of
army officers were lounging on wicker chairs near the pagoda fountain, their laughter becoming more boisterous with each toast of
schnapps. 'I went to apologise to Brundage, followed him in there,
but lost him in the dark; next thing I knew there were these men's
voices . . .'

She quickly told him the rest.

Gallico gave a slow whistle.

'Bad, huh?' she said.

'Throwing the Jews off the relay team in case they win and em-
barrass Hitler? Well, it doesn't cast old Avery in the best light . . .'
He looked down into the lobby with a face that suggested several
thoughts playing across his mind at the same time. A hearty laugh
came from one of the officers at the fountain.

'You're not thinking I made this up to get back at that jerk?' Eleanor asked.

'No . . . I'm thinking of the politics. The UP boys have generally supported US participation in these Olympics. Now that our athletes are here in Berlin and winning medals, it could look, well, unpatriotic if we break this story now. And, sweetheart, I'm just wondering what they'll say back home. The sour grapes between you and Brundage means you won't be seen as the most impartial witness . . .'

'Then *you* break the story.'

'But I'll need more proof.'

'Confront him with it, Paul, and see how he reacts.'

Chapter Eighteen

The noise of teleprinter machines filled the corridor from behind closed doors. Beneath the wire-meshed electric lights rows of hunched figures waited on benches and lowered their eyes as the sergeant passed. Pushed along without shoelaces or belt, Denham walked in a rapid shuffle. They'd taken his tie, too. *I go to my doom looking a man who sleeps in his clothes.* The sergeant stopped outside a door marked HAECKEL, knocked twice, opened it for Denham, and closed it behind him.

Inspector Haeckel was a heavy man, with a grey moustache, a boxer's jaw, and thinning hair. He had on the full black uniform: Sam Browne belt, shoulder strap, boots, gun holster, and an array of police decorations.

A minute passed as he scribbled away at his desk, dotting *i*'s, crossing *t*'s, not acknowledging his prisoner. Denham looked around, seeing a chair, which he was not being offered, and dark stains on the floor that made his stomach clench. On a cabinet to the right stood a row of trophies awarded for dog handling, except for one, which displayed two spent bullets suspended like grubs in a block of glass. On its base were engraved the names RÖHM and HEINES.

After a while the inspector selected a rubber stamp from a small rack, thumped a document, closed the file, and took another from his tray. Denham's passport was inside, on top of what looked like a hand-filled surveillance sheet.

'Richard Arthur Denham,' he said, examining the passport, then glancing up for the first time. 'As you are certainly aware, there is a press injunction on speaking to Hannah Liebermann. So would you mind telling me what you were doing at her home today?' He had the gravel voice of a man accustomed to shouting.

Sound honest, Denham thought. *No clever remarks.* 'I'm a reporter, Inspector, and she's one of the best-known athletes at the Games. I wanted a few quotes for some copy, that's all. Frankly, what reporter wouldn't?'

Haeckel seemed uninterested and leaned back in his chair.

'I'm not wasting time with you because you're not my case, or not yet anyway. You see, the oddest thing just happened, Herr Denham, and maybe you could explain it to me.'

He stood up, not as tall as Denham expected, with a solid, rounded gut, and walked to the back of his chair to stretch his legs. Boots, belt, and strap creaked and groaned.

'The minute my boys turned up at your apartment I get an urgent call from the SD, who send over this file on you.'

The SD?

'That's right. I'm to hold you until a certain SD officer gets here to interrogate you.' He leaned over the chair and picked up a sheet from the file. 'One, espionage of new German Zeppelin technology on board the *Luftschiff Hindenburg* . . .'

'*What?*'

' . . . two, using an identity not your own to infiltrate Reichsminister Goebbels's reception on the Pfaueninsel; three, attending an illegal music event convened by antisocials known to the police'—the inspector closed the file—'and this in the course of a few days' surveillance . . .'

'The espionage charge is nonsense.'

'Is it?' He picked up the paper again. 'It says here that you breached a military regulation by taking a camera on board and gave your guide the slip in a restricted area. So what were you up to?'

He waved his hand, not interested in an answer, and sat down again to a fugue of leathery creaks and squeaks.

'I'm a British subject, Inspector, and can't be held—'

'Your passport won't save you from an espionage charge.' He gave a quiet, hissing laugh. 'Annoying as this is, the SD have done me a favour here. With an espionage charge we keep you as long as we like. But the SD want you *unspoilt*'—his eyebrows rose at this veiled slur on his professionalism—'and that order comes from the top. So I'm curious, Herr Denham. What is this really about? Mm?'

Denham had absolutely no idea. The SD, the Sicherheitsdienst, was the state's intelligence service, a cadre within the SS. That's about all he knew. It was known to be a cut above the sadists in the Gestapo, attracting educated recruits.

'You seem to know more than I do, Inspector.'

Haeckel picked up a rubber stamp and began twirling it between his fingers, still observing Denham, eyes narrowed like gun slits.

'The SD don't bother with lists of stocking-fillers like these. That is the type of donkey-work they leave to me. As for the espionage, an explosive bag of gas like the *Hindenburg* has the technological value of my mother-in-law's arse. So they're keeping me in the dark about something. What makes you special, eh?'

Denham gave a shrug, and Haeckel suddenly hurled the stamp towards his head. He flinched, and it struck the door with a *clack*.

'A British agent, are we?' he barked. 'Or spying for the NKVD?'

Denham's brain was spinning, and his face must have shown it. 'I'm just a reporter.'

'All right, all right,' Haeckel said, stroking his moustache and seeming to have remembered in time his orders not to harm the prisoner. His face was crimson. 'It will all come out in the end . . . makes no difference to me.' He picked up the telephone and summoned the sergeant. Then he said, 'When the SD are done with you, sir, you and I will go over every single thing said between you and that Liebermann woman. For as long as it takes . . .'

ELEANOR RANG THE bell next to the ornate door of Kopischstrasse 5 and put her face to the glass. A small woman with trailing wisps of hair and a long shawl clutched to her chest shuffled out from a ground-floor apartment and opened it for her.

'Uh, Richard Denham? Is he here?' she said, hoping to aid communication with smiles and hand gestures.

At the mention of Denham's name, fear animated the old woman's face. She shook her head, dissembling away in German to Eleanor's bewilderment, and retreated quickly back to her apartment. Her door closed, but Eleanor sensed the rheumy blue eyes watching through the pattern in the frosted glass.

The name on the first-floor apartment was Reinacher, from whose door came the sound of a radio playing military band music; she continued to the second floor with a mounting sense that something was wrong. She found Denham's door and knocked. It swung inwards with a quiet moan on its hinges.

The place had been worked over so thoroughly it looked like a grenade had exploded, and two cigarette butts had been stubbed into the rug, leaving burn marks. She tiptoed into the mess of smashed record discs, overturned drawers, and opened books. On the floor a yellow telegram slip caught her eye. So his son had not been found. What was going on? She stood still for a moment, mystified, and a flat voice startled her.

'*Kann ich Ihnen helfen?*'

A tall, fat-headed man was standing in the doorway, holding a collection tin with a swastika on it.

He gestured to the mess in the room, speaking in a droning voice. Only the word *Gestapo* was clear to her among the alien words and made itself understood.

HIS RUMBLING STOMACH told him roughly what the hour was, but he knew he'd soon lose track of time. An electric light hummed behind a wire grill. He didn't imagine they ever turned it off. In the next-door cell a man moaned.

Every thought that came to him swirled around and slipped away.

The fears of never seeing Tom again mixed with his dread of what
the SD had in store. He drew his feet up and buried his nose between his knees, struggling to imagine why he could possibly be
here.

The espionage charge was a trumped-up ploy to stop the embassy
from getting him released in a hurry. He was fairly sure of that. The
other charges were trivial except for one—speaking to Hannah—
which the inspector seemed to think was a Gestapo matter. But who
knows what turf wars were fought in the dark labyrinths of the Nazi
state. Maybe the matter was too serious for Haeckel.

But why had they been watching him before he'd even made contact with Hannah? They knew about his trip on the *Hindenburg*;
they knew he was at the reception on the Pfaueninsel, and of his
night at the Nollendorfplatz Theatre.

What did they want?

Hours passed, and he fell into a nervous stupor, too edgy to sleep,
too drained to move. When footsteps echoed in the corridor outside, he jumped. An eye appeared in the peephole, a bolt was drawn
back, and the door opened. A man in a dark suit stepped into the
cell.

'Herr Denham?' he said with an interested smile. 'I am Hauptsturmführer Udo Rausch. I've been looking forward to meeting you.'

Chapter Nineteen

Two guards with the SD flash on their sleeves led Denham from the cell. The man in the suit, Hauptsturmführer Rausch, was perhaps a year or two younger than Denham, and looked as though he'd dined well somewhere. He greeted the sergeant and asked after his wife, joked with the orderlies smoking in the darkening courtyard, and walked with his hand on Denham's shoulder, almost friendly, as though they were professors between lectures. A new BMW, its engine idling, was waiting. Before they got in, Rausch lit a Murad and offered one to Denham.

'No, thanks. Turkish isn't my brand.'

'They're not to everyone's taste,' he agreed. 'I picked up the habit in Ankara. Served there with the German Foreign Ministry for two years.'

That solves one puzzle, Denham thought. The hempy aroma filling the car was the same he'd smelt in his apartment.

A minute's drive and the car turned into a garden courtyard off the Wilhelmstrasse, stopping outside the covered portico of an elegant classical building. Inside was a marble hallway of columns and red drapes. The uniformed woman on the front desk, blond hair plaited into pretzels, beamed at Rausch; young men in suits passed on their way out, bidding him a good evening. Denham followed him up a marble staircase overhung by an enormous chandelier, making slow progress without shoelaces. The guards were two steps behind.

'This was a summer palace of the Hohenzollerns,' Rausch said over his shoulder. 'Designed by Schinkel. A refinement that's rather lost on our Gestapo cousins.'

They passed down a long carpeted corridor, and climbed another flight to a narrow service corridor in what seemed like an old servants' quarter. At the far end Denham was shown into a room with bright overhead lights and a small barred window, and was asked to sit on a chair in the centre of the room. The only other furnishings were a table with a telephone on it, a row of wooden chairs, and a portrait photograph of Reinhard Heydrich, head of the SD, peering from the wall.

Heydrich, the Blond Beast. The man's Nordic nose was so long it almost put the rest of his face out of focus, but the tiny, deep-set eyes were as bright as pins. Heydrich the Pitiless. Heydrich the Hangman. Thirty-two years old and one of the most powerful men in Europe.

Denham's suspicion that his captor's genial manner was part of some technique was borne out immediately.

'I've always felt that interrogation is more art than science where an intelligent detainee is concerned,' Rausch began, taking a seat. 'Especially one who's a war veteran. In such cases incentive can be fruitful where intimidation is not. Perhaps not something a brute like Haeckel would understand, although I daresay he gets to the bottom of everything in his inimitable way. Chips fly when you have to chop wood.' The German gave a small, satisfied laugh.

He had a groomed, cultured appearance, tailored clothes, and a sombre tie. The German upper class, relaxed with rank. Brown hair combed back from his forehead, high cheekbones, full lips that suggested a taste for the finer things, features that might be found pleasing but for the eyes, which had an unnerving directness. Denham felt sure, too, that he hadn't risen to the rank of Hauptsturmführer in the SS on the back of good table manners and a white smile.

'Your arrest caught us on the back foot. When the Gestapo went to collect you, they forced our hand. We've been letting you run around on a loose lead, Herr Denham, waiting to see where you'll take us. But we'd have come for you shortly anyway. Your landlady reported the latest telegram from your ex-wife, and we wouldn't want you leaving the country, especially not now, would we?'

Poor Frau Stumpf. How the old bird must have lost it when the men in leather turned up.

'Please let's understand each other right away, Herr Denham, there's an espionage charge against you . . .'

'Which you know is false.'

He shrugged. 'Be that as it may. It's a serious charge. At the very least it means prison; at worst, a stretch in a KZ, a concentration camp. If you come out alive your health will be ruined and you won't work again. Do I need to elaborate?'

Denham looked at him sullenly, sensing a deal on offer.

'However,' Rausch went on, spreading his hands over the table, 'I'm certain we can spare you that in return for your cooperation with the main matter. What do you say?'

Denham sighed. 'Does she upset you so much? I won't be the last reporter who tries interviewing Hannah Liebermann.'

'Hannah Liebermann?' Rausch seemed amused. 'No fooling please, Herr Denham. Do you think we're interested in some Jew girl telling tales?'

'You tell me.'

'We're interested in *you*. Because you're going to tell us where it is.'

'Where what is?'

Rausch stared at him, waiting, the smile on his lips cooling.

'You'll have to help me here,' Denham said. 'Where what is?' Fatigue, hunger, and hours of incarceration were beginning to take their effect.

The interrogator sat back in his chair with the look of a schoolmaster given a dim answer by his best pupil. 'You know precisely what.'

'I assure you I don't—'

'Herr Denham. I will not play games. I am speaking of the dossier.'

'You've got the wrong man,' Denham said, but before the words were out he'd remembered. What that man Evans had mentioned in the back of the Humber.

A dossier which we believed had been lost or destroyed . . .

He chose his next words with care. 'There's been a rumour going round that a foreign correspondent will be handed a secret dossier of some sort. We've all heard it. So what. It wasn't me.'

'But it *was* you, of course. It was always going to be you—the reporter they would contact.'

'Now there's a *they*. Who are *they*?'

Rausch leaned towards him. 'I have a reputation for stamina, Herr Denham. I can go through the night without a break.' The man made an *up to you* gesture with his hands. 'They offered you the dossier. Irresistible to a reporter, I'm sure. But you've heard what's in store if you don't cooperate.'

'You're not listening. I don't know—'

'I'll offer you this chance once only. Tell me where it is and you walk free the moment we have it.'

'My freedom it is, then.'

'Where's the dossier?'

'I have no idea.'

Rausch watched him for several seconds, then got up from the far side of the table, carrying his chair. There was an air of finality to the way he placed it in front of Denham and sat down, as if a line had been crossed. In Denham's frayed mind, the temperature of the room seemed to drop.

'Let's start at the beginning.' His face had acquired a cold fervour. 'When did the group make contact with you?'

'Group . . . ? What—'

The slap was so hard and so fast that Denham felt the hot shame of being hit like a child. He touched his lip with his tongue, split by the SS signet ring on Rausch's right hand. Cold sweat broke out under his shirt.

'No one contacted me.'

'No one.'

'N—'

Another hard slap.

'Come on,' Rausch said, almost in a whisper. ' "Didn't we meet at a poetry reading in Mainz last year?" '

Denham's mouth opened dumbly, and he was slapped again. He put up his hands to shield his face, but Rausch knocked them aside and slapped him once more, with much more force.

'For Christ's sake,' Denham shouted.

'I'm sorry. Let's make you feel more secure.' He lifted a pair of handcuffs from his side pocket, walked behind Denham's chair, and pulled his hands back, locking them tightly behind him. When he resumed his seat he pulled it closer. He searched Denham's face, his eyes an aphotic blue, a lake in winter. 'They gave you a double password to identify yourself. We found out, Denham. We know. "Didn't we meet at a poetry reading in Mainz last year?" Your response was "We did. The poems were by Stefan George." Then they gave you the dossier.'

Denham had the sensation of being trapped in an artifice that was fast assembling itself out of fragments of reality. A muscle began to spasm just below his eye. He had to grimace to make it stop.

Rausch nodded. 'Are we getting somewhere now?'

He remembered Friedl asking the question. Odd because it was in German, when they'd been speaking English, and because of the intense look that had been in his eyes when he asked it. Denham's brain was jangled. His single, urgent thought was to keep Friedl's name out of this.

'I've never heard it.'

Rausch slapped him with the full strength of his arm.

'It's the truth,' Denham said through clenched teeth.

'The truth?' Rausch wagged his finger at this interesting point. 'What is the truth . . . ?' He stood up to remove his jacket and hung it over the back of his chair, revealing a brutally fit figure. 'The Nollendorfplatz Theatre, Denham. That's where you gave yourself away.' He began rolling up his shirtsleeves. 'We'd been keeping an eye on you since you got back to Berlin, but when you walked into that dance hall yesterday—then we knew you were the one. Because among those swing-dancing nigger-lovers was a member of the group—also under surveillance by us. You spoke to him at the bar. Or are you denying that, too? So then we do a little digging around to see where you've been the last few weeks, and what do you know? Our suspect, Friedl Christian, was reported seen in your company on board the *Hindenburg* last Saturday. Bumping into him again was a bit more than a coincidence, wouldn't you agree?' He sat back down, his knees almost touching Denham's.

'No coincidence,' Denham said, his spirits sinking. 'We got talking about swing. He invited me to the Nollendorfplatz. I went along. That's it.'

Slap.

'Did you know that Friedl Christian is a warm boy registered with the police?'

'His personal life is his own affair. We did not discuss it.'

Slap. 'You discussed something.'

'Music.'

Slap. 'He was the contact the group told you to expect, was he not? You identified yourselves to each other with the password and he gave you the dossier, or he told you where to find it.'

'He didn't give me any—'

Slap. 'Did he give it to you?'

'No—'

'Did he give you a location where you'd find it?'

'No, I don't know—'

Slap. 'A name, a contact?'

'He didn't mention anyone. He didn't mention any dossier—'

Slap. Slap. Slap.

Denham's face was stinging red and raw; his lip and nose streaming blood. 'Stop this, man,' he shouted. 'Isn't it obvious it's getting you nowhere?'

Rausch did not stop, and sweat began to soak through his shirt in wide rings.

'This morning you visited Hannah Liebermann's home in the Grunewald. Why?'

Denham's head slumped onto his chest. 'I wanted an interview. And that's the truth.'

Rausch lifted Denham's chin and slapped him so hard that he almost slid off the chair. 'Those Jews will be in a KZ within one hour of the Games' closing ceremony. If it's there, d'you think we won't find it?'

'Please listen to me. I don't know—'

'If you don't open up to us, I'm sure your American lady friend will.'

Denham stared at him. 'She has nothing to do with anything. I warn you—her father is a powerful senator, and she's the guest here of the ambassador . . .'

'You're warning me, are you, Denham?' Rausch jumped out of his chair

Slap. Slap.

'You're keeping me on my toes, are you?'

Slap. Slap. Slap.

He was panting now, face a livid pink, hair dishevelled.

'Did you *examine* the dossier?'

Denham said nothing. This was hopeless.

'Or did the warm boy tell you the content?'

'No,' Denham yelled. 'Nothing. Why don't you ask him yourself?'

'Oh, believe me—we will.'

But Denham had clocked the half second's hesitation. *You haven't found him.*

At that moment the telephone rang. Rausch stood up and answered it.

'Rausch here . . . Right away, Herr Obergruppenführer.'

He took his jacket off the back of the chair, put it on, and walked to the door. 'And just as we were warming up. Don't go anywhere.' Denham heard the click of the lock slide into place behind him.

Outside he could hear rain. He wanted to touch his face. It felt delicate in the extreme, an exposed membrane, as if the skin on his cheeks, chin, and forehead had chafed and broken. The handcuffs were cutting into his wrists. He needed the lavatory. But worst of all was his thirst. They'd given him no water.

This was surreal. Dismal and surreal. It was the insane nihilism at the heart of National Socialism. He'd been on the verge of getting a story out there that would have ruined their Olympics, but they were devoting time and manpower to some wild goose chase after a lost file. For all he knew it contained Hitler's mother's recipes, or a collection of banned jokes. Eckener cracks one of his gags about the Führer, and a whole SD department is set up to trace its origin.

We did. The poems were by Stefan George . . .

Double passwords? What was Friedl mixed up in? It would explain his eagerness to introduce himself that evening in the bar at the Hotel Kurgarten—he'd thought Denham was someone else. *Farcical*, and yet they'd become friends. God alone knew what noodle-brained naivety it took to join a resistance group. But then, warm boys generally were probably no strangers to courage. For any chance of success a group had to remain small, with contacts few and anonymous. Friedl, he guessed, would know the name of only one other member, perhaps. Two at the most. Double-password precautions. But Friedl was lucky. He'd been tipped off and fled.

Denham turned the sequence of events over in his mind. To think he'd once suspected Friedl of being a police snitch.

He sighed and shut his eyes. Another thought crossed his mind. Who telephoned Rausch just now? There couldn't be many Obergruppenführers. He looked up at the photograph on the wall.

The hitting and slapping didn't scare him. What scared him was how long he'd be able to hold out. Exhaustion would get to him soon, and pain and hunger.

His head fell forwards. He tried to empty his mind for a while and not focus on the pain in his wrists.

The door unlocked.

Rausch strode in with a dour expression. He had changed into a black uniform with silver epaulettes. And he wasn't alone. Four SS followed him, stony-faced, also in black, and Denham caught a glimpse of the rubber blackjack in the hand of one of them, with one end of it tucked up a sleeve. Each SS man took a chair, and they positioned themselves around him; two immediately behind where he couldn't see them, and two slightly out of his line of vision on each side. One of them yawned, and there was beer on his breath.

This is bad, Denham thought numbly. *This is very bad.*

Rausch resumed his seat behind the table and looked at Denham. He seemed paler, his face set grimly to his task.

'Are you going to put yourself through this?' he said, tapping the tips of his fingers together. He inhaled and asked again, 'Where is it?'

'If I knew, believe me, I would tell you.'

Rausch kept his gaze on Denham, then flicked a glance at the man to the left behind him. A chair scraped back. Leather creaked. Something swished. The blackjack struck him across his left ear.

His vision went blank. He hunched over, wanting to jam his head between his knees. The detonation in his ear was paralysing his brain, short-circuiting it.

I do not fear this, he thought, through the blinding white pain. *An old soldier does not fear this.*

'Sit up,' said Rausch. 'Look at me. Where is it?'

Denham shook his head.

Another flick from Rausch's eyes and this time all four men set upon him, bludgeoning him with blackjacks: on his head, neck, and shoulders. When the chair went over, and Denham with it, Rausch stepped in to remove the handcuffs, and the beating continued with relentless ferocity: on his shanks, back, hands, and face. A searing burn across his neck made him cry out, and he saw that one of them held a length of wire cable, which was soon lashing across his back.

Rausch shouted, 'Shall we keep going?'

I do not fear this.

But his mantra could not suppress the terror rising inside him.

'Up,' said Rausch. The four men uncoiled the ball of torment he'd become on the floor and pulled him back onto the chair. He felt a spreading gush of warm piss in his trousers. One of them grunted, '*Ach.*'

The interrogator was standing, leaning against the wall beneath the photograph, giving Denham time to absorb and savour the pain. He was holding a small rust red book.

'At Heidelberg I admired this poet. We all did. He was a cult figure, Stefan George, something of a mystic, a seer who felt the tides in the German soul. What appeal he'd have to your gang of criminals I had no idea, but listen to this.'

In a piping voice he recited:

'The Lord of the Flies is expanding his Reich;
All treasures, all blessings are swelling his might
Down, down with the handful who doubt him!'

'"The Anti-Christ," from 1907. It has power, does it not? It has prophecy.'

Still looking at the book he said, 'It's going to get much worse if you don't tell me. Now, Herr Denham, cigarette?'

Denham shook his head.

Rausch lit one for himself with a steel lighter. 'Once again,' he said softly. 'Where?' He was studying his victim through the puff of yellow smoke, and Denham returned his gaze, thinking that he detected less certainty in his tormentor's face, a little less resolution in the voice. 'Where?'

Denham gave his head a tiny movement. *No.*

He was punched right off the chair.

He tried crawling under the table but was dragged backwards by his ankle. The blows came down with monstrous savagery now, and they began to kick him as well: in his ribs, in his stomach, in his face. He howled for them to stop. Anything if they'd stop . . . Ribs cracked like ice under foot. Whip, blackjack. A forest of high boots. His kicked-in stomach winded him; he couldn't breathe. One of them pulled his head back by his hair, the flash of a dagger, a slash across his cheekbone. Behind it all Rausch was shouting, reciting from the little book.

'You'll hang out your tongues but the trough has been drained
You'll panic like cattle whose farm is ablaze
And dreadful the blast of the trumpet.'

Whatever hope he'd had of getting out vanished. He was going to die in this room.

And suddenly they stopped.

The telephone was ringing.

Rough hands heaved him off the floor and onto the chair. He spat out a great gob of blood and pressed his tongue against loose teeth. Blood poured into his right eye from where the wire cable had caught him on the eyebrow; it spattered to the floor from the gash in his cheek. Vision in the other eye was out of focus. He was soaked with piss, sweat, blood.

'Rausch here . . . No, Herr Obergruppenführer. Not yet.'

The interrogator replaced the receiver and looked at him. The last thing Denham remembered before the room went dark was the worry in the man's eyes.

WHEN HE CAME round, his body was a flowering garden of agony, from the crown of his head to the balls of his feet. Even the smallest breath came with a shot of hot pain.

Denham could hear a radio in the guards' room tuned at high volume to coverage of the Olympics. He had no idea how long he'd been out.

'. . . *I have the honour now of speaking to twenty-five-year-old Berlin policeman Karl Wöllke*'—a cheer from a couple of the guards—'*who earlier won a gold medal for Germany in the shot put . . .*'

He lay on his side on the fold-down cot and stared at the white brick wall. His brain felt as though it was listing to one side, like a boat taking on water, and there was only partial vision in one eye.

'. . . *The Führer waved to me from his box and then I knew I could beat the Olympic record of sixteen point zero three metres. It was all down to the Führer . . .*'

He had some confused notion that he might have died if the telephone hadn't rung, but the sequence of events was too difficult and tiring to recall. His entire attention was focused on the pain. If only they'd give him a glass of water. He'd do anything for that.

'Saved by the bell, eh?' said a familiar voice.

He mustered his strength to turn over on the cot. Dr Eckener was standing in the door. He was swinging Arthur Denham's pocket watch, like a hypnotist. 'You've got the luck of the devil, Richard, my boy.'

'Yes,' Denham mumbled through swollen, bloodied lips. 'I'm on a real winning streak today.' He looked out of the corner of his puffy eye to get a better look at the old man, but Eckener had gone. And Tom had come, dressed in his school uniform and cap. His shorts were covered in grass stains and dirt.

'Where've you been hiding?' Denham said.

'You know where,' whispered his son, grinning. His two front teeth were missing and his face had caught the sun, with more freckles on his nose. 'Look, I've made a drawing for you to give to those men. But you mustn't hold it and smoke at the same time or it might burn.'

'I'll be careful,' whispered Denham, his eyes filling with tears. 'Wonderful to see you, son.' He tried to get up on his feet, holding his hand out to Tom for support, but it wasn't Tom who helped him. 'Who are you? Where did my son go?'

A man with a stethoscope around his neck was standing in the cell. The coat might have been white once but was covered in stains.

'Did they find their dossier?' Denham said vaguely, feeling the room begin to turn.

The man raised a finger to his lips. 'No speaking allowed with prisoners,' he said, and began opening a black medic's bag.

'No, oh no,' Denham whispered, recoiling into the corner and beginning to weep. He had a sick dread that the man was reaching for a small saw to amputate his fingers, but instead he took out a bottle of iodine and some cotton swabs and began wiping the worst wounds above and below Denham's eye, around his lip and on his gashed cheek. Then he tapped a nickel syringe, injected a local an-aesthetic, which felt cold, like meltwater, and stitched the wounds. When he was finished he helped Denham take off his bloodied shirt and soiled trousers, and gently touched each rib to see which were broken. Chest and arms were black and blue, yellow and purple, sil-ver and grey. He was nacre that had yielded no pearl.

The pain in his left hand was acute, so the doctor rubbed it with a cool ointment and wrapped it up in a tight clean bandage.

'Nothing to be done about the cracked ribs. Time will heal them,' he said, his face without expression, and left the cell, taking the bloodied clothes with him.

Denham lay down and pulled the blanket over him. His teeth no longer fitted together when he closed his jaw, and every limb throbbed. In places the pain was dull and constant; in others it was sharp and intolerable only when he moved, but everywhere there was pain.

Chapter Twenty

Within an hour of leaving Denham's apartment Eleanor herself entered Gestapo headquarters on the Prinz-Albrecht-Strasse. The man at the reception desk looked up in surprise at the American woman in the broad-brimmed hat, sunglasses, and clothes from a fashion magazine. He scratched his jaw, dialled a number, spoke to someone, and told her she couldn't see Denham under any circumstances.

Smoking one cigarette after the other, she'd returned home to the Dodds' residence to ask the ambassador's advice, the price of which was Martha's finding out about her involvement with Denham.

'Best inform the Brits tomorrow,' Dodd told her in his dry voice. He was brushing his tailcoat, as if it were an act of extreme penance, in preparation for another diplomatic function. 'They'll make enquiries, although if your friend's lost in that system'—he glanced up at her, looking like a long-suffering horse—'information could be hard to come by.'

'Couldn't you ask Sir Eric Phipps to do something?'

'You could ask him yourself if you're coming with us to the Chancellery reception tomorrow night, although, my dear, you're perfectly excused from another night of all those nodding penguins talking bunk . . .'

THE NEXT MORNING, hoping she might encounter Roland Liebermann and find out if there had been any repercussions since her

visit with Denham yesterday, Eleanor headed to the Reich Sports
Field, where Hannah was competing in the fencing finals.

A radiant sky shone over the Dietrich Eckart stage, an open-air
amphitheatre built into a wooded hill near the stadium. The occasional cloud sailed overhead like an airship, casting a lazy shadow
onto the piste. Tall pines around the rim of the arena creaked in the
tense hush. All eyes were focused on the stage where the bouts were
in progress.

The Hungarian champion was in mid-duel with an Austrian girl.

Eleanor took a seat in the centre near the aisle steps and scanned
the stage around the piste for Hannah, using a pair of opera glasses
she'd borrowed from Mrs Dodd. She spotted the girl right away,
seated apart from everyone else, accompanied by the same potbellied little coach, who was flapping about, giving her instructions.
She seemed not to be listening. In fact she appeared deathly pale,
gazing straight ahead, seeming not to see anything.

Eleanor began searching the crowd for Roland but saw no sign of
the dark, lovely boy with the mutilated face. She wondered where he
could be and surprised herself by imagining that he was a beautiful
kisser. It was only when she was peering along the almost empty
row at the very back that she saw not Roland but Jakob Liebermann
sitting alone, a Panama hat half shading his face, and for the second time since yesterday evening she had a strong presentiment that
something was very wrong.

She left her seat and ran up the steps to speak to him.

When she reached him he stared at her with blank eyes. The
world seemed dark before him.

'Fräulein Eleanor,' he said at length, in his plangent voice. She
took his hand.

'Is something the matter?'

He looked frail, not the robust patriarch she'd met only yesterday.

'Last night . . . ,' he began, but was plunged into a struggle to
compose himself. When, after a few moments, he recovered, his

voice was very calm. 'There was a hammering on our door. We thought they were going to break it down. It was that inspector, Haeckel, with two Gestapo men, shouting something about how many lessons did they have to give us before we behaved . . . We were all reading in the drawing room, behaving very nicely. Roland lost his temper, but I could see that he was also terrified. He began shouting at them to leave us alone. Ilse was begging him to stop, and became quite hysterical. They tried to put handcuffs on him; there was a scuffle and he got away. One of the men drew a pistol . . . in our drawing room. Hannah and Ilse screamed. They shot Roland twice as he ran down the front steps of the house.'

'Oh dear God,' Eleanor cried.

'He was hit . . .' Herr Liebermann motioned to the back of his shoulder and back left-side ribs. 'He died in my arms a few minutes later.'

Eleanor was too shocked to speak. They sat still, hearing the *tick-tack-tick* of the duel being waged on the piste down below. The old man seemed stoic, beyond grief, as if he were ready to leave this world, too.

Applause rippled up from the amphitheatre to acknowledge the victory of the Austrian over the Hungarian.

She managed to say, 'And you can't go to the regular police . . . ?'

'There's nothing to be done except to bury him.'

'We can fight for him,' she said, drawing some quick looks from the people in front.

Herr Liebermann dropped his eyes to the large wrinkled hands splayed on his knees. He had told her yesterday something about acceptance being the route to wholeness, and she imagined he was seeking solace in this dictum even now.

'Naked I came into the world,' he murmured, 'naked I shall leave it . . .'

'No,' she said, putting her arm around his shoulders.

' . . . the Lord gives and the Lord takes away . . .'

'Not even Job would have stood for this.'

' . . . Blessed is the name of the Lord.'

The piste was being prepared for the next bout, and Eleanor remembered that Hannah was sitting down there.

'Hannah came here to compete today?' she said, amazed. 'After what's happened?'

'That's why I'm here. I'm worried about her and want to watch over her. We thought she'd stay in her room, but she came down this morning very pale and said she was going to fight today. The chance of beating some Austrian Nazi seems to have sealed her decision. The Austrian girl who won the last bout, in fact.'

Eleanor watched in disbelief as the judges returned to their seats and the loudspeakers announced, *'Hannah Liebermann, Deutschland; Kerstin Brückner, Österreich.'*

'This is it. The final,' Herr Liebermann said, still staring at his hands.

A tremendous cheer went up as the two opponents stepped onto the piste.

The wire mask was pulled down before Eleanor could see the expression on Hannah's face, but she got a good look at the Austrian, a mouse-haired girl with a pointed nose. *Pinched and mean*, thought Eleanor. *I hope you saw the fury in your opponent's eyes.* The two women acknowledged each other with their foils and the bout commenced.

Hannah lunged into the attack, to a surprised 'ooh' from the audience, and from there on gave the Austrian no respite. She used none of the cautious probing and testing Eleanor had seen earlier that week, in which she had even permitted herself to lose the first round in order to learn her opponent's strategy. Now, she attacked without remorse. Her footwork was light, like a ballerina's, making the Austrian's movements appear pigeonlike and dull. Hannah won the first bout.

The Austrian staged a brief rally in the second bout, pushing Hannah back over the centre line, but again Hannah gave no quarter; she was fighting as though to kill. Towards the end of the three minutes her opponent's chances were doomed.

In the final bout, Hannah's moves lost all their stylised elegance. They became impassioned with violence, a chaotic, overwhelming onslaught. The Austrian was helpless in a hail of steel, having scarcely landed a single hit, and the crowd erupted, rising to their feet to applaud for Hannah before the bout had even finished.

She'd won the final.

A first warning bell was ringing in Eleanor's mind: Hannah had been forbidden to win the gold. Now a second warning rang. The Austrian, who had removed her mask to reveal her tight, stunned little face, had proffered her hand for Hannah to shake, but Hannah ignored it. She also ignored the applause, strode away from the piste, and pulled off the mask, giving her head a shake so that her chestnut hair fell in silky coils around her shoulders.

As she left, a man in a cream suit sitting behind the judges' table sprang up and followed her. Eleanor recognised him. It was Greiser.

'What happens now?' she asked Herr Liebermann.

'There will be a podium ceremony in the stadium,' he said. Their eyes met. She could tell the same thought had just occurred to him, too.

NOT A SEAT was to be had in the stadium. Every row was rammed with spectators, so Eleanor led Herr Liebermann up the stairs to the press box, where they arrived just as the women's fencing podium ceremony was about to begin. The old man didn't seem to want to hurry, as if nothing was in his power to shape or change anymore.

She introduced him to Gallico.

'Congratulations, sir,' he said, giving the old gentleman's hand a hearty shake. 'You must feel very proud.'

The poor man, thought Eleanor, watching him take Paul's hand politely. That must be the worst possible thing he could hear today.

'Damned movie crew,' Gallico said to her. 'I was standing by the track eating my hot dog when I get handed this.' He showed her a pink slip. 'It says, "Remove yourself from where you are—Riefenstahl." Listen,' he continued in a low voice, 'your rose-bush story. John Walsh and I are going to confront Brundage.'

'When?'

'Press conference at the Kaiserhof Hotel tomorrow morning.'

In the arena the three women fencers were being awarded their medals. In third place was the Hungarian, who beamed and waved after accepting her bronze. In second place the Austrian received the silver, smiling with her thin lips, if not with her eyes.

'. . . *und auf dem ersten Platz: Hannah Liebermann, Deutschland!*'

The crowd applauded with a great cheer. Hannah bowed her head to receive the gold medal around her neck and a wreath of oak leaves that was placed upon her head. Still she did not smile. Watching through the opera glasses, Eleanor saw the wild look in her eyes.

They took their places on the podium, with Hannah on the highest step.

The first trudging note of 'Deutschland über Alles' sounded, a chord from an accordion, and the entire stadium heaved to its feet and sang, half a beat behind the band, right arms raised. The sound slurred through a great forest of Hitler salutes.

Slowly a giant swastika rose above the scoreboard on the western rim of the stadium and fluttered in the breeze.

And Hannah Liebermann's right arm stayed firmly at her side.

Even over the singing Eleanor sensed the crowd registering her defiance. The prickling hairs on her neck told her.

'Are you seeing what I'm seeing?' said Gallico at Eleanor's side.

'A courageous woman with nothing to lose,' said Eleanor. 'Shame A-dolf's not with us today.' She cast a look at Herr Liebermann and thought she saw a grim pride in his eyes.

The anthem finished and the crowd sat.

'I'm going down there before they do God-knows-what to her,' said Eleanor. But just as she said this Hannah jumped from the podium before anyone could reach her and darted to an exit near the foot of the western gate.

Eleanor stared after her for a second. And then she realised.

'The radio car,' she said, grabbing her handbag and running from the box.

She sprinted into the gallery surrounding the upper tier, round the curve of the stadium towards the western gate, and flew down the steps. Just outside, near a solitary oak on the Olympic plaza, she spotted Hannah surrounded by a large crowd accompanying her in the direction of the Deutscher Rundfunk mobile radio car. Her crown of oak leaves and her all-white fencing garb added to the strangeness of the scene, making her seem like a sacrificial virgin, or a divine being walking among believers. How many in the crowd knew of her astonishing defiance a moment ago wasn't clear, but they seemed excited by the famous face moving among them.

Just then, running out of the western gate, face shining with sweat, came Greiser, frantic, looking left and right, but in his haste he did not at first notice Hannah surrounded by the crowd. It was a few seconds later, as she was climbing the short ladder into the radio car, that he spotted her and pelted towards her, shouting and waving his hand.

He reached the edge of the throng and shouldered his way in, just as Hannah entered the car and the door closed behind her.

'*Öffnen Sie die Tür!*' he yelled over people's heads. '*Öffnen Sie die Tür!*'

Eleanor went after him, knowing she had to think of something drastic, and fast. She pushed into the crowd and managed to get almost right behind Greiser, so close she could see the golden hairs on the back of his neck, smell his cologne. Then she filled her lungs with air.

And screamed.

The most toe-curling scream she could muster.

The crowd became still in an instant. All eyes turned towards her, Greiser's included. She pointed, quivering and trembling, at the startled Greiser. 'That man,' she shrieked, 'just stuck his hand up my . . .' She mimed the action in a manner so graphic that it obviated any need for translation.

A mixture of shock and disgust spread over the faces of the men and women surrounding her and Greiser, turning to hostility as they took a good look at him. And then he recognised her.

'You,' he said just as several men's hands grabbed his jacket and someone yelled, *'Polizei.'* She couldn't understand what was shouted in the rumpus that followed but concentrated on projecting a look of outraged modesty and defiled maidenhood. She'd created complete pandemonium. Everyone was shouting, including Greiser, but just when it seemed as though his purple-faced protestations were being heard by the men holding his arms, the door of the radio car swung open and a technician appeared at the top of the steps, his eyes round with embarrassment and dread.

They've cut the transmission, Eleanor thought. *Wonder whether she got a full minute.*

As she later learned, Hannah got fourteen seconds of live airtime before the cable was pulled. But fourteen seconds is a long time on the radio.

Greiser was screaming at the technician, jabbing a finger at him, and Eleanor guessed he was ordering Hannah's confinement in the radio car until the police arrived.

Herr Liebermann was sitting exactly where she had left him, his cheeks ashen. As she explained what had happened at the radio car he sat rigid, a rolling tear the only motion on his face.

'She's done an amazing thing, sir. She has your courage. They've arrested her now.'

'Yes,' he said. 'I imagine they have.' He picked up his hat and rose.

Out of the corner of her eye Eleanor saw a group of UP boys talking across each other. *'Hold on a second. She said what?'* One of them was gesticulating with wild movements.

'I'll walk with you to your car.'

'No need,' Herr Liebermann said.

Two of the UP reporters who understood German had heard Hannah's live broadcast on the pressroom radio and were telling their colleagues and a dozen or so other correspondents. Within seconds the news was threatening to spill over the rail into the stadium crowd.

Gallico appeared next to her, his straw boater askew, just as Eleanor was walking Herr Liebermann to the door. 'Did you hear what's happened?' he said, a squeak of astonishment in his voice. 'Jesus knows how many listeners just heard that. Ten million? Thirty million?' With a loud whoop he seized Eleanor's hands and danced her around in a little jig in full view of the stadium until he caught the stricken look on the old man's face. 'Gee, sir, I'm sorry.'

Eleanor asked, 'What did she say?'

But before Gallico answered she was distracted by Herr Liebermann tapping her arm. 'We may not meet again, Fräulein Eleanor . . .'

The reporters in the box had become aware of the old man's presence—'Does he speak English?'—because one of them was now at his side, opening a notebook.

'Mr Liebermann, sir? Norman Ebbutt of the London *Times*. Have you heard what's just occurred? Your daughter used her live broadcast to . . .'

The old man gaped at him without comprehension, then turned again to Eleanor, flustered now. 'I was intending that you and Herr Denham—'

Several reporters had now gathered around them and were speaking at once, eyes and mouths animated and manic.

She was aware of Herr Liebermann's face close to hers, and suddenly he put his arm around her and clutched her in a brief, awkward embrace, his beard grazing her neck. For a second she did not know whom she was fending off.

She held out her hands in a 'stop' sign to make the reporters back away.

'Please . . . ,' Herr Liebermann said, 'keep it safe.'

'What?'

The back of his Panama hat was retreating towards the door,

and two reporters were following him. In three long strides she was among them and slammed the door shut after Jakob Liebermann had gone through. Leaning her back against it she barred the way to the reporters.

'Ma'am—'

'Leave him the hell alone.'

DENHAM DRIFTED INTO and out of consciousness, despite the noise. The radio playing down the corridor in the guards' room was kept loud enough to ensure that no one got any rest.

Something the patch-up doctor gave him had made him drowsy.

'*Hannah Liebermann . . . winner of the gold medal for Germany in today's women's fencing . . . just arrived in the radio car . . .*'

Someone was talking about Hannah Liebermann. Too loudly. He tried to chase the dream away, but then she herself was talking, also too loudly.

'. . . *began when I was expelled from my home fencing club three years ago and fled to California . . .*'

He swam away from it, and broke through the surface for a moment.

'*—Fraülein Liebermann, your gold medal . . .*'

'. . . *as if forcing me to compete wasn't enough, the Gestapo murdered my brother last night in our own home . . .*'

Denham sat bolt upright, as though a wire had just pulled him up by his spine.

'. . . *so that the Führer could deceive the world by allowing a single Jew to compete . . .*'

In the background of the radio car a man's voice was yelling something inaudible.

'. . . *robbing my father as the price for letting my family escape torment . . .*'

More commotion, and then Hannah's voice rose to a strained shout as though someone was pulling her away.

'. . . *the Führer is evil. He will bring sorrow to every hearth in Germ—*'

The click was followed by a loud buzz as the transmission was cut. A few seconds later the station was back on air playing military band music.

With those few words Denham forgot all about his pain and fear. He even forgot his thirst.

Chapter Twenty-one

The hall was warm from the heat of the day and noisy with chatter echoing off marble. Somewhere behind the din a choir of Jungvolk boys were singing German folk songs in their clean treble voices. Ambassador Dodd, Eleanor, and Martha and her mother were announced by a black-liveried major-domo holding a court sword.

'Utter hogwash . . . ,' the ambassador mumbled as their names were called.

Tall windows along the left-hand wall looked down into the Chancellery gardens, which were lit for the occasion with Chinese lanterns. Eleanor recognised some of the guests from the Goebbels party on the Pfaueninsel, but this seemed an even more select and powerful gathering. Martha pointed out Göring holding court like a Nazi Bacchus, his bulk festooned with medals that wobbled as he flirted and joked. The choir finished to polite applause, and a string orchestra took its place.

'Just look at the dimensions of this room,' Martha gushed. 'You know it was designed by Hitler himself?'

Eleanor looked around. Rows of red marble pillars lined each side, drawing the eye up to a coffered ceiling, where eagles and swastikas were set into mosaics of pale blue and gold. 'I guess some bachelors have a flair for interior design,' she said.

It struck her that the people who looked out of place in this illustrious company were the Nazis. She began scanning the crowd for the dapper figure of Sir Eric, and listening for mentions of the now highly charged name Liebermann.

Within minutes of Hannah's broadcast the wires from the stadium press box to the capitals of Europe had been jammed. And at the packed-out upstairs bar in the Adlon later that afternoon, Eleanor heard talk of nothing else. Word spread that Willi Greiser would give a statement at a press conference; then it turned out he was unavailable for comment.

Eleanor accepted an orange juice from a passing tray and handed a glass of champagne to Martha. 'Can you see Sir Eric anywhere?' she said.

Martha gave a wistful sigh, and again Eleanor sensed the reserves of jealousy just below the surface, like groundwater.

'I have to get Richard released, Martha.'

'All these available men here this fortnight,' she said, 'and you fall for the only one who's in serious trouble.'

The string orchestra was playing something upbeat and jaunty, and some couples were dancing. Eleanor threaded her way among the chattering groups and twice heard Liebermann's name spoken. She passed the broad back of Ambassador Dodd, who was stooping to hear the elderly German official who'd given the long-winded address at the opening ceremony. The old man seemed to be pleading with Dodd, who looked decidedly unimpressed.

Eleanor smiled to herself. The Liebermann Effect was spreading like a benign virus, giving these bastards a debilitating attack of shame.

At last she saw Sir Eric with a small group in the far corner of the hall, his monocle glancing from one speaker to the other. With his sash and glittering crosses he resembled some Ruritanian admiral. The pencil moustache twitched, but the poker face gave nothing away.

She was making her way towards him when a rough hand gripped her elbow.

'I don't think I properly made your acquaintance . . . ,' said a man's voice.

The hand spun her round, and she was faced with Willi Greiser.

' . . . Mrs Emerson. I do hope the sight of me this time doesn't send you into screaming hysterics.'

'Oh.' Eleanor gave a tight little laugh to hide her alarm. 'I am sorry about that. The culprit must have been someone else. It was really hard to tell in that crowd.'

His duelling scar flushed purple, she noticed.

'Would you permit me this dance?'

'Some other time—'

'Indulge me,' he said, clutching her wrist tightly and propelling her towards the orchestra, his other hand forming a fist in the small of her back. 'It's the least you could do.'

'Stop it. You're hurting me.'

Immediately he pulled her close and left her no choice but to join him in foxtrotting to the music, caged by his embrace.

'So, our friend Denham's checked into the Prinz-Albrecht-Strasse Hotel,' he said, smiling with genuine pleasure. 'I do hope they're giving him the full hospitality.'

'I expect you put them onto him.'

Greiser laughed. 'I had nothing to do with it,' he said. 'It's true. I didn't.'

'We were eager for your press conference at the Adlon earlier,' she said with acid innocence. 'What made you cancel it?'

'You didn't hear?' He swung her around to the music, screwing her hand hard into his grasp. 'I had to attend to an athlete who suffered a mental seizure during a radio interview. I fear she may spend years recovering in a secure institution.'

She tried to release herself from his arms, but he yanked her back, slipping his hand lower. 'What's the matter? Afraid I'll touch you somewhere you don't want to be touched . . . ? You'd be wise to treat me a little more sweetly.'

'Or what?' she almost shouted. 'You're gonna put me in an asylum, too?'

She pulled away her hand. Again he tried to hold her tight around her waist but hadn't reckoned on her swimmer's strength. She slung off his arms and shoved him backwards, sending him bumping into a dancing couple. Her face was flushed and hot as she strode from the floor.

Outside the light was dimming, and stewards entered carrying tall candelabras, placing them around the hall so that the flames were reflected in the red marble. To Eleanor's eyes they created a hellish glow.

Finally, she reached the British ambassador.

'Sir Eric, may I have a word?' she said, stepping into the man's circle. He was listening to a tall patrician gentleman adorned with medals and ribbons, and a younger, elegant lady with waved hair. The tall man spoke in that potato-laden Brit voice she'd heard only in movies.

Sir Eric bowed to kiss Eleanor's hand. 'She walks in beauty like the night . . . ,' he said. The trace of a smile played beneath his moustache as the taller gentleman was thrown off his stride by her appearance. Sir Eric introduced the couple as Sir Robert Vansittart, permanent undersecretary at the British Foreign Office, and Sir Robert's wife, Sarita, who turned to her politely.

For five agonising minutes they solicited Eleanor's opinion on the low cloud that had dogged the Games so far, and enquired after the comfort of her crossing, until finally their attention was drawn away, and she spoke quickly into the ambassador's ear.

'Sir Eric, it's about Richard Denham, the English reporter you spoke to at that Goh-balls party earlier this week . . .'

'Of course. I know Denham.'

She told him of the warning not to go near Liebermann, their defiance of Greiser's injunction, and of Richard's arrest by the Gestapo.

'Extraordinary,' Sir Eric said, his face as unfathomable as the Sphinx.

'You've got to help me get him released, sir. His son has gone missing in London. He has to get home. And now that Liebermann herself has told the world what happened to her, why would they need to keep him? The facts are public knowledge.'

Sir Eric looked at her carefully. The difficulty of gauging him wasn't helped by his monocle, which caught the light and appeared as a blank disc on his face.

'How did you become an interested party?' he asked, picking his words.

'We've grown . . . close,' she said.

The ambassador paused, as if choosing what to impart. 'The Gestapo don't have him,' he said. 'He's in the hands of the SD, the intelligence service.'

'How do you know that?'

He gave a discreet cough. 'The worrying question—to which my sources found no answer—is what they want with him.'

'Isn't it about Liebermann?'

Sir Eric shook his head thoughtfully. 'No. It must be something bigger than that . . .'

'*Meine Damen und Herren . . .*'

A voice booming from the far end of the hall was making an announcement, which it repeated in French and then in English. 'Ladies and gentlemen, Your Excellencies, honourable guests, please now extinguish your cigars and cigarettes. There is no smoking in the presence of the Führer.'

An excited murmur swelled around the hall.

'My word. We're honoured,' said Sir Eric. 'He's not normally much of a partygoer.'

Two gigantic bronze doors swung open and some twenty helmeted SS in white parade gloves entered the hall. Spreading out, they positioned themselves along the walls and among the crowd. Eleanor noticed with some unease that one had stationed himself only a few feet behind her.

The guests waited, facing the doors. The orchestra fell silent.

Ambassador Dodd came over to stand with Eleanor and Sir Eric, as far away from the doors as possible, and he and the Englishman exchanged a look of bemused tedium. She considered slipping away to powder her nose, but there was no chance now.

At last he entered, accompanied by an interpreter and two Olympic officials wearing chains of office. He looked awkward and ill at ease, Eleanor thought, in his white tie and tails, which didn't fit him well: the coat was slipping off his shoulders.

'He looks like a flea circus master,' she whispered to Dodd.

The face was pale, with bags under the eyes. The moustache wasn't as ludicrous as it seemed in caricature. Yet there was something outlandish about him, something about his gaze, which was expressive, hypnotic even.

Slowly he moved through the crowd, being introduced to various diplomats and ambassadors for sport. He nodded and listened, making it hard for her to connect him with the raving demagogue she'd seen on the newsreels. She wondered whether the Liebermann incident had sparked one of his famous tantrums earlier. It seemed impossible to imagine he'd taken the news calmly.

'You don't think he'll come over here, do you?' she asked Sir Eric. She felt the palms of her hands begin to sweat.

'I fear he will, if he knows I'm here. The Germans are proffering their fishy hand in friendship at the moment.'

Eleanor shifted on her heels. She had a strong sense of something malefic at work in the room. Irrational, yes, but she noticed how most of the guests stood in silence, in thrall to some mystical will emanating from this man. She could see it in their eyes, including Martha's: a type of rapture.

They waited, watching him come nearer. He gave a short bow when presented to a woman, kissing her hand; with the men he said hardly a word but looked into their faces with a pale blue beam. Every few seconds his hand would smooth the curious lock across his forehead, as if by nervous compulsion.

And then he was in front of them.

He recognised Sir Eric, took the ambassador's hand in both of his, and fixed him with an intense stare. The translator at his elbow leaned in to hear.

'Sir Eric Phipps,' he said. 'The Anglo-Saxons are much in my thoughts.'

'And you in ours, Your Excellency.'

Hitler nodded slowly. 'Do you know that today, for the second time, I watched the film *Lives of a Bengal Lancer*? My bid to discover how England gained her empire.'

'How extraordinarily interesting.'

Still he held Sir Eric's hand. 'India, a nation of half a billion people, ruled by only four hundred English public servants? *Erstaunlich.*' Astonishing.

It occurred to Eleanor how wrong-footed most people would have been by such remarks, but Sir Eric was an old hand.

'*Lives of a Bengal Lancer* . . . My wife's seen that only once, I think,' he said. 'She's a Gary Cooper fan, too.'

The gaze swept across Sir Eric's poker face, but nothing could be read.

Dodd was next, and made a remark about the American team being mightily impressed with the Olympic village. At that, a bothersome memory seemed to pop into the dictator's head.

'Yes-sy Oh-vens,' he said, looking straight through Dodd.

It was at that moment that Eleanor understood with a shock that she was about to be introduced. She had not expected this at all and suddenly felt a powerful aversion to the thought of those lips kissing her hand. There was no backing out, but was there a moment to be seized? Surreptitiously she prised open her handbag.

No one realised what she was doing until the very last moment, when the guard standing behind her darted forwards.

But it was too late.

There was an audible gasp from the people around her.

She had lit a cigarette in the Führer's face.

Chapter Twenty-two

Denham was woken from a dreamless state by the voice of a man sitting at the end of his cot. He had no idea how long he'd been asleep under the harsh electric light.

'They've patched you up, I see.'

He opened one swollen eye and saw the sheen of a jackboot. Fear surged through him, and he shrank against the wall with a moan.

'It's all right,' Rausch said, reaching over and putting a hand on his arm. There was a stink of wine on his breath. His hair was dishevelled and his uniform was undone at the collar. 'I've come to say a friendly hello, that's all. Just a friendly hello.' The man's nails were bitten to the quick, Denham saw, and stained yellow from those noxious Murads.

Rausch leaned back, his head hitting the wall with a soft thud. 'Do you know what trouble this is bringing me, Denham?' he said, almost to himself. 'Have you any idea what could happen to me? I'll be thrown down here with you, that's what. The Obergruppenführer is most displeased. Wants to have a go at you himself. Wants to twist it out of you. You wouldn't want that, believe me, Denham. You wouldn't want that.' The blue eyes dilated, struggling to focus.

'This started so well. *Outstanding* intelligence work. That's what he said. Should have got me decorated . . .' Rausch folded his arms and started shaking gently, so that whether he was crying or laughing Denham couldn't tell. Spittle foamed at the sides of his mouth, and when he spoke again his voice was ill-controlled. 'I was this close . . .' He held his thumb and forefinger with a tiny space between them. 'And then you entered the picture.'

Denham thought of protesting the truth once more, but getting the words out would have cost him too great an effort. And what was the point?

'You're one of those types, aren't you, whom beatings only make silent. Isn't that so? I've seen it before.' He sighed. 'You and I both, Denham. We'll hang for this . . .' His face reddened but he suppressed the rising sob.

A strange silence opened between them for a while.

'This dossier . . .' Denham whispered. 'Why?'

Rausch slumped forwards and cupped his forehead in his hands so that Denham thought he was about to vomit, but then he said in a distant voice, 'Wish I knew.'

He sat up, remembering something, fumbled in his tunic and pulled out a cigarette packet. 'HBs,' he said, opening it and offering one. 'Your brand, I believe.'

'Water,' Denham croaked.

Rausch struggled to his feet and opened the cell door, swaying. 'Water in here.' Seconds later he was handed a jug. Denham sat up despite the hot knives stabbing at his ribs, and reached for it. It sloshed over the rim and onto Rausch's hands, dripping to the floor. Cool, clear water.

But Rausch didn't give it to him.

'Tell me now, friend,' he said, standing in the middle of the cell, his feet set wide apart to steady himself, 'and spare us both. Once and for all. Where is it? Please . . . tell me where.'

Denham shook his head sadly without taking his eyes off the jug.

The interrogator staggered backwards, his eyes closed, as if seeing his own doom. His nostrils flared, and a drunken roar came from his chest. With a wide arm he bowled the jug, smashing it against the wall behind Denham's head, covering him in water and pieces of earthenware. The next moment Rausch was on top of him, punching and screaming.

Chapter Twenty-three

The morning after the Chancellery reception Eleanor and Gallico found standing room only at the back of the tearoom in the old Hotel Kaiserhof on the Wilhelmplatz. The place was full of foreign correspondents and newswire photographers. It was a humid day, and the room already smelled of sweat, cigarette smoke, and whisky hangovers.

Willi Greiser entered to a barrage of shouted questions.

'Sir, was Liebermann forced to compete?'

'Can you confirm that her brother was shot while resisting arrest?'

'Is she in custody? Sir?'

Eleanor noticed that he did not flinch but brazened the onslaught with an urbane smile, dismissing the matter of the Liebermann broadcast with a wave of his hand. Let's not waste anyone's time over such a thing. *This guy's good*, she thought. Speaking smoothly in English with his German-American accent, he said, to popping flashbulbs, 'After the great strain that training for these Games has taken on her mentally and physically, Fräulein Hannah Liebermann is now convalescing at a private sanatorium. She sincerely regrets any misleading impressions she may have given in her pressured state of mind, and has personally asked me to express her deep gratitude to the German Olympic Committee for once again allowing her the honour of defending her title for Germany.'

'Boys, don't fall for it . . .' Eleanor mumbled.

Greiser then took questions only from the German reporters in the room, who, right on cue, got his propaganda machine rolling with something more palatable. The *Völkischer Beobachter* was eager to know whether Ilse Dörffeldt had recovered from her disappointment in dropping the baton in the women's relay.

'She was upset,' said Greiser, 'but the Führer himself sent a car full of flowers to console her.'

He answered two more servile questions from the *Deutsche Allgemeine Zeitung* and the *Berliner Tageblatt* while his eyes scanned the room, noticing that the foreign press corps had ceased their shorthand and become restless, whereupon he suddenly thanked everyone and turned his back on the instant uproar of unanswered questions about Liebermann. As he was striding towards the exit, a female voice carried high over those of the males.

'Has the Gestapo tortured English reporter Richard Denham for speaking to Liebermann?'

Greiser was halfway through the double doors, but Eleanor saw his back tense and his neck stiffen. He'd heard the question.

The room fell still.

She had the sensation of a tide turning as every foot and chair scraped and shifted around and faced in her direction. Faces looked at her eagerly, notepads on knees and pencils at the ready. Then all the questions began at once.

'Ma'am, who's this guy? Colleague of yours?'

'Did he get an interview with Liebermann?'

'How long's he been in the cells?'

And Eleanor found herself giving her own press conference, with Gallico standing behind her, amused and shaking his head at the ceiling. The room filled with the dry rustle of 150 pencils taking shorthand.

'Did you say the Gestapo have got Denham?' said a lanky, grey-haired Englishman pushing his way through the pack, his pipe smouldering like a paddle steamer's. 'Well, who the bloody hell's getting him out?' he shouted.

*   *   *

EARLY THAT EVENING Gallico rang the bell at the Dodds' house
on Tiergartenstrasse and invited Eleanor for a stroll. The humid-
ity still hadn't lifted. They bought ice creams from a stall near the
Tiergarten and walked along the edge of the park, up the Hermann-
Göring-Strasse towards the Brandenburg Gate. Cries of parakeets
and howler monkeys reached them from the zoo.

'So you gave Brundage a hard time?' she asked.

'Well, he denied everything of course and looked like he wanted
the floor to swallow him up. First time we've ever seen him break a
sweat . . .'

Gallico's voice trailed off.

'What's the matter?'

'Sweetheart, listen,' he said, hesitating. 'You may as well hear this
from me first . . .'

'What is it?' She felt her stomach turn cold.

'There's a report on the wire of an interview your husband's given
to the *New York Post*. Said your behaviour on board the *Manhattan*
embarrassed him. Made him think you weren't the blushing flower
he married . . . He doesn't want you singing with the Herb Emerson
Orchestra anymore. Says he needs time apart.'

Eleanor exhaled loudly and realised she'd been holding her breath.

'Oh,' she said, almost wanting to cry with relief, but started gig-
gling instead, to Gallico's bemusement. 'I thought you were going
to tell me Richard had been . . .' She put her arms around him and
hugged him. 'Thanks for letting me know.'

'You're not upset?'

'Not at all. If anything, it just made my life a whole lot better.'

When they reached Unter den Linden Eleanor suggested a coffee
at the Adlon. The first person she saw in the lobby was that lanky
Englishman, Rex Palmer-Ward, talking to a group of reporters near
the fountain. He spotted her and approached trailing a veil of sweet-
smelling smoke.

'My dear,' he said. 'There's been a development.'

Chapter Twenty-four

Searchlights lit Berlin's new showcase airport, creating a theatrical effect from the blood-red flags, silver eagles, and rows of regimented windows: the hallmarks of the brutal new style.

'I haven't packed,' Denham mumbled to the three SD men escorting him in the BMW.

'You're going straight on the flight.'

One of the men showed Denham's passport at the desk, then escorted him past the brass rail, out onto the runway, and towards the steps of the plane. Its silver fuselage glinted under the lights. The baggage hold was closing and the fuel truck reversing away. The propellers began to turn. In the door of the plane a young stewardess was beckoning for them to hurry.

Denham reached the steps just as the engines began to roar, but before he could climb inside, the SD man grabbed his elbow. With his other hand holding on to his trilby he yelled, 'Make any attempt to reenter the Reich and it's straight back to the cells. Understand?'

'I'm not coming back,' Denham said, taking his passport from the man's hand.

He hobbled through the door of the plane and said hello to the stewardess, seeing the effect of his ravaged face in her eyes. Pretty eyes, too. Iceberg blue. Inside the cabin were about sixteen tall, upholstered seats, all occupied, except one. In their haste to flush him out of their Aryan paradise, Denham guessed they'd bumped someone off the flight. At least he had a window seat. He eased himself in with care, trying not to faint from the hot pokers in his ribs.

The plane began to move. It rumbled along the runway for a minute; then the engine noise swelled in pitch, there was a sudden acceleration, and they were away, up out of the Reich. Trying not to rest his stitched-up brow against the window he watched the spider's web of illuminated streets radiating from Potsdamer Platz station, the long line of car taillights passing along the Tiergarten, the dark mass of the zoo and its lakes. Drifts of cloud slipped over the wing. A few minutes later they were over the western districts of Wilmersdorf, Charlottenburg, and Spandau, and Berlin was stretching away behind them.

Iceberg Eyes asked if he'd like a drink. He winked at her and asked for a triple whisky, neat, and some aspirin.

'I'll have the same,' said an American voice. 'Without the aspirin.'

Eleanor stood in the aisle, smiling at the man seated next to him, asking if he wouldn't mind swapping seats. Denham had never seen her look so lovely. She was in a navy suit with a marocain blouse and had her hair held up by a black felt band with a ribbon.

He blinked, fearing another hallucination like the ones that had haunted his cell. Maybe in truth he was still there, doped on morphine and comatose, incapable of breaking through the surface to reality, and not wanting to.

'You sure took your time,' she said, sitting down next to him.

He touched her forehead with his finger.

'It's me, Richard. I'm real. This is real.' She kissed him gently on his swollen lips.

'How did you . . . ?'

But it didn't matter for now. He put his arms around her, and pressed his face to hers, ignoring the agony in his hand, cheek, and ribs. He began to cry.

'I don't look too grand, do I?'

She took his bandaged hand and kissed it. 'I think you're the grandest person on earth.'

They downed their drinks, and Eleanor said, 'Sleep for a while. Then we'll talk.'

Denham drifted off to the hum of the propellers and the steward-ess announcing, 'Our flight time over the Reich is one and a half hours; we land at Croydon Airfield, London, in four hours . . .'

He awoke with the word 'home' on his lips and realised that Tom had been swimming through his dream. The cabin lights were off, and he looked out of the window at great ranges of clouds, towering white in the moonlight and plunging into silvery canyons and cre-vasses. *Where are you hiding, son?*

'The stars look like ice crystals, don't they?' Eleanor said softly. She was curled sideways into her seat, watching him, a blanket wrapped around her.

'Did you get me released?' he asked.

'Uh-huh.' She nodded with a sleepy smile.

'Did they really kill Roland?'

Her face fell. 'You know about that?'

'I heard the broadcast.'

She sat up and began to tell him what had happened. The murder of Roland at Haeckel's hands. Hannah's victory and the broadcast.

She explained how Sir Eric Phipps approached no less a person than Heydrich himself, sitting behind Hitler at the Olympic sta-dium, and demanded Denham's release, or to see him the same day.

'Some people in high places like you, buddy. This SS big shot Heydrich told him there was an espionage charge against you, but it sounded so vague that Sir Eric asked if it wasn't really a crock o' shit—but in diplomatic language, of course. Meanwhile your old friend Rex Palmer-Ward and others in the press corps put pressure on that prize asshole Greiser to confirm what I'd told them about you being held in the Gestapo cells for talking to Liebermann . . . The Germans panicked, afraid of another scandal hot on the heels of Liebermann while the Games were still on. But it seems they were also worried about upsetting you Brits. Eric Phipps is the brother-in-law of Sir Fancy-Tart . . .'

'Sir Robert Vansittart?'

'Yeah, tall fellow, talks with a potato in his throat. Apparently he has a hell of a sway over your foreign policy. So the krauts made a snap decision to deport you, and I got on the same flight.'

'I'm nothing but trouble.'

'Hey . . . ,' she whispered, smoothing his hair.

'And Tom . . .'

'We'll find him.'

They sat, holding each other's hands for a while in silence, before Denham said, 'Did anyone mention a dossier?'

Eleanor shook her head. 'A dossier?'

He peered out into the darkness, but could see nothing but the reflection of his own face in the glass.

Part II

Chapter Twenty-five

It was after midnight when their taxi arrived at Primrose Hill. That had been a problem: where to go. He hadn't lived in London for nearly six years, and he doubted that Anna would open her house to a neglectful former husband and his much-younger American companion.

'How are your breaking-and-entering skills?' he'd asked.

'I can smash a window with a brick.'

A light rain fell as he looked up at the three-storey terrace house on Chamberlain Street, reminding him that he had no coat or, indeed, any luggage. With luck there would be some clothes in the house, albeit superannuated by moths and fashion.

'Who lives here?' Eleanor said, looking up at the peeling gloss and the pale-brick walls overgrown with Virginia creeper and wisteria. The windows were dark and sightless, with heavy wooden shutters behind the glass.

'It's been closed up since my father died. Couldn't bring myself to sell it.'

The front door was too sturdy an obstacle to break without waking the street, so Denham carefully descended the narrow steps that led to the basement door. At the foot of the steps he trod on a piece of buttered bread lying on the gravel. It was dusted with splinters of glass that glittered in the light from the streetlamp, and he saw that it had been employed, recently it seemed, to break the glass of the basement door noiselessly.

'We've been burgled,' he called up. Gingerly he put his hand through the broken glass and opened the door, his shoe crunching on the shards that lay on the floor inside. 'Have you got a match?'

Together they crept into the basement. Years ago his father had used it as a workshop. Now it resembled some long-ransacked tomb. The detritus of small motors covered the table, ghostly in the match light, and the air smelled musty with damp and diesel oil. Technical drawings furred in dust were scattered over the floor.

'Holy *crap*,' Eleanor cried, startled when Denham kicked a fuse box in the dark, sending it thumping across the floor.

In the hall Denham lit another match and entered the kitchen. Silhouettes played behind the old iron stove and the rows of enamelled plates. It was like having the pages of a half-remembered childhood book opened for him again.

'I think our burglar stayed for dinner,' Eleanor whispered, pointing to a plate with crumbs and smeared butter. On the table were two curling crusts of brown bread, some sour-looking green apples, and an empty tin of corned beef. On a chair was a purple kite Denham recognised, and a comic book opened to a strip featuring Corky the Cat.

'I think I know who came calling,' he said. He lit another match, walked across the hall, and, putting two fingers in his mouth, made a loud whistle up the stairs.

Silence for a few seconds, then a thudding commotion from somewhere at the top of the house, as if someone were erecting a barricade of chairs and mattresses.

A boy's voice, terrified. 'Who's there?'

'Come and say hello to your dad.'

Another moment's silence, then the sudden sound of running feet, and Tom came bounding down the two flights into his father's arms. He was clasped so tightly against Denham's wounds that the pain shot orange stars through his eyes. He didn't care.

'Oh, Tom.'

The match went out, and in the darkness Denham smelled earth and bark and liquorice in his son's hair, and when his small voice spoke it was with a soft whistle. He had lost his two front teeth, like the apparition in the cell. Maybe it was Tom's spirit that had come to him after all.

'Are you going to stay this time?'

'Yes,' said Denham, struggling under the emotion in his voice. 'Daddy's not leaving again.'

Tom's voice fell to a whisper. 'Who's in there?'

It was easier to see in the kitchen, where the city glow of the clouds shone through a window over the sink. Beyond it was a garden, dark and overgrown. Eleanor stood tall and graceful in the spectral light. A figure from a dream.

'Her name's Eleanor,' Denham whispered. 'She's from New York.' He led Tom by the hand into the kitchen. 'She's a special friend of mine.'

'Thomas Denham, how d'you do?' said Tom, stiffly offering his hand.

'Great to meet you, kid.' Eleanor took his hand and pulled him into a hug. 'Mind if we stay at your hideout?'

Denham found a penny in a drawer in the hall and went out to call Anna from the telephone box on Regent's Park Road. She wailed when he told her; her tragedy salved in an instant by the news. 'He's safe and well,' Denham said. 'I'll bring him up first thing in the morning.'

When he returned, Eleanor was chatting with Tom, who was helping her make corned beef sandwiches in the light of a paraffin lamp. The bread was stale, but with a few slices of sharp green apple as relish, and Tom's obvious joy, the meal felt like a treat. Denham tried abridging their adventures for an eight-year-old's consumption as he explained about his injuries to a concerned son, telling him the police challenged him to a boxing match, but one question led to another in the boy's eager mind, as he listed all of the ploys

Charlie Chan would have used, until it was very late and his father
was exhausted.

'We'll tell you the rest over breakfast,' Denham said. 'But now to
bed. Your dad has to sleep.'

'Will Eleanor be here for breakfast, too?' Tom whispered.

'Yes.'

'Good.'

The mattress in the master bedroom might have been a century
old and not aired in just as long. Denham sat on the edge, his hands
resting on the springs, and watched Eleanor undress in front of him
without a word, standing amid the shadows and the cobwebs.

She took out a hairpin, gave her head a small shake, and her hair
fell around her neck. She reached beneath her hem, undid her gar-
ters with a secret movement of her fingers, and slowly slid her stockings down over her smooth, long legs. He hesitated, shyness yielding
to desire, then took her hand and held it to his face. They kissed, lips
and tongues just caressing, breath quickening. She undid her blouse,
holding his gaze as it shimmered from her shoulders to the floor.
Pale breasts in a white-silk bra.

Gently he touched them, running his thumb under the silk strap.
Then she reached behind her back, and the bra, too, came away.

Getting out of his own clothes was a challenge, and he winced as
she helped him out of his shirt.

They lay back on the bed. The house seemed to creak, as if turning over in its sleep. She had on only her white-silk panties. Her
skin was translucent, as if she were absorbing the faint lamplight
from the street. Their faces in shadow, he whispered in her ear. She
gave a soft, complicit laugh, then slipped the panties off.

NONE OF THE men noticed him crouching in the corner of the
control car. They were flying blind: rain and hail dashed the windows from the darkness outside. Their faces were illuminated by
the radium glow from the dials on the instruments. The propeller
engines were making every surface tremble. One of the men turned

and saw him. It was his father, who smiled in the apologetic way he had. A slide rule and pencils in his top pocket. Denham tried to call out but couldn't be heard over the roar of wind and engines. His father winked at him sadly, opened his hand to reveal the pocket watch, and Denham understood that everything was lost. Suddenly the engines started making a violent hammering sound, and he awoke to realise that the hammering was at the front door.

He lay still, breathing fast. Tiny rays filtered through the tattered curtains. He heard the milk horse clopping down Regent's Park Road. Eleanor was still in a deep sleep next to him, her arm linked in his. The hammering sounded again.

He heard Tom running down the stairs to the hall, talking to himself.

Denham shouted, '*No*,' and started to get up but the pain in his ribs forced him back onto the mattress. Eleanor stirred.

Moments later Tom called up the stairs from the hall.

'Dad, a man wants you.'

'Who is he?'

'He's got a bowler hat.'

Chapter Twenty-six

David Wyn Evans was waiting in the Hole-in-the-Wall café near the bridge on Regent's Park Road. He got up when Denham entered, took off his hat, and muttered something, which may have been an oath in Welsh, on seeing Denham's face.

'You're getting that seen to, I hope?'

'How did you find me?'

'Ah.' Evans smiled with regret, as if he were a magician being asked to reveal his tricks.

They sat down just as the waitress placed a fried breakfast on the table. 'Full English?' Evans said to him. 'They do kidneys here, and kedgeree.'

'Just tea,' Denham said to the girl, reaching into his jacket for cigarettes and finding with a shock the full packet of HBs Rausch had given him in the cell.

He and Evans were the only patrons. The sign on the door had been changed to CLOSED without him noticing, and Bowler Hat Man stood guard outside next to a black government car.

'I'm glad to see you at liberty,' Evans said, giving his plate a liberal sprinkling of salt. 'Sir Eric kicked up quite a fuss to get you out of there, I can tell you.'

'They thought I had something that they want as much as you do.'

'Ye-es, that's what worried us.' He heaped scrambled egg onto a slice of fried bread and took a bite, watching Denham as he chewed. 'Let's hear it.'

Denham explained what had happened in the interrogation, and what little he'd learned of the resistance group. The Welshman listened with keen attention.

When he'd finished, Evans said, 'So, evidently you weren't the chosen reporter . . .'

'Good God, man. D'you think I'd have gone through this'—he pointed at his face—'if I could have told them where it was after the first blow?'

'Hmm . . . quite so,' Evans said, and gestured for the bill.

'I think I've earned the right to know what's in this bloody thing . . . this dossier.'

Evans dabbed his mouth with his napkin, his cheek bulging as he probed his teeth with his tongue, trying to dislodge some bacon. 'What we know is only from hearsay and rumour. Nothing precise. But forgive me, Mr Denham—it's best if I don't tell you even that. People with knowledge of the List Dossier have a habit of dying.'

The List Dossier.

'So you're not even sure what it is?'

'It's valuable intelligence all right. That much we know. A unit within the SD has been going to extraordinary lengths to track it down, and in secrecy, without using the police apparatus. That alone gives an idea of its worth . . .'

He paid for his breakfast and stood up. 'I thought you might like Saturday's newspaper,' he said, passing a folded copy of the *Daily Mail* across the table. A photograph of Hannah's nonsalute on the podium filled most of the front page. 'Goodbye, Mr Denham.'

'Before you go—I'd like to ask . . .'

Evans stopped, standing over him, lean and angular in his wing collar and black homburg, like a Mafia undertaker.

' . . . Would you find out what's happened to Hannah Liebermann and her family?'

He studied Denham for a moment and gave a curt nod. 'I'll do what I can,' he said, making towards the door. He put his hand on the door handle, then turned and said, 'A word of advice. The press think you were detained for interviewing Liebermann, so leave it at that. Mention the dossier to no one. If Heydrich still believes you know something . . . you are not beyond his reach.'

WHEN DENHAM GOT back it was still early. Eleanor's shoulders rose and fell gently in sleep, the hair across her cheek golden in the dusty light. He looked around the room, with all its reminders of his father. A pile of technical manuals, drawers filled with odds and ends. But it was the picture above the nightstand that sent a tingle over his scalp. He hadn't noticed it last night: a framed photograph of the project engineers at Cardington, posing beneath the control car of the R101, one of two gigantic airships built to link the capitals of the empire by air. Must have been taken sometime in 1929. His dad, hands behind his back, neat and trim with his Fairbanks moustache. His colleagues with serious smiles. The mighty ship behind them nearing completion.

'Where were you?' Eleanor's voice was thick with sleep.

'Just talking to a neighbour.' He sat on the bed, facing the picture. She brushed the hair from her eyes and stretched lazily, reaching her arm towards him.

'Did he help build that Zeppelin, your dad?'

'Yes . . . he died on it, too.'

'Oh gee, I'm sorry,' she said, sitting up.

'Took off for India in bad weather. Crashed over northern France and burned. On its maiden flight.'

DENHAM SENT TOM out for some pastries, and told him there was a shilling for him if he could get hold of any more of the weekend's newspapers from Mr Blount's shop or the neighbours. In the meantime Eleanor got the mains water running.

The boy excelled himself, returning in fifteen minutes, beaming, with the *Manchester Evening Guardian*, the *Times*, and the *Daily Express*. This last one carried a long feature on Hannah by

Pat Murphy, using the news agency snap of her standing, tight-lipped, on the podium. There was plenty of backstory, but news of what happened was thin, posing the question 'could she have been coerced?' rather than taking the words of her dynamite broadcast at face value. It cited a German press report that she had suffered a breakdown and mixed in some conjecture that this may have stemmed from the strain she felt over German policy on 'the Jewish question.'

Oh, Pat, Denham thought, guessing that his friend had been leaned on by Lord Beaverbrook. Go and work for someone else.

Laughter came from the kitchen, where Tom was giving Eleanor his tips for winning at conkers.

The *Times* scored far higher, with an article on page two by Rex getting most of the truth across. Must have cost him a fight with his editor. The bare facts were so startling that the lead column felt obliged to comment, albeit in an exculpatory tone: 'Hannah Liebermann, an Olympian not noted for outbursts of an emotional kind, has revealed the brutality and coercion surrounding her decision to participate; further evidence, if any were needed, that the German government is prepared to back policy with force, and that its grievances resulting from the Treaties of Versailles and Locarno must be taken seriously . . .' He would cable Rex later to thank him.

He put the papers down and stared at the frayed pattern of the sitting room rug, his mind working. He hadn't a day to lose. If somehow he was going to get the Liebermanns out of Germany, he must publish his interview with Hannah *now* while everyone was talking about her. It would be his biggest and best shot.

WHEN TOM HAD eaten his breakfast Denham took him on the bus up the hill to Hampstead and delivered him to the gate. Anna rushed from the front door in a sort of crouching run, her arms wide, crying at the sight of Tom's face, hugging him on the garden path. She didn't invite Denham in.

It started to rain as he hobbled back towards Rosslyn Hill, wishing he were recovered enough to make the walk down.

He'd almost reached the bus stop when a wave of dizziness hit him.

His left shoulder was seized with a bolt of pain that almost made him faint. By the time he was seated on the bus and heading towards Fleet Street, the pain was so intense, his head spinning so violently, that the lower deck rolled like a raft on the high seas.

Chapter Twenty-seven

Harry Garobedian sat behind the desk in his dingy office suite above the Olde Cock Tavern on Fleet Street. His hard brown eyes were wide now with understandable astonishment.

'My God, Ricky boy. This . . . this has got everything.'

'You wanted a human interest story . . . and I want to give the Germans a bad press week. So this one works for both of us.' The attack of dizziness had subsided, leaving him with a dull headache.

Harry picked the telephone receiver off its cradle and replaced it immediately, breathing deeply through his nose, as though smelling his mother's lamb keshkeg simmering in the pan. 'I got to hand it to you. "Hannah Liebermann—*My Story*" . . . When do I get the copy?'

'Tomorrow.'

He opened a drawer and rolled a cigar across the desk to Denham.

Denham said, 'I need this piece to go huge, Harry. To turn the heat up so high they *have* to release her. Her family, too.'

Harry lit his cigar from an enormous brass table lighter and leaned back in his chair, observing Denham through the fug. A rumble of barrels rose from the tavern cellar.

'What's happened to you?' he asked.

Denham lit his cigar and drew on it, but did not speak.

Harry continued to watch him, then leaned forwards to tip his ash. 'Okay, listen, I want a follow-up, too.' He placed his fingers in the air, as if seeing Denham's name in lights. ' "My Gestapo Night-mare," by Richard Denham.'

Denham smiled. Harry had the eyebrows of a vaudeville villain. The agent lifted a cash box onto the desk, unclipped four white £5 notes, and handed Denham an advance.

'Tomorrow then,' Denham said.

ELEANOR HAD FOUND some engineer's overalls and had tied a tea towel as a scarf around her head. She had cleaned out the iron boiler, reconnected the flue with a spanner, and got the thing burning with coal she'd found in the basement, finding the whole task oddly satis-fying. All morning it had helped clear her mind and set her thoughts on her future. On Richard . . . on Herb. 'No electricity, no gas,' she said, kissing him, 'but there's hot water. I'll just serve notice on the spiders and the place will be almost habitable . . .'

He slid his hands around her lower back and pulled her to-wards him.

That afternoon Denham cleaned the grime off his father's Ed-wardian typewriter and got down to work. The strange pain in his left shoulder was now constant, and his ribs seemed to be rubbing against needles, but he ignored it, tapping away quickly at a little escritoire in the drawing room, listening to the children playing in the street. Children without brown shirts or daggers.

By seven o'clock the rain had passed over and a sunset beckoned, sending its crimson light into the house. Eleanor was writing letters at the kitchen table. He noticed that one, already sealed, was ad-dressed to her husband. He had a fair idea of what it said.

'Get your hat,' he said. 'I'll show you the Hill.'

Clouds parted, filling the sky with drama. A flock of sheep scat-tered before them as they climbed Primrose Hill, deserted apart from a few boys flying kites in the gathering breeze. At the top of the path Denham turned her round towards the city below.

'Oh my,' she murmured, clutching his hand.

Beyond the trees of Regent's Park, dark with rainwater, London shone from myriad chimney pots to the cross on the dome of Saint Paul's, ablaze with a reddish gold.

Denham pointed out the Palace of Westminster, black with soot; the distant downs of Kent, where he'd grown up; the spires of the City churches.

They stood a long while without speaking. Eventually Denham said, 'When I was locked in that place I thought I'd never see clouds or sky again.'

'I love you,' she said, turning to him. 'I want to stay here with you and Tom.'

'Marry me, then?'

THEY HAD CELEBRATED quietly that evening, and the next morning Denham delivered the Liebermann piece to Harry, who had been on the telephone for much of the night, syndicating it to newspaper groups across the United States. By the time Denham got back home, though, the dizziness and the pain in his shoulder had reached an intensity he could no longer ignore.

'Well, isn't that the damnedest thing?' he said, after kissing his fiancée in the hall.

'What?'

'You've gone all blurred, old girl.'

'Excuse me?'

'You know, like the way they film Greta Garbo in close-ups . . .'

Chapter Twenty-eight

He thought he heard the horn of a river barge. Now and then he would open his eyes and see faces. He knew when it was Eleanor's face, and Tom's face, but others he didn't know at all. Often there came a face with an efficient smile; her breasts rested on him when she leaned over to adjust his sheets, and a man with a copper-wire beard who put his face very close and shone a light right into his eyes. He had no sense of time. He felt the tube in his arm being checked and a dressing being changed on his upper left side. His one constant sense was of Eleanor always nearby. Sometimes he could sense her crouched next to him, her head almost on his pillow, and this made him feel calm, safe. He slept most of the time.

A morning came when he could see clearly again, when his eyes remained open, and the sister fetched the man with the copper-wire beard. The blanket was folded down over his chest. He couldn't touch his upper left side. The burning itch of a major incision. A brown rubber tube led from his bandaged arm to a saline drip. To his left, a window gave a view across the river, framing the length of Westminster, all its pinnacles and parapets like an eroding black cliff on the opposite bank. The sky wore a heavy haze.

'You're very fortunate to be alive, sir,' the man with the beard said, observing him over a pair of half-moon glasses. He had a genteel Scottish brogue.

'How long have I been here?'

'Four days. Your spleen was damaged, but the main rupture was delayed. You had heavy internal bleeding when they rushed you in. I performed an emergency procedure to stanch the flow.'

Denham closed his eyes and nodded, fighting a feeling of nausea.

The pain in his shoulder, the dizziness, and the blurred vision were symptoms, the man explained, of the spleen being starved of oxygen.

'That's quite a beating you got. I take it you reported the incident to the police?'

Denham gave a faint smile. To think he was in a country now where the police were on your side and the criminals didn't wear uniforms. If the rupture had begun in Berlin, he realised, he would have bled to death at Rausch's feet. He started to thank the surgeon but was overwhelmed by a series of hacking, dry retches.

He dozed again and was roused only by an altercation near the door of his room. The sister's voice was saying, 'Certainly you may *not*.' A slight scuffling sound, and there was Rex, holding a bunch of carnations and a paper bag bulging with grapes, with some bare stems at the top.

Denham wanted to laugh. 'Flowers? I'm not dead, man.'

'Brought you a bottle of Bass, too, but that harridan just took it off me.'

He leaned over and offered Denham a skinny hand. 'How are you feeling, old chap? You look all in.'

'Don't make any jokes, Rex. I may actually split my side.'

Rex's face became earnest. 'Dashed over like billy-o when I heard. Came yesterday as a matter of fact, but you were in no state. It was David Wyn Evans who informed me.'

'You know him?'

Rex busied himself for a moment putting the carnations in a vase. 'It's, ah, confession time.' He sat down slowly and lifted the creases of his trousers off his knees. 'Evans reports to me. I'm his officer.'

Chapter Twenty-nine

The net curtain billowed in a white arc. Outside, the heavy haze was giving way before a wind that whipped the dark surface of the river, sending a draught of cool air into the room. The sun dimmed, filtered through an ominous sky of sulphur and charcoal. Rex got up and closed the window.

'All those beers and you never once mentioned it,' Denham said. 'Although I admit I had an inkling.'

Rex gave an embarrassed smile. 'Well, I'm relieved. Couldn't say *anything* until I knew you were on board. That said, we would never have made an approach if we'd known they were already shadowing you . . .'

The first drops came down, followed quickly by a deluge, which pimpled the river in a great hiss, dissolving the Palace of Westminster in a wash of grey. For a few moments they stared out the window.

Denham said, 'All this'—his hand gestured to his broken body—'over some missing dossier?'

Rex grimaced.

'Hitler must be stopped, old boy—and soon. Diplomacy will achieve nothing. And the few of us who *realise* that have been looking for other means . . .' Rex pinched the inner corners of his eyes. 'He's a madman, nothing but, yet the diplomats come away saying his demands deserve consideration. The PM is wavering, and you know how many here are sympathetic. The Mayfair set—all bloody admirers—with voices in the cabinet. The Cliveden lot, who've been whispering against Phipps.' He let out a long sigh. 'This Anglo-German treaty Hitler is after—it must not happen. If it does, we'll have paid with our souls for a shaky peace, weakened our allies, and made him unassailable into the bargain . . .' He folded his thin arms and stared into the rain.

Denham couldn't help but smile. 'I'm not surprised the *Times* won't print half your pieces.'

'Think she'll let me smoke?' Rex said, pointing towards the door with his thumb.

'I doubt it, but don't mind me.'

Rex took out his tobacco pouch and poked a clump of brown shred into his pipe. 'The Rhineland, six months ago. Our best chance to unite and stop him—*missed*. He took a gamble, but his instinct was dead right . . .' He shook his head. 'The man has an unholy sense for others' weaknesses, their cowardice. He won't stop now. Unless we make a bold move of our own, and I mean a *bloody* bold move, we're looking at a German hegemony in Europe within a few short years . . .'

'That bad?'

Rex slouched back in his chair, surrounded by curls of wood-smelling smoke. Water poured down the windows, filling the room with a veiled light.

Denham's eyes began to droop.

'Rex, that dossier . . .'

'Yes, old boy . . .'

'Why me . . . ?'

The sound of Tom laughing approached from outside in the corridor. Rex stood up.

'Almost forgot,' he said, speaking around the stem of his pipe. 'Hannah Liebermann is being kept at a sanatorium in Frankfurt called Klinik Pfanmüller. She's allowed no visitors, so we may make of that what we will. Her parents are at home under house arrest. I'm sorry, that's all we could discover . . . That was a splendid piece you wrote, by the way. Powerful stuff. But I fear not powerful enough to dent the steely heart of that regime . . .'

'Then I'll try harder . . . I'm not giving up.'

'Yes, well, get some rest, old chap. I'll see you when I'm next in town.'

THREE WEEKS LATER, on a bright day in the third week of September, Denham was discharged. Tom led him by the elbow up the steps of the house on Chamberlain Street, assuring him that he'd helped 'old people' with the Cub Scouts. Denham's movements were slow and paid for with spasms of pain. He'd lost weight.

Eleanor had transformed the house. Swept it out and expelled the ghosts. The curtains in the windows were new, and there were flowers on the hall table.

'Welcome home, Mr Denham,' she said, taking off his hat and kissing him in the hall. He felt a soft twining around his leg and saw the amber eyes of a purring tabby looking up, a stray Eleanor had taken in.

He walked through the sunlit sitting room and into the drawing room, followed by Tom and the cat, taking in the changes, the smell of fresh paint and furniture wax. Years of living in dingy Berlin tenements had not prepared him for this. A lump rose in his throat.

He stopped in front of a dark mirror in the drawing room, his arm around Tom's small shoulders, and looked at his reflection. His Berlin wounds were healing, with only the ghost of a scar likely on his brow and beneath his eye, but with a livid, uglier scar cutting down his right cheek from the corner of his eye to the side of his mouth.

Later that day, when he was propped up with pillows on the divan in the sitting room, Eleanor showed him his Hannah interview in print. It had been published over three weeks previously. The *News Chronicle* had the British exclusive.

It looked good. And the picture he'd taken of them—Jakob, Ilse,

Roland, and Hannah—exceeded all his expectations. He was no great photographer, but the play of light from the windows that morning in Grunewald had conspired to make a haunting picture of depth and shadow.

He riffled quickly through the newspapers Eleanor had kept for every day he'd been away. The interview had revived Hannah's story in the public eye, giving it new impetus for a day or two. But then worrying reports of the war in Spain began filling the headlines, infecting the national mood, dominating the letter pages, as was the news that Mrs Ernest Simpson had filed a suit for divorce. Clearly the King now wanted to marry the woman and make her Queen.

Within a week the world had moved on. Hannah's story was dead, and as far as he could see there had not been a single reaction from the German government. Just as Rex had said.

He flung the papers to the floor.

Chapter Thirty

While Richard lay in the hospital Eleanor had been busy with more than the house. With some leads from Rex she had written to everyone she could think of who might help in the matter of the Liebermanns. And once she'd started, the list only seemed to grow.

She wrote to the Berlin correspondents of the *New York Times*, the *Daily Express*, the *Mail*, and the *Herald Tribune*, urging them to keep Hannah's name alive at press briefings. She thanked Sir Eric for his efforts in getting Richard released and asked him to raise the matter of the Liebermanns with the German Foreign Ministry. She made pleas to Lord Beaverbrook and William Randolph Hearst, underlining the public interest in the case and calling for their newspapers to adopt Hannah's cause. She appealed to the president of the IOC, flattering his vanity by suggesting the Reich leadership would hear his petitions for the release of Hannah Liebermann.

As the weeks passed and the season changed, the responses to Eleanor's letters dropped like so many leaves onto the doormat: a mixed bag of general sympathy, vague support, and one or two blunt rebuffs. Sir Eric had broached the subject over tea with von Ribbentrop and had been heard with 'cold contempt.' A response from the IOC's president, Count Henri de Baillet-Latour, contained such flannel about goodwill between nations as to be almost meaningless—or at any rate, it meant he wasn't going to do anything. Only Rex seemed to be really trying, but his questions were met each time by the same statement: that Hannah Liebermann was convalescing from a breakdown and was not receiving visitors in her weakened state. Eleanor tossed each letter onto the shelf over the escritoire. At the end of October a letter from Ambassador Dodd arrived. She and Denham read it together.

> *My dear Eleanor:*
> *Life at Tiergartenstr has been most dull without you. Martha, Mattie, and I have missed your company. I can only apologize for taking so long in responding to your letter about the Liebermanns. You'll forgive me, I hope, when I tell you that we have been waiting on responses to petitions made by the State Department to the Reich government.*
>
> *Hitler's reply to our request that Hannah and her family be permitted to emigrate to the States was, I regret to say, a flat refusal. When I tried to get a private interview with him to plead the case in person I was brushed off.*
>
> *There is little more I can do. I am deeply sorry that this news will disappoint. Let us hope that Hannah's fame affords her some protection for the time being.*
>
> *We wish you well, my dear. Martha says she'll write soon. She has been much in the company of a young Russian here in our diplomatic community, which she'll want to tell you all about I'm sure. Knowing well how disapproval only emboldens her, I'm keeping my views on this latest suitor to myself!*
>
> > *Please send my fond regards to your father.*
> > *Yours affectionately,*
> > *W E Dodd*

Denham stood up, put his hat on, and went out without saying a word, but Eleanor read over it again, lit a cigarette, and sat watching the trees thrashing in the wind through the kitchen window. The cat was curled on a chair, with one eye open. A log in the stove shifted, sending a heap of ash through the grate.

Despite their efforts, it seemed the book was closing on Hannah, Jakob, and Ilse.

Chapter Thirty-one

Eleanor never seemed to tire of Tom's company, even when his persistence and curiosity exasperated Denham. On weekends he would stay over and go swimming with her while Denham rested. The boy had none of his father's taciturn nature and would chat happily for hours, so she soon had knowledge of everything from model gliders to soccer's offside rule. More than once she'd called him George without thinking. The eight-year-old kid brother she still missed.

She watched Denham recover his health and grow stronger by the week. At half term he was well enough to take Tom to see the new television mast at Alexandra Palace, driving the Morris Oxford she had bought from the automobile dealer on Regent's Park Road. By November he was working again, writing features for Harry Garobedian. The money he'd earned from the Hannah interview had barely been enough to tide them over, so she was thankful for having funds of her own.

Two matters had preoccupied Eleanor since Denham had proposed that evening on the Hill. The first, her determination to be busy and useful, had been solved with relative ease. With the help of a string pulled by her dad she'd got a job at the United States embassy in Grosvenor Gardens; nothing high level, just filing the voluminous documents pledging plight, peril, or ancestry attached to applications for visas. Most were from European Jews in transit through London to the States.

The second matter was a real headache. Herb had consented to a divorce, but there was still the problem of Reno. In a letter almost as disappointing as Dodd's, her dad's lawyer explained that obtaining a divorce in the state of New York was difficult. Most marriages were dissolved out of state. So she or Herb would have to take up residency in Reno, Nevada, for six weeks, after which the state's more relaxed laws would grant her a divorce. Of course, Herb refused to go, so she would have to, and as she couldn't leave Richard just yet, Reno, and her freedom, would have to wait, whatever her mother said about living in sin.

ON A GREY afternoon in mid-March, cold enough for snow, but not to deter the crocuses from blossoming on Primrose Hill, Eleanor was returning home from work when she saw Mr Blount putting a sign in the window of his grocery store that exhorted her to STEP INSIDE AND SEE WHY SPAIN IS FIGHTING FOR YOU!

A smaller sign announced that the shop was offering Spanish goods for sale and a service to send aid parcels to the Republican cause.

An hour later Eleanor returned with an armful of dresses, slacks, blouses, and suits to donate for Spain to the delight of Mr Blount, the grocer, whose eldest son, she learned, was with a brigade outside Barcelona.

'Are you sure, miss?' he asked, now joined at the counter by his wife, who was eyeing the bolero jacket and clutch coat. 'They're very smart.'

'I'm positive,' said Eleanor. 'And do sell them if you think the cash will be more useful.'

She was turning the corner into Chamberlain Street when the grocer came panting after her, smiling and tipping his cap.

'You left this, miss, in one of your pockets.'

In his hand was a yellowing sealed envelope.

'I don't think so—'

'It's definitely yours, miss.'

She opened the envelope, and a silver key fell into her hand.

'Excuse me, Mr Blount?' The grocer, already halfway down the road, turned. 'Which item did you find this in?'

'Your cream jacket, miss.'

Her bolero jacket. When had she last worn that? Certainly not since Berlin.

Not since . . .

And then it came to her.

The old man awkwardly embracing her. At the time she had thought it strange, even in that mêlée of reporters surrounding them, shouting questions. Now she remembered, and she understood.

Please . . . keep it safe.

'JAKOB LIEBERMANN GAVE you this?'

Denham turned the key over in his hand and examined it under the lamp in the drawing room.

'I think so.'

'You think so? Eleanor, do you realise—'

'I told you. I didn't realise. He said, "Please, keep it safe." I didn't know what he meant, and then he gave me this funny hug, and I thought how weird, but I had *no idea* he was dropping something into my pocket.'

'And it didn't occur to you that what he'd said might be significant?'

'For your information, mister, he had a pack of reporters on him like bloodhounds with only me to protect him, and it was on a day when one damn thing had been happening after the other . . .'

'Fine, darling, but how is it that seven months on you've never found this?'

Eleanor collapsed onto an armchair and pressed her fingers to her temples. 'I have a lot of clothes,' she said in a level voice. 'I didn't try *not* to find it. I'm sorry, okay? I guess it's what happens when you shack up with a spoilt little rich girl . . .'

Her eyes began welling with tears.

Denham gave her his handkerchief. 'I'm sorry. Here, I'll pour us both a whisky . . .'

He put the key down on the coffee table. It was about three inches long, heavy, plated with nickel, and had a subtly ornamented handle, as if it might open a reliquary or a jewel box.

'It's a beautiful thing,' he said, handing her a drink. 'Let me see that envelope it was in again.'

She fetched the crumpled blank envelope from her handbag. The flap had been sealed with a licked adhesive, and she'd torn it open along the top.

He held it up to the lamp, then carefully pulled the triangle flap away from the back.

'Got it,' he said.

'Got what?'

'Look.'

Written inside in pencil, in a small, faint hand, were the numbers *1451*.

'What does it mean?' she asked.

'My guess is that this key opens a safe-deposit box. The question is, a safe-deposit box *where*?' He was still holding the envelope flap up to the light. 'Hand me that key again.'

Eleanor passed it to him, and he held it under the lamp, tilting the silver object to the sharp light. Engraved along the ridge of its rounded handle he saw the words ADALBERT & SONS LOCKSMITHS, ENGLAND.

THE NEXT MORNING they were at the Public Records Office on Chancery Lane in time for its opening, and asked to see the register of all banking houses licenced to trade in England. Together they sat on a green banquette in the reading room and opened it. There was no institution by the name of 'Liebermann,' so they began to study the others, the long alphabetical list of banks maritime, merchant, public, and private.

'There are so many,' Eleanor said.

'You're in the banking capital of the world.'

When no name of any meaning leapt out they turned to the lists of stock brokerages, investment houses, and moneylenders. It did not help that what they were searching for was not at all clear.

By late morning they had almost finished the register. Feeling cast down they joined the lunchtime crowd of print workers and secretaries on Fleet Street, collars turned up and hats pulled down against the bitter wind. For a halfpenny Denham bought a bag of hot chestnuts, which they shared as they walked. Tiny flakes of snow had begun to fall, stinging their faces. The smoke from a brazier, the unseasonal cold, and the drab people trudging the sidewalk like a beaten army all seemed to add to a sense of defeat.

'What now?' she asked.

After lunch Eleanor returned alone to the Records Office to run her eye over the remaining pages of the register.

A dead loss, she thought. By the time she had reached the *Z* entries in the final columns, she had her coat on ready to leave. She closed the register with a thump, returned it to the librarian on the issue desk, and was through the lobby door to the street when something made her slow and stop in her tracks.

Without thinking, she turned around and began to walk back.

She couldn't have said where this feeling came from. Some sense was making her react to whatever she'd seen a moment ago. Years of swimming had taught her to trust her instincts.

'I'm so sorry,' she said to the librarian. 'May I see that register again?'

Eleanor turned immediately to the final page, and her eye went straight to it. Goose bumps rose on her arms.

The very last entry, on the very last line, was for the Zavi-Landau Bank, a private concern whose registered business address was 20 Idol Lane, London EC3. An asterisk next to the name referred her to a note at the end of the entry in tiny print: '*subsidiary of Liebermann-Landau Bank GmbH, Berlin.'

Chapter Thirty-two

If the Zavi-Landau Bank had chosen its registered City premises with the intention of discouraging visitors and deterring business, it could not have done much better than Idol Lane. But for the brass plaque over the bell, no passers-by would have known it was there, even if they had walked down the ancient passageway every day of their lives. The tall Georgian building, darkened by centuries of smog, shared the bend with a draper's shop and a sliver of a timber-framed drinking establishment, from which came low laughter and the smell of stale beer.

The bell produced no sound they could hear, so Denham struck the wrought iron knocker, so heavy he could barely lift it. The blow reverberated.

'Someone's coming,' Eleanor said.

Denham wondered with a sudden embarrassment how they were going to handle this. They had nothing but a number and a key, and no document to prove that they'd come at the behest of an associate of the bank. And so he found himself smiling inanely at the bearded young man who opened the door.

'You have an appointment?' he asked, giving them each a wary look. He wore a black silk embroidered waistcoat, a white shirt, and a black frock coat.

'We've come on behalf of a German client,' Denham began, 'perhaps even a director of the bank's . . .'

The man glared at them, his jaw tensing very slightly.

' . . . whose name is Jakob Liebermann . . .'

The listener hesitated, resolving some internal dilemma, then said, 'Please come in.'

They followed the man into a dim vestibule that led to a small old-fashioned banking hall with a polished wooden counter. Beyond that was an office area of desks, each lit by a green banker lamp. The four or five clerks working there were dressed the same—wearing black silk waistcoats, white shirts, and yarmulkes. One was making heavy work of a mechanical adding machine, whose noisy *tap* and *clunk* filled the room.

The young man showed them into a wood-panelled, window-less salon furnished with high-backed leather armchairs. He turned on the lights, asked them to wait, and left. They sat down, looking around. On the wall was a lithograph of the Temple Mount in Jeru-salem. A small brass bell lay on the coffee table in front of them.

Eleanor said, 'I've got the creeps already—'

'I am Abner Landau,' said a papery voice. A stooped man stood in the door. Watch and chain, white beard, and pince-nez gave him the air of a senior judge. He did not offer his hand. Behind the low white bristles of his eyebrows, his eyes were anything but welcoming. 'Please understand that we avoid using names here for our clients' own protection. Our services are conducted with discretion and, whenever possible, anonymity. But since Mr Liebermann's name has been *aired*, and because Mr Liebermann is not exactly a client, what is your business on his behalf?'

Denham felt himself back at school. 'Mr Liebermann is under house arrest in Berlin,' he said. 'I . . . believe he's given us custody of his assets at this bank.'

'I see. And naturally you've brought a notarised power of attor-ney voluntarily signed by him . . . ?'

Denham blushed.

' . . . Or a deed of transfer putting his accounts into another name?'

'Nothing like that.'

The old man eyed him coldly and stepped slightly to one side, as if to show them out.

'Then perhaps you have no business here after all.'

'Sir, he gave us a key,' Eleanor said. 'On the last occasion we saw him. It was all very desperate. We've been trying to get his family out of Germany.'

'We have nothing in writing,' Denham added.

Mr Landau's eyes narrowed very slightly. 'A key?' Again he studied Denham's face, but the scars couldn't have given much assurance.

Eleanor opened her purse and handed it to him, together with the envelope with the number. The old man wiped his pince-nez with his handkerchief and sat down.

He examined the number and seemed to hesitate, weighing the key in his other hand, as though some fear was being confirmed.

'So I take it you're here to open the box,' he said.

Denham and Eleanor looked at each other. Denham said, 'Yes. But, forgive me, I don't understand—'

'Mr Liebermann's private box at this bank is held under terms that are very specific. Right of access is reserved not solely to him, but also to the key holder.' Mr Landau glanced at them with a curious expression, caught between suspicion and trust. 'And as it would seem that the circumstances he had in mind when he made this arrangement have come to pass, that privilege of access . . . falls to you.' Mr Landau had a question forming, but something held him back. They sat in silence for a moment; then he leaned forwards and rang the small brass bell. The bearded young man who had admitted them appeared in the door.

'Mr Rosen here will take you down to the vault,' Mr Landau said, getting up.

'Shouldn't we give you our names?' Denham said.

The old man shook his head. 'The key holder's other privilege is anonymity. Good afternoon.'

Without offering his hand he moved to leave, but then stopped and turned slowly. In a softer voice he said, 'If you do hear from Mr Liebermann again, please wish him well from me . . .'

Mr Rosen led them through another door. 'Mind the steps on your way down,' he said as they descended a spiral iron staircase. At its base, set into a brick cellar wall, was a massive door of polished steel, which he unlocked with two keys and pulled, using all his weight. Lights flicked on inside, and the gleaming vault appeared before them. They stepped over the wide rim of the door. Two walls were made up almost entirely of large steel safe boxes, about a hundred of them, each with a square lock of the same silver nickel as their key. Some type of ventilation machine resonated through the floor out of sight.

The man wheeled a low trolley from a corner and followed the box numbers along the opposite wall. 'Here we are,' he said, crouching to one knee. 'Box one-four-five-one.' He slid it out, deeper than Denham expected, from the bottom tier—'Not too heavy this one; some of them weigh a ton, literally'—heaved it onto the trolley and pushed it through to a small, brick side room with a low vaulted ceiling. It was furnished with a table, a desk lamp, and two chairs.

'Ring this bell when you're finished,' he said, pointing to a button on the wall.

After he'd gone, Eleanor put the key into the lock and turned it, glancing up nervously at Denham. 'Well. Here goes.'

Air colder than the surrounding room seemed to breathe from the box.

She reached inside and removed a large, dark blue oilskin folder, grimacing as she touched it. It was filthy, stained with grime, and charred black in one corner, as if someone had once tried to destroy it in haste. She placed the folder on the table, beneath the yellow light of the lamp, and opened it.

Chapter Thirty-three

A young man stared up at them, cold, clear-eyed, and fair, wearing a military tunic undone at the collar. It was a charcoal line drawing, made with some care, with the details shaded and filled and the rest a loose impression. He looked about twenty, with unkempt hair, a wispy moustache, and an impudent smile at the edges of his lips. Freckles dotted the bridge of his nose and under his eyes. In the eyes, the artist had captured sadness and vulnerability.

When Eleanor turned it over to reveal the next picture beneath, Denham gasped. The drawing was made on the back of some official headed letter paper, yellowed and spotted with age. Along the top, in a heavy Gothic font, were the words *List Regiment Hauptquartier.*

Eleanor turned the sheets of paper, the same headed letter paper. All were drawings of young men, German soldiers of the Great War from the look of their tunics and caps, perhaps sketched in barracks or the wooden billets behind the line, or in the trenches themselves.

In some drawings the lads looked at the artist with a guileless expression, young faces worn down by premature wisdom, ravaged by the horrors they'd witnessed; others looked away and into the light, smiling with a slight frown, suggesting mild embarrassment. There must have been more than a hundred drawings in all, some made on small scraps of notepaper, but most on the letter paper of the List Regiment. Towards the end of the collection the tone of the pictures changed, becoming more naturalistic in style. In one, a lad lay convalescing from an injury; bandaged heavily around his upper chest and shoulder, he looked impassively at the viewer, a cigarette held in the tips of his fingers. The drawing dwelt on the smooth torso, the heavy arms, and the large, powerful hands. There were several more in this vein. None, as far as Denham could tell, were of officers. In one startling drawing, a crop-haired young man with a smooth face stared fiercely at the viewer, holding wide open the left side of his tunic to reveal a shrapnel wound healed above his nipple; on the right side his iron cross was pinned below the breast pocket. *Like a Teutonic Saint Sebastian*, Denham thought. Heroic, but also something else, somehow . . . A small white terrier dog featured in some drawings, sitting at the subject's feet or being held by him.

Only the final drawing confirmed what the others seemed to be hinting at. It was another young soldier, but this one had on his army boots and felt cap, with a full cartridge belt slung over his shoulder, and nothing else, save for a bottle of beer swinging in his right hand.

'My God, he's—' Eleanor said.

The descending seismographic scribble in the bottom left-hand corner of each sheet would have been indecipherable to a police graphologist, but Denham recognised it. He'd seen it before. On the watercolour hanging in Herr Liebermann's parlour.

'These drawings,' he said, 'are the work of Adolf Hitler.'

Eleanor dropped the final, nude drawing from her hand.

'They must have been made during the war.'

She looked up, not focusing on anything, before turning to him. 'You're *kidding* me.'

The ventilation machine thrumming through the floor sent a shudder up Denham's spine. He remained silent.

'Hitler drew naked men?' Eleanor said in an astonished whisper. There was the tremor of a laugh in her voice.

'He does brawn better than buildings.'

'What are they doing in Jakob's safe?'

The final, nude drawing was the most skilled in terms of its draughtsmanship. Denham picked it up and underneath found some large, sealed buff envelopes, cleaner than the shabby letter paper. There were four of them. He opened the first while Eleanor leafed back through the drawings.

It contained the two-page sworn affidavit of one Fritz Engelhardt, a former colonel of the List Regiment of the 6th Bavarian Reserve Army, notarised in Geneva and dated January 1930. The central passage read:

> Lance Corporal Adolf Hitler served under my command as a dispatch rider stationed in the List Regimental Headquarters at Fromelles and Fournes from 1914 to 1918. The artistic drawings hereto attached were confiscated by Lieutenant Karl Lippert from Lance Corporal Hitler upon the latter's return from furlough in January 1918. Subsequently, the drawings were submitted to me privately by Lt. Lippert pursuant to an application for promotion from Lance Corporal Hitler. I was unable to ignore the evidence of the drawings and as a result promotion was refused, despite Lance Corporal Hitler holding the Iron Cross 2nd Class.

Denham read it again. It took several seconds to sink in.

The next envelope contained a dense, typewritten statement, five pages long, titled Mend Protocol. As far as he could tell, it was a transcription of the evidence of one Hans Mend, also known as 'Ghost Rider,' a dispatch runner serving on the staff of the List Regiment, who had known Hitler between 1914 and 1920. On the third page someone had circled one paragraph with blue ink:

> We noticed that he never looked at a woman. In 1915 we were billeted in the Le Fèbre brewery near Fournes. We slept on hay bales. At night Hitler lay down with Schmidl, his male whore. We heard a rustling in the hay. Someone flicked on his electric torch and muttered, 'Look at those two fairy brothers.' I myself took no further interest in the matter.

He was aware of Eleanor talking about the drawings, but he wasn't hearing her. He opened the third envelope.

Inside it were around fifteen pages of yellowed notes, written on paper headed Pasewalk Military Hospital. Some sort of case notes by the look of them, but the crabbed, obsolete style of handwriting was almost illegible. This one would take some time to decipher. One thing stood out, however. Across the top of the first page another hand had written in ink: *Dr Edmund Forster dismissed University of Greifswald Feb '33. Arrested September '33. Died police custody.* Denham returned it to the envelope.

And then the final, fourth envelope.

It seemed to contain a series of arrest sheets, dating from 1920 and 1921. Mug shots. And pages and pages of witness depositions.

On 17 November, I, Jochen, nineteen years old, unemployed, met a gentleman of average height near the kiosk on the Marienplatz. He remarked that I was looking hungry and asked if I wanted a hot meal. As I had not eaten that day I accepted. He also paid for beer but he himself did not drink. Afterwards he asked me to accompany him to his home, and in return for five marks, to spend the night with him. I had been without employment for two months and there was no heating or food at home so I agreed to accompany the gentleman to his home. Signed: Jochen Krübel.

At the Alte Pinakothek museum in the Kunstareal district I, Heinz Peter, twenty-one years old, a bailiff's clerk, was approached by a man wearing an old army greatcoat who spoke an Austrian dialect. I agreed to go to a café with him where he talked a great deal about a new order of German art that would represent the true virtues of the people. When he saw that I was interested in his remarks he wanted to show me paintings made by himself and books with plate photographs of the German masters which is why we went to his lodgings.

Because it was late and the district trains had stopped running the man invited me to spend the night and I accepted. Signed: Heinz Peter Frank.

On a street near the university in the Schwabing district I, Michael, twenty-three years old, an apprentice sheet metal worker, met a man with whom I went for a walk in the English Garden and then for a meal in a small tavern. When I told him I had served as a private in the war and had hoped to become a sergeant he spoke for a long time about the need for Austria and Germany to unify. He urged me to join a new military-political force of ex-servicemen led by himself and asked if I was willing to agitate on its behalf, because Germany belonged to men such as myself and my comrades. After giving me cigarettes he invited me to his room but did not wish me to smoke there. The man wore a wide-brimmed felt hat and carried a short leather crop. One of his distinguishing features is a forelock falling over his forehead. Signed: Michael Schneider.

The mug shots, both face-on and profile, were glued to each charge sheet. A younger face, only thirty-one, but hard to mistake. The forelock and luminous stare. Arrested for soliciting, conveyed to the cells of the Munich vice squad on Ettstrasse, and charged under Paragraph 175 of the Criminal Code.

'What is all that?' Eleanor said.

'You won't believe me if I tell you . . . I can't believe it myself.'

Chapter Thirty-four

On the cab ride home they held hands in silence on the backseat. Rain came down in lead rods, hammering the roof of the car and turning the gutters into sluices. Shop awnings along the Farringdon Road fashioned small waterfalls. There seemed to be an unending supply of bad weather.

Denham wiped a gap in the misted window and saw black umbrellas clustering around the bus stops like barnacles. He let his forehead rest on the cool glass.

It was as if pieces from separate puzzles were joining, bumping together like ice floes, and carrying him along. And he himself had no power to stop the drift.

He'd been played.

So pleased with himself, that day on the *Hindenburg*, for coaxing and cajoling the Hannah story out of a reticent Friedl. The story that had set him on a trail that led to Jakob and ultimately the dossier. Surely, no coincidence. Friedl was an actor, after all. For the second time Denham had underestimated him and felt foolish.

But why had he chosen Denham? He hadn't given the password. *He wasn't Friedl's intended contact.*

The more he mulled this over, the more he thought how it didn't matter now. The group had to achieve its mission any way it could. The damning dossier was now in the hands of a journalist who could ferret it from its hiding place and exploit it. But this realisation gave him scant satisfaction. He felt angry. He could have been beaten to death, thinking the whole thing had been a dreadful mis-understanding.

THE HOUSE WAS dim and cool. A dripping sound from somewhere in the eaves. Denham lit the fire in the sitting room and sat with Eleanor on the sofa, with the cat curled on her lap.

'Where do we even start?' she said.

'With what I haven't told you . . .'

For the next half hour he explained his unwitting role in the group's mission. How his suffering at Rausch's hands had nothing to do with interviewing Hannah. She had started to ask questions as he spoke but became sullen as the story went on, looking hurt and astonished in equal measure.

'You couldn't trust me with the truth?' she said.

'I couldn't risk it. Telling you now is dangerous enough. British Secret Intelligence warned me that people with knowledge of this have a habit of dying—'

'*British Secret Intelligence?*'

Denham looked away. He was on difficult ground now. 'Our intelligence service is after it, too.'

They were silent for a long time, listening to the cat purring on Eleanor's lap.

'They want it to blackmail him,' she said at last.

'Yes . . . it's almost too incredible, isn't it? Diplomatic threats have no effect. But the dirt from Hitler's past might actually contain him. Do what no army could. Assuming, that is, that the dossier's genuine.'

'You think it could be a forgery?' she said.

Denham dropped his head onto the cushions and looked up at the old grandfather clock behind the sofa. Its hands had frozen at five past ten a lifetime ago. 'It just seems too . . . too great a secret to keep hidden.'

'Who says he hid it? Those guys in the drawings must have had a fair idea of his interest. His officers, too.'

He said, 'If it wasn't for those other documents in the folder, I wouldn't have thought the drawings that significant. Conditions at the Front were so . . . extreme that close attachments were not uncommon . . . and of course, there wasn't much else to draw . . .'

'Come *on*,' said Eleanor. 'Think about it. Hitler's a bachelor who interior-designs ballrooms. And he likes uniforms. And opera.'

Denham smiled. 'I wouldn't think that important either, if it wasn't for the criminal records . . .'

'Not *important*? What's got into you today? If this gets out it'll cause an international scandal, an outrage. A worldwide goddamned sensation.'

The wind picked up again, throwing rain against the window like shale.

'So what's the plan of action?' she said, brushing the cat from her lap and standing.

Her hair was up today, revealing her slender golden nape, and she had on a form-fitting skirt that wrapped smoothly around her hips.

He breathed in deeply. 'We'll give it to the boys in intelligence,' he said. 'They'll know how to use it. As soon as I've studied the documents in those envelopes . . .'

'Would it ever penetrate into Germany? If this got out?'

'In my experience of news embargoes, truth is like the rainwater up there. One way or another it gets into the house in the end . . .'

She sat back down next to him, kissed his hand, and pressed it to her cheek. A log split and hissed in the grate.

'Until we hand it in, *we tell no one about this*,' he whispered.

LATER THAT DAY he opened up the old grandfather clock, adjusted its weights, wound the chain, and was not surprised to find that it worked. His father had loved tinkering with clocks. With the warm tick-tock setting the tempo, he sat at the old escritoire in the drawing room with the envelopes from the dossier spread before him.

The first item, Colonel Engelhardt's affidavit, was significant because it attested to the drawings' authenticity. It also answered, at least in part, a question that had intrigued the European press during Hitler's rise. Why had he never made it above the lowly rank of lance corporal? To be awarded the iron cross for bravery—*twice*—without a simultaneous promotion was, well, unheard of.

Next was the so-called Mend Protocol, which made the most explicit allegations. It was a strange, compelling document, brimming with personal antagonism, which painted Hitler in the most unflattering light imaginable. Someone had interviewed Hans Mend at length—possibly the same man who had witnessed the document beneath Mend's signature, a Captain Kurt Rogel. The date was 30 October 1932, three months before Hitler came to power. An army captain?

Did the army compile the dossier?

Mend stated that he was the author of a book called *Adolf Hitler im Felde*, published by Huber Verlag in 1931, an official account of the Führer's selfless feats as a front-line soldier, by one who served with him. Denham knew the book. It couldn't be missed. It was in every bookshop window in Berlin, and even on the German school curriculum. Yet Mend had given this damning evidence in secret the year after his book was first published. Why? To preserve a private record of the truth?

'He struck me as a psychopath from the start' was Mend's considered view.

In the winter after the war, Hitler had turned up at Mend's digs on Schleissheimer Strasse in Munich, hungry and down at heel, asking to spend the night because the flophouse on Lothstrasse was full. He was surviving, Mend said, with the help of his iron cross and his gift of the gab. On one occasion a year later, in January 1920, Hitler came again, asking to sleep on Mend's floor because he could not go home. When Mend asked why, he made no answer.

There were plenty of reasons to doubt Mend—Hitler, of all

people, wasn't short of enemies, and Mend had clearly fallen out with him—but somehow Denham did not doubt the protocol. For all its animosity his testimony had the ring of truth.

Denham got up to pour himself a whisky.

Most who had known Hitler during the war would have been killed at the Front, but one or two, like Mend, survived and remembered who he was; *what* he was. Maybe Mend had been bought off. The book would have been a lucrative commission.

He turned to the next evidence.

The future Reich Chancellor had been arrested in Munich five times between January 1920 and the end of 1921. Twice at his rooming house on Thierschstrasse, once on the Marienplatz; twice in Schwabing.

Denham leafed through the pages again, the depositions of these young men collared by the vice squad, all pleading hard-luck stories in mitigation. With nothing but hunger and cold waiting for them at home they had accepted this man's offer of money, a hot meal, and cigarettes, and listened to him for hours.

But what of the charges? It seemed impossible that Hitler could have avoided spells in custody. And this in the year 1920, when he was becoming the star speaker of the fledgling German Workers Party. Tucked away at the back of the depositions, Denham found the answer.

An undated note from Captain Ernst Röhm of the Bavarian Reichswehr Information Department told the chief of the Munich vice squad, in the bluntest terms, to drop his objections to the release of repeat offender AH. 'Charges are dismissed pursuant to the intervention of Major General Ritter von Möhl' was Röhm's only explanation. 'Have all files on this case ready for collection by my adjutant.'

So there it was. Hitler had already won friends in high places. Men who were impressed by this rough, difficult man with his iron cross and his talent for speaking and who had found in him a voice for the speechless fury of the masses.

Hitler. Denham was starting to get a loose sense of this misfit.

The Führer is not married.

Now all the innuendos burgeoned with significance. Was this an open secret among Berlin's warm boys?

He recalled the Nazi Party being dogged by press scandals and lawsuits during its rise to power. In fact, the leadership of the Brownshirts—Röhm and those beer-hall bruisers close to Hitler in the early days—had all been warm boys and made no secret of it. They must have known. Röhm had helped make those police charges disappear.

But of course . . .

The hairs on the back of Denham's neck stood on end. June '34. The Night of the Long Knives. Hitler'd had them all shot.

He opened the final envelope.

This one contained the yellowed case notes from the Military Hospital at Pasewalk, in Pomerania, northern Germany. They were dated 1918. So, back to the war. The first clue to authorship was the note scribbled in a different hand on the front page: *Dr Edmund Forster dismissed University of Greifswald Feb '33. Arrested September '33. Died police custody.*

Taking a notebook and pencil from the desk drawer Denham began an English translation as he untangled each word. The scrawl was dreadful—that of a tired doctor writing his notes late at night, his only peace after a heavy day's caseload.

Chapter Thirty-five

This morning a requiem mass is held for Grubitz in the chapel. A depressing, meagre service. I must have heard tens of hours of his life story during our meetings and he never once mentioned he was a Catholic. The men look shaken. His 'accident' has appalled them. They know. Suicide is not a soldier's death.

The cantor sings 'Voca me cum benedictus' and Captain Gutmann is whispering in my ear: 'I've a gift for you,' and I know at once it is anything but. A blindness case. Mustard gas. When I ask why this one cannot be treated on the appropriate ward, he gives me that thin smile.

Later in the mess I learn that the soldier in question refused to allow Gutmann to touch his eyes because Gutmann is a Jew! The man's outburst on the subject (the Jews) being so emotional that Gutmann is pointing to neurasthenia as a pretext for getting rid of him. I am not pleased. I remind him that simply keeping my men from harming themselves and each other is a terrible strain on the orderlies, without throwing a racialist into the mix. Also that my ward NCO is a Jew. But Gutmann pulls rank: 'Forster, he's yours.'

21 OCTOBER '18

First thing today I examine Patient H in my office. He is pale and lean, with a long Hungarian moustache. He is deferential towards my rank.

I ask him a few questions in order to observe him. He tells me he is from the River Inn region of Austria and lived in Vienna before the war, where he hoped to become an architect. He enlisted in the Bavarian army, he says, because he did not wish to serve under the Habsburgs, having suffered great hardship in Vienna. He is silent when I ask him if he has a wife or a sweetheart.

He has no tic, twitch, or stammer that I can discern. When I put a glass of water into his hand his movements are coordinated; there is no shaking. He has no nightmares, he tells me, because he sleeps hardly at all. No outward signs of any disorders of the nervous system, though there is a slightly odd prosody to his speech. He is agitated from insomnia, which <u>may</u> indicate depression. The only observable symptom is impaired vision from the gas. Eyelids are severely swollen and inflamed, as is to be expected. Conjunctivitis will persist for some days. I warn him not to rub his eyes.

I am annoyed with Gutmann.

24 OCTOBER '18

We have a problem with Patient H. The ward NCO, Singer, complains that he is waking the ward at night with his wandering and incessant muttering, which is often very loud. Also, he will not tolerate smoking in his presence and this unnerves the men.

I summon him to my office. My intention is to reprimand him. Standing before my desk he makes a visible effort not to talk, but then to my great surprise he launches into a tirade, his words like hot steam from a boiler. I let him speak. Of course, he has found out that Singer is a Jew. He has a fierce and obsessive hatred for the Jews. When I ask him why, he becomes speechless with rage, shaking almost, but summons his will in an attempt to calm down. I too try to stay calm. His hatred repels me. His voice has a coarse energy to it—I would recoil if I heard it on the street . . . and yet . . . I listen to the whole rant.

When he is gone I realise that I have not reprimanded him. I feel cast down and wish I had not seen him.

27 OCTOBER '18

I do my evening rounds. Without him knowing, I observe Patient H in the ward. The men torment him for his eccentricity and his politics, leading him for a walk in the grounds and abandoning him, or putting meat in his bowl, knowing he is a vegetarian.

Yet I see that he has attracted a few adherents who sit near his bed listening to his monologues. When he's not speaking they spend hours reading newspapers to him. Some papers are proposing a negotiated peace. Indeed, while I am in the ward one such article provokes our blind prophet into a sermon, railing against betrayal. He refuses to be quiet.

I say 'Forster here' to announce my presence and angrily tell him that others have the same right to peace and quiet as he has. He turns his swollen eyes in my direction.

6–7 NOVEMBER '18

Rumours here all week of something momentous about to happen, of the war's impending end. A group of sailors who had mutinied at Kiel have been spreading sedition in the wards. The men are highly agitated. I go to visit Patient H.

I expect to find him spitting fire and brimstone, so I am very surprised that he is curled on his bed, silent, a newspaper torn into shreds all around him. The men leave him alone now.

I stand next to him and remark that the swelling in his eyes seems improved. He tells me simply that he is blind. I remind him that mustard gas does not harm the eyes themselves. With the tips of my fingers I open his inflamed lids, and am greeted with a dead, sightless stare.

Later:

—I cannot get that stare out of my mind.

At 10:30 p.m. I call him to my office, knowing he will be awake. One of his adherents leads him in. I see he is agitated. I half expect him to start raving, but he does not speak.

In the darkness of the room I point the electric lamp towards his face and look into his eyes with the ophthalmoscope. The cornea reflects the light, as a blind eye would. But the eyes are healthy—with no signs of damage.

So I have a genuine case after all. Because I am in no doubt that his blindness is a symptom of a psychopathic hysteria.

I've seen enough of him to know that he can be possessed of great energy and self-mastery when he needs it. And now I find myself admitting an odd thing. I am impressed with him. I think I understand. Unconsciously he has willed himself not to see. He has blinded himself rather than witness Germany's defeat.

Chapter Thirty-six

At this time of morning Primrose Hill was deserted. He peered ahead, glimpsing the bench at the top before it was shrouded again in fog, his footsteps loud in the chill air.

When he was close enough to see the bench again, a figure was seated there, silhouetted against the glow of the lamps, which were still lit.

The figure stood as Denham approached, a tall, dark stovepipe.

'Mr Denham,' David Wyn Evans said, tipping his hat. 'I wasn't expecting to meet you again.'

Denham glanced about. No sign of Bowler Hat Man.

'Let's walk,' Evans said. 'The bench is damp.'

They set off along a path beneath the trees, their footsteps waking a crow, which began a harsh cry above them.

'I assume you didn't arrange this meeting for the benefit of my health,' Evans said. Beads of dew glistened on the black felt of his homburg.

'I've got it,' Denham said. 'Here, in London.'

Evans came to a halt. A stunned pause, before he began walking again at a slower pace. 'How?'

Denham explained briefly the sequence of events. 'For now, it's secure in the bank.'

'When can we collect it from that bank?' Evans said.

'Give me a few days.'

'My God, man. Do you realise—'

'I said, a few days.'

Evans nodded reluctantly.

'Who else knows?' he said.

'Only one other person—and she can be relied upon.'

Evans sighed. 'The sooner it's in our hands, the safer for both of you.'

They were quiet for a minute; then he said, 'You've heard that Sir Eric Phipps has been recalled from Berlin?'

'I saw that.'

'He's been replaced with someone more . . . accommodating.'

'I hear the new ambassador goes hunting with Göring . . .'

'Yes, quite,' Evans muttered. 'Well, replacing our knight with a pawn is not considered the wisest move by some.'

'You mean Winston Churchill and the SIS.'

Evans looked ahead into the fog and gave a signal with his hand. Some thirty yards away the outline of a man in a bowler hat acknowledged him.

'What I mean is that it's more vital than ever that we get our hands on that dossier, Mr Denham, and as soon as possible.'

Chapter Thirty-seven

10 NOVEMBER '18

It's all over!

In a sorrowful speech the pastor addresses the staff and patients in the refectory. Every phrase he utters is a dreadful blow. The war is lost. Revolution in Berlin. The Kaiser has abdicated and Germany is a republic! We must put ourselves at the mercy of the victors, and hope they are magnanimous.

I see the relief on the faces of some; others weep bitter tears, myself included. I can scarce believe it. Were all those lives in vain?

There is a commotion and I notice Patient H stumbling among the men, feeling for the walls. The door is opened for him and he gropes his way along the corridor in the direction of the ward. I go after him.

On his bed, his head is buried in the pillows. He is sobbing loudly, hitting the mattress with his fist.

11 NOVEMBER '18

Like Patient H, I do not sleep. I am exhausted.

The armies are demobilising; soldiers are returning to their homes all over the country. But most of the men in my ward dread the world outside the hospital. They cling to me like a father. Society is in no state to care for them. I continue my duties as if with a fever.

In the long hours of the night I think how hard the peace will be for Patient H. How utterly unsuited he is to a life dependent on the care of others. A life darkened and curtailed, not able to be an architect. Maybe over time he could learn to view the defeat in context, and in the end regain his sight.

On some patients with a hysterical symptom, in particular with mutes, I have used hypnotic suggestion to free their minds from the event that caused the breakdown. But as hypnosis is effected through the eyes, how would I use it to cure Patient H? It just would not work.

Unless . . .

ELEANOR HAD SET out for work earlier than usual. Along with most of the embassy staff she was putting in extra hours in preparation for the influx of American press and guests attending the coronation in May.

She was about to turn the corner into Grosvenor Gardens when two figures in the long line of émigrés waiting for American visas caught her eye. One had on a suit faded to purple by the elements, and a hat with the rim turned up at the front. He was seated cross-legged on a bashed leather case with his head in a book. The other, leaning against the wall next to him, sported a gorse bush of tangled hair and was whistling with his eyes half closed.

'Friedl?'

Two thin faces looked her way, alert. A moment's suspicion, and then Friedl dropped the book and drew her into the arms of his old suit, releasing a heady smell of camphor and stale fish. 'Eleanor.'

'You made it out?' she said, the questions beginning to crowd her mind.

He made an effort to smile. 'I did. And here I am, bound for America. What can I say? Hollywood needs me. Maybe you remember Nat. From the Nollendorfplatz Theatre?' He nodded towards his companion, and Eleanor nodded back in response. She recognised him. The youth who'd tried to slip his arm around her at the door.

'Of course.'

A moment's hesitation. 'And Richard? He's well?'

'He is well,' she said, hearing the coolness in her own voice.

'You've heard from him?'

'Actually, we're engaged to be married.'

Both men looked surprised. Then Friedl laughed. 'Congratulations.'

'He'll want to talk to you, I'm sure.'

'Yes,' he said, colouring. 'Much has happened since we last met.'

Keeping her eyes on his, she said, 'They arrested him and questioned him for three days.'

To Friedl's credit, he looked stricken. She half expected him to make a show of not knowing what she was talking about, but he said nothing.

'Here, let me have those,' she said, taking their application forms. 'Meet me back here at four.' She opened her purse and gave Friedl a ten-shilling note. 'Get yourselves something to eat. Then you're coming home with me.'

Chapter Thirty-eight

I am restless with energy, nervous at what I am about to attempt.
Before breakfast I send for him.

He enters; he is wary and sullen. I guide him to the chair.
Through the window the dawn is beginning to light the room.

My intention is to master his subconscious . . . with an
overwhelming Idea.

I make a long pretence of examining his eyes once more. I tell
him that, on this more careful examination, I can indeed discern
physical injury caused by the gas.

He nods and clasps the iron cross pinned to his tunic, as if to tell
me that he would never feign blindness to avoid duty.

I allow a long silence to intervene. Now, dropping my voice in
the manner I use to put patients into a hypnotic trance, I speak
slowly, telling him that no doctor in the world can help him now.
There is no cure for blindness.

I watch his face fall into dejection, but I continue.

Rare indeed is the man who might overcome such an affliction,
I tell him. But wonders do happen in nature, maybe only once
or twice in the Age of Man—to those whom Providence shows
especial grace, to truly exceptional men whose destinies she throws
open to greatness. Ordinary men she does not see, I tell him, but
you are no ordinary man.

He looks taken completely by surprise. As though I have voiced a profound truth about him, a truth known only to himself.

'Yes.' His voice is a whisper.

'What need have you of medicine if you possess this rare essence, the will to rise to the call of Providence and all the power she bestows? To overcome the damage in your eyes, and use this power to see . . .'

Perspiration breaks out under the hair on his brow.

'How?'

'Trust in yourself absolutely. In your will. You alone can achieve this. See the sun in front of your eyes!'

His hands are agitated in his lap. He stands up; I take his elbow and turn him towards the window, where the first rays of the sun are shining through the bare trees.

'Do it. See the brightness in front of you.'

He is in turmoil.

'I see nothing,' he says.

'Open your mind,' I say, raising my voice. 'See everything. Let your will <u>triumph</u>. <u>There is no limit to your will!</u>'

His breath quickens, and now I see that he might do it. So I shout at the top of my voice, '<u>Now</u>, see it <u>now</u>!'

The tension on his face is tremendous. Then his eyes flare like an animal's exposed to bright light. The room is filling with light.

'Yes . . . I see it,' he says, his voice tight. 'I see it.' He turns quickly. He is seeing the desk, the books, the room.

I breathe with relief. He has done it! <u>I</u> have done it.

Laughing, I throw my hands in the air. I want to shake his hand and say well done.

But he is not smiling. He seems stunned, shaken to the core. His face has turned a dead white.

The large eyes focus on me now for the first time, as if I am a creature in an aquarium. They have a most unsettling effect. I wait for him to speak but he says nothing.

'You have your sight,' I say. 'You'll be an architect.'

My words seem to travel across a great chasm to reach him. 'An architect,' he whispers. 'You think after this total . . . unpardonable betrayal, I would be an architect?'

I know he is speaking of the war. Standing in the light he begins to tremble all over, as if from extreme cold, and his breath comes in short gasps; then he covers his face with his hands and lets out a low cry, as though he is being reborn into the world.

Too surprised to speak, I wait until he is more composed.

Go back to the ward, I say.

Without thanking me, or uttering another word, he pulls open the door and leaves.

In those few moments I was more frightened of him than of my own father.

Chapter Thirty-nine

'It all began when I met Captain Kurt Rogel,' Friedl said.

He was on the sofa in the sitting room, across from a fire Denham had made from the last of the winter's wood. After getting over the shock of finding Friedl and Nat at his door, after a dinner over which the young men had recounted the tale of their escape—on a Danish herring trawler from Warnemünde on the Baltic coast—Denham stood at the mantelpiece listening, with Eleanor next to him in the armchair. Nat had gone to bed.

'He picked me on the Ku'damm, must have been June '32. Invited me to Horchers, the best restaurant in Berlin. Got to know me over a bottle of Pfälzer. Military bearing, Prussian blue eyes, *French manners*. Forty-five years old and with a permanently amused expression. From an old family in Pomerania. Soon I was more or less living at his house in Zehlendorf. Much later, he told me about the network . . .'

Friedl turned his glass of whisky, watching the fire's light through the crystal.

'Kurt was a career army officer. Had been since the war. He'd paid little regard to Hitler throughout the '20s. I mean, there was something just *absurd* about him, so *odd* after all, and his support came and went. But by the winter of 1930 the Depression was biting deep, and Kurt and his colleagues, officer friends, became seriously alarmed by the little corporal. Every time this man spoke the crowd was tens of thousands larger.

'Who was he? The question no one seemed able to answer.

Which is why Kurt and the officers began looking into the man's past. The records of his war service, the missing years in Vienna, all that. Of course, they suspected *something*, and I can't say I was surprised. Ask a warm boy in Berlin back then and chances were he'd say the Bohemian Herr Hitler wasn't as cold as you'd think. The investigations turned up what you've now seen, and that's only what they could find. More went missing or was destroyed. They tracked down Engelhardt of the List Regiment, found some of the Munich boys who gave those police statements . . .'

'And Hans Mend?' Denham said.

'Him, too, the *Arschloch*. The idea was to show the dossier to President Hindenburg and so keep Hitler firmly out of power. But then in January '33 a deal was done behind closed doors, and this great deceiver was handed the chancellorship of Germany before Kurt and his friends could act. That dossier suddenly became a very dangerous thing to possess. Kurt needed someone with contacts abroad whose sympathy was beyond any doubt.'

'Jakob,' said Eleanor

Friedl nodded. 'Jakob Liebermann was invited to join what was becoming a small, highly placed resistance group. He used his banking network to spirit the dossier to safety.'

Friedl took a cigarette from a silver case that sparked in the light. Denham had seen it before. Those engraved initials *KR*, which had made him so suspicious when they'd first met at the Hotel Kurgarten.

'But by the end of '33 the group was biding its time. The dossier was left in its hiding place because they were convinced Hitler would soon overreach himself, take a step too far, at which point the army's support for him would crumble. Or that was the hope.

'But instead the monster's power increased tenfold. It was as if the country was under a spell, as if it still is . . . We decided to use the dossier. The question was how.

'The idea of us blackmailing the Führer was crazy—we'd have been murdered in our beds before we knew what had hit us, along with anyone who'd ever met us. But a foreign government could do it, blackmail him. The British, for example . . .'

Friedl dropped his head back on the sofa.

'For my safety I was not told everything. I was to meet a British reporter who would identify himself with an agreed password at the first meeting. The date for the meeting was the first of August, the day the Games opened in Berlin. With so many foreigners there it would seem less suspicious.

'A week before the meeting, while I was in Friedrichshafen, something went badly wrong.' Friedl sighed, looking tired, and stubbed out his cigarette. 'One of the officers in the network was betrayed and arrested. Under interrogation he revealed the names of two or three others—and the dossier's existence. On that day I believe Hitler himself learned of the dossier for the first time. Kurt got an urgent message to me . . .'

Friedl stopped. Fighting down the lump in his throat had the effect of making his eyes fill up.

' . . . warning me not to go to the house. Then they got him, too. What happened to him after that, I never found out.'

The cat leapt in a silent arc onto the sofa, looking for company. Friedl lifted it onto his lap, and ran his fingers through the tabby fur for a while. The purring seemed to calm him down.

'Who knew the dossier was hidden in London?' Richard said.

'Only Kurt, Jakob, and me. No one else.'

'Go on.'

'You could imagine—how I felt. Not knowing how much the SD had discovered through interrogation. The timing was the worst thing. Because in a matter of days I was due to meet the British reporter beneath the bell tower at the Olympic stadium. That was on the day you and I flew to Berlin on the *Hindenburg*. My task was to tell him where he would collect the key and to give him instructions for accessing the London bank.

'But by then I feared a trap. What if it wasn't a British reporter meeting me . . . but an agent of the SD.

'I didn't know what to do. Then I saw you in the bar of the Kurgarten. A British reporter by himself? I couldn't believe it. I hoped, oh I hoped that you were the one I was meant to be meeting in the stadium—because I had this sense that I could trust you. And after we spoke for so long on the airship that sense was even stronger. Of course, you weren't him; you didn't know the password, but I had to do something. So I acted on instinct . . .'

'You gave me the Hannah story, knowing it would lead me to Jakob . . .'

'Yes.' Friedl seemed to shrink into his clothes. 'And if Jakob trusted you, too . . .'

'He would give me the key.' Denham smiled thoughtfully at the fire.

'If your damned group had given the key to the British embassy instead,' Eleanor muttered, 'you might have saved us all a lot of trouble.'

'Kurt must have had his reasons,' Friedl said, looking at the floor. After a long pause he said, 'Richard, I am so sorry. For putting you in danger. Their investigation of Kurt led them to me. The moment I got back to Berlin I think they had shadows all over me, waiting to see where I led them. It was only a matter of time before they found out I had indeed met a British reporter—and it was you. I should have warned you at the Nollendorfplatz . . .'

Denham heard the soft, whirring chime of the grandfather clock in the drawing room. It now had for him the association of history turning, reconfiguring.

'Well. It's over now,' Denham said. 'Tonight I'll finish that translation. And tomorrow we'll hand the dossier to the SIS.'

'Yes, thank God it's over,' Friedl said and knocked back his whisky. 'Now please forgive me, but I'm exhausted.' He got up, said good night, and went upstairs.

A log cracked and shifted in the grate. Eleanor was staring into the fire, the light dancing across her face.

'Eleanor?'

Still looking into the flames, she said, 'I'm thinking about Jakob—and Hannah and Ilse. What are we doing . . . just handing this thing to the Brits when we could use it to save our friends' lives?'

The cat purred on the sofa.

She pulled her gaze away from the fire and faced Denham. 'Who knows what the Brits will do with it? It could rot in another old safe for years while they decide—or worse, end up in the hands of one of those pro-German suckers. I say we go to the German embassy and make an offer they won't refuse. The dossier in exchange for Jakob, Ilse, and Hannah.'

'Eleanor,' Denham said, 'this is about more than three people.'

'Do you really believe we can do this, Richard, that we can play power politics to control a head of state? Look, we've got our hands on something that could actually save the lives of three people we know. Are we going to throw that away on the off-chance of something greater?'

She plucked a cigarette from the packet on the coffee table and broke the match as she struck it.

'Jakob Liebermann gave us that key, and it's his family that's suffering now.'

After the second attempt she lit her cigarette and blew a jet of smoke at the ceiling. The firelight made a golden crown of her hair, in which Denham's gaze was lost.

'Think it over,' she said, getting up. 'But if we can't use this to rescue our friends, there must be something wrong with us.'

Chapter Forty

What rest I have is disturbed by a nightmare as lurid as any of Singer's. I am awake before dawn, and it is icy cold in my room; I warm my hands under the electric lamp and try to recall the dream.

I am surrounded by men's faces in a muddy trench, wanting to assure them that their emotions are no cause for shame; that they can shed tears and still be men—the things I tell hardened troops on the wards, to their surprise. Then I realise they are all dead, and in different stages of decomposition. The trench walls are made of corpses, heaps of them. I look over the top and see a soldier coming. I can't make him out at first because he is veiled in a green mist—mustard gas. He scrambles down over the bodies towards me, pointing his rifle with bayonet fixed. He speaks to me. His words are 'Voca me cum benedictus.' I pick up a bayonet from the hands of a corpse, lunge forwards, and plunge it into the soldier's eye with all my strength. With that, I wake.

To analyse it: the first part is simple. Its source is the conflict in my own role: between my duty to heal the men and send them back to the Front, in most cases to their deaths. For that, duty does not absolve me.

The figure emerging from the mustard gas is more complex, but it was that which brought the feelings of dread and fear, not the corpses. Of course it was Patient H. Those Latin words, from the requiem mass for the dead—'<u>Call me among the blessed</u>.'

The animus driving H's cure was his belief that he was chosen in some way, that Providence was calling him to a purpose. And I was the medium of his awakening. But it is more than that.

'Call me among the blessed . . .'

<u>Whom</u> have I called?

It occurs to me that of all my cases, Patient H is my only complete success. And I gave him more than sight. For surely, a man who believes that through his <u>own will</u> he has cured himself of blindness will believe he can achieve anything on the face of this earth.

And in the dream I had to kill him. Because he is one who should not have survived.

Chapter Forty-one

David Wyn Evans watched the track as the next race was prepared, his brow set against some doubtful thought. The conversation was not going the way Denham had planned.

An electric buzz as the hare flashed by, and seven muzzled greyhounds shot after it to roars of encouragement from the crowd.

'Slippy Boy's in the lead,' Tom shouted, turning to look up at them.

Evans leaned in to Denham's ear. 'If I'm understanding you right, you're attaching conditions to handing it over—'

'Of course I'm not.' Denham gave an abashed smile. 'King and country come first. But you can surely give me a guarantee—that you'll use it to procure the release of the Liebermanns? Once you've got it you can start demanding whatever you want from Berlin—'

'Dad, which dog did you bet on?'

'Slippy Boy.'

He rested his hands on Tom's shoulders. Evans was silent again, tall and sombre in black like a lay preacher, oblivious to the cheering tiers of flat-capped men around him.

Eventually he said, 'It may not be that simple, Mr Denham.'

He continued to watch the track, but his eyes were distant, reflecting some complex tableau of thoughts, and Denham understood. The SIS had politics of its own, and those prepared to play so ruthless and un-British a game as blackmail were probably few. He would have to trust that Evans, Rex, and whoever else was on their side would not be stopped.

The shouting rose as the dogs sped into the second lap.

'In that case photograph everything in the dossier,' Denham said. 'I will use the original to exchange for the Liebermanns.'

The tall man considered this new tack, tapping the tip of his black umbrella on the ground and slowly shook his head. 'The power of that dossier is its uniqueness and authenticity—and in the fact that we will have the original proof and no one else. Sorry. I can ask, but they'll say no copies.'

Denham felt his spirits sliding. *There goes plan B.*

Evans glanced sideways at Denham. 'Our colleague, Mr Palmer-Ward, is getting most eager to take possession of it.'

'Soon,' Denham said, distracted. He had to think.

There was a great commotion as the hounds tore past in a blur, leaving behind one dog trampled, yelping in the dust, its hind legs broken. A great 'oh' from the crowd. Denham put his hands over Tom's eyes as two men ran onto the track to put Slippy Boy out of his suffering.

THE MEETING AROUND the kitchen table at Chamberlain Street that evening felt like a war cabinet. Denham explained that they were on their own in the matter of the Liebermanns; there would be no help from the British government. Eleanor began to cuss, but Denham cut right to it: the only idea he had left.

'Tell me, Friedl, who actually knows *what's* in the List Dossier—I mean not just that it exists, but what it contains.'

'Everything in it? Only Jakob and Kurt. But most of the officers in the network read a copy of the Mend Protocol.'

'And the Sicherheitsdienst, the SD. They've never *seen* it?'

'No.'

'So how much would they really know about it?'

'Depends what they learned from interrogating that officer. That it concerns Hitler's war record and missing years. Probably no more than that. They would have been wary of learning the details until they'd informed Hitler . . .'

'That fits. I certainly got the impression that Rausch, who inter-rogated me, did not know.'

'I suppose only Hitler himself would be able to fill in the whole picture,' Friedl said.

'Yes, but he would have to confide in *someone*, wouldn't he? If he were to impress upon them the seriousness of the matter? Even tell them some of the truth.'

'Who knows? Maybe one or two very senior SD.'

'Such as Heydrich?'

'It's possible . . .'

'But the SD men tracking it down will know from him how ur-gent and serious this is—even if they don't know why.'

'Without a doubt.'

'They will know it is imperative that they recover it. For him.'

'You know that very well yourself.'

'So if, again for argument's sake, we arrange to give *a* dossier to, say, Rausch . . .'

Friedl closed his eyes. 'Richard . . . where is this going?'

'Rausch is not going to know for certain if it's not *the* dossier.'

'No, I suppose not . . .'

Denham clasped his hands together and turned to Eleanor. 'I think we'll call on our Nazi friends.'

Chapter Forty-two

The German embassy on Carlton House Terrace was being redecorated. Denham dodged the ladders and paint buckets en route to the visitors' desk and handed over a manila envelope.

'This needs to go in your diplomatic pouch on this evening's flight,' he said.

The young male official grimaced, looked at the name and address, and took the envelope by the corner, as if it might contain rat poison.

'We will need to know what's in this.'

'You could open it and take a look if you like, but Obergruppen-führer Heydrich will have you killed.'

The man looked sharply up.

'My name is Denham. *D-E-N-H-A-M.* I will return tomorrow afternoon to speak by telephone to the person named on that envelope. He will be most interested to hear from me.'

WHEN DENHAM GOT home, Friedl showed him a manuscript he'd been working on during his months in hiding. There were almost a hundred pages of *No Parts for Stella*, an experimental novel. It was the story of a high-minded Berlin actress who loses all integrity in her bid for fame. In a series of increasingly dire compromises she slips further down a moral slope, so that by the time she's a star, she's a monster. It wasn't a bad read. It explored the perils of ambition and notions of personal worth, but the lurid, uncompromising style was both its strength and its failing.

'Any good?' Friedl asked, when he was near the end.

'Ye-es,' Denham said, 'but I think it's ahead of its time. It'll need a rewrite if you want to show it to a publisher.'

'Why?'

'Well, for one thing, you've written a scene where she sleeps with all the male extras in *Frederick the Great* . . .'

THAT EVENING ELEANOR took them to hear Ambrose and His Orchestra at the Café de Paris. In the gilded red interior Denham could tell the boys thought it all very high hat: a dinner-jacketed set treating platinum blondes to champagne and eggs Benedict. Eleanor led them into the ballroom, gliding down the semicircle stairs and between tables lit by amber lamps. She'd waved her hair, powdered her face, and wore a new glossy lipstick called Havana Dusk.

'Violins,' Nat said, as though he meant *spittoons*. They found their table with a banquette of red upholstery. 'Two trumpets and only *one sax*!'

'Kid, you wouldn't know class if it kicked you in the nuts,' Eleanor said. 'Let's dance.' The orchestra had begun a pepped-up arrangement of 'Isn't It Romantic?'

A waiter brought an ice bucket and poured their flutes with a flourish while Denham watched the odd spectacle of an elegant American woman being twirled around by a shock-haired, spotty youth who wouldn't have looked amiss on the Petrograd Soviet. Nat made one attempt to swing her over his hip, but Eleanor was far stronger than he was.

Denham's mind wandered.

He pictured Rausch sitting in his office on the Wilhelmstrasse in Berlin tomorrow morning. Perhaps a corner office looking onto that pillared courtyard where the supercharged Mercedes cars pull in with pennants on the hubcaps, bringing the high SS to work.

Leather coat hanging from a hatstand; his desk with two telephones, one for the outside world, one internal—for his parallel world, the vast police spiderwebs of the Reich. He sees the envelope marked *Poste Diplomatique*, the one his secretary has not opened. Curious, he tears the flap with his honour dagger, and removes a single drawing, the very one Denham saw when he'd first opened the dossier—the lad with the charcoal freckles and the clear cold eyes. Something in the fullness of the young man's lips faintly suggests a kiss, a mocking kiss, and a man of Rausch's urbanity sees it.

He is perplexed, but then his gaze falls to the signature, which burns into his eyes. The appalling secret pouting up at him. Now he is nervous. He reads the typed note attached with a paper clip: Denham's offer to exchange the complete List Dossier in return for the safe passage from Germany of Jakob, Ilse, and Hannah Liebermann. There follows an instruction to communicate with him by telephone at the German embassy in London tomorrow at 16:00 Greenwich Mean Time. Rausch flattens the drawing on the desk, dagger upright in his hand, and stares at nothing. His nerves give way to incredulity, then to rage.

Denham had retrieved the drawing and a handful of others that morning from the bank vault. The rest of the dossier, including his finished translation of Forster's notes, he left in the vault ready to give to Evans. For the plan to work, the *fake* dossier, the one he would give Rausch, would contain . . . *what?*

Suddenly he felt the full danger of what they were doing. An insane risk that could end in their deaths. Even if it all went as planned, he couldn't shake off a fear that these marvellous months with Eleanor—the happiest of his life—were about to end.

'What's up, buster? You're as sad as a map.'

She was leaning over him, radiant, and she brushed his cheek with a kiss. Taking his hand she led him to the dance floor, where the orchestra was playing a gentle rumba. A dark-skinned woman balancing an arrangement of fruit on her head stepped up to the microphone, accompanied by three crooners in white tuxedos.

He took Eleanor's fingers in his own and put his other arm low around her waist, breathing in her perfume. Gently he moved his hips with hers.

'A penny for your filthy thoughts,' she said.

'My darling . . .'

'What is it?'

'I don't know . . . I've a feeling things can't carry on . . .'

She looked at him quickly with hurt and fear in her eyes.

' . . . the way they were. Once we've gone through with this. Somehow, it will change us. I just want you to be ready for that.'

She lay her head on his shoulder as they moved to the rhythm.

'Regret over doing nothing will change us far more,' she said.

He smiled at her, though she couldn't see his face. The melody enveloped them in its sweet cadence.

When she looked up at him again, a tear was making a track down her powdered cheek.

They stopped still in the centre of the floor, held each other close, and kissed long and deeply, oblivious to the couples shuffling in circles around them. They kissed as though they were about to part for a long time, or forever.

Chapter Forty-three

The young official at the embassy main desk sprang to his feet when he saw Denham, as though he'd been waiting for him all day, then looked confused when he saw Eleanor. He ushered both of them upstairs regardless.

The embassy's new interior seemed designed to intimidate the visitor and flatter the vanity of the incumbent, von Ribbentrop, who had impressed Hitler with his smooth hauteur, and with his ability to speak French and English, skills he'd learned from his years as a travelling wine salesman. His pompous portrait hung in the entrance hall. The oversized staircase lined with bronze torches gave onto a pilastered landing, where a bust of the Führer was garlanded with sprigs of oak and pine, like some psychotic god of Yule.

The official showed them into a large salon overlooking St James's Park, where the chestnut trees were budding with bright green leaves, and asked them to wait. When he'd gone they were too nervous to sit and paced the edge of the carpet towards the far wall, on which was hung a KRAFT DURCH FREUDE picture calendar for 1937. A family of four waved ecstatically from their Volkswagen.

The door opened and a fat man in a dark suit entered. There was a Party pin in his buttonhole. He resembled a grossly grown-up doll. He gave them a supercilious stare. *SD*, Denham thought.

'Mr Denham?' he said in English. 'I have orders to arrange a telephone call to Berlin for you at four p.m.' He turned to Eleanor with a quizzical look.

'She's with me,' Denham said.

The man gestured to a telephone on a gilded table under the window. 'You can take the call there in a moment. I've been keeping the connection open.' He left the room.

Seconds later the telephone rang. Eleanor squeezed Denham's hand. He walked towards it. It rang again, and he picked it up.

'Hello, Rausch, this is Richard Denham.'

A brief pause filled with static before a thin, high voice said, 'This is Reinhard Heydrich.'

Denham's mouth opened, but words had fled. 'I see,' was all he managed at last, clutching the receiver very tightly.

A quiet, high-pitched bray came down the line. 'You've won some admirers here, you know. After three days working you over my boys were convinced you knew nothing of that dossier.' The voice had the offhand easiness of power. 'You even had Rausch fooled. Either you've got nerves of steel, or he's going soft.'

Under his shirt Denham felt a bead of sweat roll from his armpit down to his belt. He thought of the long pale face in the photograph on the wall of that SD torture room. The tiny eyes deeply set, slanted, bright, and cruel.

Recovering himself he said, 'Well, I didn't want to make it easy for you. No fun in that, is there?'

The soft braying laugh again. 'You're making us a marvellous offer, Herr Denham. The dossier in exchange for three inconvenient Jews? How could we say no?'

Denham felt a dizzying surge of adrenaline. 'There are two conditions.'

'Go on.'

'Rausch, and no one else, is to bring the Liebermanns in a single car to the town of Venhoven, on the Dutch border, at five p.m. next Friday. There's a small hotel called Hotel Mertens, about five hundred yards from the German frontier. I'll be there with the dossier. Second, Jakob Liebermann keeps his fortune. He's not to be robbed by the Reich.'

A long pause.

'Agreed,' Heydrich said finally, 'with the exception of the location. The handover is to take place at Tempelhof Airport in Berlin . . .'

'No.'

'See it from our point of view,' Heydrich said, sounding positively reasonable. 'You are handing over property that belongs to the Reich. It is appropriate that you do so on German soil, where we can be certain of no outside interference.'

'No.'

'Really, Herr Denham, I'm a fencer myself, you know. I'm honour bound to act with chivalry.'

'We stick to my terms or . . . I go straight to the British Foreign Office with what I have in my possession.'

Another silence on the line. Behind the static Denham sensed the Obergruppenführer's mood souring.

'But who will believe any of it?' he said.

The Führer is not married.

Denham did not rise to it. 'I'll expect Rausch at Venhoven with the Liebermanns, alive and well, and no one else. At five p.m. on Friday.'

The pulse in his neck was pounding. Three, four, five seconds more of hissing silence on the line. He was about to hang up, when the thin voice spoke again.

'I was really too hasty in signing the order for your release.' And then: 'Very well then, we go with your plan. But now I must warn you.' His voice dropped. 'Try to cheat us over this and we will hunt you down. Do you understand?'

Denham placed the phone down onto its cradle. He turned to face Eleanor and she ran towards him. His hands trembled, and his shirt was soaked through.

Part III

Chapter Forty-four

The old town of Venhoven on the River Maas was a little over five miles from the German border. Denham knew it from a driving trip he'd made with his father to Germany years ago. It had been their halfway stop for the night. The country along the frontier to the east, where the hotel was located, was undulating, wide open farmland, the strategic sweep into the Low Countries that had made it the scene of countless battles. Without the cover of trees or buildings, he thought, it would be harder for the SD to pull any tricks.

It was a tiring day-and-a-half's journey, driving from London to Harwich, waiting for the car to be winched onto the ferry, and sailing to the Hook of Holland. He drove through the night with Friedl sitting next to him, having eaten a light meal on the crossing.

'Hope Nat's all right looking after the cat,' Denham said, to break the silence.

'He'll manage.'

Friedl was watching the suburban lights of Rotterdam passing in the darkness. Denham had spotted at least four cars with German number plates behind them for long stretches of the road but told himself there was nothing odd about that. They were heading east after all.

It was a leaden, dim morning with a sharp wind picking up when they pulled into the forecourt of the Hotel Mertens at 7:00 a.m. on the Thursday. They had more than a day and a half to spare before

the handover. Plenty of time to notice if there were any suspicious
comings or goings.

Friedl had been eager to accompany him, but on the strict-
est understanding that no part of the plan involved crossing into
the Reich. He seemed determined to share the danger, Denham
thought, perhaps to atone for his unwitting role in Denham's arrest
and torture. But for Denham's part, he was thankful for an extra
pair of eyes and ears.

He absolutely did not trust Heydrich. A hundred times in his
head he went over that telephone conversation. The man had agreed
to the deal too easily. And the more Denham thought about it, the
harder he found it to believe that Heydrich would simply comply.

The most exposed and dangerous part of the plan lay in the journey itself. Heydrich's men might easily have shadows on them as
soon as they arrived in the Hook of Holland. If they could do that,
then they could ambush the car anywhere along the way and simply
take the dossier. True, all they'd get was a bogus dossier, containing
a handful of genuine drawings from the bank vault wrapped around
a sheaf of worthless papers. But Denham, too, would be cheated if
he didn't get the Liebermanns. So if SD agents did stop the car, the
safest thing was to make sure they found no dossier at all, bogus or
otherwise. Then there was still at least a chance of holding them to
their word.

After a long discussion in Chamberlain Street, Eleanor had come
up with a precautionary plan. She would send the bogus dossier by
parcel courier from the US embassy in London to arrive at the hotel
the same day as Richard.

Then she would take a flight to Berlin.

Richard, preoccupied with practicalities, was slow to absorb this
last part.

'What?'

'As a precaution,' Eleanor said, 'to make sure the Germans are
honouring the deal. I want to know for certain that they've told the
Liebermanns of their impending release . . .'

Denham was incredulous. 'How? Jakob and Ilse are under house arrest.'

'I'll get a message to them . . .'

Denham flatly refused to go along with it.

'That's absolutely insane. The Germans know you're involved in this. The Gestapo probably have a file on you. You publicly humiliated Willi Greiser for Christ's sake. You can't just fly into Berlin pretending you're on a weekend's vacation. *They'll be suspicious*, my love.'

'And if I were there officially, invited by the embassy?'

Denham looked at her blankly.

She reached into her handbag and handed him a folded page of newspaper, which he opened out on the kitchen table, puzzled. It was torn from a week-old *New York Times*.

'FBI closes in on Alvin "Creepy" Karpis . . .'

'Bottom left,' she said.

Near the foot of the page was the heading U.S. AMBASSADOR'S DAUGHTER TO WED SOVIET DIPLOMAT with a head shot of a laughing Martha Dodd.

'Good God,' Richard said, holding the page closer.

Ambassador Dodd, it seemed, had surprised the State Department by announcing his daughter's engagement to a Mr Boris Vinogradov, thirty-four, press attaché at the Russian embassy, Berlin . . .

'The intelligence services will have her for breakfast,' he said.

'And look who's got herself invited to the engagement party.'

Eleanor was holding up an embossed invitation with her name inscribed across the top in a girlish hand. 'May first, US embassy, Berlin. The invitation arrived this morning. I'm staying with the Dodds.'

'You're not going.'

Denham spent the rest of the evening trying to talk her out of it, listing every risk she was running. But her mind was set firm.

They went to bed that night without talking. The next morning, when he saw that no words he could ever say would make her change her mind, he insisted she take Rex's telephone number in Berlin in case something went wrong. 'But remember he's a reporter, so his phone may be tapped.'

AFTER A BREAKFAST with Tom over which they assured him they'd be back in a few days from a driving trip, Eleanor said her goodbyes to Denham and Friedl and watched the Morris Oxford depart Chamberlain Street. Then she gave the keys of the house to Nat and left to enact the next part of the plan—the delivery of the genuine List Dossier from the vault of the Zavi-Landau Bank to the hands of David Wyn Evans. After that, she would hurry by taxi to Croydon Airfield for her flight to Berlin.

Denham had telephoned Evans two days before leaving to arrange the details of the handover. At 9:00 a.m. Evans would be waiting in his car outside the bank on Idol Lane while Eleanor retrieved the dossier from the vault. She would hand it to him inside the car.

Denham had described Evans to her, even imitating his Valleys accent. She was warned to expect Bowler Hat Man at the wheel. Partly as a joke for the diffident Welshman, whom he'd grown to like, he'd suggested a double password, more as a dig at Evans's profession than anything cloak-and-dagger. 'No password, no dossier,' Denham said. They agreed on: 'Will I see you at Biarritz this season?' to which the response had to be, 'No, I vacation in Rhyl,' a North Wales seaside town for which the words *drab* and *tawdry* fell someway short.

A sombre rush-hour crowd on the Tube. She stood swaying among men in black bowlers, drawing their glances when they thought she wasn't looking. A valise over her shoulder contained an embassy diplomatic pouch where she'd concealed five hundred reichsmarks for any unseen eventuality; between her feet a small, lightish case contained her clothes, and a single gown. It had been a headache to pack so little, but she would be back in three days, all going well. And in time for the coronation on the thirteenth. Her eyes moved between the headlines in the newspapers open around her. BASQUE TOWN NOW HEAP OF RUINS. *Four hours of bombing.* GERMAN PLANES ATTACK IN RELAYS. *Escaping villagers machine-gunned from the air.* Dear God. Why?

A mood of resignation pervaded London. Not surprising when the papers were filled daily with aggression and atrocity.

A smaller piece in the same papers baffled her but was, in its way, as depressing as the bombs. She had to squint as the carriage shook. LORD LONDONDERRY IN FRIENDSHIP TALKS WITH HITLER. On another: LORD LONDONDERRY LEADS ANGLO-GERMAN UNITY TALKS.

The silver key in her purse. Had she and Richard the means to change all this?

She arrived several minutes early at the bank and was obliged to wait ten long minutes to be shown down to the vault. She was back outside on the lane, with the dossier inside her valise, within sixteen minutes.

No sign of a car.

She glanced at her watch. Her flight was at 11:00 a.m. Not much time. It was cold here in the shade. Maybe the lane was too narrow for the car to wait. Yes, that must be it. Following the kerb to the end she turned the corner and gave a small shriek.

A broad man in a bowler hat was walking quickly towards her. He stopped when he saw her, said, 'This way, please,' and beckoned with a pair of leather driving gloves.

On a wider street at a right angle to the lane, parked alongside a wall in the sun, was a gleaming automobile with whitewall tyres. A Humber, Richard had said. Bowler Hat Man opened the back door, and she stooped to climb in, lifting her case in front of her.

'Mrs Eleanor Emerson?'

Inside, a man was offering his hand. Pinkish face, waxed moustache, and a tepid smile that said *fair play*. A folded *Times* on his lap. Tailored chalk-stripe suit, brown suede shoes, and carnation boutonnière. Definitely. Not. Evans.

'Where is he?' she said.

A small, surprised laugh. 'My name's Channing. Evans asked me to meet you.'

'Why?'

The man raised his eyebrows.

'If you must know,' he said, moving the newspaper to the seat beside him and brushing a pastry crumb from a fold in his trousers, 'he now works in another department.'

'Evans was moved?'

The man continued to smile with patience. 'Yes. Now then, I believe you have with you something that—'

Eleanor glared at him. 'Will I see you at Biarritz this season?'

A momentary flicker in the eyes, enough to tell her of his bewilderment. 'I hardly think—' He stopped.

'You know, uh, Mr Chilling, I think I've left my purse in the bank . . .' She reached for the door handle and pulled down.

'Just one minute—'

'Won't be long.'

She got out quickly, case first, and pulled the valise after her just as he made an ungentlemanly lunge for it.

Bowler Hat Man turned in the driver's seat behind the glass partition, but the car was parked against the wall. He lurched across the front seat to the passenger door.

Eleanor ran for it—back down the narrow lane she'd come from, where the car couldn't follow. Behind her a car door slammed and footsteps came after her—in a real sprint. The valise and case didn't seem so light anymore. Only a few yards ahead: the corner of the lane. She reached it, hearing the driver's breath behind her, turned the corner, and saw the busy street at the end. She saw a red double-decker and a policeman go past on a bicycle. She didn't stop running until she reached the kerb.

A pillar with a golden flame was straight ahead of her. Streetcars whirred past. One stopped to let people off, the clippie calling 'Monument,' and she hopped on, sweating and cursing. Looking back to the entrance of Idol Lane, she saw Bowler Hat Man standing still, looking at the tram, trying to find her in the window.

Moments later she got off near London Bridge and hailed a cab.

'Croydon Airfield' she said, collapsing low onto the backseat. 'And quickly, please.'

For a long while she had her face buried in her hands. *That wasn't my fault.* After a time she found herself staring at the cookie-cutter houses passing on the Brighton Road, gardens neat and colourful, and she marvelled at the twists her life had taken.

An hour and a half later she climbed the steps into the Imperial Airways de Havilland Express to Berlin. She opened the valise on the empty seat beside her as the propellers began to turn, took out the diplomatic bag with the cash, and crammed into it the genuine, complete, bona fide List Dossier.

THE HOTEL MERTENS was a three-storey white box with a glassed-over patio restaurant to one side. In its front two poplar trees had curved with a prevailing wind to point west, like index fingers. *Like a warning to turn back,* Denham thought. A gravel forecourt opened directly onto the main road into Venhoven. The only other building nearby was a large filling station where a line of heavy goods trucks waited to refuel as they entered or left Germany. From there the road led straight up to the frontier, where they could see the wooden Dutch customs house with its smoking chimney, and behind that the German border crossing with a black-, red-, and white-striped barrier and damp flags fluttering.

A yawning girl showed them upstairs to their rooms, which were spartan and worn, with a smell of rain and manure blowing in through open windows. Denham told Friedl he was going to get a few hours' sleep. Then he turned back to the girl, who was about to descend the stairs.

'Does the hotel have a safe?'

She showed him an ancient strongbox in the cupboard of a small, shabby office next to the restaurant. Quickly he checked the satchel's contents before depositing it: £50 in sterling in a large wad, and nearly 400 Dutch guilders for any expenses; his passport, vehicle documents, return ferry tickets, and finally Willi Greiser's *Sippenbuch*, his honorary SS identification. Along with the engraved pocket watch Eleanor had found this item in one of Denham's jackets on the floor of his ransacked apartment.

He looked again at the languid mug shot—the slightly hooded eyes, the duelling scar down one cheek—and his lips turned up in a half smile. It wasn't an item he had any use for, and he wasn't sure why he'd even brought it. But somehow, having it with him signified, preserved, his upper hand.

From outside came the low growl of a motorbike, and moments later the girl was handing him a parcel from London. With perfect timing, the bogus dossier had arrived.

Chapter Forty-five

J ust imagine,' Martha said with a smirk, 'having to explain the affairs of my poor heart to Washington, who naturally suspect *Bolshevik infiltration*.' She linked her arm in Eleanor's. 'No, Daddy wasn't best pleased. Mother's putting her brave face on it, though.'

She was wearing a smart dun-coloured hat with a long feather poking from the top, which, when she turned her head, occasionally caught Eleanor right under the nose. They were watching Martha's fiancé proffering a peanut to a Barbary sheep.

'Isn't he divine?' She had barely contained the squeal in her voice since meeting Eleanor at the airport.

'He's certainly outgoing,' Eleanor said with a sporting nod of her head.

The sheep turned its nose away and scampered up the crag to join the rest of its ginger flock.

'I hear all what you say,' the man said, turning to them and popping the peanut into his mouth. He was tall, brown-haired, and boyish, with Tartar eyes, broad cheeks faintly pitted, and a gap-tooth smile that had a certain charm. He wore a suit of some indeterminate fabric.

'I'm also Boris's English teacher,' Martha said, pinching him.

'Yes, and when are you going to Moscow for learning Russian? Then I am teaching you lesson.' He gave a loud laugh and put an arm around both of them. Eleanor caught a sweet hint of alcohol on his breath.

'Have you set a date?' she asked.

Martha's smile wavered. 'Actually, Boris still needs Stalin's permission to marry . . . We're waiting. Oh, here's the lions' house. I wonder what time they're fed.'

Boris whispered something in her ear, and she slapped him playfully across the chin. Eleanor looked at them with a pang of concern. Somehow, she saw some of her own past mistakes foreshadowed in Martha's little adventure. *I hope you know what you're doing*, she thought.

It was the first of May, and the day was warm and muggy. The cottonwoods and acacias of the zoo, filled with the screams of tropical birds, made her feel they were strolling through some lush estate in New Orleans. The place was quiet, near closing time. Nannies pushing prams; a few soldiers on leave taking photographs; couples walking dogs.

'If you think we're being shadowed, we are,' Martha said with an amused savoir faire. 'But at least we can talk freely here. Daddy has all his important conversations at the zoo. You'll have to be careful what you say at the party later.'

Ambassador Dodd had told Eleanor, in a loud stage whisper during her last visit, that the house and embassy were *wired* by the SD—along with every other ambassador's residence—with listening devices in the telephones and light switches.

'I'll confine my remarks to the weather and the price of gas,' she said.

DENHAM DOZED ON an overspringy bed. He had finally slipped into sleep, when he was jolted awake by the rattling of the windowpane and the wind whistling around the eaves of the exposed building. It was 1:00 p.m. on his wristwatch. Midday in London.

He lay on his back for a while with his hands behind his head, thinking of Eleanor, and Evans.

It's done.

He got up. From the window he saw the gravel forecourt still deserted apart from the Morris Oxford. An enormous goods truck rumbled up the road towards the frontier of the Reich. He saw the girl carrying in a potted tree from the steps and the gale catching her skirts and apron, ballooning them up like a jellyfish around her thighs. The poplar trees groaned and thrashed in the wind, sending leaves and twigs flying against the window.

Chapter Forty-six

Eager to know Eleanor's impressions of her fiancé now that they were alone, and to hear all about Eleanor's own marriage plans, Martha insisted they dine in style at the Café Kempinski on the Ku'damm. 'Darling, the street's Europe's largest coffee shop,' she said. 'It's where one goes to be seen.' There was an infectious gaiety about her. Martha was in love, and it was making her generous.

By 6:00 p.m. the place was crowded with chattering ladies showing their purchases from the KaDeWe department store and office workers in suits. There were a couple of blue Luftwaffe uniforms, and a party of three SS bandsmen drinking tall, frothing beers.

A waiter showed them to a table, and Martha had begun translating the plats du jour for Eleanor when their attention was caught by a stentorian voice addressing the maître d'. To the poor headwaiter's mortification, a tall, portly man in a suit from the 1920s was jabbing his thumb towards the party of SS bandsmen, the wattles under his white goatee shaking. He had drawn the eyes of everyone in the café and didn't seem to care.

Martha leaned towards Eleanor. 'He said, "Seat me as far as possible from those gangsters."'

In a flurry of semaphore among the waiters the man was ushered with swift discretion to the table next to theirs, where he struggled to fit his heft into the cramped wicker chair. The buttons on his ash-smudged waistcoat snagged against the table's edge, and his long legs and orange brogues had to stick out into the aisle, where they formed a formidable obstacle. When he was finally installed he snipped the end off an enormous Cohiba cigar and signalled the waiter for a light.

'*Sofort, Herr Doktor Eckener.*'

Eleanor looked at the man, whose large head was in profile next to her. 'You're Hugo Eckener,' she said.

He turned to her with a weary look. 'Madam,' he said in English. One eye was flinty and piercing; the other seemed to wander lazily. He gave her a grumpy smile. 'Forgive me for not recalling your face. Have I had the pleasure?'

'No, sir,' she said, offering him a light, 'it's just that I've heard so much about you from someone you know well—Richard Denham.'

Eckener's gruffness seemed to dissipate with the puffs of cigar smoke, and he raised his eyebrows in apology. 'You're a friend of his?'

'I'm engaged to him.'

'Engaged! My dear lady.' The old man's jumble of courtesies and congratulations were more than the confined space allowed, and he almost knocked the table over. Eleanor introduced Martha, and a bottle of Henkell was ordered.

'Richard *did* say that you speak your mind,' Eleanor said.

'*Ach*, these criminals would have locked me up long ago if they'd had the guts,' he said. 'I apologise. My meeting at the Air Ministry this afternoon put me in an ill temper. Göring rebuked me for never giving the *Deutsche Grüss*. I said to him, "When I wake up each day I don't say 'Heil Hitler' to my wife. I say 'Good morning.'"'

Several diners turned again to stare at him.

A cork twisted and popped; glasses were filled, and Eckener proposed a toast to the happiness of Eleanor's marriage, and Martha's. 'It would give me the greatest pleasure to entertain you in comfort and style on board a Zeppelin,' he added, explaining that he was staying one night in Berlin at the Hotel Kempinski, before heading to the new international airship terminal at Frankfurt for the first transatlantic flight of the season to New York.

'By airship to New York,' Martha said in a sigh.

*   *   *

DENHAM ORDERED A white beer to wash down the bread, smoked ham, and a great wedge of Leerdammer. Friedl asked for a Coca-Cola. News from the radio in the hotel café could only just be heard over the howls of the gale that battered the building, making the windows tremble and the ceiling groan, as if the room were gasping for air. Rain began to lash the glass roof like falling gravel, and the elderly proprietor who served them kept glancing up, fearing leaks. 'Severe weather warning on the radio,' he said, wiping his hands on his apron. 'Storm blowing in from the Atlantic.'

Friedl had been subdued ever since they'd left London.

'Do you think we're doing the right thing?' he said at last. 'I can't help thinking we're missing a . . . historic opportunity.'

Denham raised his eyebrows. Since taking possession of the List Dossier, he thought he'd had a surfeit of historic opportunities.

'I mean giving it to the British SIS is one thing,' Friedl said, 'but they'll use it to bargain, won't they. Calm down and stop your aggression, they'll say, because we've got the proof in a dossier.'

'You mean they won't destroy him?' Denham said, taking a swig of beer. 'That's *Realpolitik*. The way the world goes.'

Friedl only seemed more agitated. 'You know I'm classed as a *Volksschädlinge* in Germany, a pest registered with the police? He has to be exposed.'

'He will be. The world will learn the truth in the end, and history will judge. In the meantime, peace in Europe.'

Friedl sighed and looked out at an empty landscape blurred by moving curtains of rain. 'I suppose I should be relieved, for my own sake. Men like me . . . I'm hardly helping our cause by naming this monstrous freak as one of my own. What an irony . . .'

Denham looked at him with sympathy. 'You're angry. But you escaped. Soon you'll be in America and you'll put it all behind you . . .'

A bell was ringing in another room.

'Mr Denham?' said the proprietor from the door. 'There's a telephone call for you.'

Denham followed the proprietor into the small hotel office and was handed the mouthpiece and receiver.

'This is Rausch,' said an iron voice.

'Yes, Rausch.'

'You have it?'

'I have it,' Denham said. 'Will you be here tomorrow as arranged?'

'I'll be there.'

There was a click and then a dead line.

Denham leaned against the wall and closed his eyes. *Everything is under control.*

But the storm was starting to worry him.

Chapter Forty-seven

Eleanor waited until dark before pushing her way unseen into the Liebermanns' garden in Grunewald. It was fortunate that she remembered this gate in the wall, flaking and ivy covered from disuse; the main entrance to the house was most probably under police watch, and she wasn't going to take a risk finding out.

At the embassy party Ambassador Dodd had drily proposed a toast to the engaged couple; the Russians reciprocated with gusto, and she'd slipped out of the room just as glasses were clinking and the orchestra started playing. With luck, she'd be back before anyone noticed she was missing.

Outside was a parked convoy of Russian-built embassy cars and limousines, their drivers standing about smoking, and a single waiting taxi. She was heading straight for it when Martha's voice stopped her cold.

'Where on earth are you going?'

Damn it.

The shorter woman was standing under the lighted front porch, a full flute of champagne in her hand. Her sparkling earrings and long, pale blue gown brought out her prettiness, Eleanor thought, like a prom queen.

'Just going to get cigarettes,' Eleanor said, wincing at how unconvincing that sounded.

'What?'

She turned and continued towards the taxi.

'Wait, you can't simply vanish off into Berlin—'

ONCE INSIDE THE Liebermanns' grounds, she saw at once from the long grass, the cracked, dry fountain, and the leaves and branches ungathered from winter how the family's circumstances had changed.

There were no lights in the Gothic turrets of the house, and the curtains had not been drawn. Boats moored at the jetty rattled softly. She skirted around some mossy paving to the building's other side and saw a solitary light coming from the lower ground floor. Carefully descending the stone steps and peering through the window she saw Ilse Liebermann sitting at a long kitchen table with family photographs spread out before her. She was fingering the pearls of a necklace around her neck, her face partly obscured by the cloud of silver hair.

Eleanor wondered whether she should ring the front doorbell, but she didn't want to frighten the woman. In the end she elected simply to tap on the kitchen window, calling gently, 'Frau Liebermann, it's Eleanor Emerson.'

Ilse looked up with a start, and Eleanor pushed her face to the glass so that the old woman could see who it was. She got up stiffly and opened the kitchen's garden door.

'Fräulein Eleanor?' she said, still startled.

Eleanor put her arms around the old woman and embraced her. 'I've come to see that you're ready for your journey tomorrow. Have you heard from Hannah?'

The woman's forehead creased into puzzled lines. 'Yes, my dear. I mean no. Thank you.' She had a question forming, but said, 'Come upstairs and see Jakob. You're very welcome here.'

She switched on a light and led Eleanor up the stairs to the grand sitting room, where Hannah had given the interview last summer.

'Jaku, we have a visitor,' Ilse called.

Eleanor thought this must be a different room. Its walls were bare, and a vase of dried flowers stood where the dream blue horses had galloped over the mantelpiece. Then she noticed, with a feeling of depression, the geometric outlines of soot on the wallpaper where the collection had hung. Jakob Liebermann was sitting on the divan surrounded by piles of documents, which he was scrutinising, pencil in hand, through wire eyeglasses. The yellow light from a table lamp illuminated one side of his face, where the port-wine stain marked his hollow cheek.

The old man put his papers down and struggled to his feet. 'I am exceedingly surprised and delighted to see you, Fräulein Eleanor,' he said in his deep, resonating voice, and took both her hands in his. 'Though it is not at all safe for you to be here. What brings you back?'

He went to pour them all a cognac from the walnut drinks cabinet. They were both looking gaunt and pale, Eleanor thought.

'I wanted to see that you're ready for your long journey to the border,' Eleanor said.

Jakob put down the bottle and gave her a quizzical look. 'How is it you know about that?' he asked.

'Richard arranged it all. He negotiated with Heydrich.'

Jakob and Ilse met each other's eyes.

'Why would Herr Denham do something like that?' said Ilse. There was a hard undertone to her voice.

'He's getting you out,' said Eleanor. 'He's made a deal . . .' She looked right at Jakob. 'We got the dossier.'

The confusion on his face seemed to still. After a long pause, he said, 'Go on.'

'You're being taken over the border to the Netherlands, then to England. Hannah, too. Isn't there an official car coming to collect you early tomorrow morning?'

'The Netherlands?' Jakob stared at her, incredulous. 'An SS car is indeed coming for us, but on Saturday, the day after tomorrow, at seven a.m. It is taking us to Basel on the Swiss border.'

*   *   *

DENHAM WATCHED FROM the window of his room as the storm gathered pace. Ragged black clouds tore across the darkening sky. The gale blew unhindered over the bare land, picking up clods of earth and bark and gravel.

Suddenly a series of cracks like a twenty-one-gun salute, and he saw the farthest poplar tree topple, splintering with a slow, woody groan as it came down on the electricity cables. Sparks fell to the ground, and the lights in the hotel went out.

'BASEL?' ELEANOR TOLD herself to breathe to allay panic. She sat down slowly on the sofa.

'We know nothing about a deal,' said Jakob, shaking his head and handing her a cognac. 'My Swiss lawyer informed the SS that he would only transfer my accounts to them if Ilse and I attend in person to sign the documents in his office in Basel. He wants to make sure we are not being forced against our will. Of course, there will be SS men accompanying us all the way . . . to make sure there's no slip of the pen. Then they are bringing us back home.'

'But Richard is waiting for you at the border in Holland tomorrow afternoon,' Eleanor said, struggling not to shout, the questions beginning to cluster in her head. 'And Heydrich—he agreed you could keep your fortune . . .'

'I think you know the types we're dealing with,' Jakob said, sounding infinitely tired. 'Clearly, you have been deceived. As to the money, I have no choice, and have accepted as much. The authorities demand extortionate sums each month in fees for Hannah's confinement at a sanatorium in Frankfurt. I am turning over some accounts to them in *compensation* for the cost of her *treatment*,' he said with a feeble attempt at irony. He knocked back his cognac and sighed, staring into the lamp. 'So . . . the dossier found you in the end . . .'

'But there is one good thing,' Ilse said. 'We will be allowed to visit her on the way there. We are breaking the journey at Frankfurt. We have not seen her since last summer.'

Eleanor swirled the cognac around in her glass. She got up and paced the room, looking into the ghostly spaces where the pictures had been. She picked up china ornaments and put them down again carefully. When she turned back to Jakob and Ilse, they were watching her with an odd expression, she thought, almost with a kind of humour and admiration. Perhaps she'd done something to remind them of their daughter.

'All right,' she said firmly. 'We're going to try something. To put a stop to this. You say you're being driven to Frankfurt on Saturday, the day after tomorrow. How many hours is that from here?'

AN HOUR LATER she was riding through the warm Berlin night, her taxi speeding through the deserted streets of the Grunewald, along the Königsallee to the floodlit Hotel Kempinski on the Ku'damm, still swarming with traffic, diners at café tables, departing movie-theatre crowds, and smart girls linking arms with men in epaulettes. She flashed a smile at the hotel commissionaire and was directed by the receptionist to a room on the fourth floor. A puzzled Dr Eckener opened the door in a long silk bathrobe and slippers. The butt of a cigar was wedged into the side of his mouth.

'Dr Eckener,' Eleanor said, with the adrenaline singing in her chest. 'May I talk to you?'

Chapter Forty-eight

The morning light exposed the devastation wrought by the storm. The Venhoven road was strewn with branches and litter, and what little hedge and vegetation there was on the farmland along the frontier had been flattened. The proprietor apologised. There would be nothing hot for breakfast, as power was still cut. The telephone lines were down, too.

Denham checked that the Morris Oxford had come through the night unscathed, cleaned the windscreen, filled the tank with a petrol can from the filling station, then took the blankets from the boot to make the backseat comfortable for the arrivals. After that he returned to the hotel café to wait until the appointed hour. Five p.m. allowed plenty of time for the SD to bring Hannah from Frankfurt and the Liebermanns from Berlin. He wanted to know how far the storm had reached and whether it would stop them getting there, but there was no radio and no news.

'THE OPERATOR SAYS the lines are down,' Martha said, turning to Eleanor in the hall at Tiergartenstrasse. She still had the telephone to her ear.

Eleanor felt her panic rising. How the hell was she going to warn him? Her first thought had been that the SD wouldn't turn up for their meeting with Richard. A half second later she'd realised with a sickening jolt that they certainly would. They thought he had the damned dossier.

'Look at you, you're a nervous wreck,' Martha said, sounding irritable. Again she pressed a cold flannel to her forehead. Martha had a hangover, and Eleanor's crisis was probably the last thing she needed. 'I don't know *what* is going on but I wish you'd tell me. If you and Richard are in some sort of trouble—'

'There must be a radio mast at Venhoven,' Eleanor said, her breath fading from her voice.

She sat down on the hall chair and felt herself crumple. When she looked up, Martha was handing her the cold flannel. She took it and dabbed her eyes and swollen face, breathed in, and slowly composed herself.

'How about a walk in the zoo,' she said. 'You're right. I've got some explaining to do.'

BY LUNCHTIME THE rain had started again, coming down in even strokes. Denham paid the hotel bill, retrieved his belongings from the safe, and paced the deserted café, watching the road to the frontier while Friedl sat at a table reading Hemingway's latest, *To Have and Have Not*.

'What's it like?' Denham asked.

Friedl glanced up. 'A lot better than *No Parts for Stella*.'

Every two minutes Denham rose from his chair in agitation.

Finally, with less than an hour left before the appointed time, he could bear it no longer.

'Let's wait outside,' Denham said. 'Sitting in here is trying my nerves.'

They stood on the wet gravel forecourt next to the car, all packed and ready to go. Denham had a mounting sense of dread and returned to the hotel to use the lavatory.

At a few minutes before five they spotted a large black Mercedes-Benz, sleek with rain, approaching the frontier from the German side.

They watched as the striped barrier was raised and the Mercedes proceeded, pausing at the Dutch customs house. With a flutter of nerves Richard opened the car and took out the old satchel in which he'd placed the bogus dossier. They could see the tiny figure of a customs official speaking into the passenger window, taking the passports to check—another minute—then waving the car on. Now it sped on down the road towards them, a flash of sun catching the chrome of its fender.

Behind them was the sound of someone panting.

They turned to see a lad getting off a bicycle. He had been cycling into the wind. He took his cap off, wiped his brow with his sleeve, smiled, and said something to them in Dutch, then walked up to the hotel, taking an envelope from his shoulder bag.

The Mercedes was about two hundred yards away. They could hear the growl of its engine descending through the gears.

'Hallo.'

The proprietor was waving from the steps of the hotel and pointing at them, and the lad was ambling back in their direction, pushing his bicycle and holding out the telegram envelope. Denham took it from him and tore it open. The printed words struck a series of hard chimes in his head.

ITS A TRAP CONTACT DODDS URGENT

'Get in the car,' he shouted. *'Now.'*

Friedl didn't ask questions. They jumped in.

Too late.

The black Mercedes was turning into the gravel forecourt. By instinct both of them slunk low into their seats, hiding behind the rain-beaded windscreen. The Mercedes' long running board, polished bodywork, hubcaps, and taillights passed slowly in front of them like a hearse, purring towards the hotel building. It came to a halt, and all four doors opened at once. Four men in black leather coats jumped out and ran to the door of the hotel. The one in the lead, leaping up the steps, held a Luger in his hand.

Denham turned the key in the ignition. The starter motor whined and died.

'Go, go, go,' Friedl shouted, hitting the dashboard with the palm of his hand.

Another attempt, and a metallic strangle.

Denham tried again. The engine fired twice and spluttered into life. He revved, then released the hand brake, and the car shot forwards. Swinging the steering wheel they slewed out of the forecourt, throwing up a hail of gravel, and started turning right, towards Venhoven.

Suddenly a thundering blast of horns and a heavy goods truck was heading right at them. The car was too far into the road to brake and stop. In a reflex action Denham pulled the steering wheel left, swerving the car round with a screech of the tyres.

'Not to the *border*,' Friedl shouted, his hands clutched to the sides of his head.

'That truck's right behind us,' Denham said. 'By the time I turn around the Germans will be out of the hotel and looking to see where our car went.'

'Oh, *shit*.'

The frontier was looming before them, flags flying.

'I'm wanted by the SD in Germany,' Friedl said, his voice tight with terror.

In the rearview mirror Denham saw one of the leather coats come out from the hotel, then another. Both were looking in the opposite direction, along the road into Venhoven, but then the truck obscured the view. With a little luck, thought Denham, they had not seen which way the car had gone.

The Dutch border guard waved them through with only a glance at their passports. As he slowed for the German *Kontrolle* Denham struggled for breath. 'Think of it this way,' he said, as much to calm himself as Friedl, 'we've gone in the one direction they won't expect us to go.'

There seemed to be a Friday evening laxness at the barrier. One of the inspectors made a remark that drew laughter from the other. Denham handed over their passports with a smile.

'What's the purpose of your visit?' said the man through the passenger window, still grinning from some joke.

'Visiting friends for the evening in München-Gladbach,' Denham said as casually as he could. The inspector disappeared into the *Kontrolle* with the passports.

'It's a rural crossing,' Denham said in a low voice. 'They won't be on the lookout for you going in.'

'And coming out?'

A minute later the man emerged with their passports stamped and handed them back through the window. '*Wilkommen im Deutschen Reich—*'

The striped barrier was raised, and they drove on beneath a sign painted with an enormous black eagle, its claws splayed.

Chapter Forty-nine

In less fraught circumstances Eleanor might have found comedy in the mounting amazement on Martha's face. As soon as they had reached the zoo she told her everything—or almost everything. The dangerous truth of the List Dossier, hidden in her case in the bedroom at Tiergartenstrasse, she had kept to herself, telling Martha only that the exchange involved the return of some munitions plans. When she explained the SD trap in which Richard was sitting, Martha's mouth fell open, timed perfectly with a squawk from a nearby cockatoo. But after a few stunned seconds, she showed a resolve that Eleanor would forever after admire, and saved her questions until they'd run to the embassy and warned Richard by radio telegram.

What Eleanor told her afterwards in the embassy garden, where they'd gone for a calming cigarette, astonished her even more, if that were possible.

'How do you plan to do *that*?' she shrieked.

'I'll hire a car and drive?' Eleanor said dubiously.

Martha lowered her voice. 'Darling, this isn't like last August, when there were thousands of foreigners here. You're conspicuous.'

Eleanor was about to argue, but she knew Martha was right. And Richard had more than warned her.

They were both quiet for a minute, smoking with quick, deep drags.

'We'll go in Mother's car,' Martha said suddenly. 'It's less suspicious if I'm with you . . .'

'Oh, no, Martha,' Eleanor said, alarmed.

'. . . I'll tell Dad we're touring the new autobahn . . .'

Eleanor grabbed her friend's elbow. 'You are not getting involved in this.'

WITHIN MINUTES OF crossing into Germany Denham turned off the main route east and onto a sequence of minor roads, still strewn with branches and mud from the storm. They drove through villages with steep gabled houses, neat red-brick churches, and rolling farmland. The most glaring difference from the Netherlands, only a mile away, was the signs on the outskirts to each town and village, of warning. JEWS NOT WELCOME IN KALDENKIRCHEN; JEWS MUST NOT STOP IN HÖLST! Some villages proclaimed themselves JUDENREIN—pure of Jews.

If the SD had seen them head to the frontier, then their head start on that Mercedes-Benz was only a matter of minutes. The *Kontrolle* inspector would confirm that they'd passed into Germany. Denham told himself that this wasn't necessarily a complete catastrophe. There were some factors in his favour: he spoke the language; he knew the country. And Eleanor was here. But the truth was he knew there were dire factors against them. Friedl kept a lookout on the road behind but saw no one on their tail.

They'd been double-crossed by Heydrich. Of course they had. How did he ever think they wouldn't be? But he was consoled by one thought: it had gone wrong for Heydrich, too.

At the market town of Viersen, some fifteen miles from the border, Denham parked in a quiet street behind a church just off the town square, taking only the satchel with his documents and passport. May Day banners with emblems of spades and corn sheaves hung dripping from the lampposts.

He found a telephone booth in the local hotel—the Westfalen-Stübchen. 'They're still fixing the lines,' the landlord said, drawing beer into a tall glass. 'But you might be in luck.'

Denham called the Dodds' number at Tiergartenstrasse. To his surprise, Eleanor answered, and almost immediately.

'Oh *Budd*, darling, I'm *so* glad to hear from you. Sidney Dean is here, too. He's listening on the extension. How are you, dear?'

'Safe and well at the moment. Just came back east, but you know how it is. My old creditors are after me.'

'You're back *east*? Oh, uh, how are you fixed tomorrow, sweetheart? Martha and I are having a reunion with Lester and Eileen Linderhofer and their daughter in Hamburg. It would be a blast if you could make it. They'd love to see you.'

'Hamburg.'

'Yes, you remember. We discussed it that day we had the *picnic* during the Olympics. It'll just be a quick visit; then I thought we'd all take off together, you know, somewhere with a change of air.'

'I'll be there.'

'I'm so pleased. It's been arranged. Hotel Hamburger Hof at six p.m. Bye, Budd.'

'Bye, Eleanor. Bye, Sidney.'

Denham put the telephone down in a daze.

Friedl was waiting for him outside the telephone booth, chewing a bread roll with cheese. 'The baker over the road gave me these for free,' he said with his mouth full. 'It's the end of the day.' He offered one to Denham from a paper bag.

They walked out of the hotel bar just as a local Brownshirt Sturmführer was entering, rubbing his hands, ready to begin the weekend's drinking. He smiled at them both with a leery red face. 'Heil Hitler!'

Quickly crossing the town square towards the church, Denham explained what Eleanor had told him.

'Hamburg!'

'Ye-es . . .' Denham hesitated. And then it came to him. 'It's plaincode,' he said, remembering that far-off picnic lunch they'd shared in the sunshine after watching Hannah fence.

'Your frankfurter looks nicer than my hamburger . . .'

'She means Frankfurt, that's what she was trying to tell me. She couldn't say it because the SD had wired the telephone. What's the grand hotel in Frankfurt?'

'Frankfurter Hof.'

'We're meeting her there at six p.m. tomorrow.'

'That's a long way,' Friedl said, kicking a pebble.

'We're going to have to trust her. She was shocked to learn that we're in Germany but I think she may have a way out . . . We could drive to Cologne tonight—that's not so far—then take the train from there to Frankfurt tomorrow morning. But we'll have to ditch the car as soon as it's light. British number plates will be like fresh meat to a police dog.'

'But why Frankfurt?'

'It's a big transport hub, I guess, and because Hannah and her parents are going to be there. Don't ask me why or how.'

They turned the corner into the narrow street behind the church where they'd left the Morris Oxford, and stopped dead.

Two policemen in green Orpo uniforms were on either side of the car, one of them crouched with his hand to the side window to shield the light, looking inside. The Orpo wagon was parked behind it.

Denham grabbed Friedl's arm and together they spun on their heels and walked briskly back the way they had come.

'Did you take your passport out?' Denham said.

Friedl nodded and patted his breast pocket.

'They'll have alerted the local stations. If they've got our car, then they'll expect us to be on a train or a bus out of here . . .'

'So we steal a car,' Friedl said. They were back in the town square.

'Isn't that easier said than done?'

'We have a choice of three.'

Parked in front of the Hotel Westfalen-Stübchen were a rusted Citroën, a newish, dark blue Adler Standard 6, and a large farm truck with empty churns on the back.

Friedl walked smartly to the driver's door of the Adler and opened it. 'Who locks their car in a place like this? Get in.'

Denham threw the satchel into the passenger side and jumped in. Friedl felt in the glove compartment, then ran his hand under the dashboard, then under his seat. 'They'll be here somewhere . . .'

'Hurry.' The two Orpo men walked a few feet past the front of the car and entered the hotel.

'Hey, if I'd left it to you we'd still be out there like rabbits in a field.'

He pulled down the shade, and the keys fell into his lap.

The starter motor fired the engine at once, and he reversed the car smoothly into the square. 'German engineering,' he said.

'You've done this before.'

Friedl looked ahead, his mouth grim, his eyes determined.

'Not much petroleum,' he said, 'but maybe enough to get us to Cologne. See if there's a road map in here.'

Denham explored the contents of the glove compartment and found that day's *Völkischer Beobachter*, a Party membership book with dues paid, and some group photos from a Strength Through Joy Rhine cruise.

'Marvellous,' he said. 'We've stolen that Brownshirt's car.'

Evening was drawing in as they turned onto the Cologne road, the sky a peach colour after the storm, with feathered, golden clouds.

It was after 11:00 p.m. when they saw the lights of Cologne's suburbs winking in the distance. Friedl pulled over into a farm track. They tried dozing for a couple of hours in the car without much success. Denham knew he had to address their next, most immediate problem: money. They had no reichsmarks, and he couldn't risk entering a bank in the morning and producing his passport to exchange currency. He got out and opened the boot of the Adler on the off chance it contained sequestered cash, but instead found something almost as useful.

'You're not fat enough for this,' he said to Friedl, 'but it might look all right with the belt tightened.' Friedl turned to see Denham holding up the Brownshirt's pressed, tailored, single-breasted, light brown dress uniform. 'Think you could walk like a Nazi for a day?'

AT 6:00 A.M. they abandoned the Adler beneath the Gothic shadows of St Kolumba on the Herzogstrasse and walked through the bright, fresh morning along Cologne's old city streets towards the Hauptbahnhof, the city's main station. Denham was wearing his grey wool-flannel three-piece suit and a hat, with no luggage except an old satchel. Friedl walked with his hands behind his back in a pair of tight-fitting squeaky brown jackboots, enormous loose breeches, and a tunic pleated around his waist with a belt.

Chapter Fifty

M artha gripped the steering wheel of her mother's russet brown Hanomag with a pair of driving gloves.

For all her misgivings about having Martha along, Eleanor felt pride in this woman who had refused to be dissuaded. 'If we save three people,' Martha had said with an airy sense of her own immunity, 'it's something that just has to be done.' And for the first time trust, as unexpected as friendship, had come between them. The fact that Martha was clearly enjoying herself was beside the point.

She glanced at Eleanor. 'Put your dark glasses on.'

They had arrived in Grunewald at 6:45 a.m. and parked at the end of Winklerstrasse, inconspicuous among the other cars. Soon, they saw a dark grey BMW with an 'SS-' number plate, almost camouflaged by the half-tones beneath the trees, gliding towards the Liebermann house at number 80. Jakob and Ilse must have been waiting inside the gate, because they emerged almost immediately and got into the backseat of the car. The door was held open for them by an unsmiling, porcine man dressed in a seersucker jacket and walking breeches, as if for a hike. He slammed it shut after them and adjusted the passenger seat and mirrors in preparation for the long journey across the country to Frankfurt, and from there to Basel in Switzerland. A young SS man was driving.

Martha started the engine and moved off at a discreet distance, following the BMW through the tree-lined suburbs of Dahlem, Zehlendorf, and Kleinmachnow until Berlin became sparser and the car passed up onto the new orbital autobahn. Soon it turned off near Lehnin, and twenty minutes after leaving Winklerstrasse they were driving at top speed on Hitler's broad new superhighway heading southwest.

'Isn't this thrilling?' Martha cried.

Perspective and scale changed on the great road, making the scenery vaster and the objects on the human scale—the farmhouses, tractors, and telegraph poles—smaller, like models on a railway set. Martha managed to overtake a Deutsche Post truck, but it was soon obvious that the 1930 Hanomag's vertical windscreen and two-cylinder engine weren't designed for the velocities now possible, and they watched the powerful BMW speed away from them, accelerating up the distant slope of the autobahn like a grey billiard ball. Eleanor hoped that Ilse and Jakob would think of something—anything—to slow the progress of that car.

'At least we know where they're going,' said Martha. 'What's the name of the place again?'

'Klinik Pfanmüller,' said Eleanor. Finding in her handbag the piece of paper Ilse had given her, she added, 'Bockenheimer Land-strasse, Frankfurt-am-Main.'

Jakob and Ilse had told her that Hannah's letters from the sanatorium were so brief and vague that they feared she was being kept under sedation, until one letter in January thrilled them and gave them hope. Hannah explained that she was healthy and well and that she'd befriended someone who'd agreed to post her letter, which would otherwise be censored and returned to her by Dr Pfanmüller, who had complete charge of her. She had everything she needed, but was isolated in the 'Haus Edelweiss' part of the complex and treated like a royal prisoner, not permitted to talk to other patients or take her meals with them. At night her door was locked; the grounds patrolled; the gates guarded. On the one occasion she'd protested she was given electrotherapy and sedated for two days. She took exercise but, as a Jew, was not permitted to use the swimming pool. Doctors injected her daily with vitamins, gave her mineral supplements and mineral-water baths, and kept her on a dairy-free diet with plenty of raw spinach, so she was in good condition. All this was to maintain the fiction that she was a patient in need of a cure, and so she was given everything a luxury sanatorium could offer. Although Dr Pfanmüller told her she'd suffered a mental breakdown, her treatment did not include any form of psychoanalysis. He seemed to take satisfaction in telling her that the interpretation of dreams and the analysis of the unconscious mind were decadent Jewish ideas with no place in modern medicine. She had the impression there were other inmates of the Haus Edelweiss who, like her, the authorities had deemed it impolitic to put in a KZ. Her own outlook was uncertain. She feared that they were simply waiting for her name to fade in the world's memory before moving her to a women's camp. In the meantime, she had her health.

'What exactly is the plan when we reach the sanatorium?' said Martha.

'I'm still working on it,' Eleanor said, feeling the knot tighten in her stomach.

The List Dossier was in her valise in the trunk of the car.

'Whatever our plan, it'll only succeed if that car hasn't left by the time we get there,' she said. *And I hope to God Richard understood what I meant in that telephone call.* She was afraid something terrible had happened to make him cross into Germany.

BENEATH THE HIGH wrought iron arches of the Cologne Hauptbahnhof, a wagon-lit had just arrived from Paris. Yawning passengers were emerging amid jets of steam from cooling engines. Whistles echoed across the concourse as the early trains of the day chugged out to destinations all over the Reich, sending spark-filled spasms of smoke into the glass roof.

Denham had the creeping feeling that everything was being watched. Train guards, Reichsbahn inspectors, soldiers, Orpo men, and two conspicuous Gestapo in leather coats all seemed to be scanning faces. That Adler would have been reported stolen by now, and Rausch would guess who'd taken it.

'The train on platform two is the seven oh five express to Frankfurt-am-Main, stopping at Bonn, Koblenz, and Mainz . . .'

He looked at his watch. It was 6:55 a.m.

Friedl mumbled, 'We can't cool our heels here waiting for someone to drop a wallet on the floor. How are we going to buy tickets?'

'Wait a second,' said Denham. He'd been watching a curious party of English Girl Guides in blue uniforms with knapsacks on their backs, embracing and taking leave of their hosts: German girls of the BDM—the girls' wing of the Hitler Youth.

The English party seemed to be the charge of a middle-aged man with an RAF moustache. He wore a club blazer and a regimental tie with khaki, bell-tent shorts, and long socks.

'Hello there,' Denham said brightly, 'on your way back to Blighty?'

'Yes, as a matter of fact.' The man gave him a toothy smile.

'Look here, you couldn't do an Englishman a favour, could you, and exchange some of this sterling for reichsmarks? No chance to get to the bank, you see, and my train leaves in a few minutes.' The man hesitated. 'Happy to make it worth your while,' Denham said, beaming.

Seconds later he was pocketing a wad of crisp, unused reichsmarks.

He gave the money to Friedl to buy the tickets, and they walked separately through the barriers to the platform, without meeting the eyes of the guards.

'We mustn't sit together,' said Denham as they climbed into the train. They chose seats in two adjoining compartments of the same carriage just as the whistle blew and the train shunted forwards with a metallic screech, couplings banging together, puffing its way out of the station, past the immense spires of the Dom on the right, over the bridge crossing the Rhine.

Frankfurt in three and a half hours.

Denham closed his eyes for a moment and breathed. The only other occupant of the compartment was an old lady in a cloche hat. He picked up that morning's *Frankfurter Zeitung*, discarded on the seat. An article on the forthcoming coronation in London filled a whole inside page with a photograph of Their Majesties and a family tree stressing their German ancestry; Göring had declared himself delighted with recent test-flight manoeuvres over Spain of the new Heinkel IIIs and Junkers 52s; the Führer was to receive Mussolini on a state visit in September; the city of Coburg had proclaimed itself *Judenrein*.

The compartment door opened suddenly. Black uniform and cap. 'Tickets, please.'

Relax, Denham told himself, and gave his ticket to the conductor. Relax.

He put the paper down and watched the suburbs of Cologne give way to the lush pastures and hills of the Rhineland. Soon his eyelids became heavy as he listened to the beat of wheels on track, and his chin fell onto his chest.

'CAN'T SEE 'EM,' said Eleanor. She was now at the wheel of the Hanomag, her eyes peering at the cars along the distant stretch of the autobahn. 'They're probably miles ahead by now.' They had just passed Leipzig.

'We've been driving for hours,' Martha said. 'I need the restroom.' She'd taken off her dark glasses and seemed to be tiring.

'I'll stop there,' Eleanor said, seeing a rest stop up ahead with a café and a gas station.

They stretched their legs while the attendant filled the tank, before getting in the line for the washroom just ahead of a coach full of Strength Through Joy vacationers. Then, while Martha went to buy some sweet rolls, Eleanor found a telephone booth in the gas station, got a stack of pfennigs ready, and placed a call to Berlin.

Richard had told her to make this call if she had a problem. Well, she had a problem all right. And this was the second time she'd tried the number.

'Eleanor? My goodness.'

Rex was surprised to hear her voice—or as surprised as a reserved Brit could sound—but she interrupted before he asked too many questions. 'I need to ask a favour of you . . .'

'Is something wrong?' A noise of typewriters in the background.

'It really is a lot to ask . . .'

'Try me.'

She hesitated, then said, 'Could you come to Frankfurt by six p.m. this evening?'

TEN MINUTES LATER they'd rejoined the autobahn and were nudging the limit of the Hanomag's unimpressive top speed when Martha shouted: 'There they are!'

About a hundred yards ahead the dark grey BMW with the SS number plates was pulled over to the side of the road. The red-faced, porcine man was in his shirtsleeves, crouching next to the back wheel with the jack, and trying to heave a blown rear tyre away from the axle, while the SS driver stood behind him, holding a spanner. She could see Jakob's and Ilse's heads in the car's back window as she passed.

'Well done, Jakob,' Eleanor said, watching in her rearview mirror. 'Now, how did you manage that?'

THE KEENING NOTE of the steam whistle woke him as the train passed into a tunnel. He rubbed his eyes, confused for a minute. The old woman was still there, reading. And a man with a young boy holding a model glider now sat opposite, watching him. Maybe he'd slept through the stop at Bonn. The satchel and newspaper were still on his lap.

He got up to use the lavatory, and in the next-door compartment saw that Friedl was not in his seat. On the way back to his own compartment, he saw the carriage door at the end of the corridor open,

and a black uniform with belt and holster stepped through, followed
by another. Even from forty feet away he could see the diamond-
shaped SD flash on their sleeves. The first man was large with a broken nose, and looked as though he could kill a man with his hands.
He slid open the nearest compartment door and Denham heard him
ask the occupants for their documents.

Beads of cold sweat broke out on Denham's brow. He returned to
his seat and picked up his paper. *What to do?* It was safer to jump off
the train than show them his passport.

They had just entered the compartment next to his.

Stay calm. Completely calm.

A minute later his compartment door slid open, and the sound of
the train picking up speed came in. The men stepped straight up to
him, ignoring the old lady, the man, and the boy. '*Mein Herr? Ihren
Ausweis bitte.*'

Denham reached into the satchel at his feet, without looking up
from an article about a school for brides newly opened in Düssel-
dorf, and handed over the *Sippenbuch* with a slightly careless flick. *If
you must.*

I'm done for, he thought. I am completely done for. I don't look
like Willi Greiser. I don't even have a scar—

But of course, he did have a scar curving down his right cheek,
from his eye almost to the corner of his mouth.

The SD man examined the document and Denham felt his gaze
like heat. Fleeting shadows passed over his newspaper as the train
sped along a tree-lined embankment. He kept his eyes on the article. Seconds passed, and the print began to swirl before his eyes.

'*Danke, Herr Standartenführer,*' the man said at last, handing it
back with a click of his heels.

'Heil Hitler!' Denham said, with a casual raised palm. He resumed reading with his heart hammering in his ears.

Chapter Fifty-one

Denham hopped off the train before it had come to a full halt at Frankfurt main station and walked quickly beneath the high, iron-latticed roof to the barrier. Where in God's name was Friedl? After the appearance of those two SD he hadn't seen him again.

He passed the train guards without arousing suspicion and spent a minute glancing around the busy concourse, looking at faces. He waited, watching the passengers emerging from the train he'd just arrived on. Still no sign of him. Denham's mind began to reel through every dire possibility. The young man had no papers to bluff with, nothing.

Too dangerous to stand around. He would have to make a decision.

He was about to turn and leave the station when he saw a troop of five Brownshirts coming down the platform from the train, the last passengers. They were holding Friedl, had him by both arms, and were pushing him along. Hair a mess; buttons undone. He was dragging his feet, as if barely conscious. Denham could only watch, appalled. The bastards were laughing.

But something was not as it seemed. Now Friedl was laughing, too, talking in a boisterous voice. One of the men seemed to be using Friedl's arm to steady himself. They shambled towards the barrier howling 'Die Wacht am Rhein,' an awful tune at the best of times. Friedl spotted Denham, flashed him a look of profound relief, then bid a lengthy and rowdy farewell to his new friends, embracing them.

'What the hell happened?' Denham said.

'Don't blame me,' Friedl said, breathing beer into his face. 'Someone passed along the train. Said the police were checking the men's
papers, so I moved . . .' They emerged from the station arches and
onto the cobbled open forecourt. 'You,' he said, pointing at Denham
and swaying, 'were asleep in a newspaper. Lucky for me those gorillas
were in the restaurant car with no money for beers . . .'

Denham hailed a taxi. 'You stink like the Schultheiss Brewery.'

Friedl gave a long, deep belch. 'That's method acting.'

Denham almost laughed. 'Meet me in the lobby of the Frankfurter Hof in half an hour,' he said. 'I'm going to try getting a room.
With luck we can have something to eat, take a bath, and get some
sleep,' he said, stepping into the cab. 'Then we wait for Eleanor.'

THE FRANKFURTER HOF, an ornate relic from the Second Reich, was
a palatial edifice on the Kaiserplatz. The impression it gave was of
a dowager marchioness overdressed for a royal wedding. The desk
manager apologised, and hoped Denham would understand, because unfortunately the hotel was fully booked for the annual Hessian Vintners' Guild conference being held today, and with guests
departing on tomorrow's flight of the *Hindenburg* to New York.
But Denham smiled, explained that he was Willi Greiser, the press
chief, and that he felt sure there was something the manager could
do. A blink of the man's eyes, and his voice changed to a smoother
gear. As luck would have it, *mein Herr*, there had been a single can-
cellation. Denham paid in advance and was shown to a pilastered
room with gilded claw-and-ball chairs, a divan, and heavy, gold-
brocaded curtains. The bed could have been designed for a courte-
san of Napoleon III, and it was exceedingly comfortable.

Denham found Friedl sprawled over a brocatelle sofa in the lobby
with his boots up, and ushered him up the stairs to the room, hoping nobody had noticed the state he was in. In any smart hotel in the
world, he thought, they'd have asked him to leave, but the brown
uniform was licence for the vilest behaviour; and no one would dare
say a thing.

Denham ordered lunch from room service and had a bath in the enormous copper tub, and soon they were both in a deep sleep, with Friedl on the divan.

They were awoken some hours later by the telephone ringing on the marble dressing table.

'Herr Willi Greiser?' said a voice of smooth obsequy.

Who? Sleep had disoriented him.

'This is the manager. Forgive me, but word has got out that you're a guest of ours, and the editor of the *Frankfurter Zeitung* is in the lobby, wishing to pay his respects to the press chief.'

'Sorry, I'm busy,' Denham mumbled, reconnecting his brain. He was about to hang up, but then said, 'but you can tell him from me that today's piece on the English coronation had two factual inaccuracies, and it wasn't clear what Fat Hermann's Heinkels were doing over northern Spain.'

'Very well, sir.'

'It's nearly six p.m.,' Friedl said.

They dressed in a hurry and descended the stairs to the grand lobby, crowded and noisy with knots of high-spirited guests in dinner jackets—the Hessian Vintners come for their annual gala dinner. From his vantage point on the stairs, Denham scanned the room, looking for the women.

'*There*,' Friedl said, not daring to point. 'At the door.'

The short figure of Martha Dodd had just entered through the main doors in a raincoat and a pair of dark glasses. Eleanor followed her in and began casting her eyes around.

Denham led Friedl through the crowd of dinner jackets towards the doors and was halfway across when he felt a tap on his elbow. He turned to see the hotel manager smiling greasily and bowing with eyes closed. Behind him stood a small sandy-haired fellow in a herringbone tweed suit. Pouched cheeks and a pair of round, tortoiseshell eyeglasses made him look like a book-loving beaver.

'Herr Greiser, my apologies,' said the manager. 'Perhaps now that you're free you might spare a moment for Herr Joost, the editor of our local *Frankfurter*—'

'I fear not,' Denham said, pulling Friedl after him. 'I'm on my way out.'

'That's not Willi Greiser,' the editor exclaimed, in a voice firmer than Denham would have given him credit for.

'Let's go,' he said to Martha and Eleanor without stopping to greet them.

'Car's outside,' Eleanor said, catching the look on his face.

'Ah, just one moment, sir . . . ,' came the hotel manager's voice.

Two seconds later the four of them were through the doors, down the steps, and running along the Kaiserplatz towards the Hanomag. Martha started the engine, and they screeched into the Saturday night traffic on Kaiserstrasse.

'Couldn't pay your bar check?' Eleanor said, squeezing Denham's hand from the front seat. He leaned over and kissed her. 'Thank God you're here.' She started laughing with nerves and relief. 'I was worried sick, thinking of you at the border.'

'The telegram warned us in time,' said Denham.

'About two seconds in time,' Friedl added.

'Don't mind me,' Martha said in a petulant singsong. 'I'm just a chauffeur without a clue where I'm going. And I don't think we've had the pleasure, young man,' she added in German.

Denham introduced Friedl, who said, 'Good evening,' in English. He was holding his head now, the drink catching up with him.

Eleanor read out the address of the Klinik Pfanmüller again and while Martha stopped at a flower stall to ask directions, explained to Denham how they'd followed an SS car carrying Jakob and Ilse from Berlin, and how it was en route to Basel with a stop-off at Frankfurt, where she was hoping to intercept it. A puncture on the autobahn had, Eleanor hoped, put the car half an hour or so behind the Hanomag.

Denham and Friedl met each other's look in the backseat.

'What's the plan?' Denham said.

Eleanor outlined what she had in mind, right up to the part where Dr Eckener came into it.

'Eckener?' Denham's face dropped into his hands as he struggled to digest what she'd told him. 'Darling, forgive me, but that's not a plan,' he said. 'It's a Keystone Kops movie. Even if we can get the Liebermanns away from the SS, how are seven people going to fit in this Hanomag?'

Eleanor flared. 'For *one thing* I hadn't figured on you two turning up in Germany, and if you think you can come up with something better, you just go right ahead.'

Denham sighed and apologised. 'Well, at least we don't have to worry about fooling anyone with a bogus dossier now.'

Something in the way Eleanor's eyes closed and her mouth went rigid told him there was more.

She recounted what had happened outside the bank in London.

Martha was still outside, receiving the flower seller's directions to the sanatorium. The Hanomag's doors were closed, but over the noise of the traffic and the voices of Saturday evening revellers on the sidewalks, she heard Denham's voice.

'You brought it *back to Germany*?'

'Oh my God,' Friedl said.

By the time Martha got back into the car the shouting had transformed to silence.

'All right . . . ,' Denham said. 'It wasn't your fault. We need to think.'

'I was about to tell you,' Eleanor said with acid coolness, 'that I telephoned Rex. He couldn't get a flight here in time for six p.m., so he's meeting us at the sanatorium at seven. That's in less than half an hour. We give him the dossier. It's fine, Richard. It'll be in safe hands in half an hour. He can take it straight to the British embassy . . . Then we find Hannah.'

Chapter Fifty-two

The Klinik Pfanmüller was located just off Frankfurt's millionaires' row, a lush, tree-lined street in Westend, near the botanical gardens. Dusk was gathering as the Hanomag stopped before the gated driveway. They had driven along the approach slowly enough to see that neither Rex nor any car was waiting in the street outside.

A light came on in the guardhouse and a man emerged—round eyeglasses, veteran's medal—and peered at the car. Friedl stepped out. The brown uniform had its transforming effect—a very slight change in the set of the man's mouth, from officious to obsequious.

'Tell me, has an English reporter visited?' Friedl said.

A moment of alarm behind the eyeglasses. 'I don't know if he was a reporter, Herr Sturmführer.'

'You keep a register?'

'Of course.'

The man led Friedl into the guardhouse and turned the register round for him to see. The last name on the list was Rex Palmer-Ward's. He had arrived less than ten minutes ago.

'I told him he had to go in or leave,' the man said. 'No one's allowed to wait out here. Gauleiter Weinrich lives on this street.'

'Thank you,' Friedl said. 'We just want to check on him.'

He got back in the car, and Martha drove through the gates, past the puzzled guard.

The main building, a neoclassical villa with a modern annex and outbuildings, could be seen at the end of a long driveway.

Pine-shaded grounds and a high surrounding wall afforded the requisite seclusion. It was also, Denham thought, the perfect place to confine an inconvenient Jewish celebrity: the world could see, if need be, that she was being treated well, but they had total control over her.

Rex was not outside the main doors when they parked in the fore-court.

'He must have gone in,' Friedl said.

'Take the dossier with you,' Eleanor said, a resolute look on her face. 'Give it to him quickly before that SS car arrives here with Jakob and Ilse.' She got out, opened the boot, and took it out of her case, placing it in Richard's open satchel.

Denham and Friedl entered the building with the satchel, leaving Eleanor and Martha with the Hanomag.

Inside was a panelled hall with a reception desk. Flower arrange-ments beneath spotlit portraits of bespectacled medics. The re-ceptionist was talking to a hefty blonde in a blue and white nurse's uniform, who turned to look at them without smiling. Denham glanced around. *Where the hell was Rex?*

'What can we do for you, gentlemen?'

Denham hesitated. How to play this. Charm? Or the cold tap . . . He took out a cigarette.

'There is strictly no smoking here,' she said.

The cold tap. 'I am Standartenführer Willi Greiser,' he said. 'We're here to question the Jew Liebermann.'

The woman did a double blink. 'I'm afraid that isn't possible. She's a quarantined patient.'

'Why, does she have TB?'

'You'll have to apply to Dr Pfanmüller if you want to see her, but apart from that she's expecting visitors from Berlin at any minute.'

'Look,' Denham said, 'we can stand here arguing, and you'll be out of a job tomorrow, or you can stop wasting SS time and take us straight to her. The only thing stopping me shoving you out of the way is your size. I don't want to put my back out.'

The woman blushed scarlet, her lips forming a perfect O. She said, 'If you'll follow me.'

They walked behind her out of the hall and into a bright, modern annex, almost Bauhaus in style, with curved, factorylike windows. Shiny floors had a pleasant smell of ether. On the right they passed a gymnasium with a class in progress. A woman instructor in a leotard was saying, '*Hup*,' trying to get her millionaire ladies to do squat jumps. They left the annex through swing doors and entered the grounds along a winding stone path lit with waist-high lamps.

The lamplight dotted among the pines made the place resemble a lavish stage set. Eventually they came to a sign that read HAUS EDEL-WEISS, and some hundred yards behind it saw another handsome modern building, white and cuboid, also with a reception area but this one with a uniformed guard.

The nurse showed a pass. 'Werner, I'm taking these gentlemen to see the Liebermann patient.'

The guard unlocked a door that opened into a corridor lined with framed paintings. The nurse led the way. Turning a corner at the end she almost collided with a tall man in a white coat.

'I'm so sorry, Dr Pfanmüller,' she said.

A dark man with a square jaw and pomaded hair, he reminded Denham of Luis Trenker, the rugged star of the Alpine films. He looked embarrassed.

'I'm glad we've run into you,' she went on. 'These men are here to question the Liebermann patient, and I've told them they must apply to you—'

'It's all right,' he said with a nod. 'They can go in.'

'Oh, but you said—'

'I've sedated her,' he said to them, holding up a medic's bag. 'So you'll have to be quick. Let's leave the gentlemen to it, shall we Frau Klott?' He turned her around by her elbow and guided her at a trot back down the corridor, her face looking up at his for an explanation. Friedl met Denham's eye. What was going on? They continued along the corridor and heard dance music from a radio, one of the big Berlin dance orchestras. They could still turn back.

The apartment door was open. A narrow vestibule with a lavatory on the left, and, straight ahead, the sitting room. Friedl followed Denham through. Low lighting from a table lamp. Two armchairs strewn with magazines and books, a rug, a table and chairs, and the radio playing, its dial lit with an amber light. He turned it off.

'Hello, Hannah?' Denham called, knocking on the open door.

The window was open. Rustling foliage, and a breeze smelling of pine needles. Somewhere in the bushes beneath the sill, a thrush singing.

'Hannah?'

Another door led from the sitting room, to her bedroom, he presumed, and it was closed. They approached it, treading softly.

Something was wrong.

He tapped on the bedroom door. 'Hannah?'

There was more than a smell of pine needles in the room.

'Come in.' A young woman's voice. Drowsy.

He pushed open the door to the bedroom, dark inside, and could make out the bed facing him, and Hannah lying under white sheets. She lolled her head towards him, but it was too dark to see her expression.

A loud slam.

The apartment's door closed behind them; in front of them the bedroom door was pulled fully open. A figure stood in the dark, with the rose glow of a cigarette in his fingers. Its resinous aroma filled the room. A Turkish cigarette.

'Good evening, Denham,' said Rausch.

Chapter Fifty-three

The black form of a second SD man filled the doorway to the apartment, barring the exit. Denham recognised the same hulking figure with the broken nose who'd demanded his documents on the train.

He turned and met Rausch's face: the glazed-back brown hair, the high cheekbones, the cold, aphotic stare. A glint against the dark suit, and he noticed the gun, a Mauser automatic, pointing at him. He exhaled slowly, feeling that same strange calm he'd felt when the Gestapo came for him. Some survival instinct, perhaps. Remain still when circled by an aggressive beast, lest motion provokes it to slaughter. Terror, he knew, came later.

'What have you done with Rex?' he said.

'He didn't make it,' Rausch said. A mock sadness. 'I'm sorry to disappoint. It was I who wrote his name in the visitors' register. Now who have we here?' He looked past Denham. 'Friedrich Christian? The warm boy?' He gave a short, mirthless laugh. 'An unexpected bonus, I must say.'

'You should be more careful who you call a warm boy,' Friedl said.

Rausch stepped into the light of the lamp, a look of profound disgust on his face. He beckoned to the SD man, who walked forwards, pistol drawn, and struck Friedl hard across the head with the butt, sending him crashing to the floor. Rausch watched him writhe for a moment.

'Denham,' he said, stubbing his cigarette on the rug next to Friedl's face, 'I am filled with admiration. I wanted you to know that before we shoot you. All that time you denied knowledge of the dossier . . .'

He held out his hand for the satchel. Denham did nothing, and the Mauser's aim moved up to his face. Then he reached over and took it gently from Denham's hand.

'You were willing to sacrifice yourself if the hour demanded. You resisted even when you had no hope; you overcame pain; you did not break. In another life, perhaps, you would have made an exemplary SS man.'

Denham gave a melancholy smile. 'I really didn't know anything, Rausch. And as for the SS, I drink and smoke too much.'

Rausch sat down in an armchair, the Mauser still trained on its target, the satchel held to his chest. 'You really wanted to exchange this for a family of Jews? That's the bit we didn't buy. What was your scam, tell me. Was the old man offering a king's ransom if you helped them escape?'

On the floor Friedl moaned.

'No scam, Rausch,' said Denham. 'They're just people I like. Fellow human beings.'

The eyes narrowed. 'Fellow human beings . . .' He gave a thoughtful grunt, lit another Murad with a steel lighter, and leaned back, observing Denham through a ring of yellow smoke. 'Ye-es, I suppose the Jews are part of our species. But they are not part of our race . . . That's the point. They are sublimely clever, Denham, to survive as they do by destroying cultures from within, like parasites, like bacilli . . .' He glanced at Hannah's sleeping form through the open bedroom door. 'So few of them, and yet such influence—in the law, in medicine, in banking. We continually underestimate them . . . But here I am, talking away.'

The Mauser cocked with a fluid click.

'D'YOU THINK THEY'RE all right?' Eleanor said, not taking her eyes off the main doors.

She and Martha were still seated in the Hanomag in the fore-court of the clinic.

'Stop biting your nails,' Martha said. 'That's the fifth time you've asked in fifteen minutes . . .'

'Oh Jesus.'

The dark interior of the Hanomag was suddenly lit by the head-lights of a car coming up the drive.

Martha turned to look through the back window. 'All right, get down in your seat . . .'

The two women slid down, almost crouching on the floor of the car, as the grey BMW rolled into the forecourt and parked in a space between two other cars.

Peeking over the door Eleanor made out the heads of Jakob and Ilse in the backseat and saw the driver's door opening.

A wave of danger washed over her.

'How are we going to handle this?' Martha whispered.

THE SD MAN held his gun to Denham's neck while Rausch care-fully removed the List Dossier from the satchel. His hand trembled slightly, Denham noticed, as if it were a holy relic, or charged with some astral energy. *Führerkontakt.*

Friedl moaned again on the floor. Denham turned to him, but the SD man pushed the gun hard into his neck.

'Don't you speak?' Denham said to him, his face forced back to-wards Rausch.

Still Rausch stared at the old oilskin cover of the dossier, touch-ing the charred corner, the frayed edges, not opening it. Yellowed corners of paper, the drawings, peeped from the side.

'Go on, Rausch,' Denham said. 'Aren't you going to take a look?'

He could see the man was struggling with himself, duty fighting temptation.

Heydrich warned you not to look.

Finally Rausch said, 'It is not my place to know.'

'What, that your god, your great Hitler, is nothing but a—'

Rausch dropped the dossier, moved quickly, and punched Denham in the stomach, doubling him over.

The SD man pulled Denham up by his hair to give Rausch another hit, but the Hauptsturmführer was talking now, bare-teethed, his face crimson. 'Tonight's report was going to state that British spy Richard Denham was shot while resisting arrest. But you have just inspired me to make you an *extraordinary* offer, to accept or decline as you wish.'

He jerked the barrel of the Mauser towards the open bedroom door. 'Go in.' Denham stepped forwards, hands half raised, still gasping for air from the punch. 'Go.'

In the dim room Hannah slept, breathing in a deep rhythm, long hair covering half her face. A princess in a fairy tale, slumbering under an evil spell.

Rausch said to the SD man, 'Guard the other one.' Then he followed Denham in, still aiming the Mauser, and turned on the bedside light. 'An experiment,' he said, sitting on the edge of the bed. His face was contorted with hate. 'We're going to test your love for your fellow human beings.' He pointed the gun at Hannah's temple with a straight right arm. 'My offer is to spare you, and kill her . . .'

'No—' Denham's head reeled.

'Your life . . . for *a Jew's*.'

'Wait—'

'I'm going to count to three. One . . .'

'Rausch, you'll be well rewarded if you—'

'Two . . .'

'You've got the dossier, damn it, what more do you want—'

'Three!'

Rausch looked at where the gun touched Hannah's temple.

'All right, take me, not her.'

His trigger finger squeezed, and the sheets surged violently.

Staring at Denham, Rausch's eyes were bulbous with disbelief.

A syringe was plunged deep into his neck.

He dropped the Mauser on the bed, struggled with Hannah's fist, and pulled the needle out. The vial was empty. He'd received the full dose.

Noises bubbled from his throat as he tried to stand, alerting the SD man, who clomped in, pistol drawn.

A discharge flash-lit the small room. Denham's ears were deafened.

The SD man's head thumped softly as it hit the door. His body crumpled, leaving a red trail down the white gloss, the hole in his forehead small and dark, like a cleft cherry, his final expression surprise.

In Denham's hand the Mauser felt leaden and filthy. A sharp smell of cordite filled his nostrils.

Rausch had fallen back onto the bed, still gurgling and clutching his throat.

'You were right about one thing,' Hannah shrieked, kneeling on the bed, a knee on either side of Rausch's chest. 'You—continually—under—esti—mate—us.' Each word was punctuated with a stab of the needle—in his arm, in his shoulder.

Denham grabbed her wrist and prised the syringe from her hand, feeling all the strength in her body ebb away.

'Enough,' he said.

She threw her arms around him and sobbed. 'Horrible, horrible,' she said.

'MARTHA, LOOK.'

The pig of a man in a seersucker jacket they'd seen earlier, the one who had changed the tyre, got out of the BMW and walked towards the building's main doors, where he was greeted by a fat woman in a nurse's uniform.

'Jesus, her butt's as big as a barn.'

It was almost dark, but they could hear her explaining something urgent, gesticulating, pointing inside, and saw the alarm on the man's face. He returned to the car, spoke for a moment to the SS driver, then ran into the clinic.

*   *   *

RAUSCH'S EYELIDS DROOPED as the drug took effect.

'What was in that?' Denham said.

'Phenobarbital, I think, and a cocktail of other stuff,' Hannah said, pulling herself together. 'While the good Dr Pfanmüller was distracted talking to these men I took an empty syringe from the trash, put it on the tray, and started acting drowsy. He assumed he'd already given me the sedative.'

Friedl came to the door clutching his head. 'What happened in here?'

'Take his gun,' Denham said to him, pointing at the dead SD man. 'Hannah, get dressed. We're leaving in under one minute.'

He put Rausch's feet up on the bed and covered him with the sheets.

'Denham . . . ,' he said, a weak smile on his lips. Then his lids closed, and he began to snore.

'Your parents will be arriving at any moment,' Denham said.

'My *parents*? But—'

'I'll explain on the way. Hurry.'

In the next room Denham put the List Dossier back into the satchel, noticing that it still contained the bogus dossier they were going to exchange at the border.

He also noticed something fallen behind the armchair. A man's raincoat. Rausch's coat. Quickly he went through the pockets. A half packet of Murads, a page torn from a notebook with the clinic's scribbled address, *car keys*, and, in the side pocket, a book. A small, rust red book Denham had seen before. *Die Gedichte von Stefan George. The Poems of Stefan George.*

He opened the cover and found something that nearly made him cry out.

'I'm ready,' Hannah said. She had on a white blouse with a navy wool jacket.

He struggled to put the book in his jacket pocket, so violently was his hand shaking.

'Richard, what is it?' Friedl said.

They left the apartment, pausing only while Friedl told the guard at the reception that Hannah Liebermann was being taken for interrogation, and that the two SD still in her room were not on any account to be disturbed while they carried out a search.

'I thought I heard a shot,' the guard said.

'No, you didn't.'

Outside on the winding stone path, they began to run.

'Oh,' Hannah said, a longed-for relief on her face. She looked up at the sky, then closed her eyes, and Friedl took her hand. Together they left the path and started across the lawn in order to circle the main clinic building without going inside it. The grass was wet on their shoes.

A man was coming towards them. Probably one of the patients, from his clothes. He had on a seersucker jacket and hiking trousers. He was waving at them. From a hundred yards away they saw in the light of the lamps the suspicion on his face.

'Stay calm,' Friedl said, grabbing Hannah's arm, as if she was being restrained.

The man was fifty feet away and shouting now. 'Hey. What's going on? Where are you taking her?'

'For interrogation,' Denham said, stopping in front of him. 'Frankfurt Gestapo. Who are you?'

'I was not informed. Show me your warrant disc.' His skin looked peeled and raw, as if he'd shaved too closely.

'I have the signed order here,' Denham said. He reached into his inside pocket, clutched the barrel of the Mauser, and in a single movement threw out his arm and smashed the corner of the butt down onto the man's mouth, harder than he'd ever hit anything or anyone, bludgeoning his lips and nose. The man's head jerked backwards, and Denham struck him again.

'Richard, stop,' Friedl said.

The man was down, on his back, his face black with blood. For two seconds they stood aghast; then Friedl knelt and felt for the gun inside the seersucker jacket. A Walther, heavy and new. He switched the safety catch off and tossed it to Hannah, and she took it without question.

They continued across the lawn, now close to the wall of the main building, and passed a patients' car park. It was occupied by a Duesenberg limousine, an English Bentley, and a Mercedes-Benz Denham recognised. The black Mercedes that had come to the border at Venhoven—Rausch's car.

'We're taking the Mercedes.'

Denham had the keys in the door when they heard the shout—'*Halt!*'

Running towards them over the lawn was the guard from the Haus Edelweiss.

'WE'VE GOT TO do something—to get him away from the car,' Eleanor said, watching the grey BMW parked outside the clinic's main doors. The young SS driver was still leaning against the car, talking to the fat nurse. 'He's the only one guarding Jakob and Ilse.' She was feeling desperate now.

She glanced at her watch. It was 7:43 p.m. If her plan was to succeed they had to meet Eckener at 8:00 p.m. at the absolute latest.

'This is a *bad* idea,' Martha said as they closed the car doors and approached the BMW, their steps crunching on the gravel.

From the nurse came a hostile look as they approached. But the SS driver, a smooth-skinned, roundish lad, had his hands in his pockets and was giving them an enthusiastic grin, which Martha was returning.

And then there was a sudden whining noise, as around the corner of the building a black Mercedes-Benz approached them in low gear, careened into the forecourt, and braked parallel with the BMW, shooting a barrage of gravel at its bodywork. The SS man and nurse spun around.

Denham jumped out of the driver's side, shouted something in German, and pointed at Jakob and Ilse, whose startled faces peered from the window of the BMW.

Caught off guard, the SS man asked Denham to repeat himself and glanced anxiously towards the clinic, evidently wondering where his chief had got to. But now the nurse was pointing at Denham as if he were a rapist, talking loudly and quickly. Eleanor caught Dr Pfanmüller's name.

At the same moment a man in a guard's uniform, flushed and shining with sweat and shouting, emerged from the direction the Mercedes had come from.

Eleanor and Martha were too surprised to take another step.

The nurse screamed.

The SS man fumbled in his gun holster, but then he froze. Everyone became still, too amazed to move.

Standing on the running board of the Mercedes were Friedl and Hannah aiming handguns at the SS man and the nurse. Slowly, Denham, too, drew a gun.

Friedl jumped onto the gravel, walked around to the BMW, removed its keys, and dropped them down a drain in the middle of the forecourt. Denham then opened the door of the BMW and asked Jakob and Ilse to get out. Meekly they did as they were told, looking in astonishment upon their daughter, whose hair blew gently in the mild night breeze. She did not look at them. Her face was focused on aiming the gun, her eyes lit with certainty. Friedl helped them into the back of the Mercedes.

Denham waved Eleanor and Martha back to the Hanomag.

Seconds later they were speeding after the Mercedes as it accelerated down the long driveway, through the clinic gates, and into the street. The man at the guardhouse, head switching left and right as both cars shot through, picked up his telephone.

In a side street near the Frankfurt Hauptbahnhof they grabbed what possessions they had, abandoned the cars, and caught separate cabs to their destination—Rhine-Main World Airport—just as every street in the city seemed to start wailing with police sirens.

Chapter Fifty-four

In the echoing space lit by hundreds of electric lights, with no-where to hide except for a few freight containers on wheeled carts, Eleanor felt exposed. The seven of them, Eleanor, Richard, Martha, Friedl, Jakob, Ilse, and Hannah, stood together like castaways. Between them they had only two suitcases.

On the night Eleanor had called on Hugo Eckener at the Hotel Kempinski in Berlin, he had given her an authorised vehicle pass for the customs yard. That part of the plan had worked. At the gates, guards and inspector admitted them with a nod and no questions asked.

But where was Eckener? It was 8:10 p.m. Had they missed him by minutes? A barrage of German imperatives crackled from the loudspeaker, and she guessed the *Hindenburg* was very close to its departure time.

Finally, when she'd convinced herself that the Gestapo were surrounding the building, the tall, plumpish figure of Eckener appeared in the far end of the cargo shed and shambled towards them. With him was a young man in a brown jumpsuit.

'My dear lady, my dear Richard, friends, friends,' he said. 'No time for introductions except one: this is Ralf, who is one of us. He is a duty rigger on board this voyage. You may trust him . . .'

All eyes turned to the blond, impassive young man.

' . . . You will get into these empty freight containers, which have already cleared customs.' Eckener tapped the side of his nose. 'They will not be opened once I attach the seals but will be loaded on board directly, under my personal supervision. In about two hours' time, once the ship has cleared Reich airspace, Ralf will open the containers, and another friend, who will make himself known to you, will install you in your own cabins as my personal guests. I must ask you please to remain in your cabins until morning, when Captain Pruss will be informed of the situation. By then it will be too late to turn the ship around. Captain Pruss does not know of our plan. We are fortunate in having only thirty-six passengers on this voyage.'

'You're coming, too?' Eleanor said.

'Alas, no, dear lady. Our leaders are keeping me out of mischief by sending me on a lecture tour. Now, please everyone hurry, hurry,' he said, taking his watch from his waistcoat pocket.

Denham helped Jakob, Ilse, and Hannah into the first of the large containers, which had wooden hatch lids in the side. 'We'll be like three cigars in this box,' Ilse said.

Friedl went to give Martha a lift up, but she said, 'Uh-uh, not me, kid. This is where I say goodbye. I've got enough to explain to Dad as it is.'

'Martha.' Eleanor reached out and drew the woman's petite body tightly into her arms.

Martha's voice was tender and serious. 'Eleanor, dear, I know I've been a minx at times. I guess I envied you, you know that . . .'

'We'd never have done this without you,' Eleanor said, welling up.

'Now look, you're making me cry . . . *Bon voyage*, darling.'

'I'll see you in New York.'

Jakob, Ilse, and Hannah were installed in one container. Friedl got into the other; then Eckener helped Eleanor in.

'I waited half an hour for you,' he said, 'I confess I thought you hadn't made it.'

Eleanor kissed his cheek in gratitude, and he blushed.

'I suppose I'll arrive in New York dressed like this,' Friedl said. He was trying to tug the red armband off the uniform.

'Certainly you won't,' Eckener said. 'Nor shall you dine on board in it. I have arranged for dinner jackets to be left in your cabins. I hope they fit.'

He shook Denham's hand. 'Your father had great humanity,' he said softly. 'He would be proud of you today.'

Denham thanked him warmly and climbed into the container. He sat back against the side next to Eleanor, the satchel between them.

Ralf said, 'Please—your matches, lighters, or anything that may cause a spark.' His sombre face could not hide his shock when he was handed a Walther and two Mauser automatics.

The wooden lid came down, and Eleanor clutched Denham's hand in the dark. They heard the sound of Ralf grappling with the seals; another stream of announcements from the loudspeaker; the tow truck's engine starting.

Then a shout from the far end of the shed.

Denham's heart skipped a beat.

He pushed the lid open a crack. A uniformed customs officer was approaching, escorting another man in a shabby corduroy jacket, with long grey hair tumbling over his forehead . . .

'My God,' Denham said.

He pushed the lid wide and jumped down from the container. The customs officer was explaining the man's presence to Eckener in wide hand gestures. Eckener looked alarmed. Whoever he was, his presence was compromising.

'*What* a business,' Rex said, panting for breath. 'Sorry I missed the rendezvous.' He seized Denham's hand. 'Took a guess you'd be here, and I was right. Bloody plane from Berlin was delayed—just landed ten minutes ago.'

'We all made it,' Denham said.

'Thank *God*. I was worried to death they'd tapped my phone and heard Eleanor's call . . .'

Eleanor began to climb out, too, but Eckener stopped her. 'No time for chitchat,' he barked. 'Richard, my boy, you are about to miss the departure . . .'

Denham continued to hold Rex's hand, searching his old friend's face as though he'd never truly seen it until now and wanted to commit it forever to his memory.

Finding himself choked, he whispered, 'It's yours, Rex . . .'

'What's that, old boy?'

'What you came here for.'

'I came for you.'

He dropped his friend's hand, turned, and saw that Eleanor was holding out the satchel towards him. He opened it and put the dossier into Rex's hands.

'It's a relief to be rid of it.'

'You mean . . .' Rex nodded, solemn and honoured.

'*Richard Denham*,' Eckener shouted. '*We—are—leaving.*'

'Goodbye, Rex.'

Denham turned and got quickly into the container without looking back. The lid was closed and locked; the customs seals attached.

Five minutes later the two late items of cargo were loaded into the hold of the waiting airship. From the darkness of the containers they heard the shouts of the cargo loaders, the heaving of ropes, the closing of bay doors, followed by silence. A cool draught blew through narrow slits in the wooden sides. Then came the faint brass tones of 'Deutschland über Alles' outside on the field, followed by a muffled cheer, an infinitesimally small sway—a buoyancy—and the creaking of canvas against a vast metal structure.

'We're up,' said Denham. 'We're flying.' He touched Eleanor's face in the dark and kissed her.

'We made it,' Friedl said, laughing, and Eleanor hugged their faces to hers in the dark.

The four great propeller engines fired and began to drone, vibrating the wooden floor of the container. They were floating away from the ground, lifting westwards towards the skies beyond the Reich.

They sat for a while, listening to the propellers and the rushing wind. It was Eleanor who broke the reverie.

'Why did you do that?'

'Do what?' Denham said.

'Give Rex the bogus dossier. The real one's here. I saw. And even now in the dark I recognise . . . its smell.'

'Yes,' Denham said.

'Why?'

A long pause. And when he spoke he felt they were the saddest words he'd ever spoken.

'Because Rex betrayed us.'

Chapter Fifty-five

In his mind's eye Denham imagined the scene, early tomorrow morning in the summer palace of the Hohenzollerns on the Wilhelmstrasse. Rex enters the building unseen, perhaps through one of the tunnels that crisscross the government quarter. He is fresh and alert, nervous before his meeting with Reinhard Heydrich, the thirty-three-year-old dauphin, the Führer's rumoured successor. Satisfied, too, because through his initiative alone the mission had succeeded. He is ushered into the presence. A globe tilted to the window perhaps; equestrian trophies; even an épée, wire mask, and kit thrown in one corner. Heydrich rises to meet him. He is gangling and fair, towering in black, squinting at Rex over his long nose. An Olympian coldness. Rex presents the dossier. A word of congratulation perhaps, and then he takes it over to the tall windows and opens it, curious, but without emotion. His back is towards Rex. Inside, nine or ten loose sheets, some of the great man's drawings. He had expected those. Behind the drawings, a thick, sealed envelope. He opens this and pulls out a wad of papers tied with string. All typewritten, with corrections in handwriting. This he is not expecting. Not expecting at all.

'My dear Herr Palmer-Ward,' he says, turning round on the heels of his boots. '*What* have you given me?'

He is holding it up. Rex blinks. It means nothing to him.

In Heydrich's hand is the draft manuscript for *No Parts for Stella*, an unfinished experimental novel by Friedl Christian.

*   *   *

'THERE WERE HINTS,' Denham explained. He took off his jacket, folded it into a cushion, and made himself as comfortable as he could in the dark. 'I just didn't want to see them . . . or draw the conclusions. Lurking in the back of my mind was the question I never asked: who was the British journalist that you, Friedl, were supposed to meet at the stadium, on the day of the opening ceremony, the man who was to identify himself to you with the password? With your man, Captain Rogel, arrested, and because you feared an SD trap, you didn't show up. But waiting there in the drizzle, on his own beneath the bell tower, was Rex. I'm sure of it.'

'So it was one of my brighter decisions,' Friedl said.

'Captain Rogel, or someone in the resistance group, had contacted him and offered the dossier. Not surprising they picked Rex. He is chief correspondent of the *Times*. Maybe they also knew he's a British intelligence officer, which would have made him the perfect choice.

'That same afternoon, I got back to Berlin from my week in the south and met him for a beer at the Adlon. His disappointment at not getting the List Dossier must have been very much on his mind. But just as he was brooding over his loss: serendipity. From something I said he realised that it was *I* who had been approached that day, and he thought I had the dossier.

'With me sitting there in front of him, he couldn't believe his luck. But he wasn't completely sure. Maybe I'd hidden it—and hours later my apartment was searched and ransacked—or maybe I'd been told its hiding place. So he decided to draw me in and recruit me to British Intelligence. He introduced me to the very organisation whose operations he was secretly betraying to the SD. It was a good plan. Why not let me deliver it, out of patriotic duty, to the British SIS, of which he was the chief intelligence officer in Berlin? Hence the sudden invitation to meet Sir Eric Phipps. If that didn't work, the SD could arrest me and beat it out of me. Either way, Rex and his SD master, Heydrich, would get the dossier.

'Doubts must have set in, though, after Rausch learned nothing

from me in the interrogation. When Rex visited me at my sickbed
in London, it may have been partly to find out for himself. And in
the meantime, when the trail went cold, he ran a covert campaign to
discredit Phipps, and then to move Evans from active duty, replacing them with appeasers who would not hinder Nazi ambitions.

'Then the dossier was found. The irony was, if that nasty ambush
at the Dutch border had worked, Rex would have been thwarted.
We would've had nothing on us but the bogus dossier. But when he
learned we were fugitives inside Germany, he was just waiting for
our call for help, and it came from you, my darling . . .'

'From a pay phone on the highway . . . ,' Eleanor said.

'You told him to meet us at the sanatorium, and he primed the
trap. Against all the odds, it failed, but he saw one last chance and
made it just in time.'

'But honey . . . ,' Eleanor began. 'Couldn't all this be pure . . .
suspicion? A misunderstanding?' She shifted position on the wooden
floor without finding comfort. 'You have no proof . . . have you?'

Denham sighed. He knew she liked Rex. Everyone did, including
Tom, who was his godson for Christ's sake. But the proof was in his
inside pocket. It was inscribed in ink on the title page of the small
rust red book, *The Poems of Stefan George*. The very book Rausch
had in his possession during the interrogation. In a younger hand
were written the words: *Rex Palmer-Ward—Balliol College, Oxford—
Lent term 1919.*

'But *why*?' Eleanor said, when he'd explained. 'Why?'

Denham shook his head in the dark. 'We have to warn the SIS,'
he said.

'And the dossier?'

Denham shrugged. 'We'll find a way to get it to them . . .'

'With the appeasers in charge?' Eleanor said. 'Oh, forget that. I say
we give it to the Hearst newspaper corporation—as soon as we land.'

'DR ECKENER HAS given you these cabins,' Lehmann said, opening the door to a narrow corridor on B deck. 'They were added

during the winter refit and are the only ones with windows. You will see no other passengers on this deck.'

Captain Ernst Lehmann had been waiting for them in the cargo hold when the containers were opened. He had ushered them here, explaining that he was an old colleague of Eckener's, had been since the war, and was on board this voyage as an observer. A shortish, handsome man, he wore the peaked cap and brass buttons of a Zeppelin officer. There was a sad sobriety about him, Denham thought.

Denham's cabin was furnished with an aluminium bunk bed, a reading lamp, and a fold-down washbasin. The bed's crisp sheets had been turned down. It was no larger or more comfortable than a sleeper in a good Pullman train, Denham supposed, save for the incomparable view of the world. From the window of tilted Plexiglas, he saw Amsterdam passing below, its streets glowing arteries of Saturday night traffic, its suburbs great webs of fairy lights.

'Beautiful,' he mumbled.

'You can open it if you wish,' said Lehmann. 'There is no draught, even at an airspeed of a hundred kilometres per hour.'

The window opened with a push, and Denham leaned out as far as he dared. A moonless night, but the sky glittered with stars. To his left, two of the propeller engine cars could be seen sticking out from the gargantuan hull. The noise was tremendous, but beneath the flow of aerodynamism, the ship's skin was insulated in stillness. Ahead of the ship to his right, drifts of white vapour parted like wraiths. He closed his eyes and breathed in the smell of the ocean, and a cold, crystalline air he imagined came from the stars themselves.

'You'll excuse me,' Lehmann said, putting on his cap. Denham had almost forgotten he was there. 'Ralf will bring you something cold to eat. In the morning I will take you up to breakfast, and then inform Captain Pruss of my shock and bewilderment in discovering six additional passengers stowed on board . . .'

He gave Denham a resigned smile, then left, his face set to that distasteful task.

A minute later, there was a tap at the door. Jakob and Ilse were standing in the corridor, smiling expectantly. Ilse held on to the doorframe, still stiff from the two hours sitting in the cargo container. Denham invited them in, and they sat on the bed. A moment later Friedl appeared with a bottle of brandy and some glasses. 'Imagine leaving the bar on this deck unattended.'

'With so much drama,' Jakob said in his deep, felt voice, 'we have not yet thanked you for what you've done.' The ruts of strain that lined his face seemed less pronounced, as though he was making an unexpected recovery from a long illness. 'There is a saying in Hebrew, "Whoever saves one life, saves the world entire." We owe everything to you and to Dr Eckener,' he said, shaking his head in wonder, 'a man we had never met until tonight.'

'Does it seem so odd that a stranger is kind?' Denham said, accepting a glass. 'I suppose it does, to an émigré from Hitler's Germany. But when you reach America you will think the opposite: how strange that anyone might be so hateful.'

'I expect he is in serious trouble for helping us,' Jakob said.

'Eckener's fame and contacts have protected him . . . ,' Richard said, hiding his worry.

'After Roland died,' Ilse said, pushing a strand back into the silver puff of her hair, 'I did not wish to live any longer. It was only the thought that I could not be so selfish as to leave my husband and daughter to their fates that made me face each day. And now, we're flying away from the nightmare,' she said, 'in this marvellous ship.'

Jakob put his arm around her shoulder, and they were silent for a time.

Denham asked, 'What happened to the art?'

'We lost the paintings,' Jakob said with a wave of his hand, 'but we were not robbed of everything in Basel, thanks to Eleanor.'

Denham poured them each a glass.

'*Mazel tov,*' said Jakob.

'*Mazel tov,*' they said in unison.

'As a token of our thanks,' Jakob said, 'Ilse and I wish to fund your honeymoon.' Denham held up his palm and began to protest until he saw that it would make them much happier if he accepted.

'That's settled, then,' said Jakob, businesslike. 'Anywhere in the world you and Eleanor want to go.'

When they'd gone, Denham was washing his face in the basin when Hannah appeared in the door.

'This is the party cabin tonight,' he said. 'Come in.'

She glided in, wearing a brushed-cotton bathrobe with a frilly nightdress hanging underneath. It must have been in the case Ilse had brought for her. Her silky chestnut hair was down, coiling and slipping around her shoulders.

'There's been a mix-up over the cabins,' she said.

'Really?'

'Yes. Yours is next door. I'm to have this one.'

Amused, he went and knocked on Eleanor's door.

'Come in,' she said in a low voice.

His fiancée lay on the bed and arched her back in a long feline stretch when she saw him.

'This is the *only* way to travel.' She sighed and switched off the reading lamp. He sat next to her on the bed, his eyes taking a moment to adjust to the pale starlight reflected off the sea. She had on a silk camisole and stockings that were lacy at the top where they attached to the garter straps. Leaning down and kissing the smooth skin of her thigh, he undid one of them.

'A generous friend of ours wants to send us on a honeymoon,' he said. 'Where would you like to go?'

'Mm,' she moaned as he kissed her again, 'the South Pacific.'

'A desert island?' He undid the other strap and ran his hand up her thigh.

'Yes. Where we can . . . *Oh*, come here.'

She pulled his head towards her and kissed him, and he lay down next to her on the narrow bed, holding tight the perfect curve of her spine.

They caressed and made love, kissing without stopping. Eventually, exhausted, they lay side by side with their feet towards the head of the bed so that they faced the window.

'The stars seem so close I could almost reach up and swish them around,' she said.

'I love you,' he said.

They were lulled to sleep by the hum of the propeller engines.

Chapter Fifty-six

The airship had entered a cold front over the mid-Atlantic, disappointing the passengers, who'd wanted to enjoy the view from the promenade windows. Outside was a world of white, an empty dimension with no sensation of forwards movement. The ship seemed frozen in time over an invisible ocean.

With nothing to see, most of the passengers returned to their cabins, and only the little party of stowaways was breakfasting in the dining room at nine o'clock. Refreshed and rested, Friedl and Hannah chattered eagerly of their coming life in America. Jakob was telling them how Pola Negri had once fainted in his arms in the elevator at the Park Avenue Hotel, when Ilse tugged his sleeve. Marching towards them among the dining room chairs was a man of about fifty wearing brass buttons and three sleeve stripes. The white peaked cap, hostile stare, and wide, grimly set mouth gave the impression of a police commissioner. He was followed by two junior officers.

'Oh,' Jakob said, dapping his mouth with a napkin. 'This must be Captain Pruss.'

'Well now.' The man stopped at the table and leaned towards them, his hands on the back of a chair. Looking at each of them in turn he said, 'Whoever you are, be in no doubt of the seriousness of the offence you have committed.' Hannah blushed scarlet and kept her eyes on her plate. 'Whoever aided you will be discovered and dealt with. The company's rules on stowaways require that the quartermaster confines you in a restricted area until we land.' Ilse glanced warily at Jakob. 'However . . .' Pruss straightened up and exhaled, his displeasure giving way to an odd expression, a type of pained graciousness. 'The response I've received from Dr Eckener orders me to treat you as paying passengers until the matter can be fully investigated . . . your names will go on the passenger list . . .'

Having left them in no doubt of what he thought of the order, and after Jakob had assured him he would pay the fares in full, he withdrew.

'Oh boy,' Friedl said, starting to laugh. 'He was not happy.'

'By now Heydrich will know where we are . . . ,' Denham said thoughtfully, looking at the white sky.

'Oh, so what.' Eleanor poured herself more coffee. 'It's too late to turn around. We'll be in New York this time tomorrow morning.'

IN THE READING room after breakfast Eleanor befriended a lady who introduced herself as Miss Mather, an elegant New Yorker in her late fifties who'd booked the passage because she abhorred ocean liners and had no sea legs. She had a delicate, Old World manner.

'I'm a dedicated fan of air travel,' Miss Mather said. 'But . . . I simply can't explain it. I felt a *reluctance* to board the *Hindenburg*. It was really quite overwhelming . . .'

'You'll be fine when you find your air legs,' Eleanor assured her, but she noticed how the woman kept crossing and uncrossing her thin ankles. She seemed even less at ease when Lehmann passed and told them that the ship was battling strong headwinds. They would be twelve hours late arriving in Lakehurst.

TOWARDS LATE AFTERNOON the fog and low clouds began to lift, and cresting grey waves could be seen below, marbling the surface of the ocean.

As they were changing for dinner in their cabins the sun finally broke through, and by the time the six of them climbed the stairs to A deck and entered the hundred-foot-long promenade in time to join the other passengers for cocktails, the setting sun shone horizontally through the windows, burnishing the lounge with a reddish golden light.

The single gown Eleanor had packed was of green satin organza with a low, square neckline, set off by her pearl necklace. Hannah had borrowed earrings from Ilse and wore her fine hair swirled and piled up. The men wore the dinner jackets Eckener had placed in their cabins.

Once they'd been served martinis they gathered along the window. The ocean had calmed, and its dark surface sparkled with gold. A cargo ship whose wake they'd followed for miles sounded its horn and its crew waved from the deck as the leviathan droned overhead.

Jakob was in good spirits. Probably never in his life had he been beholden to the mercies of strangers, Eleanor thought, as he raised his glass.

They raised theirs in return.

The old man was about to speak. But then his smile wavered and began to fade, first in his eyes, and then around his jowls and lips.

He was staring into the gathering of passengers.

'What's the matter Jaku, dear?' said Ilse.

They turned to look at what Jakob was seeing. Several knots of people chatting with drinks. But among them were two men together, in black tie, glaring at them. One with a white moustache twisted into two pins, a pince-nez, and hair swept back like a professor's; the other tall and potbellied, with fleshy lips and a mane of thick, grey hair. He wore a Party pin in his lapel. His eyes landed on Eleanor: they were the grey-beige colour of dishwater. And that's when she recognised him.

'Father,' Hannah said, 'aren't those the men . . .'

'Yes,' said Jakob.

'The men who were leaving the morning we visited your home . . . ,' said Eleanor. 'The ones who took your art collection.'

The tall man turned away from them, a look of repugnance on his face, as though he'd dressed for a society wedding only to find that the street drinkers had been invited. He leaned down to whisper to his colleague. Then they both turned and walked quickly out of the promenade deck.

'They're probably going to complain to Pruss,' said Jakob. 'Ah well. I take comfort from knowing that I've spoilt their dinner as much as they've spoilt mine.' He gave a mirthless smile. 'If our collection turns up for sale in New York they know I can kick up a stink . . . which raises an intriguing possibility . . .'

Jakob met his wife's eyes, and they seemed to be reading each other's minds.

The hors d'oeuvre was an Indian swallow nest soup served with a superb Piesporter '34. When the sun fell behind the horizon trailing ragged scraps of glory, the dining room's lights came on.

Lehmann approached their table and leaned over to whisper into Jakob's ear. He left without greeting the others.

'Our friend tells me those men are in the radio room talking to Berlin . . .'

Denham said, 'We should move the dossier from the cabin and hide it elsewhere in the ship.'

After coffee, Denham and Jakob went down to the smoking room on B deck, which was deserted but for the barman.

Jakob ordered two glasses of Delamain cognac and two cigars.

'San Cristobal de la Habana,' Denham said with appreciation, running his nose along the leaf.

The old man leaned back, and for a few minutes they savoured the taste of the cigars, at peace with the world. The hum of the engines was quieter in this aft section of the ship.

The door from the pressurised air lock into the smoking room opened with a sharp suck, and the art dealer and his Nazi colleague entered. Without waiting for an invitation they seated themselves opposite Denham and Jakob. The barman came to attend to them, but the tall man with the dishwater eyes waved him away.

'We want to talk,' he said.

'Yes, I thought you might,' Jakob said. 'Two more, please, barman.'

'We don't want a drink.'

'They're not for you,' Jakob said with a chuckle.

'And you can show some courtesy here,' Denham said. 'You're not in a *Bierkeller* now.'

The man turned to Denham for the first time, and exposed a set of khaki-coloured teeth.

'Your face is familiar,' he said.

'My name's Denham, I'm a reporter. Who are you?'

The man pulled an impatient face. 'I am Lothar Koch,' he said with emphasis. 'I am the Director of the Reich Chamber of the Visual Arts.'

'Permit me . . . ,' said the other man, the art dealer with the twirled white moustache, in a manner more civil than his colleague's. He was offering his card. Denham remembered seeing it on the table that morning they visited the Liebermanns.

'Ah yes. "Gallerie Haberstock—*German* Dealership."'

'I am Karl Haberstock . . . ,' he said, 'and our business is with Herr Liebermann.' He gave a small, sour smile. His sagging cheeks drew up to the corners of his mouth like old theatre curtains.

'I know the collection is on board,' Jakob said. 'And I have to tell you that I'm claiming it back in New York.'

'That might be difficult,' said Haberstock without blinking. 'There's the matter of the assignment of title to us, which you willingly entered into.'

Jakob said, 'The assignment is a contract I was compelled to make with the National Socialist government. I'm certain any New York district judge would consider it void.'

Koch uncrossed his legs suddenly so that his potbelly rolled over his belt. 'Listen to me, you kike, you can have your hideous collection—'

'Ah, what Reichsleiter Koch wishes to say, Herr Liebermann,' said Haberstock placing his hand on Koch's shoulder, 'is that there may be an arrangement we could make that would resolve the situation to everyone's satisfaction.'

'Really,' said Jakob.

Denham folded his arms. *Here it comes.*

'You have in your possession something which is of no value out-side Germany. We've been authorised by Berlin to offer you a sim-ple swap . . . If you give it to us, your art collection will be restored to you forthwith without the inconvenience of lawyers and proceed-ings. I hope you'll agree that's a fair offer.'

Jakob knocked back his second glass of cognac and stood up. 'Gentlemen. Thank you for your proposal. I assure you I'll give it my fullest consideration.'

'We need an answer right now,' said Koch.

'I'm not given to making snap decisions in business. You may have my answer over breakfast. Good night,' he said, smiling at them both, and left the smoking room.

Koch's neck and face began to blotch with shades of mushroom and puce.

'I'm curious,' Denham said to them. 'Did Berlin tell you any-thing of the nature of this item we have in our possession? I mean, its content . . . ?'

HANNAH EXPLAINED AGAIN to Captain Lehmann why they didn't trust those two men. She told him she believed they would use force to recover some valuables from her, which they insisted should have remained in Germany.

'Do you mean they'll break into your cabin?' Lehmann said, taken aback.

'If they've got orders from Berlin, yes,' said Eleanor.

He nodded, his lips pursed.

'Does it need to be hidden now?' he asked. He looked weary after a long day on the bridge.

'I'm so sorry,' said Hannah, gently taking his elbow, 'would you mind very much?'

The captain blushed slightly.

'Very well,' he said to them. 'I know the perfect place. But you'll need warm coats.'

The air was biting cold in the long keel corridor that led to the cargo area.

Lehmann glanced only once at the strange package under Eleanor's arm. She'd wrapped the filthy old dossier in sheets of tissue paper and tied the whole thing up with the only practical item to hand: a pink ribbon.

'Poor Captain Lehmann,' she said to Hannah in a low voice. 'He'll probably think these two crazy dames fear for the safety of their shopping . . .'

They reached a ladder at the foot of an air duct and began climbing.

'This leads to the central axis corridor,' he called down, 'the spine that runs all the way from fins to nose.' An occasional electric light, but otherwise the arduous ascent was in near darkness, with the temperature falling.

'I can see my breath,' Hannah said.

'The southern tip of Greenland is down there,' Lehmann shouted. His voice was indistinct, like a voice calling in a rock cavern.

Bracing wires creaked with the drone and movement of the ship, giving a sense of its surrounding vastness. Eventually they came to the horizontal axial corridor Lehmann had mentioned, and they followed him along it towards the stern.

Eleanor stopped and looked in amazement along the corridor's length. Lit by widely spaced electric lights it seemed to reach into infinity, with far-distant stars twinkling on the aluminium struts.

On either side of them the towering gas cells vibrated. Eleanor put her hand on the trembling sac and felt a prickle of apprehension. She was surrounded by acres of hydrogen, in every direction. If there were some accident while she was standing here . . . She put the thought out of her head. Miss Mather's nerves had spooked her.

'Do they ever leak?' she asked.

'If they did, your nose would tell you,' Lehmann said. 'The gas is odorised with garlic to give it a distinct smell.'

A rigger coming from the fins passed them in the corridor, giving Lehmann a nod. It was Ralf, wearing a head-to-toe asbestos suit. An inhabitant of the hidden city.

Eventually Lehmann stopped at a small utility platform at the cross section with another vertical air duct. They were almost in the stern of the ship, near the great fins. The platform was surrounded by a rail, with gas cells to the left and right. Next to a stool for the duty rigger, a large metal chest was screwed to the floor. He opened it. Inside were yards of folded canvas covered in a silver doping agent.

'This is spare sheathing. If we get a rip the sailmaker has to venture out and patch it,' he said. 'I promise you no one at all will look in here before we land. Those men whose faces you don't like will never know . . .'

They lifted up several folds of the canvas and tucked the package with the dossier into one of them, then replaced the folds and closed the lid tight.

Chapter Fifty-seven

Passengers gathering for breakfast on the second day, some in their dressing gowns and pyjamas, were let down again by the weather. The ship had entered a bank of white fog off the Labrador Coast, and the view from the promenade windows was a swirling fug of cloud and vapour.

Denham had lain awake much of the night, thinking of Rex.

Why had he done it? Out of resentment? Maybe. It was the only explanation that made sense. Resentment towards an English establishment that had never much liked him or valued him, the bright, upstart grammar-school boy gnawed by a sense of his own inferiority.

He'd finally fallen asleep, telling himself he'd awake with a clear head and surer of everything, but the morning's fog seemed an ill omen.

With America so close, Jakob, Ilse, and Hannah were in a buoyant mood at breakfast, though Denham took only coffee. The old man picked the shell off his hard-boiled egg with his fingertips, his movements neat and fastidious, humming to himself, as if his mind was settled and he was not going to let anything trouble him.

'Here come Dr Frankenstein and Igor,' said Eleanor, her mouth full of bread roll and jam. Haberstock and Koch were approaching, walking in single file among the tables.

Koch's eyes were puffy with grey pouches, Denham noticed, and the fat lips were chapped.

'Good morning,' said Jakob.

Haberstock gave a small bow.

'Could we talk somewhere?' he asked.

'We can talk here,' said Jakob, without looking at them. Haberstock glanced uneasily at the eager audience around the table.

'Berlin awaits your answer, Herr Liebermann. I trust you've considered the benefits of our offer.' His tone was just a shade short of civil. 'Do we have an agreement?'

Jakob did not invite the men to sit but buttered another piece of toast, taking his time as the art dealer stood waiting, and his colleague huffed, growing red in the face. Eventually Jakob said, 'I fear my answer's no, gentlemen. I hold the List Dossier legitimately, on trust for others, and I've no intention of disposing of it, whether by sale or exchange. The art collection, in any event, is not yours to bargain with.'

Haberstock's lips quivered, as if he'd bitten on a piece of glass.

'Kikes,' muttered Koch in a thick voice. He'd clearly been drinking already.

'Herr Liebermann, please be reasonable,' said Haberstock. 'That surely isn't your last word on the matter?'

'I'm afraid it *is*.'

'In that case'—he cleared his throat—'I am authorised by Berlin to offer you the sum of fifty thousand reichsmarks for the dossier.'

Friedl gave a low whistle.

'Good day, gentlemen,' said Jakob.

Throughout this exchange Jakob had not looked at the two men even once. Denham was struck by how neither he nor his wife and daughter even flinched at Koch's abuse. It wasn't that they were used to such a thing, he thought—who could be?—but that they were better people, and they knew it.

At around midday the city of Boston appeared through a gap in the fog. Not long after that the ghostly whiteness vanished altogether, and the *Hindenburg* glided down Long Island Sound in fine weather, with the passengers standing along the promenade windows, chatting loudly in English or German, pointing out people, landscape features, and buildings, and returning the universal waved greeting.

At 3:30 p.m. lower Manhattan came into sight, its towers glowing in a brief interval of afternoon sun. But beyond the tall buildings the clouds were black and anvil shaped; a thunderstorm was approaching the city from the southwest, and far up the Hudson River the horizon flashed with lightning. Denham slipped his arm around Eleanor, who had said little since they'd passed Newfoundland. She seemed preoccupied, unmoved by the skyscrapers, the welcoming flotillas, or the Statue of Liberty pointing up at them, as small as a jade figurine.

'When I left New York I said I'd return in shame or glory,' she said, looking straight ahead.

'And which is it?'

She shrugged. 'I left as a girl; I've returned as a woman.'

The ship slowed as it sailed over the shadowed chasms and high formations of Fifth Avenue, bristling with spires, gables, and masts. Over the Empire State Building they flew low enough to see the faces of the tourists taking photographs on the observation deck, of parents holding up small children.

An hour later, when they were over the flat scrub oaks and pine-woods of New Jersey, the passengers began returning to their cabins to pack. Denham stayed to watch the approach to landing and noticed the ragged, fast-moving clouds. He opened the window and put his head out. A fine drizzle brushed his face, and there was a sultry, electrical smell in the air.

'Look,' said Eleanor.

Haberstock was approaching Jakob, who listened to him with obvious impatience, then shook his head.

'The man's trying one more time,' said Denham.

'We need to get the dossier,' said Eleanor.

'We won't be landing anytime soon.'

A red warning light was flashing on the hangar of the Naval Air Station, a huge building rising from the sandy soil of Lakehurst. Tiny figures of spectators and reporters held on to their hats, their coats whipped by the wind, but the field itself was deserted. The mooring mast on rails—like a miniature Eiffel Tower—was unmanned.

'The ground crew isn't there yet. It's too dangerous to attempt a mooring in weather like this . . .'

'*What was that?*' Eleanor shouted. She turned to Denham. 'Did you see that?'

What seemed like a dim blue flame had darted along the length of the promenade sill, flickering over the metal fittings of the windows before it vanished. There it was again, to shrieks of surprise from other passengers.

'I saw it,' said Denham. 'It was like a will-o'-the-wisp.'

'Ladies and gentlemen, don't be alarmed,' said Lehmann calling from the stern end of the promenade. 'That was a display of the gas known as St Elmo's fire, caused by a buildup of static electricity during a storm. Quite harmless. There is, as you've seen, too much electricity in the air at the moment. Captain Pruss is going to turn the ship away and wait for the storm front to pass. I'm afraid this will result in a further delay . . .'

Slowly the hangar moved out of view below as the ship tilted and turned southeastwards and away from Lakehurst.

Jakob and Hannah came over to them. 'Haberstock is now offering me a hundred thousand reichsmarks for the dossier,' said Jakob. 'I could acquire a Vermeer for that.'

Denham laughed. 'If he goes any higher, I'll say yes on your behalf . . .'

'I am starting to feel sorry for him. He seemed distinctly nervous when I turned him down this time.'

The ship looped away from Lakehurst, over the Toms River and along the deserted yellow beaches of New Jersey, where seaside houses were still boarded up from winter, their pastel colours faded and peeled. From behind the clouds, sharp rays made fields of sunlight on the dark sea.

Half an hour passed as they watched the ocean; then the ship turned again and began to head back.

'We've had the clearance,' Lehmann announced. 'The weather's calmer. Herr Denham, would you like to view the landing from the bridge?'

ELEANOR FOLLOWED HANNAH along the keel corridor into the draughty hull of the ship, buzzing with engine noise, and when they reached the ladder at the foot of the air duct, they climbed, retracing their steps from the night before. This time, however, there were dozens of crew running between stern and prow as the ship prepared to land. One of them asked if they knew where they were going. Eleanor flashed him her best smile, explaining that they had the purser's permission, and would only be five minutes. When they reached the metal chest at the intersection with the axial corridor they heard a series of deep blasts from a klaxon.

'Must be the Air Station,' said Hannah.

She opened the chest and with Eleanor's help lifted the heavy rolls of silver canvas from inside. In the fifth fold Eleanor plucked out the package containing the List Dossier.

'Got it,' she said as Hannah dumped the canvas back inside. 'Let's go.'

'That's far enough,' said a voice in English.

About twenty feet away, standing on the grilled floor of the axial corridor, was the tall, potbellied figure of Koch. 'Don't move.' His arm was stiffly extended. He was aiming a handgun right at them.

Chapter Fifty-eight

Denham was next to Captain Lehmann at the back of the crowded bridge, out of the way of the helmsman, the elevator man, and the officers monitoring the gas pressure and engine telegraphs. Captain Pruss stood behind the first officer, who was in charge of the landing. Lehmann was keeping an eye on the light boards that monitored ballast and hydrogen, the nerves and nuclei of the most modern aircraft ever built. More than ever Denham wished that Tom was with him now.

On the sodden landing field hundreds of tiny figures were now assembling around the mooring tower. A heavy shower had fallen just before they'd arrived, and wide pools reflected the leaden sky.

'Reverse engines,' said Pruss, and the vast ship began to brake as it moved in from the west and slowly dropped lower. They were about six hundred feet from the ground. 'Prepare to release port and starboard handling lines.'

KOCH'S THICK GREY hair was dishevelled; his forehead beaded with sweat. The long climb up the ladder after them must have got his heart racing.

'Put the dossier on the floor,' he said. There was a tremor to his voice, and he swayed very slightly, making Eleanor think that he'd been drinking.

'What kind of idiot brings a firearm on board a hydrogen airship?' she said. 'Do you know what would happen if—'

'Put the fucking dossier on the floor,' he shouted.

The bracing wires creaked. The hum of the engines could be felt through the floor. A low, filtered light seeped through in places, but otherwise the area was in a gloaming of its own.

'Do as he says, Eleanor,' Hannah whispered.

'I'VE NEVER SEEN this type of landing before,' Denham said. 'Normally we drift down and the ground crew walks us to the mast, don't they?'

'It's a new technique called a "high landing,"' said Lehmann. 'They pull us down by ropes and moor us. Requires fewer men, and saves us money.'

As Lehmann spoke, Denham's attention was caught by the view on the right-hand side: a bank of low grey cloud was billowing towards them from the southwest. 'Is that another storm front moving in?'

'PUT THE GUN down,' Eleanor said. Her eyes were locked on Koch's. 'We're not armed.'

'Not a step closer,' he shouted. The barrel trembled in his hand. 'Believe me, I will shoot you.'

'You might,' said Eleanor, 'but you might miss and hit the hydrogen. Put the goddamned gun down.'

'At this range? With this calibre?' He gave a nervous, hissing laugh. 'This is a Walther PPK semi-automatic. No, I will hit *you*. I will kill *you*.' His face was sweating streams in the cold air. 'Put the dossier on the floor.'

Eleanor was holding up the package as if it were a shield.

'Eleanor,' Hannah implored. '*Please* put it down.'

IN THE CONTROL car Denham could not take his eyes off the approaching storm, but the attention of Captain Pruss, the first officer, and the others was focused on the mooring mast, the ship's altitude, and the speed of approach. *Eckener, with his pathological obsession for safety, would not have allowed this*, he thought. The old man would have delayed for as long as it took until the danger had passed. Out of the corner of his eye he glimpsed another blue flame wriggling along the metal fittings at the back of the room.

ELEANOR SLOWLY PUT the package on the floor, but the gun stayed trained on her.

'There,' she said. 'I've put it down. Now you put the gun down.'

Koch seemed to breathe a little easier, and he lowered the gun.

'It's yours to take back to Berlin,' Eleanor said, retreating slowly.

'I'm not taking it to Berlin,' he said in a shaking voice, 'I'm going to destroy it.' His voice had an off, cracked note, sounding more than drunk; he sounded unhinged, as though something had snapped inside his head. 'As soon as we land, I will burn it . . . as if it never existed.'

As he moved forwards to pick up the package from the floor, a shadow rose in the dim corridor behind him. Friedl was creeping up on Koch, holding a small length of rope between his hands. He'd removed his shoes. Hannah looked at him wide-eyed and gave a rapid shake of her head, but he didn't notice; nor had he noticed the gun in Koch's hand. He crouched as if to gather himself, then in a wide movement took a giant step and leapt onto Koch's back, sending him crashing to the floor. Koch landed painfully on his side, with his gun arm sticking out horizontally. Friedl struggled to get the rope around his neck, with both men straining and groaning, and then he saw the gun.

The shot sounded like *Dan!*

Sparks cascaded, and a whooshing, whip-crack made the women duck and cover their heads. The bullet had nicked one of the thin bracing wires, snapping it and sending it singing through the air as its tension released. It quivered for a second like a kraken's tentacle, then tore into the nearest gas cell, making a long gash high up in the fabric.

Hannah rushed to help Friedl, stamped her heel on Koch's wrist, and pulled the gun away, sliding it back towards Eleanor.

But Eleanor was looking up, transfixed by the tear high up on the gas cell, near the very top of the ship.

Hydrogen was flowing freely from the gash, mixing with oxygen, causing rippling waves in the fabric of the cell, like a hot-water bottle emptying. The escaping flow pushed against the ship's outer sheathing, making it flutter.

An unmistakable smell filled her nostrils. 'Garlic,' she whispered.

THE FIRST OFFICER turned to Pruss. 'That's odd,' he said, pointing at the instruments. 'We're losing altitude in the stern. We're about a thousand kilograms heavy.'

'Release water ballast,' said Pruss.

A ballast toggle was pulled, then another.

'Still tail heavy,' the first officer said, and picked up the telephone to order the crew members on duty in the lower tail fin to walk to the bow in order to correct the trim.

The ship was now about three hundred feet from the ground, hovering, and close enough for Pruss to wave to the commander of the Naval Air Station sitting in his jeep at the corner of the field.

'Release starboard and port handling lines,' he said.

From the bow hatch window the heavy mooring ropes fell and splattered on the ground where the mooring crew picked them up and tied them to a capstan. At that moment the evening sun came out, filling the control car with light, even as a light rain was falling from the weather front gathering from the southwest.

Denham turned to Lehmann. 'Won't that wet rope ground us? I mean, couldn't it cause a spark?' He could feel the static on his fingertips when he touched the sill, and in his hair.

'There's no danger,' Lehmann said, clapping Denham's shoulder. He nodded at the light board. 'All cells are normal, and we have five experienced officers in here, including me.'

'Cut engines,' said Pruss. The four propeller engines died, and with that the great ship floated in silence, as if it were holding its breath.

*   *   *

'WE'VE GOT TO warn the bridge,' Eleanor shouted. She forgot the dossier; she forgot the gun. They abandoned Koch on the narrow axial corridor, groaning and clutching his wrist. The package containing the dossier lay about ten feet away from him. Hannah ran back and snatched it from the floor.

In the distance along the endless axial corridor they saw the duty riggers moving.

They clambered down the long air duct ladder that led back to the keel. For three long minutes they descended, their feet slipping on the rungs. They reached the cargo hold and were about to reenter the passenger quarters when Eleanor, who was in the rear, heard a muffled detonation far above her, like the sound of someone lighting a gas stove.

'DID YOU FEEL that?' the first officer said, turning to Pruss.

'A rope must have snapped.'

Denham stepped to the window and saw immediately that something was wrong. The hangar building was illuminated with a rose-coloured light and the ground crew were running away, abandoning the ropes. He opened the window and leaned out as far as he could, looking towards the stern, and saw a carnation of bright flames blossoming beneath the fins. He pulled himself in faster than the colour could drain from his face.

'The ship's on fire.'

The officer on the rudder wheel let out an animal moan, and before Pruss could give another order the control car tilted steeply backwards to the sound of straining metal.

AS MOST OF the passengers were on the starboard side facing the crowd come to welcome them, the lounge and reading room were almost deserted when Friedl, Hannah, and Eleanor got there.

Eleanor saw Miss Mather sitting alone at a banquette, reading a book. Before she could say a word to the woman the floor fell away and threw them violently onto their fronts. Tongues of dark red flame blew in through the rear bulkheads, caressing the ceiling.

From above came a roar like a giant blowtorch, as one gas cell ignited the next in a string of explosions. She heard the screams of people on the starboard side, and the *thump*, *thump* of bodies falling one over the other as the ship pitched steeply to stern, tipping with it a metal mangle of tables and chairs.

'*Get up*,' Eleanor shouted. Intense heat was scorching her hands and her head. '*We have to jump.*'

The earth was rising towards them. She knelt up and grabbed the sill. The window was jammed.

'*Help me, Friedl.*'

Now the ship was quickly righting itself as it approached the ground. She saw Friedl's jacket on fire, orange flames across his back. They each pushed, and the second time pushed together, and it opened. Hannah got Miss Mather to her feet. The woman was leaning against the bulkhead, trying to shield her face with an up-turned coat collar.

'*Let's go*,' Hannah shouted. The woman's face was contorted, stiff with shock.

'*Lady, come on*,' Eleanor shouted, but Miss Mather was in a trance.

The ship smashed to the ground, its back broken, and almost pitched them headfirst through the windows.

'*C'mon outta there!*' a voice shouted.

A sailor in a white cap appeared in the window, his arms extended desperately. With Hannah's help Eleanor lifted Miss Mather and shoved her through. Then Hannah jumped, and Eleanor was following when a rolling wall of black smoke engulfed her, choking her, coating her skin and hair.

The next thing she knew she was on her hands and knees on wet soil, coughing violently while the blaze raged above her.

'*Lady, run!*' said the sailor.

Behind her came the cries of people being burned alive. Everywhere, glowing balls of molten metal were hitting the ground. She got up and had a sense that Friedl was just ahead of her; then she saw him rolling on his back like a dog. When he turned over, his jacket was scorched through; glistening burns and mud covered his bare back.

'Take my arm,' she said to him.

She pulled him up and they ran together, feeling the heat become less intense behind them, the roar of the blaze breathing less fiercely. A light drizzle was falling. People were running out to meet her and the other survivors. One man's clothes were completely burned away and his skin hung off him in drapes. A woman's face and arms were charred black. She collapsed to her knees and fell forwards. Chunks of burned flesh lay in the sand, black and dark red. Two little boys, covered in blood and burns, walked hand in hand with their mother in complete silence.

'Who's got it?' said Friedl.

'What?'

'The dossier. Who's got the dossier?'

'Hannah has it,' Eleanor said, not at all sure that she did.

When they reached Hannah and Miss Mather a few feet ahead of them, safe in the arms of rescuers, there was nothing under Hannah's arm.

'Forget it,' Hannah said. 'It's gone.' Eleanor marvelled that there was scarcely a scratch on her.

'*No*,' said Friedl, and he turned and ran back towards the inferno.

'Has anyone seen Mother and Father?' Hannah said, starting to cry.

'*Friedl!*' Eleanor screamed. She started after him, but the sailor held her back. Much later she would remember that moment keenly. It seemed to happen in slow motion, his silhouette running into the glare of the fires, and she had failed to prevent him.

The *Hindenburg*, a blazing wreck of white-hot girders, looked like the fragments of a dragon's egg. Smoke braided with flames belched out of its engines, strangely beautiful in the gathering darkness. The marvellous machine, Dr Eckener's greatest achievement, had been destroyed in seconds. Incredible that she'd survived; that anyone had survived. She looked down at her filthy dress. She had a nasty burn down one arm, and her hair and eyebrows had been singed away in places, but she was otherwise all right.

But where was Richard?

Chapter Fifty-nine

The small Naval Air Station infirmary at Lakehurst was crowded with the injured and the dead. They lay on tables and stretchers in the corridors and in every room. Everything—air, clothing, hair, surfaces—was infused with the reek of charred flesh.

Eleanor refused morphine. When she did so, she was asked to sit and help swab a man's burns with picric acid. He leaned forwards, his hands in his lap, his blackened head bowed. His back was a morass of burns from his head to his lower spine. When he said, 'Thank you,' she got up and knelt in front of him to look in his eyes. It was Captain Lehmann. Apart from his voice he was unrecognisable.

'I'm not myself, am I?' he said to her.

'Nothing they can't fix,' she said, fighting the lump in her throat. 'Was Richard with you?'

'Yes,' he said, nodding, as if remembering someone he hadn't seen for years. 'I lost him in the smoke.' Eventually Lehmann was taken away, facedown on a stretcher, and Eleanor leaned her head back against the wall. A medic tended to her arm with a cool ointment and bandage. She was exhausted; her body was closing down.

When she awoke the infirmary was quiet. She stopped an orderly. 'How many dead?'

'Twenty-one so far,' he said. 'But several won't make the night.'

She wondered whether she should ask for morphine after all before entering the morgue, but dismissed the idea.

It was dark outside and raining. A man's voice was saying that the wreck was still burning on the landing field, lighting up the sky for miles around, a sight he'd never forget for as long as he lived. Slowly she walked to the morgue. The thought of being the one to find his body was too much to bear, and she began crying quietly. She realised then that she believed in her heart that he was dead. She felt no nerves, no yearning for certainty.

A marine guarded the door to the hangar.

'I'd like to identify my fiancé,' she said.

Inside, the bodies were under blankets in a row on the floor. The space was huge and dim. Other people were there, too, looking for lost ones, holding their breath with horror and expectation as they raised each cover.

She heard Hannah before she saw her. The girl's cry went up in the vast space and echoed around the walls like a spirit begging for oblivion. She and Jakob were crouching over a corpse with their arms around each other. Eleanor approached and saw Ilse's face looking up at them from the floor, pale as moonlight. She learned later that Ilse had suffered a heart attack at Jakob's side after jumping from the starboard windows.

One by one she began looking under the covers over the corpses. She found Haberstock, his head damaged horribly, revealing the bridgework on his teeth. She found an elderly man white and waxen from the heat. She found one corpse burned beyond all recognition, but it was too tall to be Richard. She found a man in a sailor's uniform, a member of the ground crew killed by the falling wreckage. She looked under every cover.

Finally, she found Friedl. His mouth was open slightly, as if there was something important he hadn't quite said; his eyes were glassy and clear; his skin shockingly pale. The fist of his right hand was clenched tight, and sticking between the fingers were torn pieces of yellowed paper. She pulled them out. Charcoal smudges on them. Maybe he'd found the dossier, but not soon enough to save himself. She checked in the pockets of his burned jacket, but nothing was there. Gently she brushed aside some of his lovely dark hair, kissed his cold forehead, and covered his face again.

But of Richard there was no sign.

Early the next morning a shouting pack of reporters with flash-bulb cameras and microphones crowded around a blackboard in the infirmary where the station commander, Captain Rosendahl, had chalked in thick letters the names of the dead, the survivors, and twelve missing. Lehmann's name, she noticed, had been added to the dead. Richard's name was among those missing. She left the building before Rosendahl gave his press conference.

Outside, dozens of radio cars and Movietone news vans, along with thousands of cars from New York, were clogging the road.

'How can he be missing?' she asked one of the sailors. She was in a daze and panicking. It was as if another universe, in which Richard had survived, was offering to let her through, but only if she could find the door.

'Maybe he hasn't given us his name yet, ma'am. There's a bunch of injured at the hospital in Lakewood. You should try there . . . Hey, lady, get one of these guys to drive you . . .'

IT WAS ABOUT midday when she found him. A young nurse was winding a fresh bandage around his head. Eleanor gave a shriek when she saw him, startling the nurse, and began trembling uncon-trollably.

'I hope you're Eleanor,' said the nurse. 'He came around again about an hour ago and kept asking me over and over if I've seen Eleanor . . .'

Eleanor leaned down and kissed his drowsy lid, dropping her own tears onto his lashes.

He opened his eyes, blinked slowly, and a smile spread over his face. She squeezed his hand.

'He's suffered a bad concussion,' said the nurse. 'And has some second-degree burns . . .'

Eleanor looked into his eyes. She mouthed, 'I love you,' and he tried to speak. She put another pillow behind him. When he'd mustered enough breath, he said, 'Let's get married before anything else happens . . .'

'As soon as you like,' she said, crying.

' . . . and our honeymoon in the Pacific?'

'Yes?'

'We're taking a boat.'

Eleanor stood at the rail of the deck, enjoying the breeze cooling her skin through her pale cotton dress. Clouds tumbled towards the horizon. Weightless white boulders on the humid air. Far in the distance the forested uplands faded in a blue haze.

During Richard's recovery she'd taken her six weeks' residency in Reno, Nevada, and had been granted her divorce. Within days she was married again. The ceremony was a quiet affair in the Manhattan city clerk's office. Her father had overcome all his reservations, as she knew he would, once he'd spent half an hour in his study with Richard. Hannah, Martha, and Paul Gallico were there, but Jakob had excused himself, saying he did not wish to bring his sadness to such a happy day. Dr Eckener, already returned to Germany after the enquiry in Lakehurst, a saddened and diminished figure, had sent a telegram and gifts.

The public enquiry began within days of the disaster, but when interviewed by German officials of the Deutsche Zeppelin-Reederei, before Eckener had arrived in New York by ship, Eleanor and Denham, who between them had conclusive knowledge of the cause of the accident, were told that they would not be called as witnesses. The Reich government did not wish to make public the reason why a high-ranking state servant should have brandished and fired a gun near Gas Cell 4, nor the reason why six people on the passenger list had apparently not cleared customs or the *Kontrolle* at Frankfurt. The Walther PPK had been found in the wreckage and discreetly removed. Denham did, however, tell Eckener what had happened, and the old man presented his conclusions on the disaster accordingly. At least he would never be tormented by not knowing the truth. They never discovered what happened to Rex. After they alerted the SIS in London of his treachery, he vanished inside Germany.

A large insect made her jump, droning past her face and landing on the rail a few inches from her hand.

A steward serving drinks laughed. 'Señora, it's not dangerous. That's a fig beetle, quite common in Panama.'

She looked at the bug. Its metallic carapace glinted with shades of gold, emerald, and sapphire, like a scarab from a pharaoh's crown. *How beautiful everything is*, she thought.

Denham stepped onto the deck, holding himself a little stiffly because of his burns. He'd changed into a linen suit, a white cotton shirt, and a Panama hat and was carrying his Leica.

'You don't want to miss this,' she said, giving him her swimsuit pose as he took a photograph. 'It's the first lock of the canal.'

They watched as the lock closed behind them and began filling with water, raising the mighty tonnage of the ocean liner up, over the rocky jungle isthmus of Panama.

'How does it work?' she said, fascinated.

'It's a matter of weight and sea.'

'Well, we've got all afternoon,' she said kissing him. The steward approached with a tray of tall iced glasses. 'I ordered us a Tom Collins.'

'Who?'

'Gin, lime juice, soda water, sugar, and ice. Cheers.'

'Cheers, Señora Denham.'

They sipped their drinks with their arms around each other's waists. 'I want to keep travelling like this forever,' she said. 'Can't you and I and Tom settle in the South Seas somewhere?'

Denham turned to the horizon.

'There's a war coming,' he said. 'Eckener thinks so, too. We can't prevent it now.' He looked back at her. 'You know what we'll be up against. I want to fight.'

She ran her hand gently over his cheek. 'My Richard will be too old for the army,' she said.

'But I'll do something. Anything I can.'

She sighed, but not sadly. 'Yes, I know. And I will, too.'

Soon the ocean liner was through to the third lock, rising higher and higher, with dense banks on either side, and finally they saw it, the Pacific Ocean, a ribbon of dark indigo between forested hills.

Author's Note

THIS BOOK AROSE from a fascination with history's footnotes—those small, intriguing facts marginal to the main narratives. The passing detail, for example, that the *Graf Zeppelin* occasionally had a stowaway on board, or that within days of coming to power the Nazis confiscated a six-volume file on Hitler from the archives of the Munich police. But it was the story of American Olympic swimmer Eleanor Holm and her antics on board the *Manhattan* in 1936 that was the catalyst to start writing. Holm had such spirit, beauty, and courage that in my mind she quickly inspired a fictional character in need of an adventure.

It would not have been possible to write this book without drawing on a number of excellent memoirs, diaries, and histories, all of which I have enjoyed reading as much as I did the writing. Those mentioned below are just a few of these works. Any liberties taken with historical fact and any historical inaccuracies in the story are entirely my own.

Guy Walters's superb *Berlin Games* (William Morrow, 2006) portrays the stranger-than-fiction incidents of the 1936 Olympics, the parties and diplomatic intrigue, and the controversial role of Avery Brundage. Likewise, Christopher Hilton's *Hitler's Olympics* (Sutton, 2006) was extremely helpful.

The romance of Zeppelin travel in its heyday and the towering personality of the Zeppelin genius, Hugo Eckener, are captured brilliantly in *Dr Eckener's Dream Machine* by Douglas Botting (HarperCollins, 2001).

On the culture of blackmail surrounding Hitler's rise, and on the question of his private life, Lothar Machtan's *The Hidden Hitler* (Perseus Press, 2001) was utterly compelling.

Regarding the fate of modern art during the Third Reich and the dealings of Karl Haberstock, Jonathan Petropoulos's *The Faustian Bargain* (Allen Lane, 2000) was essential reading.

On the mysterious nature of Hitler's blindness at the Pasewalk Military Hospital in 1918 I am indebted to *The Eyewitness* by Ernst Weiss (Houghton Mifflin, 1977), a work of historical description loosely presented as fiction. The book is intriguing because historians John Toland and Rudolph Binion have shown how its description of Hitler's cure is based on medical facts known to Weiss, a German émigré who wrote the book in Paris in 1938. Weiss's circle of German exiles was in contact with Dr Edmund Forster, the doctor who, Binion shows, had treated Hitler at Pasewalk. Forster visited the exiles in Paris in 1933.

Hitler had all files relating to his period at Pasewalk confiscated. The few people who had access to his medical file either were killed as soon as he came to power or committed suicide in strange circumstances. In October 2011, the historian Dr Thomas Weber published the first documentary evidence that Hitler had indeed been treated for hysterical amblyopia, a psychological disorder that can cause loss of sight.

I cannot recommend these books highly enough.

Notes on the Characters

Eleanor Emerson is inspired by the real-life **Eleanor Holm** (1913–2004), an Olympic swimmer who was thrown off the US team by Avery Brundage because of her partygoing on board the *Manhattan*. She was married to the bandleader Art Jarrett. Popular with the press corps, Holm attended the Games anyway as a columnist, with John Walsh and Paul Gallico doing the writing for her. She went on to have limited success with an acting career, starring in *Tarzan's Revenge* (1938) alongside Glenn Morris, but was better known for her aquacade spectaculars at the New York World's Fair. She divorced Jarrett in 1939. She did not have a senator-father, live in London, or fly on the *Hindenburg* as Eleanor does in the story.

Hannah Liebermann has a loose parallel with **Helene Mayer** (1910–53), a German fencer who was the only 'non-Aryan' athlete invited to compete for Germany in the 1936 Games (she was half Jewish). Mayer willingly did so and did not regard herself as culturally Jewish. On the podium, after winning the silver in women's fencing, she gave the Hitler salute—something she would forever after regret—and was criticised for it by Jewish groups. Recently, it has been credibly suggested that she did so out of fear of what might happen to her family after the Games.

Historical Characters

Avery Brundage (1887–1975) was chairman of the American Athletic Union and the head of the American Olympic Committee

(AOC) in 1936. On the day the Games opened on August 1 he was made the US member on the International Olympic Committee (IOC) after the sacking of Ernest Lee Jahncke, who had strongly advocated a boycott of the Games. He became president of the IOC in 1945. Brundage remains a controversial figure even today. He openly admired Nazi Germany, opposed the participation of women in Olympic sport, and was accused several times in his life of anti-Semitism. He never convincingly explained his decision in Berlin to drop the Jewish athletes Marty Glickman and Sam Stoller from the relay team.

Martha Dodd (1908–90) was the daughter of Ambassador William E Dodd. She had been the assistant literary editor of the *Chicago Tribune* before moving to Berlin, where she had a number of romantic liaisons, including some with Nazis. It was her affair with a Russian press attaché (and likely intelligence agent), Boris Vinogradov, however, that led her to become a Soviet spy and eventually flee behind the iron curtain via Cuba. She had hoped to marry Vinogradov, whom she'd met in 1934, but he vanished in one of Stalin's purges in 1938. The 'engagement party' in the story is entirely fictional.

Ambassador William E Dodd (1869–1940) was the US ambassador to Germany from 1933 to 1937. A former history professor, he had an intense dislike of the Nazis and eventually resigned his post in frustration, feeling that Washington was not heeding his warnings. He never discovered Martha's treachery, which only became public in the 1990s.

Dr Hugo Eckener (1864–1954) was the entrepreneurial force behind the building of the giant commercial airships *Graf Zeppelin* and *Hindenburg*. He was a highly vocal critic of the Nazis, but because of his fame and standing at home and abroad was not persecuted, despite several warnings.

Dr Edmund Forster (1878–1933) was a German psychiatrist who some historians believe treated Hitler at the Pasewalk Military Hospital in 1918. After the Nazi takeover of power he was dismissed from his chair at the University of Greifswald and committed suicide in dubious circumstances in September 1933 after thirteen days of interrogation by the Gestapo. His case notes on Hitler have never been found (and remain the elusive 'holy grail' for Hitler scholars).

Paul Gallico (1897–1976) was a sportswriter for the *New York Daily News* at the time of the 1936 Games and went to Berlin on board the *Manhattan*. He went on to write the novels *The Snow Goose* and *The Poseidon Adventure*.

Marjorie Gestring (1922–92) won the gold for the United States in the diving competition when she was just thirteen, at the time the youngest ever gold medal winner.

Marty Glickman (1917–2001) was a US track and field athlete. He believed he'd been the victim of anti-Semitism by Brundage's decision to exclude him from the relay team.

Dr Joseph Goebbels (1897–1945) was Hitler's propaganda minister and a well-known womaniser. At the time of the 1936 Games he had begun a torrid affair with the Czech movie star Lída Baarová.

Karl Haberstock (1878–1956) was Hitler's private art dealer. His gallery flourished during the Third Reich by acquiring old masters from escaping Jews at bargain prices and paintings looted by the German armies from European galleries. His appearance on board the *Hindenburg* in this story is purely fictional.

Karl Ritter von Halt (1891–1964) was a former Olympic decathlete and the German IOC member from 1929. Despite being a member of the Nazi Party and a general in the SA (Brownshirts), he

continued his role in the IOC after World War II with the backing
of his friend Avery Brundage.

Helen Hayes (1900–93), US movie star, was on board the *Manhattan*.

William Randolph Hearst Jr (1908–93), son of the newspaper
magnate, was on board the *Manhattan* and rumoured to have been
'an item' with Eleanor Holm during the crossing.

Reinhard Heydrich (1904–42) was a high-ranking SS leader who
became head of the SD, the German state security police, in 1936,
at the age of thirty-two. Slim, blond, and athletic, he was the only
senior Nazi to resemble the Aryan ideal. His contempt for human
beings made him cynical, calculating, and ruthless, inspiring terror
among his own colleagues as well as the victims of the regime. At
the 1942 Wannsee Conference in Berlin, he asserted his personal
control over the coordination of the Holocaust. Six months later he
was assassinated by Free Czech agents in occupied Prague.

George F Kennan (1904–2005) was a US diplomat in Moscow in
1936 and was on board the *Manhattan*. In 1952 he became US ambassador to the Soviet Union.

Ernst Lehmann (1886–1937) was a German Zeppelin commander.
Lehmann was on board the *Hindenburg*'s final flight as an observer.
He was an old colleague of Eckener's, and, unlike Eckener, mildly
supported the Nazis, although he never joined the Party. He died a
day after the disaster from his injuries.

Carl "Luz" Long (1913–43) was a German Olympic long-jumper
who won the silver medal in the 1936 Games, reputedly after giving

Jesse Owens friendly advice on how to improve his jump (Owens won the gold). Long was killed in action in World War II.

Charlie MacArthur (1895–1956), US playwright and screenwriter, married to Helen Hayes, was on board the *Manhattan*.

Margaret Mather (1878–1969) was a US passenger who survived the *Hindenburg* disaster. Incredibly, she walked out of the wreck down the gangway stairs and suffered only minor burns.

Hans Mend (1888–1942) is not a character in the novel, but his words are quoted on page 229 (my own translation). Mend was a dispatch rider who had served with Hitler in World War I, but he later fell out of favour and died in a concentration camp. The so-called Mend Protocol was allegedly dictated by Mend in 1939, after the date of this story. Few historians have taken the document seriously because Mend was a petty criminal and a fraudster. Recently it has been given credence by the historian Lothar Machtan.

Glenn Morris (1912–74) won a gold medal in the Olympic decathlon in 1936, setting a new Olympic record. He features in several close-up shots in *Olympia*, the film of the Games made by the German director Leni Riefenstahl, with whom he had an affair in Berlin.

Jesse Owens (1913–80), the hero of the 1936 Games, won four gold medals, including one for the legendary long jump against Carl 'Luz' Long described in the story.

Sir Eric Phipps (1875–1945) was the British ambassador to Berlin from 1933 to 1937 and the brother-in-law of Sir Robert Vansittart. Both of them were acerbic critics of the Nazis. Phipps was recalled from Berlin and replaced with Sir Nevile Henderson, who supported Britain's policy of appeasement.

Max Pruss (1891–1960) was the *Hindenburg*'s commander on its final flight. He was a member of the Nazi Party. He survived the disaster and remained convinced that sabotage was to blame.

Helen Stephens (1918–94), the 'Fulton Flash' from Missouri, won two sprint event medals in Berlin when she was eighteen. She was noted for her large and masculine appearance. Hitler said to her, 'You're a big blond girl. You should run for Germany.'

Sam Stoller (1915–85) was a US sprinter and long jumper. He vowed he'd never compete again after Brundage excluded him from the relay race, saying it had been the most humiliating experience of his life. He did not believe that anti-Semitism was behind the decision.

Sir Robert Vansittart (1881–1957), known as 'Machiavelli and soda,' was the permanent undersecretary of the British Foreign Office. He visited Berlin during the Games and had several high-level diplomatic meetings. He strongly opposed Britain's policy of appeasement, a stance that cost him his job in 1938.

Thomas Wolfe (1900–38) was a US novelist famous for *Look Homeward, Angel* and *Of Time and the River*. He was in Berlin during the Games and met Martha Dodd.

Louis Zamperini (born 1917) was a US Olympic distance runner. By his own admission he failed to control his appetite on board the *Manhattan*, despite Brundage's warnings about medals being lost at the dinner table, and had gained twelve pounds by the time he reached Berlin. He went on to become a celebrated World War II veteran and an inspirational speaker.